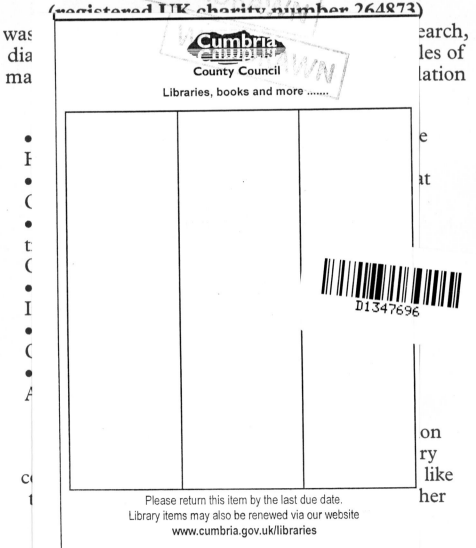

THE STEEL GIRLS

Sheffield, 1939. With war declared, brave women step up and do their bit for their country.

Housewife Nancy never dreamed that she'd end up in the Vickers steelworks factory, but when husband Bert is called up to serve, she needs to put food on the table for her two young children.

Betty's sweetheart William has joined the RAF Reserves, so she can't sit around and do nothing — even if it means giving up her ambitions to study law at night school.

Young Patty is relishing the excitement the war brings. But this shop girl is going to have to grow up quickly, especially now she's undertaking such back-breaking and dangerous work in the factory . . .

MICHELLE RAWLINS

THE
STEEL GIRLS

Complete and Unabridged

MAGNA
Leicester

First published in Great Britain in 2021 by
HQ
an imprint of HarperCollins*Publishers*
London

First Ulverscroft Edition
published 2021
by arrangement with
HarperCollins*Publishers*
London

*A catalogue record for this book is available
from the British Library.*

ISBN 978–0–7505–4897–7

Published by
Ulverscroft Limited
Anstey, Leicestershire

Printed and bound in Great Britain by
TJ Books Ltd., Padstow, Cornwall

This book is printed on acid-free paper

To every Woman of Steel, who sacrificed so much to not only ensure those at war had the munitions they needed but paved the way forward for future generations.

1

'Would you like one?' Betty asked, opening her bag of chocolate caramels and offering one to her handsome sweetheart, William.

'I bought them for you,' he said, smiling, 'but if you insist.' He winked, dipping his hand to the brown paper bag. 'They are rather good.'

The young couple had called at Harrison's sweet-shop on Green Street on their way to the Empire for a quarter of the gooey soft-centred chocolates; they had been a favourite of Betty's ever since her parents had taken her to the very same theatre house as a little girl. Tonight, of all nights, it was just what she needed. After a busier than normal week at the prestigious legal firm, Dawson & Sons, where she worked hard as a secretary, writing letters to clients and answering questions about their wills, Betty was ready to let her mind wander to a faraway place. Amiable and willing as ever, William hadn't objected when she'd suggested an evening at the Empire, where she could get lost watching James Stewart in *It's A Wonderful World*.

As she relaxed into the soft familiar seat, Betty edged as close to William as she possibly could. Just having him by her side was a sure-fire way of ensuring all her worries faded away. She had been looking forward to their date all day, knowing she could relax for a few hours with the one person who made her smile

1

more than anyone else in the world. As the main theatre lights began to fade and the heavy deep-red screen curtains slowly opened, Betty finally started to relax, happy in the knowledge she was about to escape to a fantasy world of romance and comedy.

But, just as it had for months now, the harsh introductory crackling of the Pathé newsreels interrupted the precious moment of tranquillity, terrifying black-and-white images invading the big screen. Stern-faced, menacing-looking soldiers stared straight ahead as they were addressed by Adolf Hitler, who had Poland in his sights. Hoping to deter an attack on Eastern Europe, Great Britain and France had formed a pledge to defend Poland if it was attacked. Instead of indulging in another chocolate caramel, Betty reached for William's hand, subconsciously squeezing his fingers a little tighter than normal as she stared at the incomprehensible scenes flashing before her eyes.

She understood why the public announcements had to be shown; the essential need to let the country know what was going on in the world and for people to understand once again the nation was facing the biggest risk they'd come up against since the First World War. Normally calm and methodical, Betty took a deep breath and let out an audible sigh as she looked up towards the intermittent flashing scenes. Hitler, with his pencil-thin moustache and dark, deep unreadable eyes, had signed a treaty of alliance with Italy and he was now in talks with Russia. Betty tried to placate the growing fear she felt deep in the pit of her stomach. Every time she saw that godforsaken man march his troops through another city, her heart raced a little faster. She didn't want to be the voice of doom, but she was convinced Britain was next on the evil Nazi leader's list. He seemed hell-bent on taking over the world and it seemed obvious to her he wasn't listening to anyone who tried to reason with his plans.

'He's building his empire. Are we next on his hit list?' Betty whispered to William, her voice ever so slightly faltering as she leant in even closer to the one person who always made her feel safe. Tightly clenching her free fist, Betty's neatly manicured nails dug sharply into her soft skin, leaving deep U-shaped indents in the palms of her hands. But she didn't feel a thing, her mind too overtaken by worry. It didn't take a genius to work out the months ahead could see Britain facing its worst battle since the Great War. As she sat, glued perfectly still to her chair, an icy-cold shiver ran down her spine, overwhelming anxiety soaring through her. Intuitively, sensing Betty's concerns, William turned to face her. 'Try not to worry, my love.' He smiled. 'Everything will be okay — I promise.' But, for the first time, William's kind eyes and well-meaning reassurances couldn't disperse Betty's fears. Despite only being twenty-three, in many ways she was older than her tender years might suggest. In her mind, England didn't seem ready to fight a war, despite the fact that they seemed to be perilously close to being on the edge of one.

William had already hinted at the idea of joining the RAF if war did break out, leaving his job as a trainee manager for an electrical company, and inevitably being separated from Betty. 'I've always wanted to fly,' he'd told her the last time she'd brought up the subject. 'Imagine how amazing it would be to see everything from above, speeding through the clouds.' She'd immediately regretted bringing it up as William was a dreamer who saw everything through

3

rose-tinted glasses. To Betty, though, it sounded like a pipe dream; a naive schoolboy adventure, which hadn't been thought through at all, and the dire consequences didn't bear thinking about.

As the newsreel came to a welcome end, Betty was brought back to the present, snapped out of her daydream. 'Are you okay?' William whispered, genuine concern still etched across his kind face. Betty forced a smile and nodded weakly, but the reality was she simply couldn't face the thought of losing someone else she loved. She and William had been going steady for two years now. He'd been the knight in shining armour she hadn't even realized she'd needed, so hell-bent on being completely independent and determined never to become reliant on anyone — especially after what she'd been through. After losing her mum, Elsie, at the tender age of ten, she had been left with no choice but to grow up fast. She'd helped her sister, Margaret, two years her senior, take care of their little brother, Edward — who, at eight, had been equally bewildered as to why their mother had been so cruelly taken away from them.

At nineteen, two years after securing her job as a secretary at Dawson & Sons Solicitors, Betty Clark had moved out of the neat three-bedroom terraced family home where she had grown up, and taken a small but perfectly adequate room in a smart boarding house in Walkley, the posh end of town, determined to be independent. Of course, she still went home as often as she could on a Sunday and helped her dad and Edward, now a handsome young man, prepare a traditional roast, always willing to get stuck in peeling a bag of tatties and top and tailing a saucepan of carrots.

Every few months, Betty's elder sister, Margaret, arrived from Nottingham with her husband, Derek, and their two-year-old dream of a little girl, June. The couple had moved seventy miles to the Midlands city after Derek was offered a lucrative job working on the railways. It meant the family only got together three or four times a year but, if nothing else, it made the afternoon even more special. After a modest feast of roast chicken and vegetables, followed by a jam sponge pudding with lashings of home-made custard, bought from the nearby bakery, the family usually marvelled at June as she toddled around the front room, showing off her much-loved dolly she'd received for her birthday. Betty missed Margaret; they had been so close growing up and Margaret had taken on the mother role she and Edward had desperately needed.

She recalled how, on one of her sister's visits to the family home, Margaret had looked over at Betty as she played dollies with June. 'I hope that one day you will meet a lovely man like Derek and have a little family of your own,' she'd mused, hopeful her younger sister would find someone special to share her life with.

It seemed fate had played a helping hand when Betty met William at a local church hall dance. Betty's best friend, Florence, had persuaded her she needed a night out to let her hair down after spending evening after evening with her head deep in law textbooks, secretly hoping one day to train as a solicitor. So, after Florence had somehow convinced Betty to don her best pink and cream floral knee-length dress and set her brown hair with sugar and water, they'd headed to St Michael's church hall to enjoy a night of dancing along to Fred Astaire's 'They Can't Take That Away From Me', washed down with a couple of glasses of sweet cloudy lemonade. It was while the girls were taking a break from the dance floor that Florence had spotted a keen and fresh-faced William glancing over at Betty. 'I think that lad has taken a bit of a shine to you,' she'd said with a wink, teasing her naturally shy and far more reserved best friend.

'Oh, give over,' Betty had sighed, shaking her head. It was just like Florence to read more into a situation and try to play cupid. 'I'm serious,' Florence had protested. 'If you don't believe me, look for yourself.' Against her better judgement, more to prove Florence wrong, Betty had glanced across the dance floor to where her friend had indicated. To her surprise, a handsome young man with slicked-back brown hair, dressed in a crisp white polo shirt and a pair of light-grey flannels, had caught her eye. As quick as she'd looked up, Betty had turned on her heels, colour rushing to her already flushing cheeks. 'He's probably eyeing up all the single-looking girls,' Betty had said, feeling unnaturally flustered. There was something about the young man's dashing appearance that had made her come over all of a flutter.

'Aha, so the attraction is obviously mutual,' Florence had grinned, amused by her friend's unexpected reaction. Before she had chance to tease Betty any further, a quiet, half-hearted, cough, coming from just behind them, had broken the moment.

As Betty had turned around, she'd come face to face with the handsome stranger.

'Would you like to dance?' he'd asked, his voice shaking with nerves.

'Erm, okay. Yes, I suppose one dance would be fine,' Betty had replied, and it wasn't just out of sympathy — there was something about this lad which had

6

caught her off guard, causing her usual prim façade to ever so slightly falter.

As William had led Betty to the wooden dance floor, she'd barely heard the lyrics of 'September in the Rain' echo through the hall. Instead, she'd allowed this dish of a young man to gently take her by the arm as they'd swayed to the music.

And there began a romance that had not only taken Betty completely by surprise but also left her a little shocked to say the least — it really was the last thing she had been expecting. After their first date, William had taken the liberty of asking Betty if he could call on her. 'I think I would like that very much.' She'd smiled, once again taken aback by her own willingness to let her guard down for the first time in years.

What followed were months of romantic rendezvous. Twice a week, William would appear at the boarding house, where Betty would be waiting, any creases pressed out of her skirts and a smudge of light pink rouge rubbed into her porcelain white cheeks. For so long, Betty had been fiercely independent, looking after others and politely refusing help in return, but even she couldn't resist being shown some long-awaited attention.

The lovesick pair spent Saturday afternoons strolling around the local park, and every couple of weeks they would join dozens of other cinema-goers at the Empire to catch the latest black-and-white movie. William never objected when the film showing was a romance, nor did he take any offence when he saw her eyes light up when James Stewart appeared on the screen.

As the overhead lights once again filled the theatre, William naturally turned to Betty. 'Did James Stewart live up to your expectations?' He grinned his boyish smile, hoping the film had lifted her spirits a little.

Giggling, Betty gently nudged William in the ribs, but the truth was she was still feeling rather unnerved. As William escorted her home to her room at 74 Collinson Street, Betty linked her arm with his tighter than normal.

'What is it?' he asked, concerned.

'Oh, it's nothing,' she said, sighing, yet again forcing her lips to create a forced smile.

William might have been naive but he wasn't daft; his sensitive side was one of the qualities Betty had fallen head over heels for.

'I know you better than that,' he said. 'Come on, a problem shared and all that.'

Betty knew there was no point in pretending, and the truth was she needed to vent her feelings and worries, which were overtaking her every thought. 'I know they have to show the newsreels; I just wish they wouldn't. I can't bear to see what's happening. I'm frightened of what might come next.'

Spinning Betty round to face him, he took both of her hands in his. 'Now listen up,' he said, 'everything is going to be all right. Our government won't let a war happen and, even if they did, Hitler doesn't stand a chance against the likes of me.'

Betty knew William was only trying to cheer her up — his way of dealing with any upset was to find a way of lightening the mood — but it was his endearing innocence which frightened her the most. Young men like her William saw the idea of war as one big adrenalin-fuelled adventure, a chance to take to the skies and see the world.

'Oh, my love,' Betty sighed, looking into William's

kind eyes, 'I just don't want to lose you too. I know joining the RAF feels like the right thing to do, and your bravery is one of the many reasons I love you so much.' Deep down, Betty knew she would struggle to change William's mind, but she couldn't just let him go without a fight. 'Couldn't you just take a job down the pit?' she asked, in a last-ditch attempt to convince William it was a much safer option than fighting the Luftwaffe. She knew William adored his job at Coopers, but she'd rather him take his chances six feet underground than flying across Germany's vast, perilous skies.

'You have so little faith in me.' William teased, waggling his finger from side to side. 'I will be the fastest fighter pilot the world has seen.' She'd known William long enough to give up her argument, reluctantly accepting he wasn't going to take the risk seriously. Why would he? His dad hadn't fought in the war, nor had his uncles — they had all been coal miners. The only problem was that their tales of being stuck in dark and damp mineshafts for hours at a time, nasty black itchy dust collecting in the corner of their eyes, ears and mouths — which, despite a weekly Friday night scrub in a tin bath, never completely disappeared — had put William off a career down the pit for life.

All Betty could do now was hope beyond hope that Neville Chamberlain had what it took to stop Hitler in his tracks and to avoid Britain going to war.

'Please don't worry, my lovely, sweet Bet,' William said, before he gently kissed her goodnight on the doorstep of her boarding house. For once she didn't bring their lingering embrace to a premature end, as she usually would, even if Mrs Wallis — the rather

Victorian in nature and incredibly proper and strict landlady — could see them.

Mrs Wallis kept a tight ship, refused her lodgers to enjoy any visitors, except the odd cup of tea in the communal and very formal front room, ensuring propriety was always the priority. It wouldn't surprise Betty if her landlady was hovering just a few paces behind the bright-red front door, ensuring her wards — as she liked to view those who took rooms in her rather grand townhouse — were home and safely tucked under their floral patchwork eiderdowns.

Knowing her rather stern landlady was now likely to be only seconds away from coughing or, even worse, opening the front door and catching her and William in a loving embrace, Betty finally, and reluctantly, released herself from William's warm and naturally protective hold.

'I'll call on you tomorrow,' he said, clinging to Betty's fingers, desperate to freeze time so they would never have to be parted.

But right on cue, heavy footsteps behind the door broke the tender moment as quick as a bolt of thunder. 'Goodnight, my love,' Betty sighed dreamily, giving William one final peck on the cheek.

For a few precious seconds, Betty had temporarily forgotten the foreboding thoughts that had dominated her mind all evening. But as she walked past Mrs Wallis in the corridor, bidding her goodnight and throwing her one of her most innocent smiles, the sense of uncertainty suddenly returned.

After washing her face clean with lukewarm water and lavender-scented soap in the porcelain sink in the corner of her room, Betty changed her pale-blue skirt and cream blouse, on which she could still smell

William's musky aftershave, and slipped into her long, white, crisp cotton nightdress.

Climbing into her cold but familiar bed, she tried to close her eyes as she rested her head upon the fluffy pillow — something Mrs Wallis prided herself on. But as soon as she tried to doze off, worry overcame her once more. To Betty, war seemed an obvious outcome to this whole messy situation, but where would that leave her and William? Would she have to kiss him goodbye if he did follow his heart and join the RAF, telling him she would see him soon, knowing the reality could paint a very different picture?

And what would she do? One thing was for sure: if war was announced, she couldn't do nothing. She couldn't just rest on her laurels and hope it would pass; she would have to do her bit.

Perhaps she'd have to do as the women of Sheffield did in the First World War and rise to the challenge, stepping into the steel toe-capped boots the city men would leave behind. The steel factories had relied on women to keep the foundry fires burning for four long years and Betty was determined she would be one of the first in line to ensure those sent to war, like her William, had the munitions they needed to fight the battle they faced.

2

Monday, 28 August 1939

Her arms aching, Nancy wrung the last flannelette sheet through the mangle.

'Thank the lord for that,' she said, sighing to herself, desperate for a cuppa after hours of laboriously scrubbing, washing and cleaning. It was Monday, and like most of the women on Prince Street, she had been giving the house a once-over since the crack of dawn. Even before she had safely delivered her two children, Billy, seven, and five-year-old Linda, at school, Nancy had stripped the beds and beat the front-room rug with a brush over the washing line in the back yard.

She had spent the morning scrubbing the front doorstep with a donkey stone, but despite the fact it left her knuckles red raw, and numb with cold when winter came, it was one of the jobs Nancy didn't mind. Up and down most roads across the city, women could be seen doubled over on their hands and knees, applying as much elbow grease as they did chatter with the neighbours, until their front step was spick and span. No well-respecting housewife would dream of missing the weekly ritual.

'How you getting on, Doris?' Nancy asked her good friend and weary-looking neighbour, as she trundled wearily out of her own front door

'Ah, not so bad.' Doris smiled, her eyes drooping despite it just turning ten thirty. 'Nothing a good brew and eight hours of solid sleep wouldn't sort.'

Nancy didn't need to ask why. She'd heard Doris's youngest crying through the walls in the early hours.

'Georgie?' Nancy asked, and Doris nodded. 'He'll settle soon enough,' Nancy said reassuringly, but if the truth be known, she had no idea if her well-meant words would come true or not. Little George, as he was also known, hadn't slept through a single night since his dad — 'Big George', Doris's husband — had been tragically killed at Vickers, the local steelworks. And by the look of it — neither had Doris. The heavy bags under her eyes grew darker by the day and her frail frame seemed to be visibly shrinking.

'Are you sure you're managing?' Nancy asked kindly. 'Why don't you let me have the kids over for tea and you can catch forty winks.'

'Oh, it's okay, luv,' came the reply. 'They're still all pretty needy.'

Nancy nodded. It had only been three months since Big George had died in the most tragic and unspeakable of manners. His neck scarf had got caught in one of the monstrous lathes; his workmates had tried to shut down the machine but couldn't stop the thick unforgiving belts quick enough. 'Decapitation caused by severe laceration of the neck,' the death certificate had read. No wonder Doris couldn't sleep; Nancy knew her mind must have filled with unbearable harrowing images as soon as she closed her eyes. There couldn't be a crueller way to die and now Doris was left with four children, all under the age of ten, to feed, clothe and care for. How she had time to scrub her doorstep, as well as take in washing, sewing and do the odd cleaning job for the neighbours, was beyond Nancy.

She knew there was no point telling her friend to

13

take it steady. How could she? Doris had bills to pay like everyone else and, with no husband to bring home a wage, she was juggling every ha'penny she had in a desperate bid to keep the tallyman at bay.

Doris didn't need to be told twice that if she didn't meet the rent, the debt collector would appear at the door and wouldn't think twice about taking away any possessions she had to cover the money she owed.

Nancy knew that Doris had already pawned most of the jewellery Big George had bought her over the years, including the intricate locket he'd given her on their wedding day, eleven years earlier — a family heirloom that had been passed down through the generations that had been a wrench to part with — but that she refused to let the gold band on her wedding finger go.

'Listen. Don't you be worrying about me,' Doris said, snapping Nancy out of her daydream. She didn't know how, but she was determined to find a way through the heart-wrenching predicament she had found herself in. She had no choice — she had four kids who were relying on her.

'Well, at least come and have that cuppa when we've finished cleaning later,' Nancy said. 'Bert said he'd be working late and I've got some leftover jam pudding from last night — the kids can share it between them after school.'

Doris smiled. 'Thanks, luv; that will cheer them up.'

It was the very least Nancy could do. She couldn't imagine what life would be like without Bert to bring home a steady wage from his job as a tram driver — his steadfast love and support was all Nancy had ever known.

The rest of the day passed in the blink of an eye.

14

After her doorstep almost glimmered in the bright sunshine, Nancy black-leaded the range, cleaned the windows with the previous week's collection of newspapers and a good douse of malt vinegar, before getting through the pile of washing that had mounted up. By the time three o'clock came, she'd done her jobs and was happy to put bucket and cloths away just in time to go and collect Billy and Linda from the school gates, before preparing a few extra carrots and potatoes to go with the leftover slices of beef from the day before's Sunday roast.

She's only been back a few minutes when, right on cue, as she boiled a fresh pan of water on the kitchen range, Nancy heard the giggles and chatter of Little George, Alice, Joe and their eldest sister, Katherine, come tumbling through the yard, with their exhausted mum.

'Perfect timing,' Nancy said, fetching a jug of creamy milk from the parlour and setting out her two best china cups and saucers. 'Put your feet up and have a minute,' she said, with a smile, scooping a generous spoonful of tea leaves from the old tin caddy into her trusty teapot.

'And look what I've got for you lot.' Nancy showed Doris's children, cutting the remainder of the jam sponge into squares. There was just enough for each of them, with a slightly smaller piece each for Billy and Linda. 'Now, tuck in and let your mum have a well-deserved break,' she said, knowing her neighbour's children probably hadn't had a sweet treat in weeks.

Apart from Little George, who clung to his mum like a limpet, the others all happily ran back into the yard with a trail of crumbs following them.

'Thanks, Nancy, you're a good friend,' Doris sighed,

grateful for ten minutes to sit down without fending off one request after another from six-year-old Alice, Joe, seven, and Katherine, nine.

'Don't be daft,' Nancy protested, 'you would do the same for me.' The two women had been neighbours since she and Bert had moved in the week after they had got married, eight years earlier. Slightly older, and wiser, Doris had immediately taken Nancy under her wing, something the younger woman was grateful for. Nancy's parents lived forty miles away in their home city of Manchester, not far from her elder sister, Lucy, and her husband, Jack. Nancy desperately missed Lucy; they had been so close growing up and she wished they lived nearer so she could chat to her about everyday life and any worries she had. But when Nancy moved into the neat three-bedroom terrace at 23 Prince Street, Doris had naturally slotted into the protective big sister role.

When Billy, and two years later Linda, had come along, it had been Doris who had held her hand through the painful contractions, mopping her forehead with a cool damp towel, calmly reassuring her and expertly telling Nancy when to push. And once her precious babies entered the world, yet again it was Doris who showed Nancy the ropes, until her mum had arrived to offer a helping hand.

Inevitably a close friendship had formed between the two women and now Nancy knew it was her turn to offer Doris support.

'Are you sure you're managing?' she asked tentatively.

'I've been better,' came the unsurprising reply, as Doris took a sip of her sugary sweet tea. 'The bills are mounting up,' she said, letting out an exhausted sigh.

'I'm robbing Peter to pay Paul and the kids are pulling me in all directions. It's not their fault. They are good really, but obviously need me more than ever. Alice asks at least ten times a day when George is coming home, Georgie isn't sleeping, Joe doesn't understand why he no longer has a daddy and poor Katherine is trying to be brave but every night sobs into her pillow until she has no tears left.'

Nancy took a deep breath and firmly pressed down on her bottom lip, desperately trying to fight the tears that were now stinging the back of her eyes and threatening to burst down her cheek. The thought of the heartache Doris and her children were suffering was unbearable, but the last thing her friend needed was to see her turn into a blubbering mess. Nancy tried to find the right words to ease Doris's pain, something that would give her a tiny glimmer of hope and reassure her things would get better. But each time Nancy went to open her mouth, she found herself completely at a loss as to what to say. The thought of Billy or Linda going through the same indescribable horror stopped Nancy in her tracks — no child should endure that sort of anguish, especially at such a tender age. It was hard enough for an adult to come to terms with such a gaping loss, let alone little ones, who were far too young and innocent to make any sense of how cruel life could be.

'I know I can't bring George back,' Nancy started, 'or take away what you must be feeling right now, but I'll always be here for you.' She gently took hold of Doris's tiny shaking hand. 'If there is anything you need, or anything I can do — whatever if it is, I'll do my best. Maybe I can have the children of an evening if you want to take on a couple of extra cleaning jobs?'

Not that Nancy liked the idea of Doris working all the hours God sent but she knew, now more than ever, it had become an evil necessity if she wanted to keep the wolves from the door.

'Thanks, Nancy, luv.' Doris murmured weakly, slowly stroking Little George's back, who had finally nodded off on her chest. 'You're a good friend. I might have to take you up on that if you're really sure.'

Relieved there was some practical way she could finally help her neighbour, who was more like a sister, Nancy smiled. 'Of course, I'll even make an extra jam sponge. That will keep the kids happy.' She hoped Doris would feel a little safer in the knowledge that she could rely on her whenever she needed to. After all, wasn't that what friends were for?

* * *

Long after Doris had taken the children home, and she'd tucked Billy and Linda into bed with a kiss and a bedtime story, Nancy couldn't stop thinking about her pal. She had filled the hole Nancy's sister, Lucy, had left behind when she'd moved away and now the thought of her suffering in the most agonizing of manners was just heartbreaking.

As she put the last of the dinner dishes away and settled down for her last cuppa of the day, the kitchen door swung open.

'Oh, hiya luv.' Nancy beamed at the sight of her husband, Bert, instantly jumping up to fetch his dinner from the range. 'Long day?'

'Aye,' he said with a sigh, leaning over to give his wife a peck on the cheek. 'Offering to pull a double shift wasn't my brightest idea. I've lost count of how

18

many times I've driven back and forth to the city centre today.'

Nancy smiled. Bert had always been a hard worker and whenever his manager offered him an extra shift as a tram driver, he never turned it down, grateful for the extra cash he would receive in his wage packet on Friday.

'It all helps pay the bills,' she said, carefully placing Bert's warmed-up beef dinner in front of him. Grabbing a mug for her husband and a cup and saucer for herself, she poured them each a strong brew.

'You look distracted tonight, luv. What is it?' Bert asked in between mouthfuls of mashed potatoes.

Holding her china cup to her mouth, the one small luxury Nancy allowed herself, she told Bert about her chat with Doris. 'I just wish I could make it all better for her. Apart from grieving for George, she's worrying herself sick about paying the bills. The little ones are struggling too. How on earth do you explain to them that Daddy has gone to heaven?'

Bert looked up from his now nearly empty plate. He knew how much his wife thought of Doris. 'I'll be earning an extra bob or two this week with all this overtime. Why don't you nip to the butcher's on Saturday and get an extra big joint and invite them all round for tea?'

Nancy reached across the table and squeezed her husband's arm, feeling reminded as to why she'd married him. 'That's a lovely idea,' she said. 'Thank you.'

'Ah, it's nothing in the grand scheme of things,' Bert replied, swallowing his last forkful of beef. 'It will do her good and I know how much you love seeing all the kids play together.'

He was right. Nancy had always dreamt of having

a houseful of children running around, getting up to mischief, but after Linda had come along, she and Bert had agreed two was enough. They had just enough money to live comfortably without worrying where the next meal was coming from and, despite always secretly craving holding another new-born baby for the very first time, Nancy felt lucky she had been blessed with a boy and girl.

'Besides which,' Bert added, 'I think we are all going to have to stick together more than ever soon enough.'

'What do you mean, luv?' Nancy asked, although deep down she, like the rest of the country, had felt a sense of uncertainty for months now. 'Do you really think it will happen?' she added before Bert had a chance to reply.

'Aye, I do,' he answered, almost too quickly for Nancy's liking.

She pulled her arms across her body as a cold shiver ran through her. An impending war had been the elephant in the room in the Edwards' house all summer. Bert rarely spoke about the latest developments across Europe, knowing his wife, an eternal worrier, couldn't bear to think about it. Nancy always avoided any conversation around Hitler and his power-hungry actions, all too aware Bert would be one of the first to offer his services to fight the German's terrifying regime, always wanting to do the right thing. But with the rest of her family so far away, the idea of Bert disappearing as well was one worry too many for Nancy. She would have loved to have been more like Doris, who had endless strength and determination to carry on despite how hard life was and the trauma she had faced.

I couldn't be that strong, Nancy quietly thought to

herself. I know I would crumble.

That night, after Bert had taken himself off to bed earlier than usual in preparation for another early start on the trams, Nancy sat alone at the kitchen table, contemplating her thoughts.

In the darkness — pitch black save for the glimmer of a candle, due to the newly installed thick black fabric she and Bert had fitted to every window to act as blackout blinds to comply with the new regulations — Nancy nursed the last dregs of her lukewarm tea, unable to stop her mind from wandering. Poor Doris had already lost her husband and Nancy could see the devastating effect it was having on her; the last thing she now wanted was to say goodbye to Bert as he left to fight in a strange unknown country, hundreds of miles away, not knowing if she, or their precious children, who adored their daddy more than life itself, would ever see him again.

The thought of him never coming back was too much to bear.

How could I ever tell Billy and Linda their daddy had died? Nancy silently worried, scrunching her eyes closed, just the thought of it was too much to even contemplate out loud.

Bert had also been the breadwinner since their children had come along and seeing how much Doris was now struggling left her terrified.

If the unthinkable happened, she really had no idea how on earth she would manage to put food on the table and keep a roof over their heads.

3

Eyeing up the uniform rows of Max Factor make-up, Patty mentally calculated how many weeks it would be before she could justify buying the baby pink lipstick she'd set her heart on. 'It would match my new flowery skirt perfectly,' she told her workmate and best friend.

Hattie rolled her eyes in mock jest. 'You only had a red one a few days ago. Surely you don't need another lippy already?'

'You can never have too many,' came Patty's reply. 'What's the point in slogging me guts out if I can't reward myself with something new every week or so? Besides which it might just be what's needed to teach that Tommy Hardcastle a lesson at the City Hall next week. I'm sure he's as sweet on me as I am on him but he's just playing hard to get. Last Saturday he winked at me as he led some little trollop onto the dance floor. Probably knew she was an easy catch and he could have his wicked way with her. Well, I've got me standards.'

'Maybe you should aim a little higher,' Hattie answered as soon as Patty stopped to take a breath. 'He doesn't sound very gentleman-like if he's prepared to string you along.'

'Maybe,' Patty said, barely contemplating what her friend was saying. 'He is a bit of a dish, though. I'm sure if we just had one dance, he would realize I'm far

22

more fun than some of those little wenches he's been toying with.'

Hattie gave up. There was no telling Patty. They'd worked together for the last two years at the city centre Woolworth's branch and she'd always been the same — looking for the next adventure, in search of some fun. Never content with a quiet Saturday night at home, Patty spent her week planning her outfit, how she would style her hair and whether her pink satin blouse would look more seductive than her creamy lace-trimmed camisole and matching fitted cardigan.

But who can blame her? Hattie thought to herself. She'd been the same a couple of years earlier at seventeen, before she'd settled down with her John. She too had loved to get dolled up, dab on some rouge and slip into a pair of heels for a night on the town.

Patty began emptying the latest boxes of raspberry-red Tangee lipsticks onto the waiting shelves, bringing Hattie back to the present.

'I think I'm going to wash me hair on Saturday afternoon and wear it down,' Patty said. Her dad had told her ever since she was a little girl that her long strawberry-blonde curly hair and dreamy hazel eyes would end up breaking hearts one day. 'What do yer reckon — if I wear it like Mae West did in *I'm No Angel*? She certainly had Cary Grant falling at her feet. I could clip my ringlets up and just have a few hanging down around my shoulders. My lacy top is quite fitted too, so I could always take my cardi off. That's got to get his attention,' she mused.

Just as she was about to start discussing her choice of skirts and heels, the store manager walked across the floor towards the two girls.

'Right, girls,' came his monotone command, 'less

chatting, more working.'

As he walked away, Patty repeated his headteacher-like command under her breath, using her hands to mimic his comments.

'Stop it!' Hattie hissed, trying to stifle her giggles. 'You'll get us both the sack at this rate.'

Nonchalant as ever, Patty shrugged her shoulders. 'Ah, well, it wouldn't be the end of the world. Not like we earn a king's ransom and I've 'eard a rumour the steelworks might be in need of some new young fresh blood if Hitler carries on with his crazy tirade across Europe.'

'What? Are you serious?' Hattie asked, as she carefully restocked an empty-looking shelf with boxes of a new range of waterproof black cake mascara, which came in a little tray with an intricate application brush and promised to give you movie star lashes.

'Yeah, me dad overheard one of the bosses talking about it.' Patty's dad, Bill, like his father before him, and his mom for a short time during the First World War, had worked at Vickers Steel since he'd left school at fourteen. Starting off as the tea lad, he'd worked his way up through the ranks and was now a foreman in the rolling mill. 'He reckons if we end up going to war, some of the younger lads will leave and they'll need some of us lasses to fill their places. Not that me mom is too impressed like. She told him she'd rather see me clean strangers' toilet basins than see me risk m' life in one of those huge factories.'

Carefully placing the last wonder mascara on the now rather enticing display, Hattie started dusting the normally pristine white counter, brushing off the remnants of dust from the cardboard box they had been stored in. 'I can see her point, if I'm honest,

24

Patty. Why would you want to swap working behind a make-up counter to risk life and limb in one of the dirty noisy places? I bet it's full of lecherous blokes who would be more interested in what's underneath yer overalls, than how useful you are?'

'Aye, watch what yer saying,' Patty laughed, faking her horror. 'Are you saying m' dad is a letch?'

'Course not,' Hattie sighed, knowing her friend was pulling her leg, 'but I bet there's a few wandering eyes amongst the younger ones.'

With that, a grin as big as the Cheshire cat's appeared on Patty's face. 'Well, that would teach Tommy Hardcastle a lesson, wouldn't it? I might have me pick of fellas if he's not careful.'

Hattie couldn't help but giggle — Patty must be the only person in the entire country that could be excited about the prospect of another war. 'You really do take the biscuit.' Hattie chuckled.

'Well, you've got to look on the bright side,' Patty said, grinning. 'No point worrying. Besides which, I'd take great pleasure out of telling miserable Mr Watson where to stuff his poxy job!'

Bemused, Hattie rolled her eyes. 'But can you really imagine working in one of those filthy great factories in a pair of grubby ill-fitting pair of brown overalls, working yourself to the bone every day? You wouldn't be able to paint your face on and eye up the latest lippy in there!? I've heard it's really hard work, too; you'd have to toughen up sharpish. You don't even like lifting boxes of make-up; how are you going to manage hauling heavy slabs of steel about?'

'Oh, I'm sure there will be some dashing young lad to help me out.' Patty giggled. 'And there's no way I'd turn up without my lippy and mascara on. Just because I'd be in a factory, doesn't mean I have to drop me standards, y'know.'

If only it was as black and white as that, Hattie silently thought to herself, but she knew there was no point in trying to explain to Patty the grave consequences of war.

She'd seen first-hand the terrible impact it had had on her own dad who'd sacrificed his tender years to fight against the Germans. Although he didn't say much, after one too many pints of ale on a Friday night in the local boozer, his mood would drop and his temper would get the better of him. Hattie's mum had borne the brunt of his aggression more times than she'd had hot dinners throughout their marriage. Whenever Hattie asked her why she put up with it, the answer was always the same. 'Your dad wasn't always like this,' she repeated. 'Before the war, he was a kind and loving man who wouldn't hurt a fly. But he saw some terrible things and I guess you always hurt the ones closest to you.' Hattie had always struggled to understand the logic in taking your anger out on someone you supposedly loved. She couldn't imagine her John hurting her, but she knew not to press her mum — she was suffering enough without her only daughter nagging her too.

For the rest of her shift, Patty could barely keep the grin off her face as her mind wandered to what it would be like working with a load of strapping young men. Surely then she would have her choice of dates on a Saturday night; even so she couldn't help hoping Tommy Hardcastle would show her some attention at the weekend.

At five o'clock, as the last customers left the store, Patty grabbed her red cardigan from under the counter.

26

'Any plans to see lover boy tonight?' she teased her workmate.

'Actually yes.' Hattie grinned. 'He's meeting me from work and we're off for a cuppa and hopefully a slice of chocolate cake.' As the two pals double-checked for the umpteenth time that the make-up counter was spick and span, not a mascara or lipstick out of place — only too aware Mr Watson would be the first to notice and give the girls a long and tedious lecture on how important it was to take pride in your work — Patty couldn't help but feel a tiny bit envious of Hattie. Not in a bitter way; she would just love to have someone care for her in the way John adored her friend.

As the girls finally left the store, Patty hugged Hattie.'Have an extra slice of cake for me.' She smiled as she spotted John in his smart work suit walking towards them. Patty could see why Hattie had been initially attracted to him, with his immaculately swept back brown hair, chiselled cheekbones and deep brown eyes, he was a dream to look at. From what Hattie had revealed, it was his warm and caring personality for which she had really fallen head over heels.

'You have a good evening too,' shouted Hattie. 'See ya tomorrow.'

Suddenly feeling like a gooseberry, Patty waved her goodbye before heading down The Moor to catch her bus home. As she jumped on the number 21, she felt a sense of tingling excitement at the thought of a possible new adventure ahead. She might not get a discount on her new lippies if she was working at the steelworks, but that was a small price to pay — besides which, she'd heard the wages were pretty good, so she might even be able to afford a new addition to her

27

make-up bag every week.

As Patty got off the bus at Attercliffe and headed the few hundred yards home, she had a spring in her step and couldn't wait to tell her mum her plans. But as she walked through the door at number 56 Thompson Road, her little bubble of elation was somewhat dampened.

'Milk, Mommy, milk,' came the high-pitched squeal from her youngest brother Thomas, known as Tom Tom, who was being rocked from side to side by their sister, Sally, who looked close to tears. 'Soon, sweetheart,' she said as soothingly as possible, desperately looking towards their flustered-looking mom, Angie, who was holding a pan of potatoes in one hand and trying to pour some milk into a cup with the other.

'Here, let me help you,' Patty said, rushing to her mom's side and taking the jug from her hand.

'Thanks, luv,' Angie said. 'I just need to get tea out. Your dad will be home any minute.'

Patty took her screeching brother from Sally, who instantly sighed a breath of relief, and raised the cup of what could have been pure nectar to Tom Tom's gaping mouth, to save everyone from another one of his ear-piercing demands. She smiled. 'Hey, come on. It's here now.' As soon as the first drip of milk hit Tom Tom's quivering pink lips, peace was restored.

'Thank God for that,' Angie said. 'I swear, you'd think he hadn't been fed for a month.'

'Oh, Tom Tom,' Patty sighed, pretending to be cross, using the nickname her baby brother had adopted. 'Have you been a demanding boy again?'

The angelic blond-haired two-year-old looked up at his sister as though butter wouldn't melt. 'You were just thirsty, angel, weren't you?' Patty added, grinning. 'Were they starving yer?'

'No chance of that,' Angie said. 'He's not stopped munching all day. I swear he's going to eat me out of house and home.'

'He's not the only one,' came Patty's dad's voice as he walked through the kitchen door. 'What's that you have cooking, luv?' Bill asked, giving his amused wife a peck on the cheek.

'Beef casserole and mash,' came the reply.

'Ooh, you're a darlin', cooking yer old man his favourite after a long day.'

With that the door from the hallway flew open. 'Dad, you're 'ome,' exclaimed Patty's second youngest brother, eleven-year-old John, as he ran towards Bill, just as he had done every evening from the day he could walk.

'Come 'ere, son, and give yer old dad a big hug.'

John didn't have to be asked twice. As the pair took part in their evening ritual, Angie scooped a ladle full of mash onto six plates, followed by a generous portion of beef, carrots and onions covered in a rich gravy — the aroma making Tom Tom's eyes widen, resembling saucers.

Patty laughed. 'Don't worry, little 'un. Yours is here too.' He wasn't the only one keen to tuck in; the clatter of dinner being served brought Sally and Patty's younger sister, thirteen-year-old Emily, bursting into the kitchen.

In the space of seconds, five chairs and a wooden highchair had been filled and the clatter of knives and forks being lifted from the wooden table filled the room.

'More, Pat Pat,' Tom Tom managed to articulate

as soon as he'd swallowed his first spoonful, his little mouth hanging open like a goldfish.

'His father's son.' Bill laughed, leaning over and ruffling his mop of blond curls. 'You just love yer snap, don't yer, kiddo?'

Tom Tom grinned his toothy smile, pleased he'd got his daddy and the rest of his family's attention. With that, the whole family turned to the youngest member of the household, just in time to see him wolf down another mouthful of his mom's best casserole.

A sense of tranquillity had overtaken the storm Patty had walked into just twenty minutes earlier. Picking her moment, she thought this might be a good time to share the plan she'd been cooking up.

'Do yer reckon a war is really looming?' she said, tentatively broaching the subject.

'Why do yer ask that now, sunshine?' Bill asked, using the name he'd called his eldest daughter from the moment she'd entered the world, apparently with a big grin on her face, despite Angie's insistence it was just wind. He was always keen to keep his household a happy ship but sensed his eldest daughter was about to bring the mood down somewhat.

'Well, the rumours are rife that Hitler won't stop until he's taken over Europe,' Patty started tentatively, 'and I thought I might be able to come and work with you if the factory need an extra pair of hands.'

Bill had never been a man to shout and scream or lose his temper when something upset him but the deafening silence that followed was more than enough for Patty and the rest of the family to understand she had stepped across an invisible line, which had left her normally amiable and placid dad quietly reeling.

Calmly putting down his knife and fork, you could

have heard a pin drop in what was the normally lively and vibrant kitchen, where more often than not six voices were all chattering away at the same time, all competing to be heard over one another. But even little Tom Tom somehow knew not to let out so much as a murmur, despite reaching for his spoon to quickly grab another mouthful of mash.

'Why in God's name would you want to do that?' Bill asked, doing his utmost to keep his voice from going up a single decibel but with an unfaltering tone that warned his daughter she better have a damn good explanation for her latest madcap idea.

Patty might have lived in her own little world that centred around having fun and enjoying every moment, but she knew there was no way on earth she could tell her dad the real incentive. Thinking fast, she said in her most convincing voice, 'I just thought they might need some extra help like they did in the Great War when Nannan worked there, and it would be more worthwhile than m' job at Woollies with that blinkin' slave driver Mr Watson breathing down m' neck every five minutes.'

Angie, who could count on one hand how many times she'd seen her husband in such a silent internal fury, stared across the now tense table at her husband, trying to second-guess how he would react to their fiercely independent and free-living daughter's announcement — a trait she had clearly inherited from Bill's mom, Florence.

Battling with his own conscience, Bill took a deep breath and looked Patty straight in the eye.

'I only want to say this once,' he said quietly but firmly. 'Over my dead body is any daughter of mine working in a dirty, filthy and dangerous foundry full of men, some of whom have questionable morals. I'd rather see you sweep the streets first.'

Angie quickly shot her daughter a look that quite clearly said: Now is not the time to argue. Do not say a word, not a single word. Nevertheless she already had a sinking feeling this was one battle her stubborn Patty would not give up without a fight. Once their determined daughter got an idea in her head, she would move hell and high water to make it happen.

But even for Patty, this came with a caveat. She adored the ground her dad walked on. He had been her real-life hero for as long as she could remember: from the first time she'd fallen over as a toddler, grazing her knee, and he'd been there to lovingly scoop her into his arms until her tears faded away; to when he'd appeared at the school gates, leaving work early, to give a not-to-be ignored stern telling off to the thirteen-year-old boys who had teased his daughter for her 'drainpipe' legs. He had always been the one person Patty knew would be by her side no matter what.

So, despite her seemingly far-fetched idea, which she was somehow determined not to let dissolve into thin air, Patty also knew this was not the time or the way to press her well-meaning dad. His heart was in the right place; she just had to find a way of gently persuading him to come round to her way of thinking.

Not wanting to spoil what had the makings of a pleasant family evening, Patty looked up at her dad. 'I guess I'll just have to find a way of keeping out of old Mr Watson's bad books then,' she said.

'Believe me, he will seem like putty in your hands compared to some of the foremen I've come across,' Bill replied, his tone already softening, happy his daughter appeared to have taken on board what he'd said and come to her, at times, dizzy senses.

Later, Patty tucked her little brother into bed, who with a full belly and sucking on his thumb, was finally content. As he closed his eyes, his 'Pat Pat' gently sang him a lullaby, but his sister wasn't quite as settled, her mind wandering once again.

Surely there had to be more to life than putting rows of lipsticks in order of colour and making sure every counter was devoid of a speck of dust. Patty craved adventure, and war might just be the thing to bring it, so, if the opportunity arose, she was going to take the bull by the horns, seize the moment and fly with it — she just had to convince her fiercely protective dad first.

4

'Good morning!' came William's normal cheery greeting as Betty opened the front door of her lodgings. 'How's my sweet girl?'

'You're a charmer, I'll give you that much.' Betty grinned as the man she adored reached over and quickly pecked her cheek before she could protest, worrying Mrs Wallis, her landlady, would be hovering nearby, on high alert because her youngest 'ward' had an early Sunday morning visitor.

'So, do you fancy a quick walk with yours truly?' William asked, knowing his Bet was secretly amused he took the odd risk when it came to the very strict proprietor of 74 Collinson Street.

Betty quickly glanced down at the little silver watch with the thin red leather strap, which her dad had bought her as a twenty-first birthday present. It was just after nine thirty.

'As long we're back before eleven,' she answered. 'I don't want to miss the announcement.'

William didn't need to question why. The whole country had been on tenterhooks for months, but the last few weeks, in particular, had seen a dramatic increase in tensions. Despite Neville Chamberlain's efforts to come to an agreement with Adolf Hitler; the power-hungry German dictator had ignored the repeated requests, signed a deal with Russia's equally notorious Stalin and the pair had defiantly invaded

Poland, murdering thousands of innocent Jews.

'Come on, the fresh air will do you good,' William said, reaching his hand out to take Betty's. She knew he was right. She'd barely slept the past few nights, worrying what the future held and whether the life she had carved out for herself was about to come crumbling down.

Sensing Betty's mood was about to become somewhat melancholy, William ushered her away from the door, down the steps and led her up the street.

'What about my jacket,' Betty half protested.

'You don't need one,' William said. 'It's a beautiful day. The sun is shining and, besides, you can have mine if you get nippy.'

Happy to be persuaded, Betty linked her arm through William's as they turned the corner onto Thomas Avenue, which wound its way up to the local small park where the pair had spent many an hour enjoying each other's company.

'A letter from Margaret arrived yesterday,' she said, as she and William sat down on their favourite bench.

'How is she?' William asked, genuinely interested, aware how much Betty was missing and worrying about her elder sister.

'Like me, she's feeling anxious and I think if Derek's job allowed it, she would move back to Sheffield in a flash. She hates being so far away from us all and would like little June to see more of her family,' Betty sighed. 'But the good news is that June's saying new words every day and apparently becoming a right little chatterbox — I don't think they are getting a moment's peace.' With that Betty's face lit up — talking about her much-loved niece was always a sure-fire way to bring a smile to her face. 'I bought her a new

Winnie the Pooh book this week as a treat. I'm going to pop it in the post. The drawings are just lovely and I'm sure she will love hearing about the adventures Christopher Robin gets up to.'

For the next hour the couple chatted about their week at work, how Betty's boss had praised her for ongoing efficiency and William's manager had started to hint at a promotion if he carried on excelling in the manner he was.

'Oh, that's good news,' Betty said, secretly hoping it would be enough to keep him interested and persuade him to climb the career ladder, as opposed to following his dream to serve the country. It wasn't that Betty didn't want William to do the right thing — his desire to was one of the reasons she loved him as much as she did — but it was that very love, which left part of her fighting every urge she had to beg him to forget about becoming an RAF pilot if and when the time came.

The worry of what lay ahead made Betty look at her watch. 'We better get going,' she said, almost jumping up from the bench. 'It's ten thirty. I would like to be back in good time.'

William was slightly disappointed their pleasant interlude to the park had been cut short, but he also knew Betty wouldn't be persuaded to wait a minute longer. 'Your wish is my command,' he happily conceded, without a hint of hurt in his voice. And with that the pair walked back to Betty's lodgings at a slightly faster pace than they had coming.

Knowing Mrs Wallis wouldn't hear of William stepping a single foot inside Betty's first-floor room, the couple made their way into the immaculately kept communal front room, with its old brown leather sofa and armchairs and wooden sideboard full of spare china crockery and her landlady's set of best Arthur Price cutlery that only came out at Christmas and Easter. The wireless — positioned in between two old black-and-white framed photos, one of a couple Betty assumed to be Mrs Wallis's late parents and the other of a dashing young man in uniform — was already playing.

'Can we join you?' Betty asked her anxious-looking landlady.

'Oh, yes, please do,' she replied. 'I've just made a fresh pot of tea. Why don't you both have one with me?'

'That would be lovely,' Betty accepted politely, sensing that, for once, Mrs Wallis was grateful for the company. She may have been curt and kept a tight ship, but no one could ever fault her exemplary manners. Immediately standing up, Mrs Wallis walked to the sideboard and picked out two additional dainty cups and saucers adorned with delicate pink roses. As she carefully poured the tea from a matching pot, Betty could feel the flurry of butterflies in the pit of her tummy rising. She longed to grip William's hand but wouldn't dream of upsetting her landlady by being so forward, especially when she sensed she was equally as anxious. Instead, Betty made do with taking comfort in the loving glance her sweetheart directed straight at her. Instinctively she knew William was telling her everything would be all right; they would get through whatever happened together, but no matter how hard Betty tried to remain positive, the niggling worry she'd felt for weeks was ever present.

At exactly 11.15 a.m., just as she lifted her cup of tea to her lips in a bid to quench her thirst, which had left her throat as dry as sandpaper, the music on the wireless abruptly stopped, the crackling interference that followed sending an icy-cold shiver down Betty's spine. Instantly she closed her eyes, which were threatening to erupt into tears as the feeling of impending doom she had been trying to suppress all day soared through her.

The room, which had fallen into a deadly silence, was now filled with the Prime Minister's calm and steady voice. Addressing the nation, Neville Chamberlain announced: 'This morning the British Ambassador in Berlin handed the German Government a final note stating unless we heard from them by eleven o'clock that they were prepared at once to withdraw their troops from Poland, a state of war would exist between us. I have to tell you now no such undertaking has been received . . . '

Betty was in no doubt: those initial words were preparing the country for something very grave indeed. Squeezing her cup a little tighter, but now unable to avert her eyes from the brown wireless, she listened, barely able to catch her own breath, as the words 'consequently this country is at war with Germany' echoed from the speaker.

She desperately tried to comprehend the consequences of what the leader of the country had just said. Her mind raced, her thoughts quickly recalling the look of sheer worry and panic in her dad's eyes a week earlier when news of Hitler's barbaric assault on Poland had been broadcast.

He'd sat slumped at the wooden kitchen table with his head in his hands. 'Please God, don't put us through this again,' Joseph had whispered, almost avoiding vocalizing the words, in the hope that if he didn't say them it wasn't real. 'It can only end one way,' he'd trailed off.

Betty's dad had lost two of his brothers to the First World War — both of them had gone off to fight, fresh-faced and keen as mustard, assuming they would only be gone a few months. Joseph barely spoke about Betty's uncles, but she'd picked up enough to know that within the space of two years they were both missing, presumed dead. Now it seemed her dad's recent words were becoming a terrifying reality.

For what seemed like an eternity, no one spoke. It was as though the world had stopped and the slightest movement would leave it spiralling into the unknown. Finally, Betty looked up.

William was stock-still — his eyes revealing the jumbled thoughts that he was trying to silently make sense of. For months he'd hinted at nothing but donning the esteemed mid-blue RAF pilot's uniform and taking to the skies to defend their beloved country against enemy attacks; but now his boyish dreams were beginning to feel like a frightening reality, a million miles away from what he'd envisaged as an exciting adventure.

Suddenly conscious of Betty's eyes boring into him, William smiled weakly, unable to articulate the conflicting thoughts running through his mind. 'I will be the fastest fighter pilot the world has seen' — wasn't that what he had assured his frightened Bet, when she'd expressed how worried she was? He desperately tried to suppress the fear that was now thumping inside his chest as a wave of adrenalin shot through him. This was it — his chance to do something useful, to prove he was capable of something extraordinary, that he could be a man, not a boy and show Betty that he had what it took to one day be worthy of asking for her hand in marriage.

Their gaze, which had relayed so many unspoken words, was suddenly broken by the faintest of gasps. At once, both William and Betty, who had been submerged in a trance-like state, instinctively turned to where the quietest of sobs was coming from. As they looked up, though, they couldn't help feeling they had accidentally intruded on a moment of intimate privacy, as Mrs Wallis took a deep breath and, with her embroidered handkerchief, patted away the stream of tears that were gently flowing down her cheeks.

Concerned, Betty glanced at William, then back to her troubled landlady. She had never once seen her anything but perfectly composed, with an impenetrable steely exterior.

'Mrs Wallis . . . ' Betty just about whispered, not wanting to cause her any embarrassment, breaking the hushed atmosphere that had descended on the front room of 74 Collinson Street. 'Can I get you anything? A fresh cup of tea, maybe?'

As though waking from a terrible dream, Mrs Wallis suddenly came to, blinking away her tears and slowly shaking her head from side to side.

'Oh, I'm so sorry, dear,' she started, desperately trying to stop her voice from faltering. 'I didn't mean to worry you. It's just . . . ' Before Mrs Wallis could say the words that were painfully lodged in the back of her throat, she turned to the photo of the uniformed handsome young man on the sideboard. 'Well, the announcement, you see, it just . . . it just brought back some very painful memories.'

Betty might have been at least half her housekeeper's age, but she instantly recognized the gut-wrenching

40

pain Mrs Wallis was currently enduring and desperately trying to contain. It was the same feeling that would leave Betty's chest physically aching when she thought about her own mum for too long, or recalled the evening her distraught dad had come home from the hospital and explained the person she loved with all her heart had died. The thought of never seeing her beautiful caring mummy again had left her paralysed with grief, unable to utter a single word for days.

She couldn't be one hundred per cent sure, as Mrs Wallis didn't wear a wedding ring, but she assumed the dark-haired man with the chiselled jawline and warm smile in the photo frame on the sideboard had once been her only true sweetheart. But this wasn't the time to pry or cause her landlady any further suffering. 'Here, let me pour you a fresh tea,' Betty said, gently taking the cup and saucer from Mrs Wallis's hands, which were ever so slightly trembling.

'Thank you,' came the reply, as Mrs Wallis regained her posture. 'You mustn't take any notice of me. I'm letting my silly old sentiments take over.'

All the time William stayed perfectly silent, feeling awkward, his youth preventing him from finding the right words that wouldn't sound shallow or insincere. He wanted to jump up and wrap his arms around Mrs Wallis and Betty, but somehow it felt like the wrong thing to do. It wouldn't be proper. He knew he couldn't erase the pain his sweetheart's landlady was suffering. Instead, all he could do was offer a weak smile and hope it conveyed how sorry he was for whatever had left her so unusually upset.

Sensing the anguish between the young couple, Mrs Wallis looked firmly at William. 'This isn't a time to stand on ceremony. I think you need to give Betty a hug,' she said forcefully. 'I think you'll find that's exactly what she really needs right now. None of us know what's coming and you should make the most of the time you have together as you never know when you could be torn apart through no fault of your own.'

Grateful for Mrs Wallis's intuition, William sighed wistfully as he reached across to his sweetheart, who was sat on the adjoining chair, and gently took the tips of her fingers in his and squeezed them. Unable to articulate the whirlwind of worries in her mind at that precise moment, Betty simply nodded, thankful for the small but intimate moment of comfort.

Betty allowed the poignant act of love to linger for a minute or so, as she composed herself. Taking a deep breath, she slowly released her hand from William's and refreshed her own and William's china cup, as she tried to gather her own thoughts that were racing around her mind at a terrifying rate of knots. The Prime Minister was still addressing the country, but his words were now a murmur in the background. The minutiae didn't matter at this moment — it wasn't going to alter the terrifying fact that England was now at war with Germany and their despicable godforsaken leader.

Betty knew there was every chance William would be called up or would volunteer to serve in the RAF sooner rather than later. She couldn't and wouldn't stop him — how could she? She couldn't bear the thought of being separated from William but everyone had to do their bit, herself included. She loved her job at Dawson & Sons but would that really be enough to help? She doubted it. There had to be something else she could do — sitting back in an office job would not satisfy her inevitable desire to do something worthwhile, to make a difference; she just needed to think about exactly how she could help.

'Hopefully it won't be so bad,' William said, finally finding his voice, and catapulting Betty back to the here and now.

Mrs Wallis looked up, once again alert, her usual demean-our now surfacing. 'Let's hope not,' she said, smiling weakly, 'because if it's even a fraction as cruel as the last one, the consequences will be unthinkable.'

Betty knew her beloved William wouldn't be able to grasp the gravity of what Mrs Wallis had just said. He wouldn't be able to comprehend what losing tens of thousands of men does to a country. He wouldn't be able to take on board the sheer pain and heart-ache that causes. How could he? William had lived an enviable happy and uneventful existence; he'd never endured pain or loss, had never endured the heartache of close relatives being lost to a fight they didn't ask to take part in, or even heard of any for that matter. She wasn't angry, though; William's quiet innocence and unstoppable positive take on life were amongst his most attractive and appealing qualities. It balanced her own fears, gave her something to really smile about and taught her how to relax and enjoy the simple things in life.

But how on earth could she tell her darling William that his dream to serve his country, his determina-tion to do the right thing — to embark on what he saw as an exciting adventure as a pilot — was the one thing that at the very least was likely to rob him of his pure unadulterated love of life, but quite unthinkably, could ultimately take far more?

5

'Tea's up,' Nancy called, as she walked to the back door to call in Billy and Linda from the yard, who had chalked out a hop-scotch grid in front of the outside loo.

'Just one more go,' her excited daughter pleaded, throwing her pebble, which came to a stop on the roughly drawn number nine.

'Go on then, but be quick.' Nancy smiled, never able to resist, but the reality was, right now, she was envious of her children's oblivious innocence.

Watching them while the afternoon away in the late summer sun was a welcome distraction to the overwhelming worries that had dominated her thoughts all day since the ominous letter, encased in its official brown envelope and addressed to her beloved husband, Bert, had arrived this morning. Nancy didn't have to open it to know what was inside. This was it — their simple but idyllic life as they knew it was about to change beyond all recognition. Nancy could instinctively sense her Bert wasn't going to be here for much longer.

As she watched Billy and Linda hop and jump from one square to another, depending on where their stone had clumsily landed, Nancy would have done anything to have their cheerful unblighted outlook on life. In their world, the biggest thing that mattered was who would have the last go at a playground game. Nancy's

44

feeling of mounting anxiety had reached a peak over the past three days since Neville Chamberlain had finally confirmed her worst fears and announced England was at war with Hitler.

She was grateful the life-changing decision had so far passed her precious children by, too young to understand the complexities of what a war meant; the evil and fear that would slowly ferment through every household, a new existence taking over their once happy and content normality as their lives, to varying degrees, were inevitably torn apart.

A couple of months earlier, the headteacher at the school, Mr Wood, had spoken to all the parents about the possible need for their children to be evacuated. Sheffield was thought to be a main target for Hitler, a crucial cog in the worldwide production of steel, their manufacturing now turning to munitions and parts for fighter planes.

'Your children could be at risk,' he'd said, after calling a meeting, a look of foreboding coming across his already very serious spectacled face. 'Plans are being made for them to be homed in the countryside — some will only go as far as Derwent in Derbyshire.'

Nancy and Doris, who had attended the school hall together after Bert had willingly agreed to watch over all the children, looked at one another.

'Over my dead body,' said Doris. 'I've already lost my husband. There's not a prayer my kids are going anywhere.'

'Same here,' Nancy agreed. It was just too much to think about Billy and Linda being packed off on a train to God knows where, with just a suitcase holding a change of clothes, a toothbrush, and some crockery and cutlery in one hand and their gas mask in the other, a name tag around their necks or pinned to their coat. 'They can take their chances in the coal shed or in that metal air-raid shelter up the road that's just been built, but I'm not sending them off to some random stranger they have never met.'

Nancy would do everything she could to protect her children from the atrocities that were bound to follow but she couldn't send them away, no matter how persuasive Mr Wood had been. Quite a few had, though, frightened Hitler's bombs would reduce the city to a pile of rubble.

Now, as she stood watching Billy and Linda take it in turns to throw a stone across the yard, her mind wandered back to her own childhood, and she knew she wouldn't be able to completely wrap them in cotton wool.

When she was just twelve years old, her lovely caring dad, Edmund, had gone off to fight in the Great War, full of gusto and high spirits, leaving Nancy and her younger sister, Lucy, in a state of perpetual limbo, clinging daily to the hope a letter would arrive from the trenches he'd been forced to call his home, telling them he was safe. Sometimes it would be weeks, other times months, before the airmail arrived and she would listen intently as her mum read the letter out aloud, silent tears trickling down her cheeks at the relief her beloved husband was alive, had survived another bloody battle, but terrified this would be the last letter he penned to his anxious family.

Is this what awaits Billy and Linda? Nancy asked herself. Were they to suffer the same fate? Would they ask the same unanswerable questions, and would they too wake up through the night, sobbing uncontrollably because they missed their daddy?

Nancy had never envisaged Bert would have to leave them. Even as war had been brewing, she'd told herself it wouldn't affect her family, wouldn't cause her the angst her own mum had suffered, that somehow their little bubble of happiness would remain intact.

But now, as she watched Linda hop, skip and jump to her designated spot on the dusty ground, she willed time to stop so she could stay in this idyllic moment forever and prevent her two children having to cope with the rollercoaster of emotions that now lay before them.

'How do I prepare them?' Nancy whispered, no longer able to keep the complex maze of emotions silently trapped inside her mind. She always knew her dependable husband, Bert, would want to do his bit for King and country. His strong moral compass and determination to always help others was one of the reasons she had fallen for him in the first place. He'd been a conductor back then, and when Nancy had found herself short of her tram fare, instead of hoicking her off and forcing her to walk the three miles home, he'd reached inside his own pocket and paid for her ticket.

It shouldn't then have really come as any great surprise that he'd joined the Territorial Army at eighteen, following in his dad's footsteps, who had been called up to serve in the Great War, but the letter that had arrived that morning like an unwelcome guest was now sat ominously on the kitchen table, and had left Nancy on the edge of her nerves all day.

Part of her wanted to throw it in the range, watch it burn to ashes, all evidence of the army selection papers disappearing in a puff of smoke. But she couldn't; she would never betray her husband's wishes in such a deceitful manner, no matter how tempting it felt right now. She knew Bert would eventually forgive her well-meaning misdemeanour but the unfaltering trust that had always existed between would be broken forever; and, besides which, the army wouldn't just give up on Bert — they would send an officer to the house to fetch him if he didn't respond to the orders that were about to turn their lives upside down.

'We're ready,' Linda announced as she ran past Nancy to the kitchen table, a welcome disturbance to her unsettling, troubled thoughts.

'Good girl,' Nancy said. 'Now both of you quickly wash your hands in the sink and I'll serve our tea.'

A few minutes later, her eternally hungry children were wolfing down their corned beef hash and carrots, as though life itself depended on it. 'You'd think you'd never been fed,' Nancy said with a laugh, questioning whether, in her sidetracked state, she had actually forgotten to give them each a slice of the freshly buttered bread she'd baked a few hours earlier when they'd both come home from school.

Just as she looked over to the bread board, clocking that the thick crust her two always fought over had disappeared, Nancy's thoughts were broken once again — only this time it was her husband snapping her out of her trance-like state. As he walked through the back door, Nancy felt like the nerves she had been trying to suppress all day would erupt.

'How's my lovely family this evening?' came Bert's cheerful greeting.

'Daddy!' Linda squealed, instantly jumping down from the table and wrapping her arms around her father's waist. 'I missed you.'

'Aw, I missed you too, poppet.' Bert told her as he

48

embraced his daughter in his arms. 'How was your day at school? Did you do your sums?'

Linda looked up and scowled. 'I wanted to play instead.'

Bert forced back his laughter. 'Now you must do as you are asked,' he said in a mock-stern voice.

'Do I have to, Daddy?' came Linda's pleading response.

'Yes, young lady, you do!' Then, turning his attention to Billy, Bert ruffled his son's mop of dark hair. 'And how was my little soldier's day?'

Nancy instinctively grimaced, only partially able to hold back a sigh. She'd never objected to her affectionate husband's nickname for their son but suddenly it felt bittersweet.

'What's up, luv?' Bert asked, never missing a trick.

'Nothing!' Nancy snapped, her abruptness shocking herself as well as her well-meaning husband.

'Me and Joe played tag all dinnertime,' Billy interrupted, breaking the mounting tension in the normally happy household, 'and then we did spellings, which was boring.'

'And did you get them all right?' Bert asked, half-listening to his son, as he intently watched his wife, whose somewhat stand-offish mood had left him feeling perplexed.

Instead of greeting Bert with a kiss on the cheek, she quickly turned her back and began scooping another portion of corned beef hash onto a plate. 'Grab it while it's still warm,' she said, ushering Bert and Linda to the table.

'Are you not having any?' Bert asked, spotting Nancy hadn't served herself an evening meal.

'Oh, I'm not hungry tonight,' she said, forcing a

weak smile. The truth was, since that godforsaken letter had arrived, she'd felt as sick as a dog and hadn't been able to touch a mouthful of food. Twice she'd attempted a cup of tea to calm her nerves but both times nausea had soared through her and she'd felt an overwhelming urge to be physically sick. The worry of her beloved Bert going off to war had not only zapped her appetite but left her in an unprecedented terrible state of flux all day.

Bert wasn't daft; he knew there was more to his wife's uncharacteristic behaviour than she was telling him. He knew she was anxious about the onset of war — wasn't everyone? Nancy had been on edge since the Prime Minister's announcement, suddenly aware of what everyone else had been second-guessing for months, but her mood seemed more intense tonight. In the eight years they had been married, he'd never felt such tension between them.

Bert told himself he would wait until he'd tucked Billy and Linda into bed and read them their stories before trying to talk to Nancy. They had never once had a cross word in front of the children, and he wasn't about to start now, especially when he was sure all Nancy needed was a hug and some reassurance that everything was going to be all right.

But as he picked up his knife and fork, which Nancy had positioned either side of his steaming hot dinner, he spotted the envelope that was sat ominously beside the salt and pepper pots. Suddenly Nancy's low mood made sense. He knew exactly what was encased in the brown letter addressed to him and in turn what was going through his anxious wife's mind.

Determined to lighten the mood, he pulled back his chair and walked over to Nancy, who was now washing the pans with as much muster as she used to black lead the kitchen range. Leaning over, he pecked her on the cheek, gently rubbed her back through her blue cotton blouse. 'Come on, come and sit down,' he said gently. 'I'll do the washing up later. Don't let the kids see you like this. We can talk when they're in bed.'

Bert felt his wife's body ever so slightly slump, too exhausted to argue. As she turned round to face him, he could see the tears welling in her crystal-blue eyes and her delicate pink lips starting to tremble. 'It's going to be okay. I promise,' he said, sweeping one of her stray blonde curls behind her ear. 'Now come and sit down.' Aware Billy and Linda were now watching them both with curiosity, he added jovially: 'Besides which, I want to know which one of these two monkeys had my favourite part off the end of the loaf after school today!'

'It was him! . . . It was her!' came the simultaneous duet of replies, breaking the tense atmosphere in an instant.

Linda giggled. 'Tell him, Mummy. It was Billy, wasn't it?'

'Fibber!' Billy scolded, aghast at his sister's playful untruths.

And with that Nancy's face broke into a welcome smile that turned into the happiest of laughter.

'Actually,' she teased, 'it was both of you!'

'Well, that's double tickles at bedtime as punishment,' Bert said.

The family erupted into more giggles and the proverbial elephant in the room that had been causing Nancy so much pent-up angst all day vanished. As Bert finally tucked into his wife's weekly speciality, he threw her a loving wink. Nancy nodded, grateful for her husband's infallible knack of always being able to make a bad situation seem tolerable.

A couple of hours later, after Billy and Linda had yet again successfully coaxed their willing father to read one more chapter of *Swallows and Amazons*, and Nancy had cleared away the last of the supper dishes, she poured herself and Bert a well-earned cup of freshly mashed tea. As she raised the warm milky tonic to her lips from her favourite rose-patterned china cup, for the first time that day a feeling of nausea didn't rise up through her tummy. But there was still no denying how worried she was.

Once again, glancing at the letter, which had remained intact, Nancy swallowed a mouthful of her perfectly brewed leaf tea and looked at her husband.

'It's what I think it is, isn't it?'

Bert didn't need to open the envelope to answer his wife. He had been expecting his papers to be served for the last few days. TA soldiers had been pre-warned they would be in the first wave of soldiers to be called up if war was declared.

'Yes, I suspect it is,' he answered, taking hold of his wife's soft hand that had once again started to tremble.

'I don't want you to open it but I know you have to,' Nancy said, her voice faltering. 'It's as though, once you do, it all becomes real and I can't hide from it any more.'

Bert gripped Nancy's hand a little tighter. 'We are living in a very strange time, my love. We can't ignore it, I'm afraid. It's not just going to go away.'

Nancy clenched her eyes closed, desperate to block out what she knew, deep in her heart, was inevitable. 'Okay,' she said, nodding, then staring at the envelope when she opened them a few seconds later. 'Go ahead. Let's get it over and done with.'

Bert picked up the letter and carefully tore open the envelope, pulling out the official-looking document.

As he glanced down at the mainly typed letter, his name, Bertrude Edwards, in handwritten black ink almost jumped off the paper. 'It's what we guessed,' he said. 'It says: "You should present yourself at Catterick Garrison on the above date, not later than four p.m., bringing this paper with you."'

Nancy sighed. 'What date?'

'A week today. Next Wednesday,' Bert said, trying to stay strong, but the enormity of the notice to start active service temporarily stopped him in his tracks.

'Oh, Bert,' she gasped, no longer able to hold back the flood of tears she had just about kept at bay all day. 'I can't bear the idea of you not being here. How will the children and I cope without you? And what if . . . ' but Nancy couldn't actually say out loud the words that had tormented her every waking hour and stopped her from sleeping. 'I just don't know what we'd do.' And with that, Nancy collapsed into her husband's strong, protective arms, as she finally allowed the heavy sobs she'd been fighting off with all her might to consume her.

Holding his wife, Bert calmly rubbed her back as he felt her heaving chest against his. He hated putting his wife through this trauma. It had never been his intention. Nancy, Billy and Linda meant everything to him. He would never want to cause them any pain. For the first time in his life, he felt torn. Like his dad, Fred, he was determined to do his bit to stop that goddamn man wreaking havoc across Europe, robbing innocent people of their lives, destroying families and whole communities. Bert had inherited his father's moral conscience.

In many ways, Fred had been one of the lucky ones; despite witnessing the most harrowing of scenes, watching comrades murdered, some left to rot where they'd been shot, he had come home alive. Only occasionally did he talk of what he'd endured, seen and survived, but he always said, despite the brutality, he couldn't have not gone and played his part in creating a safe future for his family. So why did Bert feel as though he was now letting his own wife and children down by doing the right thing?

The internal conflict had caused him more than the odd fretful night. He'd known Nancy would worry; and during the agonizing moments Bert had allowed himself to think about how much he would miss his beautiful wife and children, he'd thought his heart would break in two. Seeing their smiling faces, picking up his children when they fell, watching his wife sleep — these were all things he cherished and for so long had taken for granted.

But even if he hadn't joined the TA, he would have got called up eventually. He might not be twenty-one any more but he was fit and healthy and not employed in a reserved occupation. Sooner or later his military papers would have dropped through his letterbox — not that it made watching his wife sob into his chest any easier.

'I'm sorry,' he whispered, gently running his fingers through Nancy's long blonde curly hair — there was no denying Linda was her daughter, the pair were like two peas in pod, with their Shirley Temple locks and sparkling blue eyes. It had been a standing joke how not only did Linda resemble her mum, but Billy was a miniature Bert. *Those little ones didn't fall far from the tree* — if he'd had a shilling for every time someone had said that to him, he was sure he'd be living the life of a king right now, as opposed to preparing to go off to war.

But as he took in the faint floral fragrance of his wife's shampoo, instead of feeling uplifted and carefree like he had when he'd first taken in her scent all those years ago, when they'd met for their first date at Coles Corner, the popular meeting spot for all young sweethearts, he felt utterly aghast at the heartache he was causing the only woman he'd ever truly loved.

Instinctively, sensing the worry and angst her darling husband was feeling, Nancy raised her head to look at Bert, her tear-stained cheeks revealing the same fears. Taking each of his hands in hers, she tenderly rubbed his palms with her thumbs.

'Now listen,' she started, regaining a sense of composure, 'you are a good man — too good sometimes — and I know you would never want to cause me or the children any hurt, but you must do what's right.' It was as though the waterfall of tears had extinguished the anger Nancy had felt since that chuffin' letter had arrived. 'I won't lie. I don't want you to go. We will miss you with all our hearts and pray every day for your safe return, but I know this is something you have to do.'

Nancy also knew she wasn't alone. She hadn't seen this moment coming but was now in no doubt: she would be just one of countless wives or mothers up and down the country, hoping beyond hope that their husbands, sons or brothers would be returned home to them in one piece. All they had was love but surely that was something to be grateful for and would be the one thing that would keep them going.

It was now Bert's turn to close his eyes as they teared up. His sweet, sensitive, warm-hearted wife never ceased to amaze him. Just when he needed a sign, some distinctive guidance and clear direction, as always it was Nancy who was the one to provide the voice of reason.

Fully regaining herself, Nancy squeezed her husband's protective hands a little bit tighter. 'You wouldn't be you, the only man I've ever loved, if you didn't follow your conscience,' she began, instinctively knowing the words she needed to say, and her husband needed to hear. 'You have my blessing to go and fight that blasted man and know we will be waiting with open arms when you return.'

With that, the couple embraced once again. No more words were needed. As Bert pulled Nancy closer, bringing her face to his, their bodies locked as one, they both knew that, whatever the future held, their deep unbreakable love would be the one thing that pulled them through.

6

'Hiya, Mom,' Patty called cheerily as she pushed open the back door, hop-footing it over to the family kitchen, desperate to put her feet up.

'Did yer have a nice time with Hattie, luv?' Angie asked her daughter, who had spent the last few hours in town with her best friend and workmate from Woollies.

'Yer. We had a good old nosy round the shops and then went for a cuppa and a slice of chocolate cake at Davy's café on Fargate, which was delicious,' Patty replied. 'But don't worry, Tom Tom,' she added, picking her little brother up from the floor where he'd been contently playing with his little yellow replica Dinky truck, until his ears had perked up at the sound of food, 'I saved yer some.'

Plopping her little brother on her knee, Patty pulled out the half portion of gooey cake from her handbag. Tom Tom's eyes lit up as he picked up a fistful of the soft sponge and pushed it into his gaping mouth. 'You are a one,' Patty said, laughing as the happy youngster munched through the unexpected treat.

'How was Hattie?' Angie asked, as she kneaded an already swelling lump of dough, ready to leave it to prove in the brown pancheon that had been passed down to her from her own mother.

'Oh, she was a bit fed up actually. Her John has been called up,' Patty replied, still not really comprehending the impact of what her anxious friend had

57

told her. 'We're dragging her out, and I'm sure when she gets her glad rags on and has a few dances she'll be right.'

Pounding her fists into the springy cream-coloured ball, which would be magically transformed into a mouth-watering loaf of bread by the following morning, Angie didn't reprimand her daughter for her less-than-empathetic remark, but instead added: 'You'll need to take extra care of her. She's gonna find the next few months tough. A war can break the best of us, luv.'

'Okay.' Patty nodded absent-mindedly, still not fully digesting what her mom had said. Instead she took the opportunity to sound her out about her latest jackpot idea. 'Has Dad said owt else about me taking a job at the works?' she tentatively asked. 'Now that some of the men will go off to fight, there's definitely gonna be jobs going and I'm not sure how much longer I can take Mr Watson breathing down m' neck. Did I tell yer yesterday he had a pop at me 'cos a single lipstick wasn't perfectly in line with all the others?' she added, popping Tom Tom on the chair while she put the kettle on the hob to boil. 'And he gave me a right look when I took m' break, even though Hattie was manning the counter. It's not like I take very long — just enough time for a cuppa and m' sandwich.'

'Oh, luv, you know how protective your dad is over you,' Angie said. 'Just the thought of yer getting 'urt on one of those big monstrous machines would leave him in sick with worry. You were his firstborn and he's always wrapped yer up in cotton wool.'

Patty sighed, knowing her mom was right, but she couldn't let it go. Surely there had to be some safer jobs at the factories that her dad wouldn't get so wound up about.

'Anyway, have you decided what you are wearing tonight?' Angie asked, keen to change the subject as she placed the perfectly round sphere of dough into the pot and popped the Aztec-patterned lid on top.

'Well, I'm still trying to decide what skirt would look the prettiest with me lace camisole top,' Patty said, a big grin appearing across her face. 'I'm determined to show that Tommy Hardcastle what he's missin' out on.'

Angie rolled her eyes, shaking her head in mock despair. It wasn't the first crush Patty had had and no doubt it wouldn't be the last. Since she was fourteen, there had always been someone she'd taken a fancy to at school. First it was young Billy in her class, then Mikey from down the road, and when she started at Woollies she'd taken an instant shine to Sam in the warehouse.

No wonder her husband didn't want their flighty daughter stepping a single foot in the male-dominated factories where a bit of skirt would be like honey to bees. Patty thrived on having fun but was too innocent to understand the problems it could lead to, nor did she realize how her strikingly pretty English-rose looks made her a magnet for any hot-blooded man. Although Patty took a real pride in her appearance, and loved to look feminine, using what Angie gave back from her wages every week to top up on the latest fashion or lippy, she could never be accused of being vain or even remotely aware of what a natural beauty she was. Her long strawberry-blonde curls, which fell around her round face, gave her movie star good looks, complemented by her flawless and glowing peachy complexion, one of the better traits she had inherited from her mother, but Patty had never used her enviable beauty to tease the opposite sex. She might have been a bit flirty and in search of fun, but she wasn't the sort of girl who'd forget her morals.

She's just like I used to be, Angie thought to herself. She might have had put on a few extra pounds and gained the odd wrinkle here and there after bringing four children into the world since she'd settled down and married Bill, but, at thirty-eight, she wasn't too old to remember how her own good looks as a teenager had ensured she always received more than her fair share of male attention without her ever searching for it. And she was sure Bill hadn't forgotten either; after all, he had been one of the many lads who'd relentlessly pursued her until she'd finally agreed to go on a walk around the park, chaperoned from a distance by her elder sister, Doreen, as, just like Bill, her own dad didn't trust another man with either of his precious daughters.

'Do yer reckon I should wear m' cream camisole or m' pink blouse with m' new flowery skirt?' Patty, asked her mom, boomeranging Angie back to the present.

'Oh. Erm, maybe the pink one would look prettier,' she suggested, also keen that her daughter wasn't showing off too much flesh.

'It will match m' new lipstick perfectly,' she said, popping Tom Tom on the stone floor while she poured the boiling water from the kettle into the teapot to make a brew.

'I'm sure,' Angie laughed, plonking herself into a chair, as she recalled how as a carefree teenager she too would get as giddy as a kipper over what outfit she would wear to meet Bill, determined to keep him keen.

'Is anyone else going out tonight with you and Hattie?' Angie asked.

'Yer, a couple of the other lasses from work.'

'Just go gentle on Hattie,' she said. 'She'll be worried about John and anxious about when they will next see one another.'

For a split second, Patty was speechless. She hadn't meant to harp on about herself and sound so self-absorbed and thoughtless. She adored Hattie — they had become instant pals as soon as she'd started at Woollies. Two years older, she had taken Patty under her wing, shown her the ropes and how to avoid incurring the wrath of the dreaded Mr Watson.

When the make-up counter was quiet, Hattie had told Patty how she and John had known each other all their lives after growing up on the same street and going to school together. At fourteen, when they had both left, John had started work as an apprentice at Smiths, the local brewery, and made his way up from glass washer to trainee manager, but now he would be one of the first to be called up.

Always looking on the bright side of life, Patty hadn't really thought about how it might all pan out for Hattie and John. Unlike some of her friends, she'd ignored the Pathé newsreels when they had blasted onto the cinema screens and didn't really listen to the announcements when they came on the family wireless — always opting to play with Tom Tom in the other room, so her parents could listen in peace. After war had been announced, Patty genuinely couldn't envisage what it really meant, how it would impact their lives. Coming from generations of steelworkers, no one she knew of in her family had ever served in the war. She hadn't heard the tales of horror or seen

61

the after-effects that witnessing such atrocities could have on the human mind, how it could psychologically destroy someone, despite them physically surviving.

So, unsurprisingly, Patty naively assumed John would be away for a few months and then be home and life would carry on as normal.

'It won't go for on for long, will it, Mom?' Patty asked, scooping Tom Tom back into her arms as he made a beeline for the range, an element of worry crossing her mind for the first time.

'Oh, luv,' Angie sighed. She'd always loved how her daughter viewed the world around her through rose-tinted glasses, never looking beyond the surface for anything that might feel sinister or cause her any concern.'The honest answer is no one knows. The last one went on for four long years. I just hope t' God, it doesn't carry on as long this time round. They weren't good times.'

Desperately trying to find a positive, Patty mused, 'At least John can write to Hattie — that will be romantic when she gets a letter and he declares how much he loves her; it will be just like those romantic films,' but even she realized her argument sounded more like a schoolgirl fairy tale.

'Well, I hope that's how things turn out, luv,' Angie sighed, 'but I think Hattie is going to need you more than ever now.'

Quietly digesting what her mom said, Patty nodded, jiggling Tom Tom on her knee as she brought her mug of tea up to her mouth. She didn't want to see her friend, who adored John more than life itself, suffer or watch her heart get broken. Patty had assumed for months that John would go down on one knee and ask Hattie to marry him before the year was out and they would be walking down the aisle not long afterwards, followed by a seaside honeymoon in a guesthouse in Blackpool or Great Yarmouth. But now, instead of planning her outfit and matching lippy, it dawned on Patty for the first time she might have a far more serious task at hand in looking after her friend.

'I won't let her down,' she murmured to herself. Patty might not really be able to grasp what the future held, what atrocities they may all have to face, but one thing was for sure: she wouldn't let her best friend face the future alone, who to all intents and purposes had felt more like a big sister to her over the last year or so.

★ ★ ★

A few hours later, after spending an hour getting herself ready, Patty smiled as she checked herself one final time in the rectangular bevelled mirror that hung from a brass chain in the hallway, adjusting a couple of her wild corkscrew curls that kept threatening to fall over her eyes with a bobby pin. The latest rose-tinted lippy she'd spent her wages on perfectly complemented her satin Peter Pan-collared blouse.

'You look wonderful, luv,' Angie smiled, taking in every detail of her daughter's carefully put together outfit. The pastel-coloured floral knee-length A-line skirt brought out the shimmer in the creamy pearlescent buttons of her soft pink top and seemed to be colour-matched to the hint of rouge of her cheeks.

'A bit too lovely,' Patty's dad, Bill, added, his naturally protective instinct, which was never far from the surface, kicking in. 'How much mascara are you actually wearing?'

'Oh, Bill, leave her be,' Angie said, gently nudging her husband in the ribs with her elbow. 'It's how all the girls wear it these days.'

'Mmmm,' he sighed. 'Well, you just take care, sunshine, and don't forget, I want you home by ten thirty and not a minute over. I'll be waiting up.'

Patty sighed. 'I'm only going to the dance, Dad. Nowt's gonna happen to me.'

'Well, I'm yer dad and it's my prerogative to look out for my daughter. Seventeen or not, you will always be me little girl.'

Patty knew her dad meant well and the last thing she wanted was a cross word to spoil the high she was on; she was determined to feel and look a million dollars to catch Tommy Hardcastle's attention once and for all.

Patty smiled. 'I'll be as good as gold. Now I'd better be off, or I'll miss me bus and Hattie will wonder where on earth I've got to.'

'Just remember, you don't have to impress anybody,' Angie said, pecking her daughter on the cheek.

'Right, I'm going,' Patty said, finally opening the front door to leave. But just as she was about to step out into the balmy evening, a little voice could be heard from the front room.

'Cug Cug,' Tom Tom called, his arms stretching towards his sister as he frantically toddled towards her.

'How could I forget my little Tom Tom?' Patty cooed, scooping him into her arms. 'Now you be a good boy and go straight to sleep and I'll come and check on you when I get home.'

Hotfooting it out the door, Patty skipped down the immaculately clean step, just catching the tail end of her dad calling, 'Not a minute past ten thirty.'

'I'll be flamin' lucky to get there at all at this rate,' Patty muttered to herself as she dashed down Thompson Road to the bus stop.

★ ★ ★

Half an hour later, Patty was tottering as fast as she could without breaking into a sweat, her cream T-strapped heels clip-clopping on the cobbled thoroughfare that led to Barker's Pool. She could just make out Hattie, Helen and Annie, standing at the corner of the City Hall, chatting away.

As she crossed the road at the Gaumont picture house, her three workmates spotted Patty and began waving.

'Where have you been?' Hattie asked as she finally reached them.

'Don't ask,' Patty gasped. 'Between me dad giving me orders and Tom Tom wanting a final cuddle, I'm amazed I got here at all.'

Annie laughed. 'Well, better late than never. Anyway, you look amazing! Am I right in thinkin' yer out to impress?' she teased.

Colour instantly rushed to Patty's already flushed cheeks. 'Me?' she mocked. 'What do yer take me for? Anyway, before we go in, does me make-up look all right? Our Tom Tom insisted on covering me in kisses as I left the house, and I didn't have time to top it up.'

Hattie smiled, linking her friend's arm. 'You look perfect. Now stop worrying. And remember if that Tommy Hardcastle doesn't show you any attention tonight, it's his loss.'

But even as the words left her mouth, Hattie knew Patty had all her hopes pinned on her latest crush finally asking her to dance.

Walking through the doors of the City Hall, Patty felt her excitement levels rise. Tommy had been giving her the glad eye for weeks; surely tonight would be the night he actually took the next step. As she and her girlfriends made their way down the stairs to the second of the two halls, where the more modern music could be heard, Patty quickly topped up her pale-pink lippy and popped an extra spritz of the Elizabeth Arden Blue Grass perfume her mom had bought her as a birthday present.

'Go steady,' Annie said, putting her hand over her mouth, faking an over-exaggerated cough. 'He'll be able to smell you a mile off.'

'Just ignore her,' Hattie said, forcing herself to smile at Patty, despite how inwardly miserable she felt at the prospect of John going off to war, aware her anxious friend's nerves were taking over.

Walking into the huge ballroom, the big band swing music filled the air and almost on instinct the girls began moving their hips from side to side as they headed to an empty table on the far side of the dance hall, close to the bar.

'We should be able to see what talent is out tonight,' Helen winked, looking around, as the room started to fill with dapper-looking young men, their hair immaculately greased to one side, and a glint in their eyes, while the girls were dressed up to the nines, in an array of long flowing skirts, nipped-in blouses and freshly curled hair.

'I'll get us a drink, Patty,' Hattie said, hoping to distract her friend. 'What would you like?'

'Aw, thanks, Hats. Can I just have a glass of lemonade, please?' Still ten months off her eighteenth birthday, Patty didn't dare risk a shandy or a port and lemon. If her dad got the tiniest whiff that she'd had any alcohol, her life wouldn't be worth living and she had no doubt he'd never let her go to a dance again.

'I think we might go for a little meander,' Annie said, as she and Helen left their jackets on a chair each. 'Yer know — to see who's about,' she said, her smile turning into a grin the size of a Cheshire cat. With that, the two girls made a beeline onto the dance floor, attempting, but failing, to discreetly glance at who was about.

'Let me know if you see Tommy,' Patty called after them, determined to ensure he caught sight of her before the evening was out.

A few minutes later Hattie was back at the table, holding two cold glasses of lemonade.

'Didn't yer fancy anything stronger?' Patty asked.

'Nah, I'm meeting John in the morning for a walk, so I want to keep a clear head.' Her friend sighed. 'I'm just so frightened, when he leaves, he won't . . . ' But Hattie couldn't say the words that were spinning around her mind, terrified if she actually said them she would tempt fate and her greatest fears would come true.

A pang of guilt soared through Patty. She had been harping on about herself and what outfit to wear all day, until her mom had pointed out how fragile Hattie might be feeling.

'Don't think like that,' Patty said, gripping her friend's hand a little bit tighter. 'Things will turn out all right,' she added, with as much genuine heartfelt concern she could muster.

'Oh, don't you be fretting about me,' Hattie said brightly, trying to avoid bursting into tears. 'Besides which, look who is heading to the bar right now. To your right,' she added, averting her eyes towards the bar.

Determined not to look keen but unable to prevent herself from following Hattie's gaze, her senses suddenly on high alert, Patty glanced across the busy dance hall. And there he was — Tommy Hardcastle looking as dashingly handsome as ever in his short-sleeved crisp white polo shirt, perfectly cut to show off his tanned muscular arms and his tailored grey flannels. 'Oh,' Patty sighed out loud. 'He's so good-looking it hurts.'

But as Hattie watched Tommy, she wasn't as easily taken in by his movie star chiselled jawline, dark moody eyes and athletic physique. She noted how he'd spotted Patty watching him, then confidently smirked to himself, nudging his mates, telling them something that made them all raise their eyebrows and grin.

There was something about his cocksure arrogant attitude that Hattie had taken an instant distinct dislike to. Her friend, who just wanted to be swept off her feet in a fairy tale romance, deserved better, but Hattie knew she couldn't air her thoughts yet. One look at Patty's lovesick demeanour told her she wouldn't have a bad word said about Tommy chuffin' Hardcastle.

Turning round to face Patty, he gave her a sideways smile and winked, before picking his glass of beer from the bar and heading back round the crowded dance floor.

'Did you see that?' Patty said, barely able to contain her excitement. 'He winked at me. He actually winked at me.'

'I did,' Hattie replied, trying to hide her concern. The last thing she wanted to do was burst her friend's bubble of happiness, despite what her gut instinct told her. She'd seen lads like Tommy Hardcastle before — all macho and flirty, but with very few morals. Patty might have had her head in the clouds when it came to the opposite sex but she didn't deserve to get hurt — far from it. What she really needed was a true Romeo to rush her off her feet, and somehow Hattie doubted this Tommy bloke was up to the mark.

For the next hour, Patty could barely string a sentence together as she tried to secretly watch Tommy from afar. As he chatted to his equally well-suited and -booted mates, she had butterflies in her tummy — and even better, there wasn't some young floozy linking his arm and he hadn't asked anyone else to dance.

Maybe he is going to ask me after all, she thought to herself.

But what Patty hadn't spotted, or had chosen to ignore, was what Hattie had clocked: how Tommy's eye kept wandering to a girl of a similar age, who bore a striking resemblance to a young Greta Garbo, only metres from where he was stood. With her short stylish bobbed hair, sultry eyes, defined eyebrows and siren-red lipstick, there was no doubting she was a head-turner and one that was certainly catching the attention of the man Patty had set her heart on.

'Has your dad said anything more about letting you work at the factory?' Hattie asked her friend in an attempt to distract her, hoping the night wouldn't end in disaster.

'Not yet,' Patty said, rolling her eyes. 'He's convinced I'll either end up injured or taken advantage of. He still sees me as his little girl, but I'm working on him. I was hoping me mom might back me up, but no such luck.'

'She's probably just trying to keep the peace,' Hattie said, feeling nothing but sympathy for Mrs Andrews. She adored her best friend but could just imagine Patty bending her mom's ear, trying to get her on board.

Patty sighed. 'I know, but I don't know how much more of Mr flamin' Watson I can take. I'm sure he's got it in for me and just finds fault for the sake of it. Besides which, working at the factory sounds far more exciting — there's got to be more to life than stacking lipsticks in order of colour!'

But before Hattie had a chance to reply, her friend gave her a warning glance.

'How are yer, Patty?' came a deep voice from behind where she was sat. Instinctively Hattie swung round on her seat. And there he was, looking all suave and confident — Tommy Hardcastle, a waft of woody aftershave permeating the air around him.

'Oh, yer know,' Patty said shyly, her cheeks glowing, 'same old.'

'Well, maybe I can do something about that?' Tommy said, throwing Patty his most charming smile. 'Fancy a dance?'

Trying to keep her cool but internally ready to burst with happiness, she waited a few seconds before replying: 'I'd love to.'

Offering his hand, he may as well have been giving Patty a diamond ring. Grinning from ear to ear, she obligingly stood up and let the man she'd been admiring from afar for the last month lead her to the floor. Struggling to stop herself from shaking with nerves,

Patty tried to concentrate on remembering to put one foot in front of the other as Herman Darewski's 'Boogie Woogie' began playing. One of her favourite tunes, Patty would have danced to her heart's content, but as Tommy took her in his arms, the sound of the music faded away. Taking in his every detail, from his dark-brown eyes, the light freckles that were just visible on the bridge of his nose and his perfectly shaped lips, Patty felt like she was in heaven.

As the swing beat picked up and Tommy pulled her that little bit closer, their bodies now only separated by a cat's whisker, Patty's heart raced. Tommy Hardcastle was holding her, little old Patty Andrews, in his arms for the whole of the City Hall to see. She could almost feel his heart beating, his breath on her neck and his lips hovering above her forehead. Surely this meant he was attracted to her, as she was to him. There would be no reason to ask her to dance otherwise, would there? He'd been smiling at her for weeks, watching her across the dance floor, nodding when she caught his eye. Now, as they moved in their own designated exclusive space, Patty wished more than anything in the world for time to stand still, never wanting the magical moment she had only dared dream of to end.

But all too soon the track came to an end, breaking the moment of intimacy. 'You're quite a mover,' Tommy said, looking down at Patty.

'Yer not so bad yerself,' she replied coyly, trying to keep her voice level.

'Maybe we should make this a regular occurrence,' he said, leading her back to the table where Hattie was still sat, nursing her virtually empty glass of lemonade, Annie and Helen nowhere to be seen.

'I think I can manage that,' Patty replied, as Tommy glided his fingers down her neatly manicured hand.

'Right, I'll see yer next week then.' And with that, he winked, before turning round and heading back to where his mates were still stood, now mimicking wolf whistles to Patty's delight.

'Can yer believe that?' Patty asked Hattie as soon as Tommy was out of earshot, the excitement in her voice causing it to raise several octaves. 'We danced. We actually danced, and he wants to do the same next week. He must be keen. Do yer think he will ask me on a proper date soon?'

'He might do,' Hattie said, trying to manage Patty's expectations. 'But don't pin your hopes on it just yet. You know he can be a bit of a jack the lad.'

'Oh, stop being a spoilsport.' Patty laughed. 'Did you see how close he held me? We were virtually touching!'

Hattie had of course seen Tommy pull her friend towards him, but what she'd also seen, of which Patty could have no knowledge, is that, as he did so, he looked directly at the stunning Greta Garbo movie star lookalike who he'd been smiling at earlier, with a look of passion in his eye. She may not be what you would class as experienced when it came to men, but Hattie wasn't stupid either, and she would bet a week's wages Tommy flamin' Hardcastle was just using Patty as a pawn in a cruel game of cat and mouse.

She knew there was no point in trying to tell Patty this, though. As far as she was concerned, Tommy was as keen on her as she was on him and nothing was going to persuade her otherwise. Hattie didn't have the heart to pop her friend's bubble.

'Just be careful,' was all Hattie could manage. 'I'd hate to see you get hurt.'

7

The following afternoon, Nancy was just sliding the mammoth beef and vegetable pie in the oven when the kitchen door swung open, and the joyful chorus of 'got you, your turn' intensified.

'Your Bert certainly has a knack with little 'uns,' her neighbour Doris smiled as she switched little Georgie from one hip to another. 'I hope he doesn't mind another three. They were adamant they wanted to stay in the yard with your two and join in the fun.'

'Oh, the more the merrier,' Nancy said, refilling the kettle and placing it on the range. 'Anyway, you timed it perfectly. I was just going to make a cuppa. Would you like one?'

'I'll never say no,' Doris said. 'I'm parched. The kids have run me ragged all day.'

'Well, have a minute and let Bert keep the big 'uns entertained, and we can have a tea in peace,' Nancy said kindly. 'You clearly need a breather. And how's this one sleeping?' She tapped Georgie gently on the nose, who returned the affectionate gesture with an adorable giggle.

'Just the same really,' Doris said, rolling her eyes, 'but on the plus side, the crying has stopped. He only clings to me through the night now. I'm just grateful the non-stop screaming has stopped.'

'Are you looking after your mummy?' Nancy said, handing Georgie a liberally sugar-coated shortbread

73

biscuit she'd baked that morning.

'What do you say?' Doris said, looking at her son expectantly.

'Ta 'Ancy,' the gorgeous tot said, his eyes widening as he swiftly raised the treat to his lips.

'To be honest, now the tears have stopped I don't mind so much,' Doris said. 'The bed doesn't feel quite as lonely with this one next to me. And more often than not at least one of the others sneaks in part way through the night. I think they all need a cuddle and a bit of reassurance.'

Nancy bit her lip, Doris's words leaving her completely numb. Simultaneously, guilt also soared through her as she subconsciously related it to her own situation when she knew Doris was still raw with grief.

'Oh, I'm sorry,' her friend said. 'I didn't mean to upset you.'

'No, no, you haven't,' Nancy said, instantly snapping out of her temporary paralysed state, annoyed at her own selfish thoughts. 'Please ignore me. I'm being thoughtless — I'm so sorry.'

Concerned, Doris looked at her friend, sensing there was something she wasn't telling her. 'Hey, you have got nothing to apologize for. Now come in, what is it, luv? Has something happened?'

'Oh, I feel terrible harping on about m'self,' Nancy said. 'You've got enough on your plate, without having to listen to me whittling on.'

'Come on, what are friends for if we can't listen to each other's woes?' Doris smiled. 'A problem shared and all that?'

'Let me get us that cuppa first,' Nancy replied, grateful to her ever-sensitive neighbour.

After pouring the boiling water into the pot, she grabbed the jug of fresh milk from the cold stone in the parlour, two china cups and an extra biscuit for little Georgie from the tin, bringing the welcome tray of much-needed refreshments to the table.

'Come on,' Doris said, as she played mum, pouring the freshly brewed tea.

'Bic bic,' interrupted Georgie, his little chubby arms reaching towards the tray.

'Nothing gets past you, does it, sunshine?' she said, laughing and handing her wide-eyed son the tempting treat.

With Georgie now contently munching away, Doris turned her attention to Nancy. 'So, what's happened to make you look as though life has suddenly ended?'

Lifting the much-needed cuppa to her mouth, Nancy took a deep breath. 'Bert's got his papers,' she said, her voice shaking. 'He goes on Wednesday.'

'Oh, luv,' Doris said, stretching her hand across the table to Nancy's, which was wrapped around the rose-patterned cup. 'No wonder yer look as though you've got the whole world on your shoulders. You should have said something sooner, yer daft thing. You could have had a cry on my shoulder for a change.'

'I didn't like to,' Nancy said. 'You've already got so much to cope with.'

Doris nodded. 'Life can be cruel but having friends for support makes it a little bit easier to deal with.'

'Oh, Dor,' Nancy said, 'where on earth do you get your strength from? I've been a blubbering wreck for days. I'm just hoping beyond hope this isn't our last family Sunday lunch together. But as soon as the kids and Bert are out of sight, I can't stop. I know Bert has got to go, I'm just so worried we'll never . . . '

Unable to say the words, Nancy yet again stopped mid-sentence. Not only had Doris lost her husband and saying it out loud felt so cruelly insensitive but the idea of vocalizing and hypothesizing about what cruel and heartbreaking tragedies the future may hold was far too close for comfort.

'Now listen up,' Doris said, suddenly sounding the strongest she had in months, 'this flamin' war is going to test the best of us, but one thing's for sure, somehow, come hell or high water, we are gonna get through it together.'

'Yer a good friend,' Nancy said. 'I think I just needed to talk to someone about it. Bert is the only person I've spoken to and I don't want to keep going on, as I know he already feels so torn.'

Twirling one of Georgie's white-blond curls around her index finger, Doris said, 'Well, don't. Enjoy your last few days together and if you think yer about to start bawling, come round to mine and I'll be waiting with a hug and a cuppa.'

'Thank you.' Nancy smiled, grateful to her sister-like friend who always seemed to know what to say.

Before the women had a chance to say another word, the kitchen door flung open. 'I'm starving,' came Billy's familiar call for food. 'How long before tea?'

Nancy laughed. 'There's a surprise. I reckon twenty minutes and you can get your hungry gnashers round the pile of Yorkshire puddings I've made.'

The mention of dinner must have echoed through the kitchen and into the yard as seconds later the room was a sea of grubby but happy little faces, all of whom looked as though they hadn't been fed for a week.

'Oh, as a special treat and because we have guests, you can all have one biscuit each to tide you over.'

Nancy chuckled as she handed out the shortbread to five grateful pairs of hands. 'I hope there's one left for me,' Bert said with a wink, pecking his wife on the cheek, as he dipped his hand into the rapidly diminishing tin of goodies. 'This lot have worn me out!'

Doris laughed. 'Ay, you're a good 'un. I'm sorry for leaving my lot with you too. I hope they at least behaved themselves?'

Taking a bite of the soft crumbly biscuit, Bert shook his head. 'Not at all. It's no bother. They were as good as gold — I think I'm just getting old.'

Bursting into giggles, causing little Georgie to follow suit, Doris chuckled: 'I think you've got more energy than the lot of 'em put together.'

'Not sure I've got their stamina though,' Bert said, flopping into one of the wooden chairs, as the horde of giggling children ran back into the yard, playfully arguing who was 'it' for their next game of tag.

'Right.' Nancy stood up as she took her last mouthful of tea, which was no longer hot but an unappealing lukewarm. 'This dinner isn't gonna get itself out of the oven.'

'Let me give yer a hand, luv,' Doris said, handing a delighted Georgie to Bert, who was already making the toddler burst into raptures as he pulled one funny face after another.

Doris caught Nancy's tender gaze towards her husband. It was easy to see why she was so worried and upset about him going off to war. Just like her lovely 'Big George' had been, before his life had been so cruelly cut short, Bert was a real family man, who loved nothing more than making his wife and children happy.

She knew only too well the heartache Nancy was

about to endure: how hard she would find going to bed each night without the man she loved dearly by her side; how several times a day she would go to call out his name, before suddenly remembering he wasn't there when one of the kids scraped their knees or she needed a bucket of coal bringing in from the shed — only to realize, before she finished her sentence, that he wasn't there to answer her. He wouldn't be able to come running, to pick up their distraught little one or plod into the kitchen, arms wide open, to greet the kids with a hug and a kiss and his cheery smile.

Doris didn't know if the worry of wondering whether you would ever see your husband again or if your children would ever receive another bedtime story from their first and only hero, was any worse or better than knowing as a matter of fact he was never coming home. At least, Doris told herself, she had some closure, some finality, despite how utterly heartbreaking it was, but poor Nancy would be on tenterhooks every minute of every hour of this godforsaken war. She was about to face the biggest challenge of her life and in the absence of her parents or sister being on hand to help her, Doris was determined to do what she could to help her kind-hearted neighbour, who had been more than a shoulder to cry on for her over recent months.

Doris had no idea how she was going to keep a roof over her children's head and food on the table, but one thing was for sure, she would find a way, just like she would always be there for Nancy. Now, more than ever, friends and neighbours had to stick together — who knew what problems Hitler would cause them all, what unthinkable atrocities lay ahead and horrors they would all have to face. Doris was old enough to remember the First World War. Her own dad had been one of the lucky ones — he'd been a steelworker since leaving school and, being in a protected job, he'd been saved from the trenches. However, his brother, her Uncle John, had sadly lost his life in one of those rat-infested hellholes, after enemy forces had raided his squalid lookout in the dead of night. Doris could still recall the piercing gut-wrenching sobs from her Aunt Freda when the news came that her brave, courageous husband had been killed in action.

Heaven forbid this is what awaited Nancy. The poor woman and her lovely children didn't deserve that — no one did. All she could do was hope beyond hope that someone would be looking down on Bert, would protect him and shield him from whatever Hitler and his armies had in store. The thought of another good man being taken before his time was one too many for Doris and she wouldn't wish that pain on her worst enemy, let alone someone she cared for like a sister.

'More bic bic, more bic bic.' Georgie's cheeky demands pierced Doris's thoughts.

'I don't think so,' she said, laughing, turning to face her wide-eyed son who was staring intently at the blue-and-white-striped tin, which Nancy was now removing from the kitchen table, taking temptation out of the eternally hungry youngster's grasp. 'Yer dinner's coming any minute now.'

Fifteen minutes later six little faces and three smiling adults were all crammed around the table, which normally only held four at the most, but there were no complaints as each one of them tucked into their Yorkshire pudding starters, covered in a thick beefy gravy and a dollop of Nancy's home-made bread sauce.

'I knew there was a reason I married you, Nancy Edwards,' Bert joked as he loaded another forkful into his mouth.

'You betta remember it,' Nancy said with a laugh, never tiring of her husband's compliments, quietly praying this wouldn't be their final supper, and that — whatever lay ahead — he would one day return home, the same man who always managed to make her smile, no matter how much her heart ached with a sense of terrible foreboding.

8

Her hand tightly encased in William's, Betty squeezed her neatly filed and polished fingernails deeper into her palms. Biting her lip, she tried to fight the dam of tears that were building up behind her eyes. She knew there was only one reason her sweetheart had insisted they came for a Sunday morning walk to their favourite bench at their local park.

From the moment she'd answered the door, twenty minutes earlier, the concerned and slightly anxious look on William's face had conveyed the news he was about to deliver. But, without saying a single word, the pair knew the doorstep of Betty's lodgings wasn't the right place to have the conversation. Instead they had walked, quicker than normal, their newly allocated gas mask boxes slung over their shoulders, to the spot they had come to think of as their special place.

Unable to bear the awkward tension a second longer, Betty took a deep breath. 'Am I right in thinking your papers have arrived?' She swallowed hard, trying to stay composed.

William spun round and gently caressed Betty's cheek. 'They have, but please don't be so sad, my lovely, sweet Bet. It's not the end of the world. I'll be based in England to start with and will get leave. You'll hardly know I'm gone.'

'Oh, William,' she said, the tears she had tried so hard to hold back now flowing uncontrollably down her cheeks. 'It's not the training I'm worried about. I know you will work hard and do the very best you can. I'm just scared of what . . . ' But like countless girlfriends, wives and mothers up and down the country, she was unable to finish her sentence. Instead Betty brought her hands to her now flushed and blotchy face, covering her watery eyes, trying to prevent passers-by seeing the state she was in.

'Oh, Bet, please don't think like that,' William said, pulling her close. 'Have you forgotten? I'm going to be the best fighter pilot the world has ever seen. Hitler and his Luftwaffe will have nothing on me.'

Betty stifled a smile. It was typical of William to make light of the situation, but Betty was wise enough to realize it was more out of innocence than fear. Reaching for her neatly embroidered handkerchief, she dabbed her now streaky tear-stained cheeks, patting away the black mascara that had run down her face.

'You will of course be brilliant, my love. Your bravery is intoxicating.' Despite her reservations — which had caused her weeks of sleepless nights and left her days a haze of worry, weighing her down to the point she could barely concentrate of anything else — Betty also knew, now more than ever, that she had to take control of how she felt and offer William the support and encouragement he needed.

It might have been the last thing she wanted and she would much rather keep William at home in Sheffield but how could she take away his dream, extinguish his passion or dilute his determination to do the right thing? Weren't they the qualities she loved about William? The traits that had not only drawn her to him in the early days but cemented the love she had for him? To stop William pursuing his dream, no matter how much she wanted to keep him close and safe, would be wrong and would only end badly — eventually he would resent her and she too would never be able to live with herself.

'You absolutely are.' Betty looked up adoringly at William. 'The RAF don't know how lucky they are.'

'Well, they soon will,' came her sweetheart's reply. 'I start in three days.'

The words threatened to knock Betty off-kilter once again. 'So soon?' she asked, her heart racing. 'Where will you be based?' she added, trying with all her might to keep her voice calm, disguising the heart-aching upset that was bubbling away inside her chest.

'Not far,' William said reassuringly. 'RAF Finningley near Doncaster, so I'll be able to get home and see you a fair amount.'

Betty breathed an audible sigh of relief. William would only be forty miles away — that didn't seem so bad. He was almost within touching distance. For the time being, he would still have his feet firmly on British soil — well, when he wasn't in one of those cumbersome noisy aircraft that somehow defied all laws of gravity.

'Oh. I am pleased,' she said, wrapping her arms around William, unable to hide her emotions, despite the disapproving glances from the pair of rather prim elderly ladies who happened to be walking past at that very moment.

Betty secretly hoped that William, with his office management skills, might be deemed more useful in an organizational or strategical role in the base, but she also knew this was as much a pipedream as William's adventurous fantasy of flying over the skies of Europe would be, which had been further reinforced by the fictional First World War Biggles stories that he had become obsessed with reading, convinced he too could become Captain Johns. She knew, though, she had to take comfort in the fact that the man she loved with all her heart was only going to be a train journey away, for the time being at least.

'I've actually been thinking about how I can help with the war effort too,' Betty said, turning to William.

'Have you? he asked, intrigued, but not in the least bit surprised.

'Yes,' Betty said, nodding hesitantly, the thoughts she had been mulling over for days not finally made up. 'I've heard the steelworks are looking for female workers so I thought I might nip down to the Labour Exchange and see if there was anything I was suitable for.'

'Gosh, Bet, are you sure?' William asked. He'd heard the horror stories of how dangerous the factories were — they didn't seem like a safe place for his beautiful and gentle Betty to be spending her working days.

'I can't just sit around writing wills and filing paperwork,' Betty quipped. 'I need to do something more worthwhile. If you can go and learn how to fly a fighter plane, the least I can do is help keep the city's steel production going. I've heard the works will be making engine crankshafts for the very planes you and all the other RAF boys want to pilot.'

William had known Betty long enough to know that once she had made her mind up, there was no changing it. Her strong moral conscience was one of the things he had always admired but it still didn't stop him worrying.

'Please just be careful,' he said, gently squeezing her

hand. 'The steelworks are renowned for accidents — I don't want you getting hurt. Maybe you could take an office job in one of the factories instead?'

Betty threw him one of her looks, which silently said 'don't try and stop me', and, without sounding like a hypocrite, how could he? Instead, all William could do was openly support his sweetheart while at the same time hope and pray his only true love would survive unscathed.

'Just promise me, you will be careful,' he pleaded.

Betty didn't know whether to laugh or give her William an affectionate dig in the ribs. 'I'm not the one about to learn how to fly a plane!' she said, bemused by his kindly warning.

'I know but I'm a man and . . . ' but before William could finish his sentence, the horrified look Betty threw him stopped him in his tracks. 'Sorry!' he said instead. 'I didn't mean that. The words just, you know,' he said, tripping over his own sentences.'I just, you know, worry. I don't want you to end up getting hurt and putting yourself more at risk.'

'I know you are only being protective.' Betty knew her William didn't mean any harm and took no offence though his remarks could have been deemed condescending, to say the least. Besides which, she knew going to work in one of the huge factories that stood shoulder to shoulder along the River Don was an alien concept for most people. However, she'd heard from her older colleagues at Dawson & Sons that during the Great War women had done their bit. It had been a while since the women of Sheffield had been permitted to walk through the gates of the city steelworks; over twenty years to be precise. These days, the foundries that lined the east side of the city, through the industrial landscape of Attercliffe and Tinsley were seen as purely a man's domain. She'd heard rumours on the tram as she went to work of how unsavoury horror stories like workers losing limbs, being knocked unconscious or being scarred for life from the hot molten steel were commonplace, confirming they weren't a place for the fairer sex.

'I'll be fine,' Betty said, before adding, 'Us women are just as capable as doing those jobs as any man, you know.'

'I don't doubt it, Bet,' William conceded, knowing not to cross the line. 'But what sort of man would I be if I didn't worry a little about the girl I love?'

Betty grinned, raising her eyebrows. 'I'll let you off.'

★ ★ ★

That afternoon, after William walked Betty back to her boarding house, she went and sat in the communal front room, no motivation to go and bury her head in a pile of law books — her heart was no longer in it. Staring out of the window, her long-held ambition of becoming a solicitor suddenly didn't seem relevant. Already, fabricated steel air shelters were being erected in almost every street; coal sheds were being turned into safety bunkers and everybody had been fitted with a gas mask and tin hat, so if Hitler's air force, the Luftwaffe, attacked, they would offer some form of protection. Her sweetheart was going off to fight an unknown battle, against a power-hungry dictator, alongside hundreds of other fresh-faced men, all determined to do the right thing.

I need to do my bit, too, Betty silently mused.

'Penny for them?' came Mrs Wallis's voice, transporting Betty back to the here and now.

Ever since they had sat together and listened to Neville Chamberlain announce the country was at war, Betty had seen a different side to her landlady, a gentler side which revealed a sensitivity she had never witnessed before.

'Oh, I'm okay,' Betty said, rather unconvincingly. Mrs Wallis raised one of her eyebrows. 'You don't make a very good liar,' she said with a smile. 'Shall we share a pot of tea?'

'That would be lovely, thank you,' Betty said, grateful for some company. It was at times like this she really missed having a mum around, someone she could turn to when she needed a shoulder to cry on. Betty was sure she would have known just what to say, would wrap her in her arms just like she used to when she fell over or woke up crying after a nightmare, and reassure her everything was going to be okay. The loss she'd felt after her mum had died had never disappeared and, now more than ever, she wished she was here by her side. Betty's sister, Margaret, had been a substitute mother figure for most of her life, but now she lived further away, Betty felt a little lost at times like these.

'Here we are, dear,' Mrs Wallis said, now back from the kitchen with a fresh pot of tea, neatly laid out on a tray. 'I thought you could do with a little treat too,' she added, glancing at the two scones she'd also brought in, with a little ramekin each of jam and butter. 'Freshly baked this morning too.'

'Aw, that's very kind,' Betty said, feeling as though she could erupt into tears at the thoughtful gesture.

'So,' Mrs Wallis said, pouring them both a nice hot

cup of tea, 'can I take it your William will be going off to fight this awful war soon?'

'I've been trying not to mope, but is it that obvious?' Betty asked.

Mrs Wallis nodded. 'Oh, I've been around a few more years than you, and it doesn't take a genius to see when someone's heart is breaking.'

'I just want him to come home safe. Is that so bad?' Betty said, holding the warm pretty floral china cup in her hands.

'Not at all, dear,' Mrs Wallis said, momentarily looking to the sideboard, at the photo of the handsome man in uniform.

'Oh, I'm sorry,' Betty said. 'I'm being insensitive. I really didn't mean to be.'

'No, no, you're not,' came the kindly reply. 'That is a story for another day. However, my advice for you is to do something to keep you busy and give yourself a sense of purpose. The time will go much faster that way.'

Betty couldn't help but smile. It might not have been the hug she was craving but, like Betty, her landlady was the practical sort. Maybe they had more in common than she'd initially realized.

'Well, I have been thinking of something,' she said. 'I know I can't just ignore the fact that we are at war, so I've thought about seeing if I can get a job at the steelworks. Apparently us women will be needed with all the men going off to war.' Sheffield had a long history of producing steel, which was shipped all over the world. They were now being depended upon to make munitions, parts for Spitfires, tanks and shells. 'That way, I wouldn't only be keeping my mind busy, I'd be doing something to help William and the war effort.'

'But what about your dreams of becoming a solicitor? Isn't that what you have always wanted?' Mrs Wallis asked, a note of apprehension in her voice.

'It is, but it can wait. There's nothing stopping me doing it later when all of this is over. I just think I won't be able to settle if I don't do something constructive. It will niggle away at me.' And as Betty said the words, she felt a sense of overriding relief and purpose. She now knew what it was she had to do.

'Well, dear, I can't say that's what I had in mind,' Mrs Wallis said. 'I was thinking more that you would be able to concentrate on your studies with William going away, but I would be lying if I didn't say I admire your spirit. I was never brave enough to volunteer in the last war. They took women into the factories then too, but I was worried that I wouldn't like it. Instead, I stayed on in service for a few years. I take my hat off to you for wanting to do the right thing — it's an admirable trait.'

'Thank you,' Betty said, warmed by her landlady's empathetic reaction. 'I've told William, but I haven't told my dad yet. I can imagine he will worry. He's always been very protective over myself and my sister, but I guess that's understandable — he just doesn't want either of us to come to any harm.'

Mrs Wallis sighed. 'I'd have loved to have had children to look after and care for.' Betty was too polite to try to quiz her landlady any further but couldn't help but feel a pang of sadness. Whatever had happened during the Great War had clearly taken its toll, and the latest developments had brought back some painful memories. 'I think that's why I was happy to take on this place when my parents got too old. The thought of looking after my lodgers seemed like a nice idea.'

Betty barely knew what to say. War could do funny things to people — it had even managed to soften Mrs Wallis's sharp edges and Betty no longer found her stand-offish and as fearsome as she once had but instead someone in whom she could now confide. She'd gone from being strict and quite aloof to some-one Betty actually felt she could talk to and grow fond of.

'I had no idea,' Betty said. 'I'm so sorry.'

'Oh, don't be dear,' came the reply. 'I'm perfectly fine. I sometimes just get a little melancholy. Anyway, enough about me. What are you going to do about your plans?'

Finishing her tea, Betty carefully placed the dainty flower-patterned cup back on its matching saucer on the table. Between William going off to war and her own determination to do something productive, she'd thought of nothing else for weeks. 'I'm going to hand my notice in tomorrow at work and then go and sign on at the Labour Exchange. I just hope Mr Dawson isn't too upset with me.'

'Well, I'm sure he will be sad to see you go,' Mrs Wallis started, 'but I'm sure he will also understand. Don't forget, dear, our generation have seen this before and appreciate the sacrifices we all have to make.'

'I just hope it doesn't go on as long as the last one,' Betty said. 'The idea of all those lives being taken away, let alone worrying about William, feels too much to cope with.'

'Only time will tell,' Mrs Wallis replied. 'But one thing's for sure: we all need to stick together.'

9

'Come on, kids,' Nancy called up the stairs of their even neater than normal three-bedroom terraced house. Ever since Bert's papers had arrived, she had been cleaning incessantly in the hope it would keep her mind off him going away. 'Your breakfast is ready. Be quick before your dad gets it!'

'I'll race yer,' came Bert's voice from the landing. Seconds later, between fits of giggles and the trampling of feet, came Nancy's husband, dressed in his green army khakis, holding an excitable and very wriggly Billy in one arm and a delighted Linda in the other.

'Did you say there was extra toast for me?' Bert winked at his amused wife, as two smiling faces looked up in fake horror from the crooks of their dad's elbows.

Nancy smiled. 'Oh, I don't know. What do you think? Is there anybody else that would like some?'

'Me, me!' came the unison of excited squeals as Bert gently released his two children and they raced to the table to claim their breakfast, which was sat waiting for them.

Bert laughed. 'Oh, well, as long as I've got the crust, I might let you both have a slice each.'

As Nancy poured herself a china cup of freshly brewed tea and a mug for her husband from the pot, she was, once again, grateful for Bert's permanently cheery demeanour. She'd barely slept the night before

91

and had got up before the crows, silent tears cascading down her drawn cheeks, unable to sleep, knowing that in a couple of short hours she would be waving her husband off, not knowing when she and the children would see him again.

'I'm only going to Catterick in North Yorkshire,' Bert had reassured her, as she'd encased herself in his arms as they'd got into bed.

But what Bert hadn't said, what Nancy didn't want to even whisper, was that it was only a matter of time before he was moved from his temporary base to God only knows where. TA soldiers like Bert had been training and preparing for a potential war for months — they were one step ahead of the young men who were being called up in their thousands to join the fight against Hitler's armies. Nancy knew only too well that Bert would be amongst one of the first waves to be sent into combat.

'Dad!' came Linda's half-laughing, half-protesting gasp, catapulting Nancy back into the moment. 'That's my toast,' she said, playfully tapping his hands away from her plate. 'You've got your own.'

'What about my little soldier?' Bert asked, edging towards his son's half-eaten breakfast. 'Will you share your crust with your old dad here?'

For a second, Billy contemplated it — eyeing up his piece of mouth-watering toast and strawberry jam, glancing suspiciously at his dad. 'Only if you give me a shoulder ride to the bus stop,' he said, weighing up his bargaining power.

'Aha,' Bert said, reaching for his son's round of toast, pretending to take a bite. 'That's a deal. But on second thoughts, how about I just let you sit on my knee and we share my breakfast too?'

Billy didn't have to be asked twice. Within the blink of an eye, he'd jumped from his own set place at the kitchen table and was snuggled up with his dad.

'What about me?' Linda said, looking somewhat dismayed.

'I have two knees,' Bert said.

And that was that — the three of them perched on one chair while they wolfed down as much toast as they could manage. As Nancy slowly drank from her china cup of tea, the one little luxury she allowed herself, she wished with all her heart that time would stand still. She would have given her right arm to freeze-frame the happy moment and store it away in a bottle so she could take it out again whenever she wanted. Seeing her perfect little family so happy and content was all she had ever hoped for — she didn't need a big house or plenty of money. Her husband and children were more than enough, but not knowing when this very picture of perfection would be repeated was ripping her heart to shreds.

However, as she stood up to put her now empty cup into the sink of hot soapy water, Nancy vowed that today of all days she would put aside her fears and emotions, for a few hours at least.

'Right then,' she said, painting on her bravest smile, 'are we nearly ready? The bus leaves in fifteen minutes.'

'Go and get your shoes and jackets on, kids,' Bert said, aware his wife was holding herself together by the most fragile of threads. Doing as they were told, Billy and Linda jumped from their dad's knee and ran into the hall, instinctively sensing this wasn't the day to put up a protest.

As soon as they were out of earshot, Bert stood up

and walked over to his wife, who was now wiping up the breakfast dishes. Wrapping his arms around her waist, he leant his head on Nancy's shoulder. 'I promise I will come home,' he whispered. 'I won't leave you.'

Nancy clenched her eyes shut as her body naturally tensed, determined to fight back the flood of tears that were threatening to erupt. 'But what . . .'

'Shush,' Bert said, turning his wife round to face him. 'Don't think like that. There is no way on this earth I am not coming back to you, Billy and Linda. If I have to crawl back on my hands and knees, I will.' He held Nancy's face, which was on the brink of crumbling, in his strong, warm hands.

'Do you promise?' Nancy asked, her voice on the verge of faltering, as the thoughts of what the future held tormented her.

'Have I ever lied to you yet, Mrs Edwards?' he said, using his pet name for her, which he reserved for when he needed to reassure her.

Scared her words would merge into tears, Nancy shook her head, not trusting herself to stay composed if she looked into her husband's eyes. 'No,' she whispered.

'So, you must believe me now,' Bert replied, pulling her close. 'You must have hope and trust and know I won't let you down.'

Nancy allowed her head to rest on her husband's chest, breathing in his musky aroma, allowing herself to feel encased in his arms, once again wishing the moment could last forever.

For a few seconds neither Nancy or Bert spoke, but remained perfectly still, both fully aware the intimacy they had shared from the very first moment they had kissed all those years ago, something they had come to take for granted, was now a precious commodity.

'I love you so much,' Nancy whispered, her eyes closed, allowing herself to be completely supported by Bert's embrace.

'And I love you with all my heart,' came his steadfast reply.

But they both knew the moment couldn't last and, as if on cue, the pitter-patter of two pairs of feet indicated their moment was over and it was time to face the day ahead.

'We're done,' came Billy's cheery announcement, delighted he and his sister had been allowed the day off school to take their dad to the train station.

'Right then, soldier,' came Bert's response, 'let's get going.'

★　★　★

Fifteen minutes later, Nancy, Bert, Billy and Linda were all squished together on a row of seats designed for two people not four, as the number 52 made its way down Saville Street and under the Wicker Arches, taking them into the city centre.

As the driver pulled in alongside the train station, in no rush to say their final goodbyes, the family waited for the flux of other passengers — many of them soldiers, their bags slung over their shoulders — to leave. As the bus emptied out, Bert carefully lifted Billy and Linda into the aisle, before grabbing his own kit bag from underneath the seat in front. Nancy, who had been sat by the window, was the last to stand up. Her knees threatening to buckle, she took hold of the nylon-covered headrest of the seat in front.

95

Come on, she told herself, keep it together. Bert needs you to be strong now.

Crossing the road into the Midland Station, the family of four held hands as they joined the throng of families, young soldiers with arms wrapped round their sweethearts and parents guiding their fresh-faced adventure-seeking sons, all heading in the same direction.

'Gosh, it's busier than I expected,' Nancy said, taking in the sea of bodies in front of her.

'Are they all going to fight that horrible Hitler?' Linda asked innocently.

'Quite a few of them are, poppet,' Bert said. 'He doesn't stand a chance, does he?'

'No way,' Billy said. 'Will you drive a tank, Daddy?'

'Oh, I don't know yet,' Bert said, carefully guiding his family onto platform one, trying to find them a space where they could all stand together amongst the bustling crowd.

A mixture of excitement and tension filled the air, the two emotions almost battling against one another. As Nancy glanced round, the feeling of anxiety she had been trying to subdue all morning was replicated on faces of wives, girlfriends and mothers wherever she looked. Knowing her fears and worries were shared by dozens of others, who now surrounded her, gave her a fleeting feeling of comfort. She wasn't alone; she wasn't the only wife or teenage sweetheart who was petrified this could be the last time they saw their loved one.

But the short-lived united feeling of being in it together wasn't enough to make Nancy feel any better right now. Every fibre of her soul ached, every tiny hair on her shaking body was on edge and she was fighting back every single overwhelming urge to beg her Bert not to go, to stay at home, to return to his safe secure job as a tram driver, and allow their tranquil life to carry on undisturbed.

But as the tannoy burst into life, announcing the connecting train to Leeds was approaching, Nancy knew she couldn't make this any harder for Bert or their two children, who were now gripping onto their daddy as though life itself depended on it.

'Come on then, you two,' Bert said, once more scooping Billy and Linda into his arms. 'Give your old dad a kiss and a cuddle.'

They didn't need to be asked twice. Both of them wrapping their arms around his neck, they smothered him in kisses, almost knocking his dark-green felt beret to the floor.

'Be good for your mummy,' was all Nancy could hear through the muffle of arms and faces, no longer able to hold back the dam of tears that were now flowing down her normally rosy, but currently ashen, cheeks.

Easing their two children to the floor, letting them cling to his thickset thighs, Bert gently pulled his wife to him. 'Be strong now,' he whispered. 'Today will be hard but tomorrow will be easier, I promise you.'

'We are so proud of you. Please just take care,' Nancy said between sobs. 'And come back to us.'

'You try and stop me.' Bert smiled, gently easing away, but still clasping his wife's trembling hands.

Nancy nodded, blinking back the tears, knowing she now had to do the one thing she had dreaded for weeks and let her Bert go.

'I love you so much,' she mouthed for the second

time that morning.

'And I love you,' came the reply, a slight tremor in his voice.

Nancy knew she couldn't let Bert crumble now. She had to allow his strength to stay intact.

'Come on, kids.' She smiled, summoning up all the courage she could muster. 'Stay next to me now as we wave to Daddy.'

Bert nodded, no need for words, a mutual understanding of thanks passing between them.

'We'll write to you every day,' Linda said.

'And I'll send you the crusts with jam,' Billy added, breaking the heart-rendering tension.

'Make sure you do,' Bert said, releasing his hands from Nancy's to ruffle his son's mop of dark hair as he bent down to gently plant a kiss on Linda's forehead. 'I'll see you all very soon.' He nodded, trying to stay strong but the look on his face betrayed his true feelings. Keeping his family in sight, he began to step backwards, trying to find his place in the crowd of soldiers, who were all now moving closer to the edge of the platform, as the screeching of metal on metal indicated their train was easing into the station.

'Mummy,' came Linda's eruption of heartbreaking sobs as Bert edged further and further away, until Nancy could just make out his beret.

'It's okay,' Nancy said, as she lifted her distraught daughter up for a cuddle.

'Will we see Daddy again soon?' Linda cried.

'You will, angel,' she said, scooping her little girl onto her hip, then with her free arm, pulling Billy close to her side, his body starting to tremble. 'Now we must be brave,' she said. 'Wipe those tears away; Daddy wouldn't want us to be sad.'

Just then, as if by magic, a slight gap appeared in the line of people filling the platform. At the end Nancy could just see Bert's heavy army bag slumped over his shoulder as he was about to board the train. 'Come on, kids,' she said, seeing her opportunity. 'Let's give your dad one last wave.'

Weaving through the crowds that were starting to spread out into the little space that had emerged, Nancy kept a tight hold of Billy's hand as she focused on the back of her husband's head.

Please don't go yet, she thought pleadingly. Just one more kiss.

Ten steps and she would be in touching distance.

'Bert,' she called, as though life itself depended on it. 'Bert!'

For a split second, Nancy thought her husband wouldn't hear her above the overwhelming din of loved ones all saying their final farewells to one another. But as Billy shouted 'Daddy' at the sight of his beloved father stepping onto the train, his cries pricked Bert's ears and instinctively he turned to see his wife and two children less than an arm's length away.

'Oh, my loves,' he gasped, jumping from the train, flinging his arms around the three of them, kissing each one of them in turn. 'Thank you,' he said, smiling. 'Thank you.'

A tangle of bodies, the four of them held each other tight, their tears merging, until their tender moment was interrupted by the sound of the station master's sharp high-pitched whistle. 'All aboard. Last call for the eleven o'clock to Leeds.'

'I have to go,' Bert said, no longer able to remain composed, his face drenched with emotion. 'But I'll be back soon. I promise.'

'It's okay,' Nancy sobbed, giving her husband her blessing. 'You will always be in our hearts.'

After tightly squeezing each of their hands in turn, Bert reluctantly let go of Nancy, Billy and Linda, jumping backwards onto the train. Pulling the metal door shut, he leaned his head out of the rectangular window. 'I'll write tomorrow,' he said, the roar of the engine threatening to drown out his voice, his fingers just making contact with Nancy's.

'We love you, Daddy,' Billy shouted, as the black metal train started to move. Plumes of steam filled the air and a mass of people all followed, all shouting their goodbyes as the packed carriages, full of soldiers, began edging out of the platform.

As her husband waved, his hand disappearing into the untouchable distance, Nancy watched with their two children until he was finally out of sight.

For a few seconds no one spoke, as Nancy and the children were frozen to the spot, the sound of the steam engine fading, the echoes of multiple *Good-bye*'s and *I love you*'s coming to an end. The deafening cacophony of noise that only minutes earlier had filled the station was replaced by an eery quiet as mothers, daughters, sweethearts and children were left feeling empty, wondering what the days, weeks and months ahead had in store for their loved ones.

Nancy only snapped out of her trance as the sounds of muffled sobs on her left shoulder broke the stillness.

'Oh, sweetheart,' she whispered, leaning her head into her daughter's, their combined mass of blonde curly hair entwining. 'Daddy will be back before you know it.'

But even as the words left Nancy's lips, she knew

that in reality she couldn't hand on heart be sure, but, as a mum, whatever her fears, she owed it to her children to stay strong and give them hope.

10

As the pair walked into the busy train station, her arm linked through William's, Betty glanced round. The central concourse seemed to be much busier than normal, with families and couples crossing paths as they made their way to the exit or a platform, all looking equally forlorn and teary. One family in particular, who were leaving the grand Midland Station, caught Betty's eye. It was the woman she noticed first — a blonde-haired lady, dressed in a navy jacket, her curly hair twisted into a clip, but the odd stray ringlet falling around her flushed cheeks. She was carrying a little girl, the double of her, and had a boy, a couple of years older, by her side, who was clinging to her thigh. His face was as crumpled as his mum's, hers stained with lines where her make-up had obviously streaked from tears shed. The sight stopped Betty in her tracks, her heart immediately going out to the poor woman, who looked visibly distraught and was carrying the weight of the world on her shoulders.

It's hard enough saying goodbye when I only have myself to think about, Betty thought inwardly.

The idea of having to comfort two children, whose daddy had just departed on a train with no return ticket or idea when he might be home, caused an icy-cold shiver to run down her spine. Is that how her dear dad had felt after Mum had died, only a million times worse? She could still recall how he'd sat her, Margaret and Edward down, his voice shaking, to explain how her mummy wouldn't be coming home.

102

For weeks afterwards, Betty had cried herself to sleep, tears soaking her pillow. Some nights Edward, only eight, had crawled in beside her, with his raggedy teddy, his little body shaking in his blue and white cotton pyjamas — the pair of them hugging each other until sleep finally gave them some respite from the pain that had left a gaping hole in their hearts.

'Please don't let this be the fate those poor children have to suffer,' Betty said to herself. She couldn't bear the thought of any youngster losing their parent — it just wasn't right. It wasn't what nature intended. It shaped your life, defined your personality in a way that had a long-lasting impact. Isn't that why, after all, Betty had grown into a fiercely independent young woman, determined to take care of herself, and never feel so emotionally reliant on anyone else ever again?

So, now, as she stood next to William in his dashing mid-blue uniform of jacket and trousers, ready to say her final goodbye, she steeled herself.

For weeks, if not months, Betty had been frantic with worry, terrified what would happen when her William, her first and only true love, finally followed his childhood dream of joining the RAF and soaring across the skies. His determination to go into battle against Hitler's Luftwaffe had left Betty unable to sleep at night, terrified his ambition would literally be the death of him. But now, as he stood tall and proud, she could see her young innocent William had found his rightful place in the world, despite her fears.

'Just please take care of yourself,' Betty said, gripping her sweetheart's hand.

'I will, my lovely, sweet Bet,' he replied. 'You too. I can't bear the thought of you getting hurt in one of those huge factories.'

But Betty had already made her mind up and was now more determined than ever. As soon as she'd waved William off, Betty was planning to go straight to the Labour Exchange in town, hoping it would have the dual purpose of signing up for a role in one of the city's factories as well as keeping her mind busy.

If the truth be known, though, she too had felt a little anxious about what lay ahead. When she'd told her colleagues at Dawson & Sons her plans a couple of days earlier, they had all thought she was barmy to give up a nice secure job to go and work on one of those 'dirty horrible places', as one of the other secretaries had phrased it.

The announcement over the tannoy interrupted Betty's thoughts. 'The next train to arrive on platform two is the midday to Hull.'

As the deafening sound of the steam engine's brakes echoed through the station, William swung Betty round to face him.

'Be brave now, my love,' he said. 'You will be in my thoughts every minute of the day and your photo will be next to my heart continually.' He pressed his right hand against the pocket, which was hidden by his new perfectly pressed pilot's jacket.

'And you with me,' Betty replied, her voice threatening to falter, despite her best efforts to stay strong.

'One last hug.' William smiled, wrapping his arms around his lovely sweet Bet, as she rested her head against his firm muscular chest, exactly on the spot where the black-and-white image of the two of them walking down the promenade at Cleethorpes a few months earlier lay. Not long afterwards, the beaches had been closed as mines were planted in the sand to deter enemy troops coming ashore. The normally bustling seafront, full of ice cream vans and shops selling sticks of rock and candy floss, was no longer full of courting couples and holidaymakers but replaced by eagle-eyed soldiers, guarding the shores, ensuring nobody stepped on an explosive and potentially fatal device.

As the couple embraced, Betty felt her heart race.

He's only going to Doncaster, she told herself over and over again. You will see him again soon.

As William passionately kissed her on the lips, Betty closed her eyes and let herself fall into his arms, for once ignoring her normal sense of decorum, which would make her shrink from such public demonstrations of affection. For a few seconds the world around them disappeared, the couple oblivious to the hustle and bustle that had picked up pace as a sea of passengers, many of them in identical blue uniforms, were shuffling closer to the edge of the platform.

It was only the harsh shrill of the station guard's whistle that transported the lovesick couple back to reality.

'I wish we could stay like this forever,' William said, 'but I must go. I don't want to get into trouble for being late on my first day.'

'No, you must not,' Betty said, determined not to fall to pieces at the last minute. 'Go, before you miss your train.'

'Final call for those travelling to Hull,' came the guard's call. 'Anyone not travelling as a passenger must leave the train now.'

'Go on,' Betty said, kissing William's hand as he slowly moved it down her cheek. 'I'll be fine. I promise.'

'Okay, you take care now, Bet. I love you so much

and I'll be thinking of you, every minute of every day.' He nodded, taking a step towards the waiting train. The momentum of the other passengers pushed William further away from Betty, until he was side-stepping up the step of the open carriage.

She caught one last glance of her sweetheart before another trainee pilot jumped onto the train, blocking her view. A few seconds later there was a loud gasp as a plume of steam burst from the front of the engine, and a roaring noise indicated the train was about to depart.

'Goodbye, my love,' Betty whispered, her voice barely audible.

Waiting until the steam engine was completely out of sight, leaving a fog of smoke in its wake as the only reminder of its presence, Betty wiped away the tears that were now gently flowing down her cheeks.

Well, this isn't going to win a war, is it? she thought, chastising herself, making her way towards the brown brick arches of the Edwardian nineteenth-century station façade as she buttoned up her smart tweed jacket.

There was only one thing on Betty's mind, and she was determined that before the day was out her mission to do something worthwhile would be accomplished.

* * *

Twenty minutes later, Betty was walking through the doors of the city centre Labour Exchange. A line of desks were set up at the end of the huge room, with a queue of mainly women forming at each.

I'm clearly not alone, Betty thought, walking to

the nearest line. In front of her, two girls, who she assumed were late teens, were chatting.

'I've heard it pays better than the cotton mills,' the auburn-haired girl, whose denim skirt barely covered her knickers, said.

'It better chuffin' had,' her mate said, taking a drag of her cigarette. 'I ain't riskin' me life in a hellhole for a bloody pittance. It's gotta be worth me while.'

'Aye,' said the first girl, who was also wearing far too much coral rouge and siren-red lipstick in Betty's opinion. She was signing up for a job, not entering a beauty pageant. 'I want some spends left for me fags and a night out after tipping up to me mom every week. No point slaving me guts out otherwise. I may as well stay put at the shop.'

Betty composed herself. It felt like these girls were from a different world to the one she inhabited. Dare she say they were a bit on the rough side. They spoke a different language and lived a different life — were these the type of people she would be working with in the not-too-distant future?

No wonder William and Mrs Wallis had been so concerned when I told them my plans, Betty thought to herself. And that's before I even attempt the work.

The queue seemed to quickly move forward. Betty watched with curiosity as each woman and teenage girl left holding a small blue card.

A passport to their future, she mused. Where is it taking them?

The city was famous for its steelworks but now more than ever they were playing a crucial role in supplying munitions for Allied forces. Rumour had it they were responsible for making parts for Spitfires and Hurricanes. As the thought sunk in, it made the hairs on

Betty's arms stand on edge. Is that what her William would be flying one day? Were the women of Sheffield going to be making the very aircraft her sweetheart would take to the air in to fight Hitler's Luftwaffe? If she didn't already have a reason, this was surely the confirmation Betty needed to reassure her she had made the right decision.

'What are yer up to tonight?' asked the girl with the minuscule skirt, who couldn't have been more than nineteen, snapping Betty from her thoughts.

'Well,' came the reply, 'I'm off to see Mick, and yer never know — his luck might be in!'

Betty's eyes nearly popped out of her head. She glanced down at the left hand of the girl, whose low-cut, very fitted pillar-box red top left nothing to the imagination, as she took another drag from her cigarette. No wedding ring! Not even an engagement ring. For Betty, who had only allowed William to kiss her, the idea of such a public announcement of sexual intentions left her utterly speechless.

What type of girl was she? she wondered. Didn't she have any morals at all?

Before the neighbouring woman could reveal anything more about her not-so-clandestine relationship, she and her amused-looking friend were called up to the desk and a few seconds later they were gone, holding their little pieces of card, the entry ticket to their new jobs.

'Next,' called the plump dark-haired woman who looked a similar age to Mrs Wallis, beckoning Betty forward.

'I would like to work in a steel factory,' Betty said, suddenly full of assertion.

'Well, lass, that's what most of you young 'uns are

ere for,' she said, giving Betty a knowing smile. 'And what a grand job you'll all do. If I was yer age, I'd be queuing up on the opposite side of this desk m'self. It's important work.'

'I agree.' Betty smiled, the thought of William once again flashing through her mind. 'My boyfriend has just gone off to Doncaster to train as a pilot. I would like to do my bit too.'

'Well, duck, take this to Vickers on Monday morning at eight o'clock sharp, not a minute after, and they will find you a role. They need all the help they can get right now.'

'That soon!' Betty said, unable to hide the shock in her voice. It was only five days away.

'That's right.' The woman nodded. 'Those planes and tanks aren't going to build themselves. Now do you know where yer going?'

'No, but I'll find it,' Betty said, determined not to sound completely incompetent.

'It's at the bottom of Attercliffe,' said the kindly-looking woman, whose gentle crow's feet around her warm eyes revealed she'd probably been around to see the factories fill up with women during the last war.

'Thank you,' Betty said, taking the piece of blue card with the name of the factory typed into it in bold black capital letters.

'Take care, duck,' the woman said, already waving the next person in the queue to come forward.

'I will,' Betty said, as she walked back out of the building, still a little stunned her new role would start so soon. She had naively assumed she would serve a couple of weeks' notice at Dawson & Sons.

Oh, well, she thought, no time like the present.

An air of nervous excitement filled her. She needed to go and tell her kind boss she wouldn't be returning to her job, before breaking the news to her dear protective father that she had given up her nice comfortable position to take on a role in one of the city's great factories.

* * *

An hour later, Betty left the solicitor's office where she'd been employed for six years for the last time, a box of chocolates in one hand and a leaving card, encased in a baby pink envelope, in the other.

To Betty's surprise, Mr Dawson had already assumed his much-loved legal secretary wouldn't be returning to work, after she'd revealed her plans a couple of days earlier, knowing how desperate the steelworks were for a new army of workers since the younger men had started leaving in their dozens. 'Make sure you pop in and see us if you get a spare minute,' he'd said. 'We are going to miss you. And don't forget, if you change your mind, your desk and typewriter will be waiting for you.'

'Thank you,' Betty had answered, a tinge of sadness coming over her.

But now she had to go and see her dad and break the news.

Walking along Surrey Street to the Town Hall tram stop, in her mind Betty mulled over how she was going to break the news to him. He'd been so proud when she had secured her job at the solicitor's firm, a respectable role in a nice office, with long-term prospects — a far cry from a mucky job in a huge dirty factory or from the daily toil he and Betty's youngest brother had down the pit.

She knew he'd worry; it was in his nature. If he could have had his own way, after Betty's mum had died he would have wrapped her and her big sister, Margaret, in cotton wool, but he hadn't envisaged how fiercely independent both his daughters would turn out to be. In his eyes, they would always be his little girls.

Continuing to mull things over, Betty joined the half a dozen or so other passengers as they jumped on the end of the tram. Taking a window seat, Betty reached into her soft leather handbag, a Christmas present from William, and found her purse. Taking out the few pence to cover her fare, she waited for the female conductor, or clippie, as some called them.

Absent-mindedly, Betty stared out of the window. As the route took her through the bottom of Pitsmoor, the black pointy hands of the red-brick clock tower of the Northern General Hospital came into sight. Just as it did, every time she passed it, a vision of her beautiful mum flashed before her eyes, knowing this was where she had slipped away. Betty would have given anything for her to still be here, to give her the courage now as her William started a new and terrifying chapter of his life. Although her memories were scarce, she could picture her mum being there with a cup of tea, just like Mrs Wallis, and telling her everything would be all right.

'Fare please,' came the voice of a girl, not much older than herself, in a navy-blue shirt and matching trousers, with a battered tan-brown leather bag hanging horizontally across her body, bringing Betty back to the present.

'Oh, just a single to Firth Park, please,' she said,

111

handing her the right change in coins.

'Thanks, luv,' the female conductress replied, handing Betty her rectangular paper ticket.

Slipping it into her coat pocket, Betty looked at her watch. It was three o'clock. Her dad and Edward should be home from their early shift at Tinsley Park Colliery. The kettle would be on and no doubt a ready-made pie from Johnson's butcher's in the oven, a bag of potatoes ready to be peeled and boiled on the side.

She didn't have to wait long to find out. The sharp shrill of the bell indicated the tram was pulling into Firth Park and a few minutes later Betty was making her way up the tree-lined hill to her family home at 58 Queen Street. As she reached the house, Betty walked past the black front door and down the side ginnel, into the back yard, knowing exactly where she would find her dad and brother.

'Aw, look who it is,' said Joseph, his eyes lighting up as his daughter opened the back door that led straight into the kitchen.

'Hiya, Dad,' Betty said, walking over to where he was sat at the kitchen table, and giving him a peck on the cheek. 'How are you both?' she added, turning to look at her younger brother, who, like her father, was still in his mucky coal-stained overalls.

'Aw, not so bad, luv. Same as ever. Nothing much to report. How about you? Did William get off okay?'

'He did, thanks.' Betty smiled, trying to conceal the heartache she was really feeling. 'Is there some tea left?' she added, glancing towards the pot in the centre of the table, covered in a pink and white knitted cosy, which must have been as old as the house.

'Aye, there is indeed, luv,' Joseph said, scraping his pine-varnished chair backwards, going to stand up.

'Let me get you a mug.'

'Stay sitting down. I'll get it,' Betty said, walking over to the kitchen cupboard next to the range, where, as she'd predicted, a mince and onion pie was cooking away, the tempting smells reminding Betty she hadn't eaten since the slice of toast and butter she'd had for breakfast. Picking out a dark-blue cup, she pulled out a chair to join her dad and brother and helped herself to a Rich Tea biscuit from the half-empty packet that was open on the table.

'You're very quiet today,' Betty said, looking at Edward as she picked up the milk jug.

'Sorry, sis. It was an early start and I'm jiggered.'

'Early night for you then?' she asked.

'I'll be lucky if I'm still awake at six at this rate,' Edward replied, resting his head in his hand.

'Anyway, luv, are you going to tell us to what we owe this unexpected pleasure?' Joseph prompted, knowing all too well his daughter hadn't popped in out of the blue just for a cuppa and a biscuit.

After taking a sip of her tea and a quick bite of the much-needed biscuit, Betty took a deep breath and announced: 'I have got some news, actually.' Suddenly a sleepy-looking Edward was all eyes and ears. 'I've taken a job at Vickers. I start on Monday.'

For a spilt second Joseph and his son were completely speechless as Betty anxiously took another mouthful of her tea, her throat suddenly as dry as sandpaper.

'But . . . but what about your job at Dawsons?' her dad finally asked, more than a little shocked by his daughter's unexpected revelation.

'I've left,' Betty said. 'I went to see them before I came here to explain I'm required straightaway at the factory. Actually,' she added, reaching into her bag, suddenly the remembering the box of Milk Tray Mr Dawson had given her, 'would you like to share these?'

'Yes, sure,' Joseph said instinctively, more out of politeness, not even giving the generous-sized box of chocolates a second glance. 'What will you be doing?' he asked, concern spreading across his weathered face, which had already suffered more than its fair share of worries over the years.

'I don't know until I get there on Monday. I was just told to report to the main desk.'

'Chuffin' 'eck, sis,' Edward finally said, eyeing up the purple box with the fancy gold swirly writing containing his favourite caramel swirls, which looked far more appealing than another bland Rich Tea. 'You don't do anything by 'alves, do yer?'

'Well, I couldn't just sit around and do nothing while everyone else is doing their bit. It wouldn't feel right.'

Carefully considering his words, knowing it was too late to change his daughter's mind, Joseph poured himself the last muddy brown dregs from the teapot.

'It wouldn't be what I'd have suggested,' he started. 'You know I'll worry about you constantly, but your mum would be so proud of you.'

The words took Betty by surprise, burning tears welling in her eyes for the umpteenth time that day. Knowing her beloved mum would approve felt like she was giving her daughter a blessing from above.

'Thanks, Dad,' Betty said, reaching over to squeeze his arm, grateful but also acutely aware that he would be hiding his own fears.

'I don't think I've ever told you this,' he added, 'but your nannan, your mum's mum, worked in one of

114

those factories during the last war.

'Did she?' Betty asked, momentarily speechless. Her dad had never mentioned this before.

'Aye, she did. I can't remember which one, but the story goes she was making shells and the chemicals turned her skin yellow.'

Betty had heard tales of the munitionettes, or 'Canary Girls' as they became commonly known, named after the tuneful household pets, whose skin became almost fluorescent after handling the TNT used in shells, but she hadn't realized her nannan Gloria, who had died when she was a toddler, had been one of them.

Despite knowing it had probably caused her maternal grandmother lung damage, the reason she'd ended up with severe jaundice, Betty couldn't help but feel it was almost fate that she too was about to embark on a job in one of the city factories, which had only allowed women to cross their thresholds for the first time during the Great War. The revelation served to cement her thoughts that going to work at Vickers was absolutely the right thing to do. It was obviously in her blood to follow in her nannan's footsteps — after all, she and female workmates had paved the way for women like Betty.

Betty smiled at her dad. 'It feels like it's meant to be.'

'Maybe,' he said, sighing. 'But you just take care, luv. At least I can keep an eye on this one when he's underground,' he added, glancing at Edward, who was now helping himself to a second chocolate from the double box, 'but I won't be able to look out for you.'

'How about I pop home more often on a Sunday

and we can all have lunch together?' Betty said, hoping the idea of his daughter visiting once a week might help. 'I'll even peel the potatoes for you.' She was fully aware that, since she'd been courting William, her visits back to her family home had become less frequent.

'That would be lovely and would make yer old dad very happy.'

'But only if you bring chocolates,' Edward said, already eyeing up which gooey-centred treat he could have next.

'Well, I can't promise you that,' said Betty, 'but I'm sure I could pick up a jam sponge from Mrs Loxley at Queen's Bakery on a Saturday afternoon.'

★ ★ ★

As Betty made her way back to her lodgings on the other side of town later that evening, some of her anxieties about leaving her comfortable clean job at Dawson & Sons to join Vickers had started to ease. Although she had swapped her safe job to enter a new and dangerous world, she felt exhilarated at the thought she was about to do something that would actually make a difference and mean something, like her nannan before her. The idea she was going to make a real contribution to the war effort and repeat history gave her all the courage she would need to walk through those big heavy gates the following week. Her dad might worry but she was determined to make him — and her mum, wherever she was — as proud as could be.

11

'That's 'em all done,' Patty told her mom, drying the last of the teatime dishes.

'Thanks, luv. Shall we have a quick cuppa before I settle Tom Tom for bedtime?'

'Why not,' Patty said, already filling the kettle and putting it on the range to boil.

'You can tell me what your plans are for the weekend,' her mom added, as she fetched the jug of milk from the parlour.

Patty's eyes lit up. She'd thought of nothing else for the last six days since Tommy Hardcastle had led her across the dance floor at the City Hall the previous Saturday night. She'd been over it time and time again in her mind, bending Hattie's ear all week at work, to the point where Mr Watson had told her if he caught her gossiping once more in front of a customer, he would dock her wages. But Patty didn't care — the lad she'd had an eye on for weeks had not only shown her some attention but hinted — no, more than hinted — *suggested* they meet up again tomorrow night. 'Just don't get too excited,' Hattie had warned, when their crotchety boss was nowhere to be seen, but Patty refused to let her more conservative and sensible best friend dampen her spirits. 'I can't wear the same outfit,' Patty had mused, oblivious to Hattie's warnings, already picturing herself instead in her powder-blue skirt and cream blouse, which showed

117

off her slender waist.

'Well,' said Patty as she sat down at the now cleared and freshly wiped table with her mom, 'I reckon Tommy — '

But before Patty could finish her sentence, the moment of peace was disturbed by the still strange interruption of the spine-chilling shrill of the air-raid siren.

Panic instantly replaced the look of calm on Angie's face.

'Bill,' she instinctively called, scraping her wooden chair against the stone floor. 'Get the kids, quick,' she cried, dashing to the hooks by the back doors to grab all six gas masks that were hanging in their cardboard boxes.

Although there hadn't been many sirens since war had been declared, Patty knew the routine. She quickly filled the flask that lived in the cupboard by the range with the now freshly boiled water over a tea strainer full of loose leaves, before adding in a generous splash of milk.

By the time she had tightly screwed on the top, grabbed a packet of biscuits, and made her way to the back door, her parents were already waiting with her brothers and sisters.

'Have you got the documents bag?' Angie asked, turning to her second eldest daughter, Sally.

'Yep,' she said, holding up the old brown battered suitcase that was now the home of the family's most important paperwork.

'Pat Pat,' cried Tom Tom, who was clinging to his dad's legs.

'Come here.' Patty lifted her little brother into her arms, quickly pulling on his navy woollen jacket.

'I've got his teddy,' said their other sister, Emily, handing him his favourite snuggly friend, which was now more grey than pale blue.

'Right, let's go,' Bill said, leading his family from the relative comfort of their home onto Thompson Road, where the intermittent screeching of the siren was louder than ever. Their neighbours and friends were all heading in the same direction, their heads down, protecting themselves against the late-afternoon drizzle, to the top of the road where a big brick and concrete communal public shelter had been erected a few weeks earlier.

As they got closer, the newly appointed air-raid warden, Fred Williams, who'd served in the First World War, was at the entrance.

'That's it. Everyone in,' he said, with military precision, in his new navy-blue overalls, with a red ARP stitched into the left chest pocket. 'Move up and make room for the next person,' he added, ushering Patty and her family down the concrete steps into the cavernous structure. Sitting on the slatted wooden bench, Patty shuffled along so she was as close to her mom — who she could feel physically shaking underneath her overcoat — as she could be, with Tom Tom on her knee, and Sally, Emily and John beside her, before her dad wedged himself on the end.

Across from them, Patty could make out their elderly neighbour, Mrs Bradley, who had already started knitting; the click clack of her needles could just be made out above the mumbled chat between friends and family.

'We'll be okay, won't we, Dad,' Emily said, her voice trembling.

'Of course, we will, sweetheart,' Bill said, reaching

across his son to rub his daughter's leg. 'It's probably just another practice run.' The first one had rung out through the city on the night Neville Chamberlain had announced war.

'Your dad's right, lass,' Fred said, shutting the metal door, temporarily putting the shelter into darkness.

'Pat Pat,' Tom Tom screamed, his chubby little fingers digging into Patty's arms, terrified by the sudden onslaught of blackness.

'It's okay, Tom Tom,' she cooed, bringing her little brother close to her chest and rocking him.

'Sorry,' Fred said apologetically, as the beams from torches began lighting up the crowded shelter. 'I didn't mean to scare the little 'un.'

'Can't be helped,' Patty's dad answered. 'He'll be okay in a minute, won't you, Tom Tom?'

But in the place of an answer was a sniffly whimper as Tom Tom cuddled in closer to his beloved Patty, as she quietly sang 'Twinkle Twinkle Little Star' to her little brother, a tried and tested guarantee to calm his sobs.

As a dozen or so torches created a soft flow around the makeshift sanctuary, Bill spotted one of his workmates, Frank, a fellow foreman who worked in one of the other workshops from Vickers, sat next to Mrs Bradley.

'Nah then, how yer doing?' Frank asked. 'Not how yer planned yer Friday night, I should imagine?'

'No,' laughed Bill. 'Not when I've got another early start tomorrow.'

'Aye, it's getting busier by the day, that's for sure. We are losing lads right, left and centre but the workload is increasing.' Frank sighed. 'If we don't get some more hands on deck soon, no matter how many hours a day we work, we won't be able to keep up with the orders and now more than ever we can't let the side down.'

Patty's ears perked up. She held back saying a word, still singing her brother's favourite nursery rhyme as his whimpers turned to the odd little gasp of breath as he began to relax.

'It's certainly the busiest I've known it,' Bill agreed. 'The worksheets are coming in thick and fast in the rolling mill.'

'I've heard we are taking on some lasses now; needs must and all that,' Fred said, mockingly rolling his eyes. 'Not that I mind. I don't care who does the job as long as they do it, and it looks like we are going to need a load more yet.'

Patty was now on high alert as she looked down the bench at her dad to gauge his reaction.

Bill sensed his daughter's piqued attention. 'It seems risky to me,' he replied. 'Those jobs involve hard labour that leave the strongest of men exhausted and risking their lives.'

My plan is doomed, Patty thought to herself, looking down at Tom Tom, who was now on the verge of dropping off, his heavy eyelids drooping and only occasionally springing open, before quickly closing again.

'Aye,' Fred chirped up, 'but without the women we won't be able to make the munitions for our lads.'

Patty instinctively looked up, glancing sideways at her dad. He looked deep in thought, as though he was battling against himself.

She wasn't wrong. Bill couldn't bring himself to argue. He recalled his own mom telling him with pride how she had worked in a steel rolling mill when the

Great War broke out, making parts for munitions to 'help the men'. He could still clearly remember how delighted she had been when, years later, he, her son, had started working at Vickers as an apprentice. 'Following in yer mother's footsteps,' she'd said proudly. 'That's m' lad.'

And Frank was right. He'd watched so many of the young men he'd trained up over the last few years leave in recent weeks to go and fight Hitler's troops, to defend the country. They were going to need all the help they could get now. Yes, the factories were dangerous and there was a fair selection of men he'd rather his eldest daughter wasn't mixing with, who, given half a chance, would see his sweet-natured naive Patty as easy bait, but could he really stand in the way of her 'doing her bit'? He knew, only too well, if his mom, as he had always called her, was still alive what the answer would be. She'd be giving him a piece of her mind, and wouldn't hold back if she got wind of the fact he was stopping Patty entering the factories on the basis she was a girl!

It didn't stop him worrying though. As a father, it was his job to protect his daughter, make sure she didn't come to any harm. The conflict swirling around in his mind was driving him to near distraction. He'd never forgive himself if something happened to Patty, who he still saw as his little ray of sunshine, despite her no longer being a toddler, waking him up every morning with cheery kisses, but he couldn't ignore the fact the steelworks and the Allied troops needed women to help them win this chuffin' godforsaken war.

'What about your Patty there?' Frank said, interrupting Bill's conflicting thoughts.

Patty didn't dare move a muscle, let alone smile or nod. Whatever was going on in her dad's mind, she wasn't daft enough to air her opinion now; and more to the point, she didn't fancy being on the receiving end of her dad's angst or being given short shrift in front of all her neighbours. She knew, whatever he decided, it ultimately came from a place of love.

Bill looked down the bench, his eyes portraying the confusion he felt. 'Well, I know what she would like to do,' he sighed, 'but . . . yer know. She's me daughter and in my eyes still my little girl.'

Frank chuckled to himself, turning his dimly lit torch to Patty, as she sat stock-still, her arms tightly wrapped her little bundle of a brother, whose chest was now gently rising and falling in a deep slumber. 'Well, if she comes to Vickers, you can at least keep a lookout for her. We all will. She'll be in safe hands.'

Patty was longing to speak, to plead with her dad while she had some support, but she was also wise enough to remember her mom's advice. Looking sideways to her right, the message in her mom's eyes was crystal clear: '*If you push yer dad now, he will dig his heels in,*' came the silent warning.

'You've got a point, Frank,' Bill smiled, diverting his attention to Patty. 'Probably more so than when she goes off gallivanting every Saturday night to the City Hall, dressed up to the nines,' he added, winking at his daughter.

'Really?' Patty gasped, reading between the lines and understanding the hidden meaning in her dad's comment.

'In principle, yes,' Bill finally relented. 'But the first sign of danger or any shenanigans and you will be begging that tyrant Mr Watson for a job back quicker than yer can say yer name. Is that clear?'

'Yes! I promise,' Patty replied, half squealing, half talking.

'Don't let him down,' her mom whispered, gently squeezing her daughter's leg. 'You'll never be able to persuade him twice.'

Frank smiled. 'Well, lass, I look forward to you joining the gang. If yer anything like the reports I've heard about the other young ladies, you'll do a grand job and make yer dad dead proud.'

'Thank you!' Patty beamed, already relishing in the satisfaction she would gain from telling Mr Watson where to stuff his job, although she would miss Hattie, and knew she would have to make sure they stayed in touch, especially now her sweetheart, John, would be joining the scores of lads being sent off to war. Hattie was going to need all the support she could get.

Right on cue, as if those responsible knew what needed to be decided had come to an end, the welcome alert that any potential threat had passed filled the shelter. 'Must have been another test,' Fred said, standing up and moving towards the door, ready to let the residents of Thompson Road and the neighbouring roads make their way home.

As the early evening light flooded the cavernous hut, a bewildered and now very sleepy Tom Tom stirred in Patty's arms.

'It's okay,' she said, giving him a gentle rock, as she waited her turn to stand up and leave. 'You're okay. I'm here.' Making their way out onto the pavement, Patty smiled to herself. At least it had stopped raining and it was still dusk, so they wouldn't have to make their way home in a cloak of darkness, abiding by the blackout rules that had been recently implemented.

Thankfully, as Frank had rightly surmised, there was no evidence that her beloved Sheffield had been the victim of Hitler's terrifying Luftwaffe, but, nevertheless, she couldn't help feeling proud that it was now only a matter of time before she could do her bit to help defend the city she had been born and bred into.

12

Sitting at the formal mahogany dining room table, Betty nibbled at the slice of hot buttered toast she had made herself a few minutes earlier in between sips of her freshly poured cup of tea.

It was the first Monday in years where she hadn't been mentally planning what paperwork she would need to get through for Mr Dawson when she arrived in the office. Not only that, as she looked down at her legs, she still couldn't get used to the fact she was wearing navy-blue trousers. She couldn't remember the last time she had worn anything but a skirt or a dress but knew there was no point turning up to her new job in a factory looking like a secretary or as though she was about to go for a walk around the park.

With her weekends no longer planned around meeting William, she had nipped into town on Saturday to find a pair of slacks that didn't make her feel overly masculine. There was more choice than Betty had imagined — according to the perfectly manicured sales assistant at Cole Brothers: 'They are quite in vogue and designed to slip over your hips just like a skirt would.' They were very comfy, Betty would give her that.

'How are you feeling?' asked Mrs Wallis, making Betty jump, as she sprung back to the present.

'Oh, I'm okay,' Betty told her. 'Well, a little bit

nervous, if I'm honest, but quite excited too.'

'You will be fine — they are very lucky to have you. I've made you this,' she said, handing Betty a small brown paper bag.

'What is it?' Betty asked, curiously looking inside.

'Your lunch,' her landlady replied. 'I took a guess that your mind would be too preoccupied to make anything and I didn't want you going hungry.'

'That's so kind of you, thank you,' Betty said, quite taken aback. Over the last couple of weeks the change in Mrs Wallis had been quite remarkable; she had provided an empathetic ear and more recently she had been a tower of strength when Betty had expressed her concerns over William, and now here she was taking on a motherly role.

'Well, someone has got to look out for you,' she said, smiling. 'And you need to keep your strength up. It's not going to be easy work.'

'I think that's only just dawning on me,' Betty replied. She had been so determined to do the right thing, she hadn't really thought about the ins and outs of what it entailed, just that she needed to do her bit.

'Talking of which,' Betty said, checking the time on her silver and red watch and noticing it was dead on seven o'clock, 'I better get going. I don't want to be late on my first day.'

Mrs Wallis laughed. 'No, that wouldn't stand you in good stead with your manager. Don't worry about your plate and cup, I'll clear them away once you are gone. You just get on your way.'

'Thank you,' Betty said, 'but I really didn't mean to cause you any extra work.'

'You haven't,' came the adamant reply. 'If I can't take care of my lodgers on their first day in a new job,

127

there's something very wrong.'

With that, Betty slipped on her tweed overcoat and tied her silk scarf — another gift from William, which she hoped would bring her luck today — and picked up her gas mask.

'Right then,' she said, making her way out of the dining room and down the black and white tiled hall, to the front door, 'I will see you around teatime.'

'I'll have a hot meal ready for you,' Mrs Wallis called back as Betty stepped out onto the street, the early morning chill hitting her.

'Okay, Betty,' she said to herself, 'time to pull on your big girl pants and tackle what's ahead.' If William could go off to fight a war, she was sure she could roll her sleeves up and get her hands dirty.

* * *

Betty didn't have long to find out. Half an hour later, after taking the tram to Attercliffe, she joined the moving sea of bodies — mainly made up of men in mucky brown overalls, scuffed black steel-capped boots and an array of dark coloured flat caps — as they made their way down Brightside Lane towards the huge factory that towered above many of the other dirty buildings that stood side by side, with its great grey chimneys emitting a fog of heavy smoke into the city skyline.

Betty looked to her left, taking in the stench of sulphur that hung in the air, stretching her neck to look for her entrance over the mass of heads that were bopping up and down amidst a hum of morning chatter. Gate three, her little slip of paper said.

'Can't be far now,' she whispered to herself, passing

the sign for number three.

Slowly zigzagging through the crowd the black painted number on a black background came into sight. Betty felt a flutter in her tummy, nerves kicking in. 'No point getting in a tizz now,' she told herself, weaving her way through the body of people and into the huge gateway entrance.

'Where next?' she said aloud, without realizing.

'Are you lost, duck?' came a voice from the side.

Stunned, Betty looked up. A man old enough to be her dad was beckoning her.

'I assume you're one of the new girls?' he added.

'Is it that obvious?' Betty said, suddenly conscious of her smart new trousers and tailored jacket.

'Well, we aren't used to you young ladies yet,' he added.

'I'm not sure where I'm supposed to report,' Betty said. 'I was just given this slip of paper.' She held it out as evidence to prove she was permitted to enter the city's historical club of workers.

'It is confusing, duck,' the well-built but kindly man said. 'Go straight ahead and through those double doors at the top of the yard. There will be somebody waiting to meet you in there.'

'Thank you,' Betty smiled, grateful for his fatherly assistance.

'No worries, duck. Hope your first day goes well and take no notice if some of the younger lads get a bit lairy — they're harmless enough and don't mean owt by it.'

Betty nodded, walking in the direction she'd been pointed in, desperately trying to ignore the apprehension that was now soaring through her. *What does he mean, 'if the lads get lairy'?*

She didn't have to wait long to find out. The sharp shrill of a wolf whistle a few metres away caused Betty to almost jump out of her skin.

'Would you like me to escort you t' door?' A skinny lad, who must have been all of eighteen, grinned, winking at Betty, as though he was the cock of the north.

'Er no, thank you. I think I can manage myself,' she said, throwing him a sharp look in return, taken aback by his outright brazenness.

'Oooh she's a hoity-toity one,' the lad laughed, to the amusement of his mates, causing Betty's white porcelain cheeks to redden.

'Right, lads, that's enough,' came a stern voice from the doors Betty was heading for. 'Get moving or you'll find your wages are docked and you'll be working through your breaks.'

'All right, all right, I was just having a bit of fun,' came the reply from the now sheepish-looking lad, who looked as though he'd just been caught with his hands in the biscuit tin.

'It must be Betty, is it?' the burly but friendly-looking man asked, his weathered face transforming from one of flustered annoyance to a beaming welcome.

'Yes, it is,' Betty replied, relieved to finally get to where she was supposed to be.

Beckoning her through the double doors, the second kindly looking man Betty had been acquainted with in the space of minutes introduced himself.

'I'm Frank,' he said, offering Betty his hand to shake. 'I'm going to be your foreman and will be showing you the ropes this morning. I'm just waiting for — '

But before Frank had time to finish his sentence, the doors flung open again.

'I'm not late, am I, Frank?' came the flustered voice of a young girl brushing back the mass of long strawberry-blonde curls that were playing around her face, and dropping her bagged gas mask to the floor. 'Me dad'll kill me if I am — especially on me first day. I'll be back at Woollies quicker than I can say m' name. It's just our Tom Tom wouldn't let me leave until he'd 'ad at least three cuddles and God knows how many kisses.'

'Don't worry, the hooter hasn't gone yet. You've just made it in the nick of time.' Frank smiled, secretly amused by his colleague and friend's whirlwind of a daughter. It made a change from receiving lip from some of the arrogant young lads he was normally in charge of. 'But whatever you do, get here on time in future. If you don't clock in before your shift is due to start, your wages will be docked, and I won't be able to cover for you.'

'I won't be late. I promise,' came the chirpy reply. 'Oh, I'm sorry,' she added, turning to face Betty. 'Did I interrupt you? I'm not doing very well for my first day, am I?'

'Don't you worry, lass,' said Frank. 'I was just explaining to Betty here that I will be your foreman and teaching you what you need to know this week.'

Turning to a bemused but smiling Betty, he added: 'This is Patty. As you might have guessed, it's her first day too.'

'Hello,' Betty responded politely but was secretly wondering why this dizzy, young girl had turned up looking as though she was ready for a Saturday night at the picture house as opposed to a day's hard labour in a factory.

'I must admit,' the older and more conservative

woman added, remembering the manners she'd been brought up with, 'I'm pleased to see another girl. I was a bit worried I was going to be the only one.'

'Aw, don't you worry, duck. A few others started last week, and I believe there's a couple more lasses arriving in one of the other workshops today,' Frank said reassuringly. 'We need as many of you women who are willing to work with us as possible. We're losing lads in their droves, but our workload is getting bigger by the day, so it will be all hands on deck, girls.'

'I hope not all the lads have gone off to war.' Patty giggled, before she realized what she was saying in front of her dad's pal.

Betty's eyes nearly popped out of her head. This wasn't a knocking shop! They were going to have to roll up their sleeves because there was hard work to be done.

Frank chuckled, shaking his head in mock jest. 'I'll pretend I didn't hear that, young Patty. Your dad will have you out of here quicker than you can say your name! Right then, no more time to waste,' he added. 'First things first. We need to get you two kitted out in the right gear. You can't go onto the factory floor in that good clobber — it will be ruined in minutes.'

Well, that was a needless shopping trip, Betty thought to herself.

Turning round to the wooden desk behind him, Frank picked up two bundles of clothing, and handed a set each to Betty and Patty. 'There's a changing room just through that door and some metal lockers. Why don't you go and get changed and I'll meet you back out here when you're done?'

'Thank you,' Betty said graciously, despite the mucky

brown look of the overalls, the colour resembling a muddy puddle.

'Oh,' Patty added, not even attempting to hide her look of absolute horror at the uniforms.

As the two women trundled into the small room, which reeked unforgivingly of lingering sweat and a hint of meat pasties, Betty audibly gasped.

'Chuffin' 'ell, it stinks in here,' Patty said, voicing her thoughts. 'Yer can tell it's only been used by dirty blokes — the smelly buggers.'

Betty couldn't help but laugh. 'That's one way of putting it.' It's not quite how she would have worded it but it did perfectly sum up the foul-smelling claustrophobic changing room with its dirty grey floor, which was speckled with clumps of dried mud and splinters of steel and the odd Smiths crisp packet that had been left on the well-worn wooden benches.

Finding the cleanest section she could, Betty rubbed her hand over the surface, sweeping away a layer of grime before sitting down to take her shoes off, as she realized there were no private cubicles.

'As you've probably guessed, Frank knows me dad. He works here too — in the rolling mill,' Patty said, as she pulled off her coat.

'It really is lovely to meet you,' answered Betty, bemused by her new workmate's excitable nature.

'What made yer want to come and work 'ere?' Patty added, slightly suspicious why someone as hoity-toity as Betty would warn to step foot in a filthy great foundry. 'You do look a bit posh for a place like this, if yer don't mind me saying.'

For the second time in the space of ten minutes, Betty chuckled to herself. She had never been referred to as posh before — respectable maybe, especially now she lived at the better end of town, but she was the daughter of a coal miner — hardly what she would call the epitome of upper-class society. Betty may have worked hard over the last few years to better herself in a legal firm, reading law books in the hope of one day becoming a solicitor herself, but she had put that to one side for the foreseeable future.

'Well, I just felt it was the right thing to do.' She smiled. 'I couldn't let this war rage on around us and do nothing. How about you?'

Momentarily bewildered, Patty was slightly taken aback. She hadn't really considered the bigger picture, but whether she overanalysed it or not, it had played in her favour.

'Well, two reasons really,' Patty finally said, a mischievous grin appearing across her face. Her reasons may not have been as commendable as Betty's, who seemed very serious and probably not much fun at all. 'Firstly, I hated my boss at Woollies — he was a right miserable old tyrant, always finding fault with everything I did; and secondly — for the lads of course!'

Yet again, Betty's eyes widened in shock. 'Oh,' she said, discreetly taking her new trousers off and quickly pulling on the oversized overalls.

'Although, looking at these things,' Patty added, holding up the manly brown all-in-one, 'I don't stand a chance of getting a second glance from anyone, let alone a strapping young steelworker.'

Despite Patty's seemingly immature comment, Betty had to admit, as she quickly buttoned the get-up she now found herself wearing, it was a far cry from the tailored skirts and fitted blouses she had worn every day for the last six years at Dawson & Sons. Her new unflattering uniform hung straight down, with no hint to her slender figure beneath.

'Well, I guess they just need to keep us protected,' Betty said, trying to remain pragmatic, despite her own less than enthusiastic views on her new uniform.

A couple of minutes later both women made their way back out into the reception area where Frank was waiting.

'Right then, girls — are you ready?'

'I think so.' Patty grinned, pulling the belt on her baggy overalls as tight as she could in an effort to show off her tiny waist.

'Would you like to know what jobs I've got in store for you both?' Frank added, secretly hoping his plans wouldn't end in disaster.

'Yes, please,' said Betty, impatient to just get on with her new role and concentrate on something other than the horrible thick material that was already causing her to itch.

'Well,' he started nervously, 'we need a couple of new crane drivers.'

'What?' Patty gasped, unable to hide her shock. 'I thought I'd be cutting up steel or sweeping the floors. You told m' dad I'd be safe!'

Frank stifled his laughter, amused by Patty's outburst. 'You will be safe, duck. I'm not just going to send you straight up one of those monsters without teaching you the ropes first.'

Betty didn't say a word, but she too was feeling less than confident about being sent thirty foot in the air. It wasn't that she was particularly scared of heights — it just didn't seem natural to be so high off the ground.

'Come on,' Frank said, ushering his two new apprentices through a single door opposite the desk.

'Let me introduce you to the team.'

The two women followed as he led them down a corridor and into what looked like a warehouse.

'It's not as big as I thought,' Betty said, pleasantly surprised. The cranes were only around ten foot off the ground.

'You see,' Frank said. 'Nothing to worry about.' What he didn't reveal was these were only used for training and only a fraction of the size of the ones used every day to lift slabs of steel.

No point scaring the living daylights out of them yet, he thought to himself.

'We need every worker we can get. Pete,' he called across the hall to a bloke a similar age to himself, who was sat in one of the crane cabs, 'come and meet your two new trainees.'

Climbing out from behind the controls and down the ladder, Pete stomped across the yard, curiously eyeing up Betty and Patty.

'So,' he started as he got close, 'you reckon you can take on a man's role and handle one of these?'

'Pete!' Frank said, an air of warning in his voice. 'Give them a chance. Without them we are all going to be pulling in some long shifts.'

'I'm only pulling their legs,' Pete said, breaking into a smile. 'Just teasing them, that's all.'

'Well, there's no need,' Betty finally said, her patience wavering, never one to be told she couldn't do something because of her sex. 'Just because we are women doesn't mean we can't scale those ladders and get on with the job in hand.'

'Doesn't it?' Patty asked, still looking slightly terrified by the sight in front of her. It was now her turn to be startled by her new colleague's feistiness.

'No, it doesn't,' Betty said firmly, shocked by her own confidence but refusing to be judged just because she wasn't a big strapping bulk of a man. 'We simply need to be taught what to do and then we can do what we're here for,' she added, determined to start as she meant to go on.

'Well, that's told you!' Frank laughed, looking at Pete, who now looked as though he had been slapped around the face with a wet fish. 'You know what they say? Don't mess with the fairer sex and remember what side your bread is buttered.'

'Aye,' Pete finally answered. 'You certainly put me in m' place, duck,' he said, trying to weigh up whether Betty was going to be more trouble than she was worth. She didn't look as though she would say boo to a goose but, as he'd just discovered to his peril, looks could be deceiving. 'Shall we get started then?' he added, hoping he didn't have eight hours of lip ahead of him.

'No time like the present,' Betty said, feeling rather proud of herself and already imagining relaying the story to William in the letter she was planning on writing to him that evening.

As the two women followed Frank across the dusty warehouse, Patty's initially cautious opinion of Betty started to change. They were entering a new, dangerous and daunting world, and one the traditional male workforce had dominated for decades. She gently nudged Betty.

'You told that Pete what for there, didn't ya?'

'Well,' Betty said, 'I'm not being put down just because I'm a woman. And neither should you.'

Patty looked at her new workmate in awe. She hadn't really thought too much about being criticized for her sex and certainly wouldn't have argued about it, but she was now glad to have a female workmate who wasn't scared to stand up to the more opinionated blokes and who would have her back when she needed it. It was clear women were going to be heavily outnumbered by the blokes, and she and Betty, like all the other girls who took jobs at Vickers, were going to have to support one another in this traditional man's world. She just hoped she didn't let Betty down, because, looking at those cranes, she didn't fancy her chances of being as apt and efficient as Betty was hoping.

At the same time, a surge of guilt soared through Betty as she realized her flighty new workmate wasn't really daft, just young and anxious, and despite how different the two women were, they would need to stick together to get through the weeks and months ahead of them.

'Right, first things first,' Frank said. 'To get into your cab you need to climb up the ladder and climb in safely.'

'Well, that's not a problem,' Betty said, already halfway up the metal ladder.

Frank smiled. He should have assumed his new ward wouldn't want mollycoddling. 'Patty,' he said, 'you stay down here for now. I'll go up with Betty and explain what the controls are for, then you can swap over.'

'That's fine with me,' Patty said, more than happy to keep her feet firmly on the ground for as long as possible. She took her place on the bench and looked round, hoping to spot any good-looking lads who might be working nearby. Her hopes for another dance with Tommy Hardcastle at the City Hall on

Saturday night had been extinguished like a candle in a sudden downpour of ice-cold rain when she'd seen him walk in with a stunning blonde-haired woman who could have easily passed for Greta Garbo, with her sultry 'take me to bed' eyes and siren-red lipstick. He'd barely taken his eyes off her all night, not giving Patty a second glance. She'd gone home deflated, her week-long excitement replaced by a long face and the feeling of complete rejection. 'He's not worth it,' Hattie had said, as they'd walked to the bus stop. But that was the problem — in Patty's eyes, he was. She was sure he'd been keen on her after their intimate dance a week earlier.

'Oh, well, there's plenty more fish in the sea,' Patty tried to convince herself, as from afar she now half-watched Frank show Betty what all the handles and buttons were for in the cab, while keeping another on what was going on at ground level, just in case the man of her dreams happened to walk past.

But apart from Frank, the only other bloke in sight was Pete, who must have been at least forty, with a protruding belly and a balding head.

★ ★ ★

An hour must have passed before Betty came down the ladder.

'How was it?' Patty asked, her nerves starting to resurface.

'It was really quite wonderful,' Betty replied, a huge smile on her face.

'Come on, Patty,' came Frank's kindly order from above. 'Your turn.'

Sensing her fear, Betty rubbed Patty's arm. 'You'll

be fine. I promise.'

Taking a deep breath, Patty momentarily closed her eyes. 'You can do this,' she told herself, putting her left foot on the first rung of the ladder.

'Just count to ten and you will be at the top,' Betty said, encouragingly.

'One,' Patty muttered, 'two, three . . . ' By the time she got to five, she was halfway up. Betty was right.

'That's it, duck,' Frank said as Patty reached the top and climbed into the back of the cab. 'Nice and steady. There's no rush today.'

'Crikey — ' Patty sighed as she wedged herself into the seat '—that was a bit hairy. Are you sure there aren't any less terrifying jobs going?'

'You'll get used to it,' Frank said, beginning to wonder if he'd done the right thing persuading her dad to let Patty start at the factory. Maybe Bill had a point — this work wasn't right for young girls, although Betty was proving him wrong so far. She seemed to be as tough as any man at Vickers and certainly wasn't afraid of a day's hard graft.

Determined to persevere, Frank attempted to ease Patty's nerves by patiently repeating the same tutorial he had just been through with Betty, not daring to tell her the height she was at now would feel like a breeze in comparison to where she would find herself next week.

'The principles are simple in theory,' Frank started.'There's just three handles to get used to. Once you get used to what they do, the rest is just fine-tuning and making sure you use them with care.'

'That doesn't sound too daunting,' Patty said, relieved there wasn't a whole array of mind-boggling buttons and controls to get her head around, which were bound to confuse her. It was one thing sorting out lippies and mascaras into neat rows but controlling a great heap of complicated machinery was another thing.

'It's not,' Frank said, smiling encouragingly. 'But be warned, one wrong move and it could be fatal.'

'Oh, crikey,' Patty exclaimed, 'that's the last thing I need to hear.'

'I don't want to scare you, duck,' Frank continued, 'but you need to be aware. These factories are dangerous places but if we all take care and concentrate on the job at hand, we'll all stay safe. Let's start with the basics.' Pointing to the two front levers, he explained, 'This one to your left is to control the movement of the hook and the one next to it lifts the hook up and down.'

'Okay,' Patty said; that didn't seem too hard to remember, at least. 'What about this big one 'ere?' She pointed to the handle behind the front two.

'Good question,' Frank replied. 'That one allows the whole crane to travel.'

'Oh, Lordy,' Patty said, already envisaging the terrible mess she would get herself into.

'Don't worry, duck,' Frank added. 'I won't be letting you loose on your own until I'm one hundred per cent sure you know what you are doing.'

Patty half laughed, half sighed. 'Yer might be waiting some time.' It had seemed like a good idea to get a job at the steelworks and be surrounded by such strapping fellas but now she was questioning what on earth she had let herself in for.

141

13

'Good time for a natter?' Doris asked, popping her head round her neighbour's door.

'Always,' Nancy said cheerily. 'I've just popped the kettle on and was about to have ten minutes before sorting the kid's dinner.

'I've left the big 'uns in the yard with your two,' Doris said, pulling up a chair with one hand, and propping up little Georgie on her hip as he dozed on her shoulder with the other. 'We might even get a bit of peace if this one stays asleep.'

'How's he doing of a night?' Nancy asked. 'I haven't heard him cry for a while now.'

'Oh, he's been a little angel,' Doris said, gently stroking her toddler son's rosy cheek. 'I think he's finally got used to George not being around.'

'And how are you?' Nancy asked, in awe that her friend was managing to look after four children, all under the age of ten, so well, despite the pain they'd all suffered over the past few months.

'I'm getting there,' she said, smiling weakly. 'The nights are still the hardest. I dream about George all the time and how he died. When I wake up, for a spilt second I tell myself it was just a nightmare, but then I realize he isn't here.'

'Oh, luv,' Nancy said gently, reminding herself her own worries were nothing in comparison to what Doris had endured. Popping the freshly brewed pot of tea on the table, she nipped to the pantry to fetch the milk and grabbed her only two china cups and saucers from the cupboard. 'I'm not surprised. It's going to take time.'

'That's the hardest bit to be honest.' Doris sighed. 'I'm almost wishing the weeks and months away, hoping the pain will stop but then I feel guilty as it means I'm taking us further away from when George was still with us. Does that make sense?'

'It does,' Nancy answered, as she poured her and Doris a strong cup of tea each. She couldn't have put it better herself. Since Bert had left a week earlier, all she had done was pray time would fly by, so he would be home again but at the same time she would have given her right arm to rewind the clock so they could be in each other's arms once more.

'Oh, look at us,' Doris said, and laughed. 'We're a right pair of miseries. I actually do have some good news.'

Nancy perked up. 'What is it?' she said, taking a mouthful of tea. 'Spit it out — I could do with something to put a smile on my face.'

'Well,' Doris started, 'I might have worked out a way I can stay here and not move back to live with my family.'

'How?' Nancy asked, her interest well and truly piqued. She knew she was being selfish when her mood had dipped after Doris had first told her she might have to move away. It's just she'd become close to Doris over the last few years. And now with Bert off training to fight in this godforsaken war, and her sister and parent's forty miles away, across the Pennines in Manchester, Doris had become her closest friend — the idea of her disappearing too was one thought she didn't like to dwell on.

'There was a notice in the corner shop, some wealthy woman looking for someone to do her ironing. Anyway, I got in touch and she's going to be sending me three enormous piles a week.' Nancy grinned. 'And that's not all. A few of her friends have now asked if I can take their laundry in too. If it works out, I might just be able to make enough money to make ends meet.'

'Oh, Doris, luv,' Nancy said, her eyes welling up as she reached across to touch her friend's arm, 'this is the best news I've had in ages. You might be able to get a right little business going if word gets round.'

'Well, don't count yer chickens yet, but I really hope it works out,' Doris said, an excited grin replacing the sadness that had filled her eyes minutes earlier. 'The kids are happy here. They like school, and, more importantly, this is their home; it's full of memories of their dad.'

'It is,' Nancy replied. 'We would miss you all so much too, so let's hope half of Sheffield want an ironing lady!'

With that the two women gently clinked their cups.

'I'll drink to that,' Doris said. 'Anyway, enough about me. How are you getting on?'

Nancy placed her dainty floral cup back on its matching saucer. 'I'm not going to lie — ' she quietly sighed, her meeker side surfacing one again '—it hasn't been easy. I tried to be brave while Bert was still here, I didn't want to make him feel any worse, but I've felt utterly wretched since he got on that train.

'I'm putting a brave face on for our Billy and Linda, but as soon as they are tucked into bed, the tears start, and I can't stop them. The kids have been so much

144

braver than me. Occasionally one of them sneaks into bed with me through the night for a cuddle — but to be honest, I'm grateful. I hate being in that bed by myself — it just doesn't feel right.'

Doris nodded sympathetically. Nancy didn't need to explain; it was probably the main reason she still let Georgie, who still sound asleep snuggled into her chest, sleep with her.

'Do you think it would help if you had something to keep your mind busy?' she tentatively asked Nancy. She knew only too well how long the days, and nights, felt when your life had been suddenly turned upside down. She'd spent weeks looking at the clock on her bedside table, wondering how on earth a minute passed so slowly.

'Maybe,' Nancy said, nodding. She topped up hers and Doris's cups with the last of the tea from the pot. 'I probably should try and earn some money. I think Bert's pay will be less now. He always used to top up his basic wage with all the overtime he did, to make sure we never wanted for a thing. But what would I do? I need to be around for Billy and Linda and I'm not really sure what I'm qualified for. I suppose I could look for a cleaning job or something in a shop, if they are flexible with hours, and I've heard the steelworks are looking for . . .'

Nancy stopped herself, inwardly chastising herself for being so insensitive and putting her giant size sixes in it. 'I'm so sorry, Doris,' she said, her voice faltering at the thought of upsetting her friend. 'I wasn't think-ing. I'm just whittling on about myself. I didn't mean to bring it all back.'

'Don't be daft.' Doris waved the apology away. 'What happened to George was awful, I won't lie, and there isn't a second of the day I don't wish to God he was still here, but it was a freak accident. I'm not saying they are the safest or nicest of places, far from it, but you can't let what happened to my George put you off. He had so many good years in the works and loved every minute. They paid him well and in turn we had a nice life. He'd have stayed there until they booted him out to draw his pension. He never had a bad word to say about the place.'

For the second time that afternoon, Nancy couldn't help but admire Doris for her relentless determination to find the positives in the sea of worry she had found herself in. She had no idea where she got her strength from. No one would have blamed her for hating Vickers and cursing them for the death of her lovely husband, but instead, quite remarkably, she refused to get bitter. She might have been heartbroken, but she certainly wasn't angry.

'It's all hypothetical anyway,' Nancy said. 'I need to think about Billy and Linda.'

Doris stared at her friend as if she was on cloud cuckoo land. 'Listen, yer daft bat, do I have to spell it out to you?'

'What?'

'I will help you out with the kids,' Doris gasped, in mock exasperation. 'It's the least I can do after everything you and Bert have done for me over these last few months.'

'But —'

'No buts,' Doris stopped her. 'You've already said you need to keep your mind busy. You would and have done the same for me.'

'Oh, I know,' Nancy started to argue, 'but haven't you got enough on? I don't like to add to your load.'

'Now listen up,' Doris said, pretending to get cross, 'I need a reason to stay. You will be doing me a favour. Besides which, Billy and Linda are no bother. I've already got four,' she added, gently kissing the top of little Georgie's head. 'Another two won't make any difference.'

For a second Nancy was speechless, a combination of nervous trepidation about looking for a job but also because of the selflessness of her friend and neighbour, who had been to hell and back since losing her husband yet was still thinking of others.

'Believe me,' Doris said, 'the hours and days are going to go a lot faster if we are both busy.'

'You're right,' Nancy agreed. 'I can't bear the thought of moping around for however long it takes for this wretched war to come to an end. If you're absolutely sure, I will pop down to the Labour Exchange tomorrow after I've taken Billy and Linda to school and see if they have any vacancies. But if it does come off, I want to pay you; you can't just do this out of the goodness of your heart.'

'Oh, shush,' Doris said, rolling her eyes and shaking her head simultaneously. 'If you can't help yer mates out, there is something very wrong.'

'Well, let's work something out when I know what I'm going to be doing,' Nancy replied. Friend or no friend, Nancy wasn't going to take advantage of Doris. She knew her pal was on her uppers and if she could make life easier for her, she was determined to do so; in fact, it was even more of a reason to go and get a job.

That night, after Nancy had tucked Billy and Linda into bed, watching from the bedroom door as their eyes closed in turn, she couldn't help but wonder

147

what lay ahead.

Their whole lives had been turned upside down in the last week and God only knew what the next week would bring.

'Well, Bert,' she whispered, 'it looks like we're both venturing into the unknown.'

14

'Right, kids,' Nancy said, as she tentatively led them round to her neighbour's back door, 'be good for Doris and I'll be home at teatime.'

'Are you going to be making Spitfires?' Billy asked, not in the least bit fazed that his mum was going to work for the first time since he'd been born. 'Or guns? Will you send one to Dad to fight Hitler? That'll show him what for, won't it?'

Billy hadn't stopped asking questions since Nancy had explained a few days earlier that she was now going to be working and had taken a job at Vickers — the biggest steelworks in Sheffield. If it wasn't for the fact she knew they hadn't taken a step out of Attercliffe, let alone the city, in the last week, she would have been convinced he'd kissed the Blarney stone.

She laughed, ruffling his mop of dark hair, that fell to the side just like Bert's did. 'I don't know yet, sunshine, but I promise I will tell you all about it as soon as I get home tonight.'

As they knocked on Doris's kitchen door, Linda, who unlike her big brother had barely said a word all morning and only eaten a few mouthfuls of her generously buttered toast, tugged on her mum's coat. As Nancy looked down, tears were filling her daughter's normally happy eyes.

'Hey now,' Nancy said in her naturally gentle and serene maternal tone, kneeling down on the cold

149

stone doorstep so she was face to face with her little girl, 'there's no need to get upset. Mummy will be home not long after you finish school, and you can tell me all about your day.'

'But I'm going to miss you,' Linda whispered, her voice teetering on the edge of breaking.

'And I'm going to miss you too, angel, but I promise you will have a lovely day, and, as a special treat, I've popped one of those delicious jam tarts we made yesterday in your packed lunch.'

The makings of a smile appeared on Linda's face.

'Did I get one too?' Billy asked, the mere mention of food pricking his ears to high alert.

Nancy laughed. 'Of course. But in return, I expect you to take extra special care of your sister today. She might need an extra hug or two. And you both better be on your best behaviour for Aunty Doris — if I get word of any trouble you'll be in big bother.'

Screwing his face up, Billy went to say something, but thought twice as he clocked his mum giving him one of her warning looks. 'Course I will.' He smiled cheekily, thinking better of making a joke out of the situation.

'Right then,' Nancy said, standing up to knock on Doris's back door, hoping she had done a good enough job of hiding her own nerves, which had nearly stopped her from taking the plunge into the unknown at least a handful of times this morning alone. 'Let me give you both a kiss now,' she added, pulling both Linda and Billy close to her.

Just as she gave them a final hug, Doris's six-year-old daughter, Alice, swung open the door, still dressed in her pink cotton nightie.

'Linda,' she squealed excitedly, 'come and see the

new bed I've made for my dollies.'

Nancy could have kissed her too as Linda's eyes suddenly lit up.

'Okay,' came her now cheery reply. And with just one glance back towards Nancy, she ran into the house, gas mask in one hand and her school bag, holding her lunch, in the other.

Seconds later, Doris appeared, Georgie in one arm, and a mug of steaming hot tea in the other.

'Come on in, Billy,' she said, beckoning him indoors. 'Joe's just devouring his third piece of toast. There's some extra on the table. Help yerself.'

'Thank you so much again for this, Doris,' Nancy said, the butterflies that had been performing somersaults worthy of a circus performance in her tummy momentarily easing, taking on a calmer pace in the knowledge Billy and Linda were going to be okay.

'It's nothin',' Doris said. 'Now get yerself off. You don't wanna be late on yer first day!' She wasn't deliberately shooing Nancy away but she knew if she stepped foot in the house it would make leaving her Billy and Linda even harder. 'And don't worry; the kids will be fine and so will you!'

'Okay,' Nancy said, nodding, 'I really am very grateful.'

'I know,' came the kindly reply. 'Just go and have a good day. It will be four o'clock before yer know it.'

Nancy looked down at her watch. It was nearly half past seven. She had half an hour before she was due to report for her first day at work, and Vickers was only a twenty-minute walk away. Buttoning up her coat against the crisp early morning air, she gave Doris one last smile before heading out of the yard and down the ginnel onto Prince Street.

Lost in her own little anxious world, Nancy barely noticed the throng of other workers heading in the same direction to the industrial side of Attercliffe. She had never left her children to go to work before — in fact, it had been nearly eight years since she'd worked after she gave up her job at the Co-op when she found out she was expecting her first. But after her chat with Doris last week, she'd taken herself off to the Labour Exchange and was told the steelworks were in desperate need of women to fill the roles left empty by the young lads going off to war.

Digging her hand into her pocket, Nancy felt for the piece of card she had been given — the passport to a new and different life. That same night, she had written a letter to Bert, telling him her news. She could just imagine his face as he read the words: *I am starting a job at Vickers. Doris has agreed to look after Billy and Linda before and after school. I've never felt so nervous in my life, but I think it will help keep my mind busy while you are away. Billy is very excited; he thinks I'm going to be making you a gun . . .*'

Nancy hadn't heard back from Bert yet. She wasn't surprised and knew it wouldn't be for lack of trying on his part. The post was slow, and he would be up to his eyes in training, but she could imagine the look of shock on her husband's face when he read her note. His wife going to work at the steelworks! It would be the last thing he was expecting but she had no doubt in her mind that Bert would be proud of her too, knowing she loved nothing more than making a home for him and their children, but was now bravely stepping out of her comfort zone into unknown territory.

The back of her eyes filling with water — which had nothing to do with the plumes of heavy dark smoke emerging from the factory chimneys — Nancy's nerves threatened to explode again as she joined the sea of bodies walking up the cobbled path of Brightside Lane. The image of Linda's crumpled face flashed before her.

Was she being a bad mum, she wondered. Would Linda think her mummy wasn't there for her any more?

She knew without a shadow of a doubt that Doris would take more than good care of her and it was only for an hour or so before and after school, but that wasn't doing much to ease the aching tightening pain in her chest that was literally tugging at her heart. It was the same feeling that had forced her to fight back the tears on Linda's first day at school, when she'd clung to her legs and begged Nancy to take her home — the complete opposite of her brother whose biggest concern was whether he'd still be able to make paper aeroplanes all day. The two of them were like carbon copies of her and Bert, with Linda inheriting her mum's overly sensitive side and quiet homely traits, while Billy was keen as mustard to lap up every adventure that came his way — just like his dad.

Suddenly, unable to recall a single step of the walk to her new place of work, Nancy found herself outside gate number three. Looking up, her worries about Linda were overtaken by the enormity of what she now faced. The great red-brick building, blackening in places due to all the dirt and smoke, was huge.

'What on earth have I let myself in for?' Nancy muttered to herself. 'I'll never find my way round it all.' She tried to hold back the tears she had fought since waking in the early hours, unable to sleep, worrying about the day ahead.

153

'Are you lost?' a gentle voice came from next to her.

Nancy looked round. Next to her was a kind-looking woman, at least ten years younger than her, wearing a pair of brown mucky overalls that didn't look right against her immaculate dark-brown coiffed hair and flawless complexion.

'Er, well, I know I need to report to reception,' Nancy said, her voice barely above a whisper. 'But apart from that I haven't really got a clue.'

'You can follow me if you like. I only started last week, so I'm still pretty new myself, but I can show you where you need to go now if it helps?' Betty offered, convinced she had seen the clearly terrified-looking woman somewhere before.

'Thank you; that would be wonderful, if you don't mind,' Nancy said, grateful for a friendly face. 'I'm Nancy, by the way.'

'I'm Betty, and, honestly, please don't worry. It's not as daunting as it looks,' she added, all the while trying to place where she had seen Nancy before.

'Oh, who are you trying to kid?!' came another far chirpier voice from behind. 'I'm dreading today!'

Nancy spun round to see who the mystery addition to their conversation was.

'Sorry,' said the even younger girl, whose English-rose face was enveloped with a mass of long strawberry-blonde curls, not too dissimilar to Linda's.

'Patty!' Betty quipped. 'It's Nancy's first day. Don't make her any more anxious than she already is.'

'Sorry, I didn't mean to, but we've got to up those chuffin' — '

'Stop it,' Betty intercepted. 'At least let Nancy get through the door. You are going to put her off before she even steps foot in the place.' She turned to Nancy.

'This is Patty, and don't worry — things aren't as bad as she's hinting at.'

But judging by the somewhat questionable look on the younger girl's face, Nancy wasn't convinced.

Well, it's too late now to back out, she thought.

In a state of bewilderment, Nancy let Betty lead her through the main reception doors, where Frank was propped up against the desk with a mug of steaming tea in one hand and a copy of the *Daily Mirror* in the other.

'Aw, good morning, girls,' he said, as the doors flew open. 'Are you all set for your big day?'

'No,' Patty said, dramatically sighing, her voice going up a couple of octaves. 'Are you sure we don't need some more time practising?'

Frank chuckled. 'Absolutely not, you're ready. Have faith, duck.'

'Have faith.' Patty laughed. 'Yer about to send me up — '

'Patty!' Betty exclaimed, stopping her rather vocal workmate. 'Frank, is this the new worker you were expecting?' she added, introducing a now very pale and petrified-looking Nancy, who was holding out her rectangular piece of paper as though she was about to be sent overboard on a ship.

'Ah, yes, I think it might just be. Nancy Edwards, is it?' He smiled, turning his attention to Nancy. 'Now, duck, don't be listening to this one getting herself in a tizz,' he said, glancing at Patty. 'There's absolutely nothing to be worried about. Yer in good hands, I promise.'

'Okay,' she replied meekly, but the lack of conviction in her voice wasn't fooling anyone.

'Has Patty here told you what you will be doing?'

155

Frank asked.

'No,' Nancy said, slowly shaking her head.

'We weren't sure if Nancy was definitely with us,' Betty explained.

'No point scaring her before she gets through the door,' Patty said. 'As soon as she sees what lays in store, there's every chance she'll do an about-turn quicker than she can say her name!'

'Patty!' Betty chided for the second time in as many minutes.

'Oh, don't mind her, duck,' Frank said. 'As I'm beginning to discover, she likes to make a mountain out of a molehill.'

'It is a chuffin' mountain we've got to climb today, from what you said on Friday,' Patty muttered, knowing the only reason she could so abruptly vocalize her thoughts was due to Frank being a pal of her dad's.

'Well,' Frank said, 'I'll cut to the chase, duck. You will be working with Betty and Patty here, as a crane driver.'

'Oh!' Nancy gasped, almost speechless at the unexpected revelation. 'I . . . I had no idea.'

Seeing the colour visibly drain from her new workmate's face, Betty touched her arm.

'It's really not that bad. If anything, it's quite exciting.'

'If you like putting your life in the hands of the gods,' Patty interrupted, astonished by how calm her workmate was.

Frank chuckled, raising his grey bushy eyebrows. 'Right, before little Miss Drama Queen here scares you out of your wits, why don't you go and get changed into these.' He handed her a big bundle of brown material. 'And then I can let you know what's going to happen today. The changing room is just through that door.' He pointed towards the same room he'd sent Betty and Patty to exactly a week ago.

Ten minutes later, Nancy emerged, having donned her baggy ill-fitting overalls, looking slightly perturbed, especially when she saw how her new colleagues' boiler suits were all nipped and tucked to show off their feminine curves.

'Oh, don't worry,' Betty whispered with a smile, immediately picking up on why Nancy looked so disgruntled,'Patty had an absolute hissy fit when she tried hers on too.'

'Well, you can't blame me, can yer?' Patty scowled, her hair now neatly twisted in a top knot, but the odd, beautiful corkscrew curl effortlessly falling onto her shoulders. 'They are hardly the most glamorous, are they?'

'In comparison to mine, they don't look half bad,' Nancy said, her face a complete picture.

'Oh, I looked like a chuffin' sack of coal too —' Patty sighed '—until I got my m' mom onto it. Over my dead body was I wearing this when it made me look like a bloke!'

Patty repeated the story of how she had gone home from work after her first night and sobbed until her already harassed mom had agreed to get her sewing machine out and give her daughter's new uniform an overhaul. She'd been up half the night nipping and tucking the thick mucky brown overalls in all the right places.

'She's done a great job.' Nancy smiled, rather envious of Patty's more shapely 'uniform'. 'And I'm guessing you did the same, Betty?' She looked towards the calmer of the women.

'I did, but I waited until the weekend and my land-lady helped me.'

'Right then, I can see what I'll be doing once my two are in bed tonight,' Nancy said, pulling at the excess material that would comfortably allow at least one other person to fit inside.

Frank laughed, 'Okay, girls, now you've sorted out how to look like models, shall we start work?

'I guess now is as good a time as any,' Patty said. 'No point putting off the inevitable forever.'

'Come on,' Frank encouraged, rolling his eyes. 'Let me explain, Nancy . . . '

The burly but fatherly foreman explained how for the last week he had been teaching Betty and Patty how to operate cranes on the training floor. They had moved on from understanding the controls, to lifting small weights and even moving the cargo across the warehouse.

'So, today we will just go through it all again with Nancy and then tomorrow take you into the actual factory and be partnered up with an experienced crane driver.'

The look on Patty's face bestowed the relief of being given another day of reprieve. 'Thank the Lord,' she muttered, to Frank's tolerant amusement.

He guided the three women into the windowless hall where Betty took Nancy by the arm.

'Don't listen to Patty,' she told Nancy, 'it's really not that bad at all.'

'Thank you,' Nancy replied gratefully. 'I must admit I have been really quite nervous. I had no idea what to expect.'

'Well, let me show you,' Frank added.

For the rest of the morning, despite worrying her

own fears would get the better of her, Nancy was taken up and down the sturdy metal ladder leading to the cab, ten foot off the ground, and learnt how to use the three main controls. By dinnertime she'd even managed to lift a small steel coil and move it up a few metres without dropping it.

'You're a natural,' Frank praised her, as he led her back down to ground level.

'Do you think?' Nancy asked in disbelief, light-headed, suddenly feeling exhausted after concentrating so hard all morning, determined to do her best.

'I do. In fact,' he added, looking towards Betty and Patty who were sat on one of the black metal benches, 'you all are. Some of my lads are a bit heavy-handed, but you three are just what I need — you treat the steel with the care it needs. I spend 'alf my day telling most of the lads to be careful. I reckon you are going to give them a run for their money.'

Patty smiled, thinking to herself how this would play right into her bigger plan.

They will be putty in our hands, she thought.

Betty could guess what Patty was imagining, but she wasn't so sure. She just hoped the niggling feeling that was creeping into her thoughts was a simple case of nerves.

'Anyway, why don't you grab your lunch now and this afternoon we can have one last go at moving steel plates,' Frank suggested.

'Well, I wouldn't say no to that,' Betty said.

'Me neither,' Patty added. 'I'm chuffin' starving. I feel like me throat's been cut.'

Betty turned to Nancy. 'Did you bring a pack-up?'

'I did,' she said, nodding, suddenly conscious of how much her tummy was rumbling. Her early morning nausea, triggered by what lay ahead, had prevented her eating more than a mouthful of dry toast.

'Come on then. Since we started we've been having lunch outside in the yard while it's still sunny; you're welcome to come join us.'

Ten minutes later, the three women were sat perched on a wall, enjoying some much-needed fresh air, after a morning trapped indoors, dust and steel shards already catching in the back of their throats, distorting their taste buds.

'So, what made you want to come and work here?' Betty asked Nancy, unwrapping the greaseproof paper from her ox tongue sandwich, which Mrs Wallis had made her. Ever since she'd started at the works, Betty had gone home to a hot dinner on the table and woken up to wrapped sandwiches for the day ahead.

'I needed to keep my mind busy,' she explained, reaching into her bag for her lunch. 'My husband got his papers and I knew I would send myself to distraction if I was home all day. There's only so many times I can black-lead the range. And, if I'm honest, we could do with the extra cash now Bert will be earning less on an infantry soldier's salary, with no bonuses for overtime. My children, especially our Billy, could eat me out of house and home at the best of times, so I need to make sure I can keep food on the table.'

'Oh, I'm sorry,' Betty said, knowing all too well how Nancy felt. It was only taking the job at Vickers that had stopped her mind running away with itself, thinking about how long it would be before her William risked life and limb, taking to the skies. In his first letter, which had arrived a couple of days earlier, he'd explained how his training had begun in earnest.

'I know exactly what you mean,' she said with a

sigh, explaining her own predicament.

And it was then Betty suddenly remembered where she had seen Nancy. 'I know this might sound odd but all morning I have been trying to work out why you look familiar. Is your little girl the spitting image of you? I think I saw you at Sheffield train station a couple of weeks ago?'

'Yes. I was there,' said Nancy. 'I was waving off my Bert with our children, Billy and Linda.'

'Oh, I'm sorry,' Betty said, inwardly chastising herself for bringing up what would have obviously been a difficult and heart-wrenching moment. 'I think I saw you. Was it a Wednesday? I was saying goodbye to my William — he's based at Doncaster now, he's a trainee RAF pilot.'

'Yes, it was.' Nancy smiled weakly, biting her lip as the painful reminder of bidding her husband farewell came flooding back. 'Bert's been sent to Catterick, but I should imagine he won't be there for long before he's sent off to fight. He's been in the TA for a while so I should expect they'll be the first to the front line. I couldn't just mope about. I realized I needed to keep my mind busy so signed on at the Labour Exchange.'

Betty nodded. 'Same here. And I felt I needed to do my bit too.'

'I can definitely relate to that,' Nancy agreed, secretly hoping by working in a steel factory, she would somehow be helping her Bert. 'And what about you, Patty?' she asked, turning to the youngest of the three women, who was devouring her doorstep-like jam butties. 'What persuaded you to come and work in a foundry?'

'Well — ' Patty smiled, a glint of excitement twinkled in her hazel eyes '—whatever yer do, don't tell me dad this or he'll have me back at Woollies in a flash, but I thought I might finally meet Mr Right!'

'Oh,' Nancy laughed, remembering how at Patty's age she too had been excited at the thought of being swept off her feet by the right fella. 'Well, I suppose there will be a fair few lads to choose from.'

'Exactly!' Patty giggled. 'It's the only good point about starting on the main factory floor tomorrow . . .'

Betty raised her eyebrows for the umpteenth time in mock jest. She'd unfairly judged Patty as a bit daft when they had been introduced a week earlier, but she could now see that Patty was just making the most of life, and she couldn't really begrudge her that.

'Well, one thing is for sure, girls,' Betty said, 'whatever the reason we have found ourselves here, we are now a team and we need to stick together and help each other through whatever is thrown in our path, especially by some of the more bolshy blokes in this place.'

For the first time that day, Nancy's nerves eased about what she had let herself in for. She might feel like a fish out of water, but she was grateful she was working alongside two lovely girls, who, despite only having met them hours earlier, she had quickly forged a strong bond with and felt incredibly loyal towards.

15

Rubbing the sleep from her eyes, Patty instinctively reached for her now tailored overalls from the end of her bed. The springs in her old mattress creaked under her weight as she released her legs from the comfort of her warm flowery pink eiderdown onto the less welcoming rag rug. Her little brother, who shared her draughty attic bedroom, started to rouse from his deep slumber.

'Pat Pat,' he murmured instinctively.

'Morning, Tom Tom,' his big sister said, stretching her still heavy arms above her head. 'Did you have a good bo bo's?'

'Cuggle,' came his usual muttered reply, as flickers of light seeped in under the door of the dark window-less room.

Well, if that wasn't a cue for Patty to pull herself out of her sleepy stupor, nothing would.

'I'm coming,' she said with a yawn, quickly pulling on her boiler suit before taking the few steps across the scratchy floor to her toddler brother's cot.

His chubby little pyjama-clad arms already stretched out in front of him, Patty lifted Tom Tom into her arms, welcoming his warm snuggly body, which felt like a hot water bottle.

'Let's go and get some brekkie,' Patty said, holding Tom Tom close as she made her way down the two flights of cold bare-wood stairs to the inviting smells

163

coming from the family kitchen.

'Morning, you two,' came Angie's cheery greeting. As always, she had been up with the lark, warming up a pan of stodgy porridge she'd prepared the night before and toasting slices of home-made white bread.

'Milk,' came Tom Tom's no-nonsense response, hankering for his favoured morning comfort.

'It's here,' Angie said, handing her youngest son his cup as Patty sat down at the table with Tom Tom still safely enveloped in her arms.

'How are you feeling about today?' asked Bill, who was tucking into a steaming bowl of porridge with a crimson-red swirl of jam bleeding into the top of the thick white gloopy breakfast.

Patty had been determined not to reveal how anxious she was to her protective father who'd had been more than hesitant about her relentless determination to work at the foundry. But she also knew that her dad could read her like a book and there was no point in trying to bluff him.

'I won't lie,' she confessed, 'I'm brickin' it. Frank keeps telling us we have nothin' to worry about, though.'

'He'll look after yer, sunshine.' Bill smiled, despite his own simmering concerns. He knew only too well how dangerous those factory floors were, especially for a young woman. But he also knew that this morning his anxious daughter needed to be bolstered not frightened. 'Yer in safe hands with Frank — he's one of the best.' It was true, the two men had started out together at Vickers, and he would trust him with his life. 'Just do as he says, and you won't go far wrong.' More than anything, he needed Patty to take heed and not get distracted. Many a man had been left

164

with crippling injuries and scarred for life after taking their eye off the ball.

'I will,' Patty said, nodding and pouring herself a much-needed early morning cuppa.

Bill hoped to God she truly would — he knew only too well what a scatterbrain his fun-loving flighty daughter could be.

★ ★ ★

Half an hour later, just after the kitchen clock chimed, indicating it was seven-thirty, Patty and Bill were already by the back door, pulling on their coats and picking up their gas masks.

Angie bustled towards them, holding two old biscuit tins and two flasks of tea. 'Don't forget yer snap.'

'What would we do without you?' Bill chuckled, pecking his wife on the cheek.

'Well, you'd probably starve for starters.' She rolled her eyes in mock jest.

A few minutes later, Bill and Patty were making their way up Thompson Road, the shared silent fear they both felt, bubbling under the surface.

'Dad' . . . 'Patty', the pair said in unison, turning to look at one another.

Bill spoke first. 'Please, just be careful. This isn't a game or a bit of fun. I want to see yer walking out of those factory doors in one piece at four o'clock.'

'I promise, Dad, I will. But will I be okay? I mean, we've only been practising on those little cranes. Are the real ones enormous?'

Bill knew there was no point lying to his daughter; she would see soon enough. 'They have to be, sunshine. It's the only way they can move steel across the

165

factory floor.'

Patty audibly sighed, starting to question whether begging her dad to let her leave Woollies had been a good idea after all.

'Come on, luv,' he said gently, putting his arm over Patty's drooping shoulders. 'You won't be on yer own. You will have a partner and Frank will be keeping a close eye on you.'

'Thanks, Dad,' she said, trying to placate the millions of butterflies that were fluttering around her tummy.

Just as the pair reached King Street, they spotted Nancy walking towards them.

'Hiya,' Patty called, waving enthusiastically at her new colleague. 'Dad, this is Nancy,' she added as Nancy reached them.

'Hello, Nancy, lovely to meet you,' Bill greeted her. 'I hope you aren't as nervous as this one?'

'I won't lie, I am quite anxious,' Nancy said, sighing, 'but I've been run off me feet since I got home last night so haven't had two minutes to really think about it.'

'I can imagine. Our Patty here tells me you have a couple of little 'uns and a husband away, ready to go off to war. Are they coping okay with you taking on a job at the works?'

Nancy bit her lip. She knew Bill hadn't meant to upset her but leaving Bill and Linda this morning for work hadn't been any easier now that she was in her second week on the job. Despite Doris's offer of freshly made bread and jam, minutes earlier Linda had been clinging to her legs, silent tears trickling down her cheeks. It had taken every ounce of strength she had to hand her distraught little girl over to her neighbour and walk away. She just hoped that bit would get eas-ier with time as they all got used to this new, and at times bewildering, arrangement.

'I'm not sure I'll ever get used to leaving them, if I'm honest. I feel like the cruellest mother alive right now,' Nancy sighed, unable to shake the image of Linda's crumpled face from her mind.

'I know I'm a bloke,' Bill started, 'and I leave m' wife, Angie, to sort the kids out most of the time while I'm working, but from what I can tell they're more resilient than we think. Our Tom Tom sobs every morning when Patty here leaves for work but within minutes he's happily playing again. They just know how to pull on yer heartstrings, duck.'

'Oh, I hope yer right,' Nancy said, a little more hopeful. 'I barely slept a wink last night.' After get-ting home after her first day, she could have kissed Doris, who had not only generously made an extra big bone stew but had also insisted Nancy sit down and eat a bowlful with her and all their kids after she had arrived to pick up Billy and Linda.

It had been gratefully received, especially when she saw the mountain of washing and ironing Doris had somehow managed to scale despite her youngest, Georgie, being at home all day too, but Nancy knew, even with the extra income, she couldn't expect her neighbour to prepare her a meal every night.

So, after she had tucked Billy and Linda into bed with an extra chapter of *Swallows and Amazons* as a special treat, and to relieve her own guilt, she had peeled a bowl of potatoes, swede and carrots for a broth to last her and the kids a couple of nights, before penning a letter to Bert, telling him all about her first day.

By the time she had collapsed into bed, Nancy had assumed she would be out like a light, but despite being dog-tired she couldn't drop off, with worrying about what the weeks ahead had in store for her beloved husband, and whether Linda would ever forgive her for going to work. It was the early hours before her worries gave way to a few short hours of unsettled sleep.

'The future just feels so uncertain,' Nancy mused.

'It will get easier, duck,' Bill said as reassuringly as possible. And in many ways, especially when it came to her job at Vickers, he was sure he was right, but he couldn't be as certain about Nancy's husband. Hitler and his wretched troops were already causing havoc across Europe and they seemed hell-bent on destroying whoever got in their way. After suffering a nasty leg injury that had taken months to heal in the Great War, Bill knew he'd been lucky to get home in one piece and back to the relative safety of the steelworks. He doubted he would ever forget the atrocities he'd witnessed; even now he still woke in the night, shaking and sweating, haunted by terrifying flashbacks.

Joining the crowds of workers that were now making their way down the cobbled pavement of Brightside Lane, Bill, Patty and Nancy all momentarily found themselves lost in their own little worlds, their individual worries acting as an invisible barrier to everything else around them.

But as they were about to turn into the main gates of Vickers, a friendly voice interrupted their thoughts.

'What's with all the long faces?' came Frank's cheery voice. 'You could turn milk sour between yer all.'

'Sorry, mate,' Bill said with a laugh, transported back to the present moment. 'I was away with the

168

fairies there for a second.'

'And how are you two feeling?' Frank asked, turning his attention towards his new recruits.

'I'm fine, honestly,' Nancy lied, doing her best not to let her true feelings penetrate the smile she had painted across her sleep-deprived face.

'And how about you, young Patty?' he quizzed.

'Well, I can't say I'm overly excited about what you'll have me doing today!' She sighed, whipping out her baby pink lipstick and putting a quick slick across her lips.

'Patty,' Bill quipped, 'I've told you Frank will take care of you and let's not forget who wanted this job in the first place.'

'I know, Dad. I'm sorry — I'm just a bit nervous,' she added, quietly, trying to remind herself why she had begged to join Vickers in the first place.

'Right,' Frank jumped in, sensing his youngest prospective crane driver was questioning her decision to come and work at the steelworks, 'let's get you clocked in and find Betty so we can get started without any further ado.'

Instinctively Patty looked towards her dad for reassurance.

'Go on, sunshine.' He kissed the top of his daughter's head. 'I'll see you at four o'clock. You'll be fine.' He glanced towards Frank. 'Look after her, pal,' he added, more to reassure himself, as there was no one else he'd rather have looking after his eldest daughter.

'I'll guard her with my life. Don't you worry,' Frank said reassuringly, tipping his brown flat cap towards him.

As Bill made his way through the door that would take him to the rolling mill, Frank led Nancy and

Patty to a separate entrance round the corner from the reception they had been reporting to. Just as they arrived, he caught sight of his third new trainee. 'Morning, Betty duck, come this way.'

A few seconds later the three women were waiting in line as a queue of boiler-suit-clad workers all took it in turn to collect a piece of card from a metal rack to their left on the wall.

'Right,' said Frank as they reached the front, 'this is the time clock and how you clock in and out at the start and end of your shift.'

Picking up a card with Betty's name and a unique personalized number at the top, he demonstrated how to slip the card into the slot below, waited for a second until he heard a little sharp click and quickly pulled it out, stamped 7.58 a.m. 'Then you put it on the rack here,' he said, slipping it into the right-hand side. 'The key is never to be late else your wages will be docked, no matter what yer excuse.'

Betty didn't say a word, but a feeling of agitation came over her; weren't women sacrificing enough without being penalized for being a couple of minutes late? But she noticed there was no look of frustration on her more compliant colleagues' faces. Copying Frank, Nancy and Patty did exactly as they had been shown without a single word of objection.

Frank smiled. 'Right then, girls — are you ready?'

16

Taking what lay ahead in her stride, Betty turned to her workmates. Nancy was unreadable, her face not revealing a thing, unlike Patty who looked as white as a sheet, her rosy-coloured cheeks now pale and clammy.

'It won't be so bad,' Betty tried to reassure her youngest workmate, but her words of gentle encouragement didn't seem to do a thing to ease Patty's anxiety.

In silence the women followed Frank into the room they had been training in, through a door and into an enormous windowless warehouse that seemed to reach the sky and was as long as the eye could see.

'Chuffin' 'eck!' Patty gasped, the ear-screeching cacophony of noise hitting her like a high-speed thunderbolt, instantly stopping all three women in their tracks. Frozen to the spot, the continual deafening thuds from the great steel monstrous machinery they faced and the high-pitched grinding of metal on metal was like nothing they had ever heard.

'My word,' Betty whispered when she finally found her voice, barely able to make out her own words over the ear-splitting noise. Despite her normally hardy determination, she was stunned by what she faced. 'It's much bigger than I expected.' Frank had certainly done a good of job the week before of protecting them.

No matter what direction the women looked in, there was something to take their attention, a new eye-popping sight to acclimatize and adjust to: the acrid smell of molten metal that instantly hit the back of their throats; ladders that seemed so tall they could only be a stairway to the heavens; blistering hot furnace fires, which could have easily been the gates to hell; huge machines that were surrounded by packs of men with mucky faces barely visible beneath oversized umbrella-like headgear, handling cumbersomely heavy poker-red rods of steel. Everything was enormous and filthy, and the heat, which left them sweating within seconds, was blistering.

Unable to fully take in and absorb everything before her, Nancy caught Betty's eye.

'It's really not what I was expecting,' she muttered, horrified by the loud and monstrous scene that enveloped them, like a dark and terrifying dungeon, a million miles from the comforts of their own homes.

'Yer not wrong there,' Patty quipped. 'I can see why me dad wanted me to stay at Woollies now. Mr Watson feels like a walk in the park compared to this!'

'Don't you be telling yer dad that now,' Frank chortled. 'I put m' neck out to persuade him to let you start here. If he had his way, you would still be on that make-up counter.'

Patty sighed. 'I know, I know. It's just, I didn't expect all of this.' She stared straight ahead, her eyes transfixed by a huge cavernous burning furnace in the far corner, where white flashing sparks were emerging like fireworks.

'What's that for?' she asked.

'It helps soften the steel so it can be shaped and put in the mould,' Frank replied, 'but don't worry, you won't be going near that.'

A synchronized sigh of relief came from all three women.

'There is a god after all,' Nancy half laughed, half gasped.

'Come on, girls, let me show you where you will be working and introduce you to your partners, before yer all do a runner,' Frank said, ushering his nervous trio of recruits to the far left-hand side of the warehouse.

As they walked the few metres across the dusty floor, Betty started to understand why the Sheffield steelworks were so important to the war effort. She knew Vickers was home to the only drop hammer in the country and rumour had it the beast of a machine — which weighed a mammoth fifteen tonnes and was steam-powered — was now being used to forge crankshafts for Hurricanes and Spitfires. While they had been training, Frank had also explained orders were coming in for parts for tanks, warships, bombs and an anti-tank gun.

Betty had felt an overwhelming feeling of responsibility, which reassured her she'd made the right move. If William was going to one day fulfil his dream of taking to the skies in a fighter plane, then she was going to ensure the parts that made up his aircraft were top-notch and would offer him as much protection as possible from the German Luftwaffe. The idea that she would soon be contributing to making the very aircraft he could end up manning as he protected the country against Hitler gave her all the incentive she needed to do the best job possible.

'This, girls, is one of the cranes you will be responsible for,' Frank said, boomeranging Betty back to the noisy shop floor.

'Yer kidding, right?' Patty gulped, dropping her gas mask in shock as she peered up to the dizzying heavens of the warehouse ceiling.

'It's not as bad as it looks,' Frank offered reassuringly. 'And I promise yer, duck, once yer up there, it doesn't feel 'alf as bad.'

'That's easy for him to say,' Patty whispered to a bewildered Nancy, the butterflies she had been trying to ignore all morning now whizzing around her belly at breakneck speed, performing somersaults and making her feel increasingly nauseous and faint. Gripping her workmate's arm to stop herself dropping to the mucky floor, she took a deep breath, her throat dry as parchment from the burning heat, combined with the taste of dry metal in her throat, mixed with paralysing nerves. 'He hasn't got to risk life and limb getting up there,' she croaked, pulling her bottle of water from her cloth bag with her free hand.

'Come on,' Betty said, mustering up as much courage as she possibly could, which was no mean feat, considering the perilous environment she was facing. 'It feels like a shock now but I'm sure we will get used to it. Let's remember what good we can do.'

Keen to help the women feel secure on the back of Betty's encouraging comments, Frank beckoned over three strapping lads to the bottom of the steep ladder, which had the immediate and almost magical effect of arousing Patty from her lightheaded weak state.

'This is Jack, Harry and Archie,' he said, introducing the three well-versed steelworkers to his new female recruits.

Now on high alert, Patty was suddenly brought back to her senses as she eyed up the most good-looking of the trio, once again recalling the very reason she had been so keen to start at Vickers. Although each one of them was the epitome of movie star handsome,

174

there was one who caught Patty's attention. With his chiselled cheekbones, strong Roman nose and oh-so-dreamy crystal-blue eyes, she was instantly captivated, her tummy now fluttering for a completely different reason.

'These lads are going to be your partners for the first few weeks you're up in the cranes,' Frank interrupted Patty's delightful heavenly state. 'They will show you the ropes and teach you all you need to know. You will be in safe hands.'

You'll get no arguments from me there, Patty mused to herself, already besotted by the Gary Cooper looka-like.

'Betty, you will work with Jack here,' Frank continued, introducing the pair. 'Nancy, I've partnered you with Harry, and Patty, Archie here will look after you.'

It was only when the muscly lad with the dreamy eyes and charming smile took a step forward that Patty realized Frank had inadvertently made all her dreams come true. As she looked over at Archie once again, Patty was sure the world had stopped as he caught her glance and an invisible spark ignited between them.

The moment didn't go unnoticed as Nancy and Betty swapped knowing smiles, immediately spotting the magnetic connection between the two.

Frank's romantic days may have been long gone after losing his beloved wife ten years earlier, but he hadn't failed to spot the first signs of true love between Archie and Patty.

God help me! he thought. Bill will never forgive me, setting his daughter up.

'Right,' he started, determined to at least temporarily dissolve the chemistry that was sparking as bright as one of the red-hot steel rods that had just been taken out of the furnace. 'We've got a lot of work to get through, so I'll get you all going on your cranes.

'Betty and Jack, you will be working on Myrtle here, as we like to call her. All the cranes have nicknames and this one is one of our old timers, a bit of a stalwart of the factory.'

'Okay,' Betty said, now keen to get going, popping her coat underneath a nearby metal bench along with the cloth bag containing her lunch and gas mask.

'If you make your way up the ladder and climb into the back of the cab, Jack will follow you. He will man the controls to begin with but will gradually let you take over,' Frank explained.

Turning to Jack, he added: 'Now take care of Betty here. I don't want any of my new girls feeling worried or scared.'

'Don't yer worry, gaffer,' Jack replied, winking at Betty, a little too confidently in her opinion, 'she'll be just fine with me.'

There was something about the way her new co-worker was smirking at her that was making her feel uncomfortable.

'Well, no time like the present,' Betty said assertively, starting as she meant to carry on, putting her first foot on the bottom rung of the ladder. 'See you at dinnertime, girls,' she called to her workmates. And with that she flew up the ladder, determined to set an example to the others as she scaled the full height of the factory without a glimmer of fear.

'Crikey,' Frank called up after Betty, 'I didn't expect that.'

Turning to Jack, he laughed: 'Looks like your trainee is going to give you a run for yer money, son.'

'Never,' Jack replied, clearly put out after naively

assuming the new girls being recruited would be far more submissive and needy.

Not wanting to look redundant or surplus to requirements, Jack raced up the ladder after a waiting Betty, trying to disguise the look of flustered frustration on his face.

Frank watched with intrigue, confident Betty would very quickly be worth her weight in gold and give 'Jack the lad', as he was known, a run for his money.

'Okay, right, Patty luv, your turn next. Why don't you all follow me over to Marlene?' Frank said.

The two women lined their gas masks, bags and coats up next to Betty's, and, with very obvious hesitancy, followed their foreman, Archie and Harry.

Despite her new distraction, Patty's nerves were once again bubbling away as they came to a stop at the foot of another set of equally tall ladders.

'You ready, duck?' Frank asked.

'Am I 'eck,' came the too quick reply.

'It's not as bad as it looks,' Archie volunteered, hoping to soothe Patty's worries. 'I promise, I won't let you come to any harm.'

Oh, my! Patty silently thought, her mind resembling a swirl of candyfloss as she tried to balance the fear that had left her frozen to the spot with the sheer excitement of working with this absolute dreamboat.

'The longer you put it off, the harder it will be,' Frank encouraged. 'Why don't you head up the ladder and Archie will follow close behind?'

'You'll be all right,' Nancy added, giving Patty's slender arm a gentle squeeze. 'Just take a deep breath and don't look down.'

'Okay,' she whispered, placing her hands, which were now shaking like a leaf, on the side rails of the ladder, desperately trying to avoid making a fool of herself in front of Archie.

Come on, Patty Andrews, she quietly scolded herself. You can do this.

Carefully she put her left foot on the bottom rung, tentatively followed by her right on the one above.

'That's it. One step at a time, duck,' Frank gently encouraged, his voice calm and soft, knowing only too well what a daunting task climbing the stairway to the factory heavens felt like. He'd seen many an apprentice get a case of the heebie-jeebies on those endless ladders.

Keeping her eyes firmly focused straight ahead on the wall of slate-grey corrugated iron, Patty slowly moved her hands and feet, gradually propelling herself upwards. 'Just keep going,' she repeated to herself, moving higher and higher.

Just as Patty thought she was going to make it, a sudden vibration on the ladder caused by Archie slowly following her shot through her arms and legs, causing her whole body to go into panic mode.

'What's that?' she screeched, her terrified gut-wrenching scream reverberating around the shop floor.

Instinctively Patty looked down. Realizing how far she was off the ground, red-hot fear scorched her cheeks. Feeling light-headed all of a sudden, she gripped the side rails for dear life, convinced she was going to drop backwards onto the hard stone floor.

'It's just me — Archie,' came the soothing voice from below her. 'I'm so sorry, I didn't mean to scare you.'

'Oh!' Patty replied, now frozen solid. 'Well, you chuffin' well did!' One part of her wanted to flamin' well throttle him, dashingly handsome good looks or not, but the other part was grateful he was there.

'I don't think I can take another step,' she trembled, her anger replaced with sheer terror. 'I just need to get down and fast.'

'I promise you're going to be all right,' Archie replied. 'Trust me. Just take a big deep breath, slowly count to ten and start climbing. I'll be right behind you to make sure you don't fall.'

There was something reassuringly calm in Archie's kind words, which seemed to slowly put the brakes on Patty's heart, which had been racing ten to the dozen.

'Okay,' she said, her voice now no more than a whisper. 'I'll try.'

If she was honest, Patty wasn't sure what made her take control of her newly discovered phobia of heights: the idea of humiliating herself in front of Archie and destroying her chances of making a good first impression on him; or the fact that if her dad caught the slightest inkling of how scared she was, he would have her back at Woollies under the relentlessly tiresome eye of Mr Watson.

Determined to try anything, Patty started counting. 'One . . . two . . . three . . . ' once again looking straight ahead. By the time she'd reached 'ten' her hands were at the top of the ladder and the relative safety of the crane cabin was in touching distance.

'You've done it,' Archie congratulated. 'No need to worry now. The rest of the day will feel like a doddle.'

Patty wasn't quite so sure but didn't argue as she lifted one leg and then the other into the rather snug two-seater cab.

'All good here, Frank,' Archie shouted down to their worried-looking foreman, who could finally take a huge sigh of relief, knowing his most anxious new recruit was safely where she needed to be.

'Now then, duck,' Frank said, turning to Nancy, 'let's get you and Harry across to Mildred.'

Frank led them to the other side of the shop floor.

'What's with the crane names?' Nancy asked.

'Well,' Frank started, thinking fast, not daring to explain they were the 'Three M's', short for 'monsters of the factory', due to their colossal height and ability to lift the heaviest and biggest of solid steel bars, in case it left Nancy in a similar terrified state. 'I just thought it would be a bit of fun to give them nicknames — good for the lads to know it's always the women who really wear the trousers — metaphorically speaking.' He winked at Nancy as Harry petulantly rolled his eyes.

Swallowing her amused laughter, not wanting to upset her new workmate on their first day working together on Mildred, Nancy just smiled. 'Well, I think it's fair to say my trousers still aren't doing me any favours,' she lamented, tugging at the excess of ghastly thick brown itchy material that swamped her petite five-foot-five frame.

'Par for the course,' Harry quipped. 'If yer gonna do a man's job, yer need to get used to 'em.'

'Nah then, lad,' Frank jumped in, 'we'll have less of that tone. If it wasn't for these lasses you'd be pulling double shifts from now 'till Christmas.' He nodded at Nancy. 'Ignore him, duck. He's always got the face of a wet weekend until he's had his mid-morning brew.'

Nancy kept her thoughts to herself — this was no time to give ammunition to the unnecessary and unpleasant remark — but she quietly noted it, taking the measure of her clearly highly opinionated and brazenly sexist partner.

'Also, Harry lad, I need you to take extra care of Nancy. Although she's shown herself to be a natural, she's still only had one full day of training, so you need to be patient and show her the ropes. Take her through the controls and be sure to let her start with the lighter lifts until she gets the hang of it and feels confident, but I have an inkling it won't take long.' He quickly turned to Nancy and threw her a reassuring wink. Frank could spot a promising crane driver when he saw one and was sure his gut instinct wasn't about to let him down.

'Thank you.' Nancy blushed, not used to such high praise but it was just the encouragement she needed.

'Shall I head up first like Betty and Patty did?' she asked courteously, now feeling slightly more confident about starting work and getting on with the job in hand, if for no other reason than to prove to a now dry-faced Harry that she wasn't some feeble young girl, incapable of a hard day's graft.

'Absolutely,' Frank agreed, pleased to see the third of his new recruits not rise to Harry's bait, or be put off by the sheer enormity of the crane that was to become her work station for the foreseeable future. Nancy appeared to be a natural and he had no doubt she would be a good worker — he just needed to find a way to bolster the confidence she seemed to be lacking.

With that, Nancy took to the ladder and steadily climbed to the top. She wasn't as quick as Betty but equally not as terrified as Patty. She just wanted to do what she intended and that was to keep her mind busy while her Bert was away.

After a moody-looking Harry followed, Frank

181

finally breathed a sigh of relief. For now at least he'd achieved what he'd told the factory bosses he could do, and that was to train up the new female workers who had started filing through the foundry gates, filling the vacancies left behind by the young thrill-seeking lads who had all abandoned ship, full of high spirits and vigour, to go and fight the Nazis.

17

Once in the cab, encased by metal, and not quite as exposed to the thirty-foot drop between her and the factory floor, Patty felt like she could breathe again.

'It does get easier,' Archie said softly as they sat side by side, the noise from the monstrous machinery and workers below somewhat diluted.

'I'll take yer word for that,' Patty said, praying he was right, unsure how on earth she was going to manage to scale that godforsaken ladder each time she had to start work.

Archie smiled as he checked all the controls. 'I'll let you into a little secret: the first time I climbed into one of these cabs I thought I would pass out, I was that terrified.'

'Really?'

'Yep, m' tummy was churning and if it wasn't for the fact I'd 'av 'ad the Holy Michael ripped out of me, I'd 'av bolted back down that ladder quicker than I could say m' name.'

'But you were so calm. I don't think I'd 'av made it to the top if you hadn't been so kind.'

'I've 'ad a fair bit of practice,' Archie said modestly, revealing his more sensitive side.

'How long 'av you been doing the job?' Patty asked, wondering how many shifts it would take her to get over the feeling she was about to fall from the skies.

'I started when I was seventeen, so a little over three years now, but I don't just work on the cranes. I've been working on the drop hammer too. I'm only over

183

here until you get the hang of handling Marlene here and then they will have me back on the floor.'

A wave of disappointment surged through Patty. Archie seemed like the perfect gent and more than enough reason to drag herself up to the heavens of the factory each day. After all, wasn't this the reason she had fought her dad tooth and nail to let her join him at Vickers?

But that wasn't the only reason Patty was feeling somewhat deflated.

'I can't be up 'ere by m'self,' she gulped. 'I'll be a nervous wreck and won't last a minute.'

'Let's not worry about that now,' Archie said, flicking a switch and jolting Marlene to life. 'I promise you, by the end of the week yer nerves will have vanished and you will wonder what on earth you were so worried about.'

Patty wasn't so sure but she also didn't want to look completely pathetic in front of her new, and somewhat gorgeous, workmate.

'Anyway, we best get crackin'. Word has it we're working on some new parts for Spitfires.'

'Really?' Patty asked. She'd heard her dad talking about the fighter planes and how they were being labelled as a secret weapon for the RAF and would give them more than a fighting chance against the Luftwaffe.

'Well, no one tells us anything for sure. We aren't supposed to know, but that's the rumour.'

A few seconds later, a shout from below caught Archie's attention.

'Right,' he said, his face now a picture of concentration. 'Our first load needs lifting.'

Nodding, Patty didn't say a word but instead

watched with sheer admiration as Archie began moving the left-hand crane control nearest to him, so the heavy claw-like hook began to gently move until it was perfectly in line with the waiting slab of steel that had just been wheeled onto the floor.

'That's it, lad, nice and steady,' came Frank's strong but supportive command from below.

Not daring to move a muscle, terrified of distracting Archie as he expertly commandeered the job in hand.

'Watch what I'm doing here, Patty,' he said, his tone calm and his movements distinctively precise.

Patty desperately tried to ignore how light-headed she felt. In a bid to stop herself swaying in time with the hook that was being pulled this way and that by a group of men on the shop floor as they carefully attached it to thick coarse ropes that had been circled around the giant girder like pieces of silver metal, she gripped her seat so tight her knuckles turned white.

'Ready,' came the next holler from metres below.

Archie quickly shifted his hand to the right control, his long manly fingers now centimetres from Patty's trembling leg. Focusing all her attention on the slow smooth movements, Patty allowed herself to fall into a trance-like state in a bid to halt the feeling of vertigo that was threatening to make the huge room swim.

His eyes concentrating on the cargo, Archie expertly manoeuvred the great hunk of steel across the floor towards the red-hot furnace where the same men were waiting in position to direct it into the giant fire.

'A gnat's whisker to yer right, son,' came Frank's latest instruction. Carefully Archie moved the black knob, Patty noting how the muscles in his forearm were now tense, showing off his strong athletic physique.

'Perfect. Jobs a good 'un,' came the foreman's relieved call as the team of strapping workers untied the ropes. 'Pull her back in, Archie lad.'

Doing as he was instructed, Archie moved his hand back to the control nearest his right leg and lifted the hook out of harm's way from the sea of men below.

'That was incredible,' Patty finally dared to whisper, in complete awe of her workmate, and not just for his heart-wrenchingly good looks. 'I'd have made a right dog's dinner of it.'

Archie laughed at his greener than green, and unknowingly beautiful partner. 'No, you wouldn't. Besides which, it's my job over the next few weeks to make sure you don't get it wrong. Frank will have me guts for garters if I don't get you up to scratch by the time I'm needed on the floor again.'

Unconvinced, Patty bit her lip nervously. She really hadn't thought this job through at all, despite how much her dad had tried to tell her how arduous and labour-intensive it would be.

Sensing her concerns, Archie started: 'Look, we shouldn't have another heavy load for a while. I'll get the lads to line up some smaller steel plates and we'll have a practice together and I promise you that you'll get the hang of it — you'll be a natural in no time at all.'

Patty didn't know whether to cry with relief or wrap her arms around Archie in thanks for being so kind. Of course, she didn't do either for fear of making a complete fool of herself. Instead she fought back the sea of salty tears that were now threatening to erupt, and pinched her pale-pink fingernails into her now clammy palms.

'Thank you,' was all she could manage, no more

than a whisper, her cheeky innocence and infectious confidence of a few weeks earlier now in tatters, replaced by sheer dread of what was still to come.

For the next couple of hours, Archie patiently demonstrated to Patty how to lift and move sheets of steel and she soon realized, apart from the great height she had been propelled to, there was actually very little difference to what she had been taught in the training room.

★ ★ ★

'Well, apart from how hot it is and the dirt,' Betty had exclaimed, taking a long gulp of water, when Patty shared her thoughts as they all broke for lunch. Again, the two women had led Nancy out into the yard, desperate for some fresh air, in search of relief from the dust gathering in the corners of their eyes, in their noses, and casing their tongues.

'I've never seen anything like it,' Betty scoffed, brushing down her overalls, a million particles of dust erupting into the air around her. 'I swear the muck was a foot high on the girders.'

'I'll second that,' Nancy agreed, grateful for some fresh air, the breeze that gently billowed round the yard. 'I don't think I'll ever get the grimy taste out of me mouth, and the heat is like nothing on earth.' She and Harry had been positioned the other side of the furnace. 'I've been sweating buckets all morning.'

'How was Harry?' Betty asked. 'He looked as miserable as sin this morning.'

'That's the understatement of the century,' came Nancy's reply. 'He's made it perfectly clear he doesn't think women have a place in the factory, and we won't last the month out.'

'Cheeky blighter!' Betty exclaimed. 'I hope you told him he's lucky to have us!' It hadn't taken Betty long to work out that her initial instinct to do the right thing and contribute to the war effort wasn't just a way of supporting her country but also of vital importance to the city's main industry.

'I didn't really know what to say,' Nancy said, still feeling somewhat out of sorts and rather upset by the snide comments.

'Don't you let him get to you,' Betty replied firmly. 'We can do this job as good as any man. We will show him, girls. I'm not being told I'm not up to the job just because of what sex I am.'

Nancy looked at Betty in awe. She may have been nearly ten years Betty's senior, but she didn't have a fraction of her guts or steel resolve. Biting the inside of her lip, she knew she was going to have to come out of her shell and toughen up to survive.

'To be fair,' Patty groaned, interrupting Nancy's thoughts, 'Harry's got a point. I was a chuffin' wreck getting up that ladder, and, every time I looked down from the crane, I thought I was going to faint. I felt as sick as a dog and I really don't know how many times I can put myself through that level of torture.'

Betty nearly swallowed her mouthful of cheese sandwich whole. 'Don't you dare give up now,' she said, her voice rising an octave, determined Patty and Nancy would stick out their new roles — just as she would. 'You've done the worst bit — it's bound to get easier now, and you can't tell me that your new partner isn't making the job a little less laborious,' she added, her voice softening, appealing to Patty's flighty nature.

As Betty expected her young workmate's look of resignation was quickly replaced by a sparky smile and she could have sworn a glint in her eye appeared in the afternoon sun.

'Well, he is a bit of a dream,' she gushed, suddenly forgetting about the prospect of telling her dad he had been right after all.'And a perfect gent too. He was so patient when me nerves overtook me, and he didn't once get huffy when I got confused over what control did what.'

'Really?' Betty laughed. 'Well, it sounds like your plans to find Mr Right might work out after all.'

Once her nerves had finally gone from boiling point to a gentle simmer, the thought had crossed Patty's mind too, but she had convinced herself Archie was far too handsome and kind to be single.

'I'd be stunned if he wasn't already snapped up,' she mused. 'What girl wouldn't want him?'

Betty and Nancy simultaneously burst into giggles. 'Well, I'm too old for starters,' Nancy said.

'And I wouldn't dream of looking at another man,' Betty added.

'Oh, well that's a shame,' Patty replied.

'What do you mean?' Betty gasped, once again taken aback by Patty's hare-brained comments.

Patty grinned. 'Well, I saw Jack giving you the eye. There was definitely a sparkle there and he couldn't stop gazing at you as you headed up the flaming ladder.'

'Oh,' Betty muttered, feeling niggled. Maybe her initial instincts about Jack hadn't been wrong after all. She'd told herself she had imagined how intently Jack had looked at her, holding her gaze for a second too long when they'd sat shoulder to shoulder in the cramped cab, as he'd explained how to keep a steady hand when moving a tonne of steel.

Betty sighed. 'I had rather hoped it was a figment of my imagination. Well, he has another think coming if he believes I would give him a second glance. I'm here to do my job, nothing else.'

'Speak for yourself,' Patty joked, her thoughts the polar opposite to her more prudish workmates.

After finishing their lunch, the three women made their way back onto the factory floor, a world away from the comfort and relative safety of the training workshop they had waved goodbye to days earlier. Their minds a whirl, the three women couldn't help but wonder what the afternoon had in store as they quietly contemplated where they had found themselves, unable to second-guess what the weeks and months ahead had in store for them.

18

'Well, that was a baptism of fire if there ever was one,' Patty exclaimed as she and her two workmates pulled on their coats and picked up their boxed gas masks and bags.

'Wasn't it just?' Nancy sighed, relieved the hooter had finally indicated the end of their shift. Her head was pounding from the constant thudding, bellowing of instructions and suffocating heat, let alone having to put up with Harry's condescending comments for the last eight hours.

He'd made it abundantly clear he thought Nancy would be a complete disaster and couldn't handle Mildred, so instead of showing her how to use the controls, as Frank had asked, he'd taken great pleasure in barking a running commentary at her about what he was doing, determined to show off his arrogant male supremacy.

'No improvement?' Betty asked.

'Sadly not,' Nancy exhaled, mentally and physically exhausted, her petite frame ready to collapse. 'Maybe tomorrow will be better,' she added, her gentle voice barely audible above the ear-splitting, relentless screeching of machinery, which was running twenty-four hours a day to apparently keep up with all the new orders. But even as the words left her mouth, she knew it was wishful thinking. Harry clearly had a bee in his overinflated chauvinistic bonnet, and he was going out of his way to prove a point by showing Nancy who was boss.

As the women trudged out of the factory through the main gates, Betty rubbed Nancy's arm. 'We could always have a word with Frank.'

'Oh, Lord, no, but thank you, though. I don't want to cause any trouble and, if Harry gets word of it, he's bound to make my life a complete and utter misery between now and the end of this horrible war.'

Betty and Patty instinctively threw each other a concerned glance, both feeling protective of their new colleague.

But the older of the two women knew now wasn't the time to push the point: Nancy looked dog-tired and on the verge of tears.

Betty smiled kindly, 'Okay, let's see what tomorrow brings.' However, she was already working through options on how to put a stop to Harry's out of order and unacceptable behaviour. *How dare he make any-one feel inferior, let alone a woman who had sacrificed time with her children to risk life and limb for the good of the country?*

'See you in the morning, girls,' Nancy said, waving as the three prepared to go their separate ways.

'If you hold fire, my dad shouldn't be too much longer and we'll walk part of the way home with you,' Patty offered.

'Thanks, luv, but I best get going,' Nancy replied. 'I feel bad enough leaving Billy and Linda with my neighbour as it is. I don't want to put her out for a minute longer than I need to.'

'Of course,' Patty nodded, sensing how keen the oldest of the three women was to put the day behind her.

'We'll meet you on the corner of King Street just after half seven tomorrow.'

192

'See you then,' came the weary reply as Nancy turned right along Brightside Lane, yearning to be back in the safety and comfort of her own four walls, away from the relentless criticism she had been subjected to for the last eight hours.

Despite feeling as though she'd climbed Mount Everest, she picked up her pace, weaving her way through the sea of workers all heading home, hungry for a warm meal and a hot cuppa.

Head down, looking at the dust-ridden ground, the tears she had fought back all day now filled the rims of her eyes and cascaded down her flushed cheeks. *What have I done? I've been such a fool to think I could cope in a steel factory.*

If Bert was home, she knew exactly what he would say. 'You are doing more than enough being the best mum in the world to Billy and Linda, you don't have to do anything else.' She could hear his strong voice as clearly as if he was stood next to her.

Oh, why did you have to go? Nancy silently asked.

Life had been just perfect before Hitler had marched his menacing-looking troops across Eastern Europe, causing unimaginable mayhem, and Neville Chamberlain had made his earth-shattering announcement. They might not have had much money or lived in one of those grand houses at the posh end of town, whose occupants were now paying Doris do their laundry for them, but they were happy.

Nancy's old simple life now felt like a distant dream and one she would have given her right arm to have back.

By the time she trudged up the ginnel at the side of Doris's house, her eyes were red raw and her cheeks blotchy and puffy.

'What on earth has happened?' her neighbour gasped as Nancy walked through the back door that led into the kitchen, which now resembled a Chinese laundry, with piles and piles of freshly starched and immaculately folded white, blue and pink floral sheets everywhere she looked.

'Oh, Doris,' Nancy erupted, after holding it together all day, 'I think I've made a terrible mistake.'

'Come on, sit down,' her worried-looking neighbour said, swiftly moving a pile of ironing from a chair with one hand while holding a wide-eyed Georgie on the other hip.

'Where are the kids?' Nancy asked between heart-wrenching sobs.

'They're all playing upstairs,' Doris said, knowing Nancy wouldn't want Billy and Linda seeing her in such an emotional state. 'Don't worry. Last time I looked my bed had been turned into a boat and they were re-enacting a scene from *Swallows and Amazons*.'

The thought of them all taking on the roles of the fearless and adventurous John, Roger, Titty, Nancy and Peggy broke Nancy's blubbering snivels, bringing the faintest of smiles to her crestfallen face.

'Here,' Doris said, as if by magic popping a mug of freshly brewed tea on the wooden table in front of her. 'Get that down you and then you can tell me all about it.'

'Thank you,' Nancy whispered. 'I never imagined it would be so exhausting and difficult. The lad they've partnered me with is a complete and utter brute. He's taking great pleasure out of making me feel utterly worthless. I'm not sure how much of it I can cope with,' she added, bringing what tasted like pure amber nectar to her lips.

194

'Come on now, luv,' Doris said, 'today has been tough but tomorrow is a new day — you'll feel better after a good night's sleep.'

'Oh, I hope so,' Nancy sighed wearily. As she sipped the hot brew, some of the tensions of the day started to slip away; was there anything in the world a good cuppa couldn't cure?

Whether it was the comfort of a good ole Brooke's brew, the much-needed sight of a friendly face or the fact she'd now had a little cry, things didn't feel quite as bad.

'So, what did this little upstart say that has left you so upset?' Doris asked, handing Georgie a home-made shortbread biscuit with the faintest sprinkling of sugar on top to keep her eternally hungry son entertained while she focused on her friend.

'Oh,' Nancy said with a sigh, once again lifting her mug of tea to her lips and taking another quick sip. 'Well, he has made it very clear he is not happy about women working with him and is hell-bent on making my life a chuffin' misery. Every time he let me take control of the crane, he huffed and puffed and must have told me a hundred times I was doing it all wrong and someone would be seriously injured if he wasn't there to take over. I'm now wondering if he's right and I've gone and got daft ideas above my station.'

Doris's expression changed from sympathy to one resembling that of a stern headmistress.

'Now you listen up, Nancy Edwards,' she started, raising her voice an octave, 'are you going to allow some young jumped-up whippersnapper, who was more than likely still in nappies by the time you were holding down your first job, to put you down?'

Hearing Doris get so authoritative stopped Nancy mid-slurp. She wasn't sure what she'd been expecting but had assumed it would be more sympathy than encouragement to pull up her britches and stand up to Harry.

'What would your Bert say?' Doris added. 'Because I've got a good inkling he would be telling you in no uncertain terms to go and put this little twerp in his place!'

'Well, when you put it like that,' Nancy half laughed, realizing she would have to toughen up and quick, 'I know yer right. He'd be chasing me into the yard to put Harry in his place and give him a piece of my mind.'

Doris smiled. 'Exactly. And if Bert was here right now, he would be telling you not to let this Harry lad get one over on you, but, because he isn't, I'm going to say it for him.'

'Oh, Doris,' Nancy said, 'you really are a good friend. I left that factory tonight thinking I couldn't go back and face another shift being patronized and listening to his snide remarks, but now I feel I can at least cope with another day.'

'You absolutely can,' Doris said, reaching her free hand across the table and rubbing Nancy's arm.

And right on cue there was a charge of footsteps coming down the stairs, twinned with calls of 'this is our island' and 'we will not be conquered'.

'Your time is up,' Billy, posing as a rather jubilant John, screeched as he chased an adrenalin-fuelled Linda and Alice through the kitchen door.

Nancy laughed as the trio pounded in, followed by Doris's eldest two, Katherine and Joe.

'Well, hello. You've all been having fun then?'

'Mummy,' Linda squealed, running towards Nancy, her arms open wide. 'I've missed you.'

'I've missed you too, poppet,' Nancy said, pulling her daughter into her chest, instinctively taking on her husband's pet name for their daughter.

'That's cheating,' Billy said, gesturing towards his younger sister, pretending his arm was a sword.

Linda giggled. 'Oh, I surrender then, but Mummy will save me from you.'

Nancy laughed. 'Yes, I will, though before you two cause any more havoc we should be getting home,' she added, pulling her chair backwards.

'Oh no you don't,' Doris said, standing up, and popping Georgie on the floor on his bum. 'I've made a big enough mince and onion pie to feed the entire army.'

Nancy looked across at her friend. 'No, no, you can't!' she protested. 'You've fed us all enough already this week. You won't have enough left to satisfy this hungry horde.'

'Just hear me out — I've had an idea,' Doris began, as she leant down to the range and opened the oven door, releasing a mouth-watering aroma.

Intrigued, Nancy looked across at her friend as she lifted the golden pastry-covered dinner out of the oven.

'How about,' Doris started, 'I make yours and the kids' dinner in the week for when you get home from the factory if you are happy to buy the odd joint of meat and a few veggies or help out with the shopping bill?'

'Oh, my goodness, Doris,' Nancy said, 'I can't let you do that. You have enough on.'

'Let me be the judge of that,' came the quick reply.

'If I'm cooking for five, I can cook for eight. And you'll be doing me a favour — I miss having adult company since George . . . ' Doris quickly checked herself, conscious of her four children. 'It's nice to have a natter.'

'Please, Mum, can we?' Billy piped up. 'It means I can shoot down Joe and make him surrender once and for all.'

The two women looked at one another and burst into fits of laughter. 'Well, I'm not sure how I can argue with that,' Nancy said. 'As long as you allow me to give you some money. It really is the very least I can do.'

'Right, well, that's a deal then,' Doris said, pulling seven plates and a small circular plastic bowl out of the cupboard. 'Be a good girl, Katherine, and set the table.'

'Let me help,' Nancy said. 'It's the very least I can do.'

As she placed the cutlery and crockery on the table, Nancy thought about Doris's offer. Now she was earning a wage, she could afford to give Doris some money for food every week, and a little bit extra on top, which would help her out financially, and hopefully, alongside her new sideline of taking in laundry, would be enough to keep the wolves from the door. The thought of her friend moving away was inconceivable — they had supported one another through some of the hardest times of their lives in the last few months, cementing their already unbreakable bond.

The government were also encouraging women who couldn't go out to work to help out those who could, and Nancy knew this would alleviate Doris's guilt about not taking a job in the steelworks — not that anyone could blame her, considering the factory had taken her husband and left her with four kiddies to care for single-handed.

Maybe someone is looking down on us after all? Nancy thought. Was it Big George's way of making sure his family would be okay?

Twenty minutes later the two households were crammed around the kitchen table, which was really only designed for six people, but was full of happy chatter and talk of how hard the maths lesson had been at school and how Billy intended to become the king of the island tomorrow.

As Nancy looked across at Doris, she saw a smile emerge that she hadn't seen since George had died. It was obvious now that sharing a meal every night would be a godsend for Nancy, not having to worry about cooking something after a long and arduous day at Vickers, but she could see it was also a huge tonic for her neighbour who had held her family together by the skin of her teeth over the last few months. They were both missing the men in their lives but maybe, somehow, their late-afternoon chats and a hearty tea was what they both needed to lighten their load and give them a reason to smile.

'Well, that was delicious,' Nancy said, mopping her plate clean with a slice of home-made bread to swallow up the last specks of thick gravy. 'With meals like that, I'm not sure I can ever refuse your home cooking.'

'Good!' Doris laughed. 'Then we have a deal?'

'We most certainly do,' Nancy replied, happy they had found a solution that worked for them both.

Half an hour later, after Nancy had helped wash and dry the mountain of dishes, she finally managed to round up Billy and Linda, and say goodnight to her neighbour and friend.

'See you tomorrow, bright and early,' Doris said, handing the kids their jackets and boxed gas masks with string handles as she opened the back door.

Walking back into her own house, Nancy felt the most settled she had in weeks.

'Right then, you two, I think it's time to get in your pyjamas, then a quick glass of milk and a story,' she said, as she closed their back door.

But as Nancy followed her now sleepy-looking children through the kitchen and into the living room to usher them upstairs, an envelope lying face up with instantly recognizable handwriting caught her eye.

Bert! Normally she would have ripped it open, sitting Billy and Linda on the couch, and together they would have read every word at least three times, but something stopped Nancy; a sense of foreboding sent a cold shiver down her spine. In his last letter, he had explained he didn't think it would be long before they would get news on where they were being sent.

This is it, she silently thought to herself, the settled and calm feeling she had experienced minutes earlier now completely gone and replaced with sheer dread and fear.

Picking up the white envelope, she quickly stuffed it into her overall pocket, mentally preparing to read it once Billy and Linda were safely tucked up in bed.

It was another forty-five minutes, after another chapter of *Swallows and Amazons* and lots of goodnight kisses and cuddles, that Nancy made herself a fresh cuppa and sat down at the kitchen table, wrapping herself into her blue woolly cardie, which she put on over her overalls, the early-autumn temperature now dropping.

200

Pulling the letter from her pocket, Nancy took a deep breath as she carefully put her thumb under the corner of the seal, gently tearing open the envelope, careful not to damage the contents.

My dearest Nancy,
I do hope you, my little soldier Billy and gorgeous poppet Linda are all okay?
I'm writing after the longest day training today. You can tell Billy I'm really becoming a soldier now and have learnt how to run up hills, carrying all my equipment and how to drop to the floor safely — I'll teach him when I come home.
And as for you, my love, I hope you are managing to keep busy and not fretting too much . . .

He hasn't received my letter yet telling him about my new job, Nancy thought to herself.

I can imagine you scrubbing that doorstep until you are blue in the face, trying to keep your mind from wandering, but I promise you I am in safe hands and we are all enjoying the training, even if it is exhausting at times.
But, my love, it is with a heavy heart I have to tell you it's nearly time for me to go and fight the real battle that is raging across Europe. We have been told today we will be on the move before the week is out and the next time I write won't be from England.
I will send you a letter as soon as I reach my next temporary home, so to speak and let you know I have arrived safely and that all is well.

I know these words are going to hit you hard and you will no doubt worry, my love, but I promise you I will be okay, we all will be, and before long I will be home again, holding you in my arms.

Please stay strong and give Billy and Linda the biggest kiss each from me. I miss you all so very much and there isn't a single minute of the day when I don't think of you all.

I hope Billy is concentrating at school, but I imagine it will be Linda doing all the hard work while he is playing soldiers.

I love you all with all my heart. Please look after yourself as well as our two children. I will be home before you know it.

Your ever-loving husband,
Bert

Reading the letter for the second time, Nancy didn't try to stop the cascade of tears that were now flowing down her cheeks like a waterfall and silently dropping onto the table.

'Oh, my love,' she gasped, 'when will I see you again?'

She knew Bert couldn't say a lot in his letters about where and what he would be doing, knowing they were checked and any information about what the forces were doing to combat that godforsaken man, Hitler, would be scribbled out.

But in the best way he could, Bert was telling her he was now off to fight Jerry and that he was ready and prepared. *'I'm really becoming a soldier now . . . '* — that was Bert's way of saying, 'I'm off to fight the war'. He couldn't say exactly where in Europe and what role he had been given.

Nancy gently folded the letter into its envelope and held it closely to her trembling chest, her heart thumping through her cold skin.

'Please take care, my love,' she whispered, her voice breaking, 'and please come home soon.'

She knew the German leader was hell-bent on making his mark in France; maybe Bert wouldn't be right in the thick of it. All she could do was pray that, wherever he was, it was in a more shielded than active role.

'Don't you dare take my husband,' Nancy said, voicing her quiet threat to the hard-faced German leader, who seemed to take pleasure in taking over whatever town, city or country he had his eye on.

It was past midnight when Nancy finally pulled herself up from the table, switched off the light and climbed the stairs up to bed, the house now eerily still and in complete darkness, with all the windows having been blacked out.

But despite how worried she was about her beloved Bert, as soon as Nancy's head hit the pillow, she was out like a light, exhaustion setting in after a long and hard day at the factory.

19

'Morning,' Patty chirped more cheerfully than normal, as she and Nancy walked in unison towards the time machine to clock in, where Betty was already waiting.

'Hello. I thought you wouldn't be far behind. Are you both feeling a little better?' Betty asked.

'Well, at least I have a rather dishy companion, so it might make climbing the chuffin' ladder a little easier,' Patty whispered, conscious of who else might be listening as she flashed her workmates a cheeky wink with more than a glint in her eye.

Betty laughed. 'Oh, Patty, it didn't take you long to change your tune, did it?'

'I'm only messin'.'

'I'm not so sure about that!' Betty chuckled as she and Nancy simultaneously raised their eyebrows in mock jest — they could spot a teenage crush a mile off.

'You are a case,' Nancy laughed, her exhaustion temporarily forgotten as she clicked her timecard into the machine before slotting it into the right-hand-side rack.

'Well, I can't blame you, luv,' Nancy added. 'I'd do anything to have Bert by my side right now.'

Betty nodded. 'I'll second that. It feels so odd not having our loved ones around.' The two older women exchanged knowing smiles. They didn't need to say anything else: the shared worry of their significant other away serving their country was something that didn't require words; their unspoken fears weighing heavily on their minds, already forging a natural bond between the two crane drivers.

'Anyway, we have about three minutes to get on that factory floor,' Betty muttered, determined to try and stay focused, 'so we better get a shufty on, besides which I'm intrigued to see how quickly you get into the crane cab today.'

Patty giggled. 'Okay, well, maybe I do have a new incentive.'

'You are utterly incorrigible,' Betty said with a grin, shaking her head as the three women hurriedly made their way down the corridor.

'And how about you,' Betty added, turning to a pale-looking Nancy. 'Are you ready for another day in the heavens? How are you feeling about Harry?'

'I can't say I'm looking forward to spending the day listening to him harp on as he patronizes me but I've got bigger fish to fry right now.'

Patty and Betty quickly shot each other a quizzical glance.

'Is everything okay?' Betty asked gently.

'Oh, if I'm honest, not really, but I promise I will fill you in at dinnertime,' Nancy replied as the tremendous ear-splitting noise from the factory floor hit them.

'All right, let's chat then over a flask of tea,' Betty said kindly as they each took off their jackets and placed them with their gas masks near to Myrtle — the monstrous hunk of metal machinery that would be her home for the majority of the next eight hours.

Right on cue, Betty's partner, Jack, arrived.

'You came back for more then?' He winked, a little too familiarly for her liking.

'Well, of course,' Betty said, slightly perturbed by the innuendo, 'I'm here to do my bit and that's exactly what I'm going to do. Now, are you going up that ladder first, or shall I?'

'Ooh — looks like I've got a stroppy one here.' Jack laughed, taking great pleasure from Betty's defensive reaction. 'I'll see you up there, then,' he replied, making sure his hands were firmly on the rails before hers.

Feeling slightly irked before her shift had even really got going, Betty tried to ignore the condescending and, in her opinion, frankly quite insulting comment, forcing herself to keep focused on the job in hand.

'Right, girls, I'll see you all in a few hours,' she sighed before quickly following Jack up the ladder, determined he would not get the better of her.

'We best be getting on too,' Nancy said, despite the heavy feeling that was dragging on her heart like a ten-tonne weight and how much the day ahead filled her with dread.

'Yeah,' Patty agreed, as they walked across the noisy floor, already a mass of industriousness, with orders for 'this way' and 'ova 'ere, mate' being yelled in every direction. 'I really hope it's not too horrible for you with Harry today.'

'Thank you,' Nancy replied, her eyes betraying how weary she felt. 'I'll survive, I'm sure.'

As the pair approached Marlene, Nancy could have ignited the air with a single match, sparks of electricity flying as her clearly lovesick workmate spotted a very happy-looking Archie, who was courteously waiting at the bottom of the crane.

'How are you feeling about climbing this ladder

today?' he asked, a hint of colour appearing on his almost porcelain chiselled cheeks.

Her nerves threatening to erupt once again at the thought of being suspended metres off the ground, Patty took a sharp intake of breath. 'Well, I can't say I'm overly excited about it, but it can't be as bad as yesterday.'

'That's the spirit,' Archie beamed, his sea-blue eyes positively sparkling. 'Would you like to go first, and I can follow you, so if you start to worry or feel faint, I'll be right behind you?'

Nancy couldn't help but smile as she thought about how much Archie reminded her of Bert and how he too had been the perfect gent, coy and courteous when they'd first met, and still was to this day. But the happy memory that provided so much comfort was soon replaced by yet another paralysing surge of anxiety as the words of his previous day's letter flashed before her.

Nancy swallowed hard, resisting the urge to tear out of the factory and back to the safe haven of her home, where she could think about Bert in the privacy of her own kitchen and let the tears flow, which were on the verge of once again breaking free, leaving her an inconsolable mess for all to see.

Come on, pull yourself together, Nancy Edwards, she silently chastised herself, knowing in reality she couldn't afford to let her worries take over this morning — whether she liked it or not, she was going to have enough on her plate with Harry today and she needed her mind to be clear.

'Are you going to be okay?' Nancy asked, turning her attention back to Patty, who was beginning turn a paler shade of white.

'Of course, she is, aren't you duck?' came a friendly voice from behind.

'Oh, morning, Frank. I didn't see you there.' Nancy was glad the kindly father-like foreman was on hand.

'I'll look after her,' Archie added, but as soon as the words passed his lips, the colour on his cheeks increased to a deeper shade of red, as he realized he'd revealed more in that short telling sentence than he'd intended.

'I'm sure you will, lad,' Frank chuckled, resisting the urge to say anything more, amused by the clear attraction developing between one of his best workers and his friend's daughter.

'Right, well, I'll get on,' Nancy said, looking to Patty. 'If you're sure you'll be okay?'

'I'm going to try to be brave,' Patty said, grimacing as she glanced up the perilously steep steps of the metal ladder, which felt like a pathway to hell — or would have been if it wasn't for the fact she had the complete opposite of the devil offering to take care of her.

'You can do it,' Nancy encouraged, giving her new friend a final reassuring smile. 'I'll look forward to hearing how you get on when we stop for some snap.'

'And so can you,' Patty called, as Nancy made her way towards Mildred. 'Don't take any messin'!'

'Is everything all right?' Frank asked, a look of concern appearing on his age-weathered face.

'Yes, nothing to worry about,' Nancy jumped in quickly before Patty could say anything else. She had enough on her plate without rocking the boat here too, besides which she had only been in the job two minutes — Frank was bound to think she was just tittle-tattling if she voiced her concerns about Harry, and, if the truth be known, she didn't really have anything concrete to report. She couldn't risk her boss seeing her as a troublemaker and letting her go, assuming she was more trouble than she was worth.

But as she walked across the shop floor, the intuitive foreman was determined to get to the bottom of the passing comment, especially as he watched Nancy's shoulders sag like a ten-pound sack of potatoes. There was something bothering his newest recruit and he resolved not to let it go until he'd sorted it.

Seconds later Nancy was standing beside her moody and antagonistic workmate.

'Still fancy yourself as a crane driver then?' Harry smirked.

Determined not to give him the response or ammunition he was obviously fishing for, Nancy completely ignored the pointed question.

'Good morning, Harry,' she smiled sweetly, mustering up every ounce of steely resilience she could find. 'Shall we get started?'

A disgruntled expression appearing on his face, Harry made his way up the ladder, heavily placing a foot on the first rung. 'Well, I suppose I should attempt to see if you can learn anything today.'

Taking a deep breath, Nancy reluctantly followed Harry up the ladder, trying to push away what Bert would say or do if he heard how her workmate was talking to her, knowing any thoughts of her husband today would leave her sobbing inconsolably.

★ ★ ★

The rest of the morning went as Nancy expected. When the first orders came for a steel girder to be

209

moved, Harry greedily grabbed the controls. 'This is too important for you to mess up,' he sniped. 'I'll sort it. Besides which, we don't want Frank having a pop at you.'

'Well, I've got to learn at some point,' Nancy replied. 'There's no point in me being here otherwise.'

Harry glanced at her as he moved the crane hook into position, and laughed in a way that made the hair on Nancy's arms stand on edge.

He really is repulsive! she thought.

She wasn't quite sure what she could do about Harry, so instead she focused all her attention on trying to pick things up by watching how he handled the crane, gruffly moving the big metal handles backwards and forwards as calls of 'a touch to yer left' and 'down a bit' were hollered up to the crane.

But the more she watched, the more Nancy realized Harry wasn't the expert he made himself out to be. He wasn't as quick to respond to directions as she'd expected, and when he didn't move the hook as adeptly as he should have, he arrogantly cursed, not in the least bit bothered about the mistakes he was making.

When he finally got the girder in position and the hook was released, Nancy decided she couldn't just sit like a stuffed duck all day long.

'Can I have a practice, please, while there is nothing attached?' she asked Harry, in as neutral tone as possible.

Surprised by her request, for a split second he was lost for words.

'Probably the best option,' he finally muttered but ensured his underlying message was clear — *she is a woman and not to be trusted with an actual piece of steel.*

Ignoring Harry's sexist attitude, Nancy spent the rest of the morning carefully handling the heavy controls, moving them left and right, backwards and forwards, until she knew instinctively, without looking down, what did what.

Harry didn't say a single word, only offering the occasional grunt and the odd spiteful snigger when he sensed Nancy hadn't got the movement or swing quite right.

'Rise above it,' she repeated to herself, focusing on mastering the trade she had signed up to, hoping if she could just get through today, tomorrow would be easier.

By the time midday arrived, she was mentally exhausted and more than ready for a break.

'Right, I'll see you in half an hour,' she said, feeling rather proud of herself, despite the wave of tiredness that had just hit her.

Five minutes later Nancy, Betty and Patty were huddled in their usual spot in the yard.

'So,' Betty said, pouring tea from her flask into the attached cup. 'Are you feeling any better, Nancy? You really didn't look yourself this morning.'

'Well, I wasn't particularly looking forward to a day with Harry — he's just so awful and takes great pleasure in criticizing me — but it's nothing compared to what I was faced with last night when I got home.'

'What is it?' Betty asked, her heart suddenly racing, worry soaring through her on behalf of her new friend.

'I got a letter from Bert.' Nancy sighed, desperately trying to stay composed, but her voice faltered. 'He's being sent off now to fight Jerry.'

'Oh, I'm so sorry,' Betty said, putting her tea

down and touching Nancy's hand, which, despite the unbearable heat they had all been working in, was now as cold as ice.

'I'm just so worried,' her anxious-looking workmate added, her voice cracking. 'I can't bear to think of — '

'Now, come on,' Betty cut in, knowing exactly what Nancy was worrying about. It was the same fear that left her awake at night, shivering under her eiderdown, staring blankly at the cream ceiling, praying the war would be over before William was fully trained and signed off by his superior officers to fly. 'You mustn't think like that.'

'I know,' Nancy gasped, taking a sharp intake of breath, her words catching in her throat. 'I just want him home. Me and the kids miss him so much — the house feels so empty without him. Harry is being a pig and making things quite difficult, but I don't know what I'd do without my neighbour and this job to keep my mind busy.'

Betty squeezed her hand once more. 'Talking of which,' she said, hoping a change in conversation would help Nancy get through the rest of her shift, 'how's your morning been?'

Nancy didn't know whether to laugh or cry. 'Well, Harry still clearly thinks us women aren't worthy of factory jobs and he's hell-bent on letting me know.'

'The bloody cheek of it,' Patty gasped, taking on Betty's firm stance from the day before. 'Who does he think he is, the jumped-up little twerp!'

Keen to hear something that would make her smile before she faced the afternoon with Harry, Nancy added: 'I'm guessing your morning has been slightly more pleasant?'

With that, Patty's face lit up with an enormous grin.

'Well,' she said conspiratorially, tucking a loose curl that was blowing across her cheek behind her ear, 'Archie is an absolute dream. He's so kind and patient. When I sent the hook flying, he didn't flinch and just laughed at how hopeless I am.'

'Sounds like he might be keen on you too then.' Nancy was delighted to see her young colleague so happy.

'Oh, do you think? I just don't know. I still think a lad as good-looking as him must already be snapped up. He must have lasses falling at his feet.'

'I'd say the way he is giving you the glad eye and stuttering over his words when he talks to you might be a clue.' Nancy laughed, happy to think of something other than Bert's safety or Harry's condescending attitude.

'Well, I have a funny feeling time will tell,' Betty added, folding up the piece of brown greaseproof paper that Mrs Wallis had carefully wrapped her cheese sandwich in.

Twenty minutes later, the three women were all back at their respective cranes, the afternoon proceeding as the day had started: Patty wondering if Archie was sweet on her; Nancy ignoring Harry's disgruntled comments; and Betty trying to fight off the feeling Jack was too close for comfort, his hand edging closer to her thigh as he handled the crane controls.

Not a minute too soon, the hooter echoed through the factory at four o'clock, indicating the end of the working day.

'Have you got any plans tonight?' Nancy asked her younger colleagues as they made their way out of the gates onto Brightside Lane.

'I owe William a letter,' Betty said, 'then I'm getting

213

an early night — my body is aching.'

Nancy knew what she meant. Operating the cranes didn't take a lot of physical strength but she too felt the tension across the top of her shoulder blades and into her neck from sitting bolt upright and concentrating so hard.

'And how about you, Patty?' Nancy asked.

'Actually, my friend Hattie is meeting me any minute and we're going for a cuppa and a cake at Brown's Tea Rooms up the road. I haven't seen her for a while and her fella has gone off to war, so I'm hoping a chat might cheer her up.'

'Aw, that will be nice, luv. She'll need a good friend,' Nancy added, thinking about what a tower of strength Doris had been for her.

But as Patty looked up and down the road, it wasn't her friend who caught her eye.

'Tommy Hardcastle!' she muttered under her breath, as, a few steps ahead of her, the tall, slick-looking cad turned to talk to a similar-age bloke who was walking alongside him.

At exactly the same time, the overall-clad movie star lookalike caught the young lovesick worker's eye.

'Patty!' he exclaimed, clearly as shocked to see her as she was to see him. 'I'd heard the gaffers had taken on a few lasses. I didn't realize you were one of them.'

Suddenly very conscious of her appearance, a blushing Patty smoothed down her grubby boiler suit with one hand, and patted under her eyes with the other, aware her face was undoubtedly speckled with specks of dust, as it was by the end of every shift.

'Well, I wanted to do m' bit,' Patty said, thinking on her feet, obviously unable to reveal her real reasons, although it wasn't lost on Nancy and Betty, who didn't say a word as the scene before them played out.

'I'm sorry I didn't see you at the last dance,' Tommy replied. 'I'm hoping to be at the City Hall this week, though,' he added, giving Patty his best smile, accompanied by a confident wink.

'Oh, yes,' she said, grinning coyly, blood rushing to her cheeks as she mentally put together what outfit she could wear, despite the fact he'd been joined at the hip with another woman. 'I think me 'n' Hattie were planning on going on Saturday too.'

'See you there then,' Tommy said, oozing confidence and swagger, his muscular forearms on display as he tucked his thumbs into the pockets of his overalls.

'Yes,' was all Patty could timidly manage, trying not to show her excitement at what she had just perceived as a date with the bloke she'd been keen on for months, memories of their last dance sending excited shivers down her spine, despite his caddish behaviour only a week later.

As Tommy returned to the conversation he was having with his mate and walked away, it wasn't just Betty and Nancy who had witnessed the moment.

A couple of paces behind Patty was a crumpled-looking Archie, his usual happy go-lucky-smile replaced by a disappointed frown, his mouth turned downwards, and his broad shoulders heavily drooped, any hopes he'd had stolen from him by Tommy flaming Hardcastle — who continually boasted about having a different girl on his arm every week.

How could he compete with that? he thought. Patty was too good for Tommy; she would end up being another victim of his charms and the topic of smutty conversation the following Monday morning on the factory floor.

Archie had no idea how Tommy did it, but he only had to look at a girl and they would fall at his feet, hypnotized by his smooth-talking charm, which left one girl after another mesmerized under his spell one minute and heartbroken by his rebuff the next, when he got inevitably got bored and moved on to the next gullible girl.

His heart aching, Archie put his head down, despondently pulling the collar of his coat as high as possible, joining the crowd of workers leaving the factory, Patty completely oblivious to his presence as she spotted Hattie walking towards her.

★ ★ ★

Twenty minutes later, over a cup of sweet tea and a slice of chocolate cake at Brown's Tea Rooms, Patty recounted the conversation with Tommy in minute detail. As always, Hattie had listened but it was obvious to Patty her friend hadn't shared the same level of excitement.

'Please just be careful,' Hattie warned. 'I don't want you to get hurt.'

Patty assumed her friend was simply missing John and didn't want to hear about another bloke, even if it was the one and only dreamboat Tommy Hardcastle!

'But you will come to the dance with me, won't you?' Patty had pleaded. She would need Hattie for Dutch courage.

'Of course,' Hattie promised, worried Patty may need her for very different reasons than she was imagining. She didn't trust Tommy flamin' Hardcastle as far as she could throw him and was worried her trusting and innocent friend may just be a pawn in some twisted selfish game he was playing. 'I actually bought you this,' she added, handing her a new candy-pink lipstick from Woollies.

'Oh! Thank you.' Patty jumped up to hug Hattie. 'This will definitely match my flowery skirt.' But suddenly she was overwhelmed with guilt. Her head had been in the clouds as she'd harped on about Tommy Hardcastle and the dance, pondering over what outfit to wear and whether her lippy would match, barely asking her kind and thoughtful friend how she was.

I really must try and be a better friend, she silently scolded herself, and stop just thinking about myself!'

20

The next morning, just as they had done twenty-four hours earlier, the three women made their way through the maze of corridors until they reached the factory floor that was fast becoming their second home.

'Did you have a nice time with your friend last night? Betty asked Patty as they approached Myrtle and Marlene.

'Oh, yes!' the youngest of the three crane drivers beamed. 'She is a bit down in the dumps with her fella gone but she is going to come to the dance with me on Saturday and even bought me a new lippy!'

Once again, Betty and Nancy locked glances, fully aware of their teenage colleague's naivety when it came to the fear this war was evoking.

But before they could say a word, Patty's dashing workmate appeared, ready to tutor his new trainee through another shift.

Patty's eyes lit up. 'Morning, Archie.'

'Shall we get started?' he said abruptly, not unkindly but certainly not with the bashful tenderness Patty had become accustomed to over the last couple of days.

'Yes, yes, of course,' she replied, the obvious change in his tone instantly piercing her bubble of happiness.

Patty wasn't the only one to spot his more abrupt manner. Betty looked quizzically to Nancy, who looked equally baffled.

'Take it steady and look after her, Archie,' the older of the three women said, hoping to break the suddenly ice-cold atmosphere.

'Will do,' he muttered without even a hint of a smile. 'We better get on, though. Busy day ahead.'

Taking that as a clear sign they needed to make a start, Betty and Nancy also headed off to their respective cranes, but both of them were acutely aware something had well and truly unsettled Archie, who only yesterday was outwardly swooning over Patty.

Waving to her concerned-looking friends, Patty tentatively headed to the ladder, rightly sensing Archie wasn't about to offer his normal words of softly spoken reassurance and comfort; instead the pair climbed the rungs in deadly silence, the atmosphere as heavy as the crane they were about to command.

Once safely positioned in the cab, without making eye contact with Patty, he said: 'You can do the first lift today.'

'Really?'

'Yes, you're ready. You don't need me.'

In more ways than one, Archie sadly thought to himself.

'Okay,' Patty replied, unable to comprehend her partner's extreme and hurtful change in attitude towards her.

He's obviously got a sweetheart, she surmised to herself, and she'd got word he's been partnered with a girl and had given him a stern warning.'

'I just hope I don't make a mistake,' she said out aloud. 'I don't want Frank getting mad at me.'

'I'll take over if necessary,' Archie said, his voice slightly softer, but still devoid of any emotion or compassion.

For the rest of the morning, in between moving small plates of steel across the factory floor, Patty tried to cheer herself up with the thought of the upcoming weekend and meeting Tommy Hardcastle at the City Hall.

It was those thoughts that kept her going as the hours passed at a snail's pace as she wished the morning away, longing to talk to her workmates, who she already classed as friends, over a sarnie and a cuppa.

It wasn't just Patty who was having a miserable morning.

Over on Myrtle, Betty's senses were on high alert. Unlike Harry, Jack had been nothing but friendly — too friendly. The way he looked at her made her feel uncomfortable. There was something distinctively lewd and lascivious in his dark narrow eyes; he was almost leering at her, making her feel on edge and uncomfortable.

Just concentrate on the job in hand, Betty told herself, wishing her William was right here by her side to protect her, to tell this cocky Jack the lad not to mess with his sweetheart. For years she had trained herself to be independent, to be strong enough not to rely on others but right now, metres above the ground, alone in the metal cab, out of the eyeline of others, she felt incredibly exposed, her vulnerability open to exploitation.

'Are you ready up there?' came Frank's order from below, pulling Betty back to the moment.

'Always,' came Jack's confident reply.

'You can take this one,' he added, smirking at Betty. 'It's only a baby; you're more than capable.'

'Got it,' she replied, peering over the side of the crane at the glinting slab of steel that had been brought onto the factory floor on a Lister truck.

'Straight lift and over to the furnace,' Frank bellowed over the continual thud, his arms and hands pointing in the direction of one of the many foundry fires, backing up his instructions.

Carefully, using her left hand to move the arm of the crane into position, she dropped the hook for the waiting men below to attach it to the thick ropes and wire, which were already tightly positioned around the hunk of silver metal.

'Ready,' came the next order, Frank's palms facing upwards. Instinctively, Betty slowly manoeuvred the controls, carrying out the instructions with precision.

'Well done,' Jack whispered, placing his big rough calloused hand on top of hers. Stunned, Betty froze, glued motionless in her plastic clammy seat.

'You did it,' he leered, nodding his head slowly to the same rhythm his thumb caressed her index finger.

Instantly feeling nauseous, Betty couldn't speak. Time seemed to stand still. For a few seconds, though it felt more like an hour, Betty didn't move an inch, though she wanted nothing more than to swipe his hand away from her, but his grip was sickeningly strong.

Do not let him do this, Betty thought to herself, but in those few sickening moments, she really didn't know what to do.

Then as quick as it had started, it was over, Jack jerked his hand away, shoving his clenched fists in his pockets, creating bulging lumps on his already thick-set thighs.

Betty's heart was racing so fast, if it wasn't for the fact the noise in the factory was already ear-splittingly loud, she was sure every one of her colleagues would be able to hear the thud of it thunderously banging against her chest.

In a state of shock, it took the normally determined Betty a couple of minutes to regain her composure. For the rest of the morning, she barely said a word, simply obeying orders from below when Jack made it clear he couldn't be bothered to. Betty didn't mind — it helped pass the time as she concentrated on manoeuvring the cargo back and forth.

By the time midday arrived, and the call for lunch echoed through the warehouse, the exhausted young worker felt like she had been working non-stop for a week, as opposed to four hours, mentally and physically fatigued from being on her guard.

As she made her way down the ladder, Nancy and Patty were waiting for her, their perturbed faces equally forlorn, replicating her own despondent mood.

'Girls, what's with all the long faces?' Frank said, walking towards the three women, taken aback by the gloomy images standing before him.

Betty, Nancy and Patty looked at one another in turn. There was no denying it, anyone would have thought they had been sucking lemons. The silence deafening, unable to bear it any longer, Nancy muttered, 'I think tiredness is just setting in Frank.' She smiled weakly.

But as his three new recruits stared at him blankly, not giving away a thing, the concerned foreman wasn't buying the tepid excuse. Something was definitely amiss. His trio of female amigos had gone from chatty, positive, and at times incorrigible, to completely unreadable.

'Oh, I'll cheer Betty up this avo,' Jack chirped in as he hopped down the ladder, throwing his workmate a wink.

Over my dead body, Betty silently fumed, something finally snapping in her mind. How dare he?

Turning to Frank, Betty found her voice. 'Don't you worry,' she said assertively. 'It's nothing a strong cup of Brooke's tea won't cure.'

'Okay,' Frank replied, but as the women headed towards their normal spot for lunch, he was determined, come hell or high water, to discover the real reason for their downturn in moods. Apart from being valuable assets to Vickers to ensure they got through their ever-increasing and demanding workload, he had also developed a fatherly soft spot for them all.

As soon as they reached the relative privacy of the yard, Patty burst into floods of tears and Betty could tell it wasn't going to take much for Nancy to follow suit.

'Oh, goodness, whatever is the matter?' she asked, temporarily forgetting about her own problem.

'It's Archie,' Patty sobbed, in between deep intakes of breath. 'He's barely said a word to me all morning, let alone looked at me sideways. I really don't know what I've done but I can't stand another minute of being in that chuffin' cramped cab with him.'

'He did seem a bit grouchy this morning, but I'm sure whatever it is, it will pass,' Nancy chipped in, putting her arm around her distraught young co-worker, instinctively morphing from her exhausted state to her natural motherly mode. 'Yesterday he could hardly keep his eyes off you. Maybe something has happened at home and he's a bit upset.'

'Or his girlfriend is giving him a hard time working with another lass and he's under strict orders not to speak to me more like,' Patty quipped.

The thought had crossed Nancy's mind too, feeling sure if Archie did have a sweetheart, she probably would be a little nonplussed, to say the least, he was working in such close proximity to Patty. She might not have realized it, but she had the innocent and unassuming ability to turn the eye of any potential suitor.

But she didn't say a word; instead she gently rubbed Patty's arm with one hand, and tucked the now fly-away curls that were draped limply across her clammy wet cheeks behind her ear with the other.

'I hope your morning was a little better, Nancy?' Betty asked, hoping a change in conversation might take Patty's mind off Archie's confusing change in attitude.

'Well, I've had better days.' She sighed. 'Harry is a truly obnoxious little twerp! Every time I move one of the controls, he sighs or grunts so deeply, you'd think I'd knocked a slab of steel across the factory floor.'

'You should tell Frank or let me speak to m' dad,' Patty said, lifting her head from the crook of Nancy's arm.

'Oh, no, I don't want to cause any trouble,' she said, sighing. 'I'm sure it will pass soon enough.'

'What is it with these flamin' men this morning,' Betty said, unable to keep it in any longer.

It was now Patty and Nancy's turn to look up at their workmate in astonishment. 'Not Jack as well?' Nancy asked.

Betty took a deep breath, before taking a gulp of her steaming tea, a sharp contrast to the early-autumn chill in the air, hinting colder weather was on its way.

'It's nothing I can't handle,' she insisted, 'but definitely a headache I could do without.'

224

'What's happened, luv?' Nancy probed further, questioning once again what they had all let themselves in for.

'Let's just say Jack is a little too free with his hands.'

'What?' Nancy gasped, her protective caring instincts kicking in. 'You can't be putting up with that, Betty. That's outrageous!'

'I'd take that over being ignored,' Patty spurted out, a tinge of teenage envy flooding her.

'Patty!' Nancy gasped, shocked by her young colleague's ill-thought-out words, revealing her innocent immaturity.

'Oh, I'm sorry,' Patty whispered. 'I didn't mean it like that. I just wish Archie would show me some attention.'

Flabbergasted, Betty and Nancy looked at each other, temporarily rendered speechless.

'There's a right type of attention,' Nancy explained kindly.

'And this type is far from welcome,' Betty added, ripping a corner from her sandwich, which she'd barely touched, despite their lunch break rapidly coming to an end.

'Are you going to be okay?' Nancy asked, concerned.

'Yes,' Betty replied, assertively. 'Jack has messed with the wrong girl.'

It was now Nancy's turn to feel a pang of jealousy, not because she wanted to be the recipient of unwelcome attention but she simply wishing she had even a smidgeon of the fighting spirit Betty possessed.

As the three women made their way back to their respective workstations, Nancy touched Betty's arm. 'Please be careful,' she said. 'You can always speak to

225

Frank.'

'Oh, he will know soon enough,' Betty said. 'Don't you worry.'

As she climbed up to her cab seat, the determined factory worker was fiercely adamant she would not be used as a plaything by her rather vile workmate.

'Hope you got a hearty lunch,' Jack said, as Betty got herself into position. 'Looks like we have a heavy workload this afternoon. It's going to be full-on — do yer reckon you can handle it?'

'Yes, I'm quite sure I can,' Betty answered matter-of-factly, looking straight ahead, determined not to give Jack any reason to feel he had gained the upper hand.

A few seconds later, the first orders from below were yelled up, adding to the echo chamber of noise Betty was now slowly becoming accustomed to.

Focusing entirely on the job in hand, she adeptly took to the controls with the consummate proficiency of someone with years more experience.

But as Betty safely manoeuvred the block of solid steel into position, she felt something warm and clammy cover her knee and firmly squeeze her lower thigh.

Despite how violated and vulnerable Betty felt in those few horrifying seconds, she remained as cool as a cucumber, not even a hint of a flinch.

But as soon as the great hunk of metal had been unleashed from the workers below and the call came to raise the hook, Betty swiftly turned to face Jack, whose hard chiselled face was now adorned with an arrogant sickening smirk that made her blood boil.

Not raising her voice an octave above her normal calm tone, she said very firmly: 'I am warning you right now, Jack, if you do not take your greasy filthy hand off my knee this instance, I will push you over the side of this crane cab myself!'

Utterly gobsmacked, Jack's mouth dropped open as he stared at Betty, whose pointed glare bestowed, without a shadow of a doubt, how serious she was.

Coming to his senses, Jack quickly moved his hand, stunned this young softly spoken slither of a girl had dared to stand up to him.

'No need to get so narky,' he muttered under his breath, without a hint of an apology. 'You should be counting your lucky stars I'm even giving you a second glance. I've got lasses queuing up for a date with me.'

Bemused by his blatant lack of self-awareness, Betty took a silent deep breath. 'Well, mores the pity for them,' she said, sympathizing with whatever poor girl fell for Jack's lecherous sleazy charms.

'Ha,' Jack laughed. 'Maybe they just aren't prudes!'

Betty had the good sense to stop the conversation in its tracks, the little life experience she had telling her it wasn't going anywhere.

The rest of the shift passed without so much as a word passing between the pair, Betty taking to the controls as soon as a new order came in, confident in her own capabilities to do what was required.

But when the final hooter came, it wasn't a minute too soon as far as Betty was concerned. She had shared more than enough oxygen with her obnoxious workmate for one day.

In a furious mood, his advances spurned, Jack pushed past Betty, greedily making for the ladder first, any sign of courteous chivalry a million miles from his angry and rejected self.

Betty didn't care one jot — she wasn't going to be intimidated by Jack or any man. If losing her mum at such an early age had taught her anything, it was that there was no greater pain in life, so she was damn sure some cocky, egotistic, jumped-up little pipsqueak was not going to hurt her.

As she calmly made her way down the ladder, she spotted Frank waiting for her, a look of genuine concern on his kind face.

'Ay up, Betty duck, are you okay?' he asked. 'I've just seen Jack march across the floor with a face like thunder. Has something happened?'

Betty had no inclination to protect Jack and his disgraceful behaviour.

'Actually, Frank,' she started, 'something has happened that I need to speak to you about.'

'What is it, luv?' he said instantly, worry reflecting in his narrowing brown eyes, which were normally full of laughter.

'It's Jack,' Betty said, her voice now positively sanguine. 'He's been a bit too familiar with his hands. I've put him in his place this afternoon but I'm not willing to put up with it for a minute longer.'

'Oh, duck, I'm so sorry.' Frank sighed, bringing his right hand to his forehand, a look of utter exasperation appearing across his face. 'I'd heard the odd rumour from some of the other lads that he was a bit too sure of himself and fancied himself as the cock of the north, but I promise you, I didn't for one second think he would try it on with one of you lasses. I really am sorry — I feel terrible that I've put you through this. I shouldn't have been so naive. I wouldn't blame you for being angry at me and never stepping foot in here ever again.'

'Over my dead body!' Betty gasped. 'This isn't your fault, Frank. You cannot be held responsible for that little twerp. But if it's all the same with you, there is one thing you can do for me.'

'What is it? Anything at all, duck. You just have to say, it's the very least I can do.'

Betty smiled. She didn't feel any anger towards her foreman who had shown her, Patty and Nancy nothing but kindness since they had started at Vickers.

'Can you please ensure I never have to work with Jack again?' she asked.

'Oh, Betty,' Frank responded. 'That goes without saying. I can assure you, right now, that little upstart won't be working anywhere near another one of you lasses again.

'He's chuffin' lucky I'm not giving him his marching orders right 'ere and now. If there wasn't war on and we weren't so flamin' desperate for every worker we can get our hands on, he'd never step foot on this factory floor ever again, but we've got orders coming out of our ears and a right job on to meet the demands.'

'That's all right, Frank,' Betty said. 'I understand and I'm just grateful that I won't have to see him again, let alone share a crane cab with him.'

'Consider it done,' Frank said, bereft he'd let down one of his new recruits but eternally grateful she had the strength and fortitude to carry on. 'And once again, I really am sorry, luv. But you did the right thing telling me and consider it sorted.'

'It's forgotten, let's just draw a line under it,' Betty replied. 'Tomorrow's a new day.'

'What's forgotten?' came a familiar voice.

Turning to face Patty, Betty linked her younger

colleague's arm. 'Let's go clock off and I'll fill you in. You still look down in the dumps — did things not improve this afternoon?'

'No such luck,' Patty muttered, utterly perplexed by Archie's sudden change in attitude towards her.

21

The rest of the week passed painfully slowly for Patty. Archie barely looked at her and only spoke when absolutely necessary, so much so that Patty questioned whether she'd now imagined how kind and sensitive her workmate had been when they'd first been partnered up.

By the time midday on Saturday came, her fear of heights may have been placated but she couldn't wait to walk out of the factory, so she didn't have to suffer Archie's indifference to her until Monday morning.

'At least I've got the dance to look forward to tonight,' she said to Betty and Nancy as they collected their bags and gas masks and headed to the time machine, her downturned lips now turning upwards at the thought of seeing Tommy Hardcastle again. Patty hadn't bumped into him again at work but, with Archie giving her the cold shoulder, her mind had wandered to the steelworker who had made it crystal clear that tonight could be her lucky night.

'I don't know how you've got the energy after this week,' Nancy said, stifling a yawn. 'I just want to put my feet up and get an early night before the onslaught begins again on Monday morning.'

'Was Harry any better today?' Betty asked, a surge of guilt flooding her. Now Frank had moved Jack into a different warehouse, where he had been told he would never work within arm's length of another

231

woman again, Betty felt she could really focus on her job. Not only was she free from Jack's wandering hands but Frank had told her she no longer needed a partner at all, male or female, as she was more than capable of operating Myrtle by herself.

As much as she had been relieved, pleased to just get on with what she had signed up for, it didn't stop her worrying about Patty and Nancy, who, despite trying their best to be cheerful, had been utterly miserable.

'Sadly not,' Nancy said with a sigh. 'He literally can't help himself. I'm trying not to rise to the bait, but I won't lie — I'm sick to the back teeth of him and I'm glad the weekend is finally here so I get a complete day off from him tomorrow.'

'Are you sure you won't speak to Frank?' Betty suggested, hating seeing her newfound friend so fed up. 'He was ever so good when I told him about Jack. I'm sure he would be exactly the same with you.'

'I feel I need to deal with this myself. I don't want Frank to think I can't handle the job, and there's also a part of me that doesn't want to be defeated by him.'

Betty was wise enough not to press the matter any further. Nancy was clearly exhausted after putting up with Harry and his utterly obnoxious comments all week. If only Betty could think of a way to solve the problem as efficiently as she had dealt with Jack, but she knew it would be wrong to go against her workmate's wishes.

'Okay,' Betty said. 'I hope you can have a nice couple of days with Billy and Linda and get some sleep.

'Thanks, luv,' Nancy replied, slipping her timecard into the machine, and waiting for the click to indicate her last shift of the week had been recorded. 'And you have a nice one too. Have you got any plans?'

'Well, I owe William a letter,' Betty said. 'I haven't had a chance to write and tell him what happened with Jack yet and I've promised Mrs Wallis a walk at Rivelin Valley tomorrow.'

'Sounds perfect,' Nancy said, as the three women were heading to the big black metal factory gates. 'And there's no need to ask what your plans are?' she chuckled, turning to Patty.

'I need a bit of fun after the last few days,' the youngest of the new crane drivers announced. 'With any luck I'll be dancing with Tommy Hardcastle all night long.'

'Well, just be careful,' Nancy warned.

'What do yer mean?' Patty asked, her innocent naivety shining through.

'Oh, luv,' Nancy replied. 'He's clearly been round the block a few times and I don't want him hurting you — you're too nice for that.'

'Hopefully he'll be sweeping me off m' feet, not breaking my heart,' Patty gushed, Nancy's warning clearly falling on deaf ears.

'I'm sure you will fill us in with all the juicy details on Monday,' Betty said as she waved a goodbye to her colleagues. 'Just do as Nancy said and don't let him mess you about.'

★　★　★

Half an hour later, Patty was sat at the family kitchen table, with Tom Tom clinging to her as though his life depended on it.

'He misses you, luv, now you're out six days a week,' her mom, Angie said, passing her eldest daughter and youngest son a plate of finely sliced cheese sandwiches.

'And I miss you, too, don't I?' Patty cooed, plonking a kiss on her brother's crown of blond curls as she squeezed him tight.

'My Pat Pat,' came the usual reply.

'So,' Angie started, 'have you planned your outfit for tonight? Daft question I know . . .'

'I have,' Patty said, in between a giant mouthful of her lunch. Nearly six hours had passed since she'd wolfed down a bowl of home-made porridge and she was ravenous after her shift at Vickers.

'Hattie bought me a gorgeous candy-pink lippy so I'm going to wear my flowery skirt and cream blouse. Do you think that will match?'

'I do.' Angie smiled, secretly pleased her daughter, despite how naturally pretty she was, didn't have an inflated sense of her own appearance. There was a lot to be said for being modest and she was glad all her girls hadn't grown up with overinflated egos. She did worry, however, that Patty's overly trusting approach to life, seeing the good in everyone, would cause her heart to get broken.

'You will look the belle of the ball,' Angie added, still recalling how wonderful it felt to get dressed up for a night out.

'Aw, thanks, Mom,' Patty said. 'I'm hoping it will do the trick.'

'Just be careful,' Angie warned cautiously. She too had caught more than a whisper of Patty's lovesick yearnings for the infamous Tommy Hardcastle and, from what her husband Bill had said, he was far from the ideal match for their lovely sweet-natured daughter, but she also knew if she tried to put her off, it

234

would have completely the opposite effect and make Patty lust after him more.

'Not you as well!' Patty said, rolling her eyes. 'I've already had Hattie, Betty and Nancy trying to put me off — it's only a dance!'

'It's only because we care, luv,' Angie replied, as lightly as possible. 'Anyway, do you have time to help me with a few chores this afternoon before you have a bath?' she added, keen to change the subject before upsetting Patty.

'Of course,' came the willing reply. Patty knew how hard her mom worked, keeping the house spick and span and preparing meals for a constantly hungry household of seven. 'What needs doing?'

'Where would you like me to start?' laughed Angie, rolling her eyes.

For the rest of the afternoon, Patty worked like a Trojan, beating the living room rug in the yard with a carpet beater until her arms ached, sweeping the wooden stairs, clearing out the fireplace and black-leading the kitchen range until her face reflected back at her.

By five o'clock, Patty was tired but exhilarated. It gave her a boost knowing she was lightening the burden for her mom, who never complained, despite being continually run off her feet looking after everyone else.

'Right, luv,' Angie said, 'I'm going to run you a bath in front of the fire so you can get yourself ready for tonight.'

Normally, as in most working-class houses up and down the country, bath night was always after tea on a Friday, when everyone in the household took it in turns to have a thorough wash down, starting with the head of the family, followed by the mom, before all the children took it in turn in order of age — poor Tom Tom always squealing with startled fright as he was dealt the raw end of the deal, the mucky water being somewhat tepid by the time Angie dunked him in for a much-needed scrub.

But Angie had made an exception this week, knowing what a tough old time Patty was having at the factory and how much a night out with her pals, feeling glamorous and special, would do her good.

Twenty minutes later, Patty was immersed in the welcome tub of warm water. Using the lavender soap her mom set aside for birthdays and Christmas, Patty scrubbed herself from top to toe until every sniff of steel, sweat and toil had been replaced by the delicate but sweet perfumed scent, before washing her long strawberry-blonde curls until they fell into perfectly formed ringlets around her slender milky shoulders.

Afterwards, she gently smoothed Ponds cream into her arms and legs, glad that she still had a hint of a tan from the summer sun she'd managed to catch on her days off and wouldn't have to use gravy browning to give the appearance of nylons that were becoming increasingly hard to come by.

Slipping into her satin Peter Pan-collared cap-sleeved blouse and A-line pink floral skirt, with a wave of cream flowing through the rose design, Patty felt an eruption of butterflies take flight in her tummy. It was her one chance to really catch Tommy Hardcastle's eye, knowing he would be looking out for her.

She spent more time than usual applying her shimmery pastel-pink eye shadow, carefully dabbing matching rouge onto her porcelain cheeks, and then finished off with a lick of the candy-sweet lipstick

236

Hattie had bought her.

'Wow! You look like a princess,' said Sally, her fourteen-year-old sister, who, unbeknown to Patty, had been quietly watching from the slightly ajar door. 'I can't wait to be old enough to come dancing with you. Will you do my hair and make-up, too?'

'Of course.' Patty smiled, clipping a few locks of her now shining hair into a diamanté slide, hoping her appearance had the same impact on her intended beau.

★ ★ ★

An hour later she was once again tottering through Barker's Pool in her T-bar cream high heels, clutching her matching handbag.

'You look an absolute picture,' Hattie said as she caught sight of her friend, who now also adorned a natural glowing flush to her cheeks.

'Aw, thank you,' Patty flushed further. 'Do you think it will do the trick?'

'Well, if it doesn't, I don't know what will,' Hattie replied as she linked her arm through Patty's. 'Let's get inside before it gets busy, so we can bag a table.'

Making their way down the majestic staircase, Patty's eyes darted left and right, hoping to catch a glimpse of the dashingly suave and handsome Tommy Hardcastle, a feeling of teenage excitement tingling down her spine at the thought of seeing him. Would he be wearing a short-sleeved polo shirt, revealing his tanned muscular biceps? The thought if it made her as giddy as a kipper and her heart go all of a flutter.

'What would you like to drink?' Hattie asked, as they approached the long mahogany bar.

'Oh, a lemonade would be lovely, thank you. I think I need to cool down.'

'Oh, you are a case, Patty Andrews!' Hattie said, laughing. She turned to the barmaid who was smiling at Patty, used to seeing girls hold a penchant for their dream date. 'Can I have two lemonades with extra ice, please?'

After collecting their drinks, the two girls made their way over to a vacant table that gave them a bird's-eye view of the whole room, which was now filling up with girls dressed up to the nines, and a similar number of suited and booted young men, a spring in their step, perfectly complementing the hopeful glint in their eyes as they scanned the dance floor for any potential and willing lasses.

'Can you see him?' Patty asked. There was no need to ask to whom she was referring.

Hattie searched the bar area and dance floor as 'Strange Fruit' by Billie Holiday was now attracting a crowd to the dance floor, but there was no sign of the cad, who she was convinced would break her friend's far too-easily-stolen heart.

'He's probably just playing it cool,' Hattie said, trying to manage Patty's expectations. 'But just remember — there's plenty of other available blokes to choose from. You should keep your options open.'

Patty rolled her eyes in mock horror. 'You know I only have eyes for one man tonight,' she gushed. 'He did promise me a dance after all.'

Hattie knew there was no point in arguing but she had an overwhelming feeling in the pit of her stomach the night was going to end in disaster after the last time Tommy had ignored her friend.

'How's work?' she asked, hoping to keep her

238

friend distracted.

Patty sighed. 'Oh, it's awful.'

'Really?' Hattie quizzed. 'But I thought you were enjoying working alongside this Archie fella? Are the cranes still terrifying you?'

'Mmm,' came the slightly muted reply, 'I don't like them but I'm getting used to the heights. It's Archie that's making me miserable. He's been really mardy with me for days. He won't look at me and whenever he does speak to me it's only to give me instructions.'

'Oh!' Hattie answered. 'That is odd. Maybe he's got problems at home — that would explain it.'

'Or maybe he's got a sweetheart who's giving him a hard time for working with another lass!' came the petulant response.

Hattie nearly swallowed the ice cube from her lemonade whole. 'Patty Andrews, that isn't a hint of jealousy I detect, is it?'

'Maybe,' she confessed, with a tinge of humility. 'He was so nice to me when we were first partnered up and I suppose I did wonder if, yer know, he might have had a soft spot for me, but I'm under no illusion now — he's made that perfectly clear!'

'But,' Hattie started, 'you're here tonight hoping to get off with that flamin' Tommy Hardcastle. You can't have it both ways.'

'Oh, I know,' Patty said. 'I'm just so confused. You really don't like Tommy, do you?'

Before Hattie could answer, the look of utter heartache on Patty's face stopped her in her tracks.

'What is it?' she asked, but as Hattie followed her friend's bewildered gaze, her throat went dry and she instinctively reached out to hold Patty's now trembling hand.

Not only had Tommy Hardcastle just walked across the dance floor, tightly holding onto the Greta Garbo lookalike he'd been with a few weeks earlier, he was smirking directly at Patty as he did so.

'The rotten swine!' Hattie gasped. She'd always sensed there was something intrinsically unsavoury about Tommy but never in a million years did she think he, or anyone for that matter, could be this out-rageously cruel. He really was the lowest of the low.

'Oh, Hattie,' Patty said, erupting into floods of tears. 'Can we please just go home? I can't bear to be here another second.'

'Of course,' she said. 'Come on. Don't you dare let him see you this upset. He's an absolute guttersnipe and doesn't deserve a second of your time. You are worth a million of him.'

Walking round to Patty's side of the table, Hattie gently coaxed her distraught friend to her feet, picking up her handbag that was lying on the plush red-cushioned chair where she'd been sat.

'Let's go,' Hattie whispered, but as she gently tried to usher Patty through the sea of happy Saturday-night revellers towards the door, they came face to face with Tommy and his strikingly beautiful date, who from top to toe looked like she had walked straight off a Hollywood movie set.

Unable to keep her sadness locked inside the chamber of her own mind, Patty stammered, 'How could you?', tears chasing one another down her now bright-red cheeks, her mascara forming ugly black blotches under her puffy eyes, which had ten minutes ago looked so radiant.

'Do what?' Tommy answered, a look of faux shock on his face, as though he had absolutely no idea what

240

Patty was talking about.

'You know exactly what I mean,' Patty gasped, stunned he could be so brazenly complacent. She knew herself what a dreamer she could be, but she had not imagined his flirty proposition just days earlier.

'I really have no idea what you are talking about,' Tommy said, half-laughing and turning his attention to the puzzled-looking woman who was casting her eyes from her evening's date to the heartbroken sobbing girl in front of her.

'What's happening, Tom?' she asked, clearly confused by the scene before her.

'I've no idea!' he lied. 'But shall we get that drink I promised you? I'm parched.'

'Sure,' she muttered, but as Tommy speedily led her away she glanced back at Patty, a mixture of concern and annoyance etched across her model-like face.

A few minutes later, Patty fell into her friend's arms as they stopped for breath, having finally made their way outside the City Hall.

'How could he be such a horrible rat?' she cried, in between sobs.

'I don't know,' Hattie said, hugging her tight, wishing more than anything in the world her gut instincts about the fella Patty had set her heart on had been wrong. She hated seeing her closest friend this distraught. 'Some men are just utter swines and Tommy Hardcastle is most certainly one of them. But don't start thinking all men are like him. There's plenty who aren't and I know Mr Right is out there somewhere, just waiting for you.'

'I'm not sure I ever want to look at another fella again,' Patty sniffled, pulling herself upright, wiping her runny nose on a tissue that Hattie — who had sensed the evening wouldn't end well — had pulled from her own handbag.

Hattie laughed. 'Now, if I had a shilling for every time I'd heard you say that, I'd be living the life of Riley now.'

'I mean it this time,' Patty sniffled, but even as she said it she knew in her heart of hearts she wasn't destined to grow old a lonely bitter spinster, even if every bloke she had set her eyes on lately seemed determined to break her heart.

22

In the blink of an eye, it was Monday morning again, and Patty was sat at the kitchen table, moving her spoon from one side of her bowl of stodgy porridge to the other, never once raising it to her downturned lips.

Sat opposite his sullen daughter, Bill glanced across to his wife, who was stood at the white Belfast kitchen sink, already peeling a bowl of turnips and carrots, despite it only being just turned seven in the morning, ready for tonight's tea of hash and veg. Like every good hard-working housewife up and down the country, she would have her work cut out with today being wash day and when that was done, if she had time, Angie would spend an hour on her hands and knees with a donkey stone, scrubbing the front doorstep.

'Come on, luv,' Angie encouraged. 'You have a heavy day in the factory ahead. You need to get something in that stomach, or you'll be fit for nothin'.'

Patty had barely eaten a thing since Saturday night when that sodding Tommy Hardcastle had so cruelly humiliated her. She'd spilled her heart out to Angie when she'd arrived home in floods of tears, less than two hours after setting off full of high spirits and excitement.

Bill had made himself scarce, taking his *Sheffield Star* into the front room, burying himself in the sports pages, not because he didn't know how to comfort his

243

teenage daughter — he absolutely did; it had always been his job to stem her flow of tears as a little girl when she'd fallen over or come off her bike. No, it was to prevent himself marching down to the City Hall and giving this Tommy flamin' Hardcastle a piece of his mind, and possibly a bit more, if he listened to Patty's heartbroken sobs.

This cad, who didn't deserve a second glance from his little girl, had a name for himself at Vickers for counting the notches on his bedpost of how many girls he'd managed to seduce. Although Bill was relieved to hear his Patty had not become another victory for Tommy, a steel turner by trade, he quite frankly wanted to knock his bloody block off for the way he'd treated his innocent and naive daughter.

Heaven forbid if he bumped into him at work. The chances were slim as they worked at opposite ends of the city's biggest factory, but Bill swore to God that if he clapped eyes on the bloody little toerag any time soon, he couldn't be held responsible for his actions. There was no stronger bond than that between a loving and protective father and his daughter.

'I can't face it, Mom,' Patty answered, catapulting Bill back to the scene before him. She sighed, pushing her bowl towards the middle of the table. 'Let Tom Tom have it.'

At the mention of his name, the cheery youngster, who had parked himself on the floor next to the welcome and inviting heat coming from the range, stopped playing with his yellow Dinky car, and looked up, never once known to turn down a scrap of food.

'Not even a few mouthfuls?' Angie asked, pleadingly. 'I popped some carnation milk on top for you.'

'I'm just not hungry,' Patty muttered. Normally she

would have wolfed the extra special treat down, relishing the sweet creamy topping, but every time she thought about being made to look a fool by the man she had set her sights on, her stomach churned and her eyes filled with salty tears, instantly suppressing her normally insatiable appetite.

Worried, Angie wrapped an extra thick slice of homemade bread in brown greaseproof paper with a generous helping of beef dripping left over from yesterday's roast. Patty didn't have a pick on her as it was — she definitely couldn't afford to lose any weight from her already waif-like figure.

'Well, at least have your cup of tea,' came her mom's response, as she stirred a rather generous heaped spoonful of sugar into her daughter's blue-and-white enamel mug.

'Okay.' Patty gratefully accepted. Hell itself would have to freeze over before she turned down one of her mom's famous Brooke Bond brews.

★ ★ ★

Less than an hour later, Patty was joined by Betty and Nancy as they clocked in for their first shift of the week.

'Well,' Betty asked, 'how was Saturday night?'

'Oh, don't ask!' Patty sighed. 'It was a complete disaster. Tommy Hardcastle was no more interested in me than flying to the moon. He made that abundantly clear.'

The two older women swapped concerned glances.

'Why don't you tell us all about it over dinner?' Nancy suggested. 'And no matter how bad it feels now, I promise in a few weeks' time, it won't feel a faction as hard.'

'Well, that's a relief,' Patty muttered, 'because right now between Tommy chuffin' Hardcastle and a day with Archie barely able to look at me sideways, life feels pretty rotten. I'm beginning to wish I hadn't been as hell-bent on leaving Woollies — since starting here it's been one flamin' disaster after another.'

'Maybe today will be a better day,' Betty said, smiling optimistically, but even as the words left her lips, she knew herself that her words didn't hold the level of conviction needed to persuade Patty.

'I suppose I can live in hope,' came the despondent reply.

For the next four hours, Patty fought back the tears that were stinging the backs of her eyes like red-hot pokers, as she and Archie sat side by side, only exchanging the odd sentence as and when necessary for the work required.

'Your lift.'

'Take it steady.'

'I'll take this one.'

The short, sharp staccato sentences left Patty feeling like her heart was being pierced over and over again, but it was all Archie could allow himself to mutter.

He assumed Patty's sullen mood was down to the fact she now hated being in his presence, especially after her date with factory Lothario and all-round heart-throb, Tommy Hardcastle. He assumed the pair had danced the night away at the City Hall. Wasn't that what Tommy had indicated to Patty in their flirty conversation last week?

How on earth can I compete with him? Archie asked himself. He only has to look at a girl and they fall at his feet, all gooey-eyed and acting as though all their Christmases had come at once.

Archie had spent his Saturday evening miserable as sin, sat at home with his parents, Alfred and Grace, and his beloved nannan, Martha, who also lived with them in their neat three-bedroom terraced house on Howard Street, Attercliffe. He'd fallen hook, line and sinker for Patty from the second he'd seen her that first morning on the factory floor and the first few days had been blissful working alongside her — until he realized she was stepping out with Tommy and didn't have the least bit of interest in someone like him. There was no way he would have gone out on Saturday to City Hall to see them together.

Patty had barely uttered a word to him for days, staring straight ahead, resisting the urge to ask for help even on the most difficult of manoeuvres. Once or twice, she'd over-shot the swing of the crane hook, narrowly avoiding a disaster with a slab of steel and the lads who were perilously close to the red-hot and deathly furnaces.

Archie would have dearly liked to place his hand on hers, on top of the handles, to regain control but his pride had kicked in. He wouldn't play second best to Tommy Hardcastle — not for all the tea in China. He knew he couldn't compare with the tanned muscle-bound steel turner, who had the gift of the gab and 'take me to bed' eyes.

What chance does little old me stand? Archie asked himself, his confidence taking yet another hammering.

He'd always been the quietest lad at school, never quite hitting the mark to fall in with the 'in-crowd' due to his clumsy two left feet, making him a poor substitute on the football pitch and his adolescent spots leaving him last in line for the pick of dates from his female classmates.

An only child, he had no brothers or sisters to ask advice or pick up clues on how to react around girls, only adding to his shyness and inability to know how to act around members of the opposite sex, explaining why he couldn't see how he had completely misread the situation with Patty.

Instead of bestowing her with kindness, which is what he really wanted to do — and which Patty would have welcomed with open arms — Archie had stubbornly engaged the solid and insurmountable brick-like barriers he had used all his life to protect and keep what little self-esteem he had intact.

The result was an icy-cold atmosphere, the silence unbearable even with the cacophony of noise all around them, which, unbeknown to Archie, left the hairs on Patty's slender neck, standing to attention, despite the unforgiving factory heat from the blisteringly hot furnaces that naturally rose to the heavens of the vast warehouse.

By the time the welcome screech from the hooter came at midday, both he and the woman he secretly adored couldn't get down the steep metal ladder fast enough, allowing them to escape the tense cage-like cab they had both been trapped in all morning.

In silence they descended to the safety of the busy shop floor, not even exchanging a cursory nod, the distance between them increasing, before they both headed in different directions to have their snap.

Patty played with the bread and dripping sandwich her mom had so meticulously packed for her as she retold the sorry story from Saturday night.

'What an absolute ratbag,' Betty calmly raged. 'Don't you ever give him a second glance now. He isn't worth the ground you walk on.'

'Betty's right,' Nancy added, pouring a cup of steaming tea from her stainless-steel thermos flask. 'Men like that never change. You are worth a million of him — don't ever forget that.'

Patty sighed. 'Well, I don't feel it at the moment. Between Tommy flamin' Hardcastle making a complete and utter fool of me, leaving me the laughing stock of the City Hall, and Archie barely looking in my direction, only talking when he needs to bark some sharp chuffin' order at me, I'm destined to die a lonely old spinster!'

Nearly choking on her tea at Patty's response, Betty managed to say, in between splutters, 'Oh, Patty, you really are quite the drama queen. You would think you were pushing forty, not seventeen. You've got years to find Mr Right, and I'm fairly sure he won't be a million miles away.'

'She's right, luv,' Nancy nodded in agreement. 'I can assure you we've all cried more tears than we care to remember over blokes who don't deserve a minute of our time, but I promise you there's plenty more fish in the sea — it might sound like an old cliché, but I swear it's true.'

'Do you think?' Patty quizzed, ripping the smallest of corners off her thickly sliced bread. 'I just seem to be having a right run of bad luck when it comes to men at the moment.'

'It will happen when you least expect it,' Nancy said reassuringly. 'These things always do.'

23

Their short twenty-minute dinner break over, the three women made their way back inside the factory, which seemed to be getting busier by the day. As they passed through where the turners worked shaping steel for tank guns, Patty noticed a few more women had been taken on.

'Poor mites,' she whispered, still feeling deeply sorry for herself. 'They haven't got a clue what they're letting themselves in for.'

But as she walked past, one strikingly beautiful young woman stood out from all the rest, her envious height and perfect figure obvious despite her khaki overalls, which inexplicably seemed to emphasize her perfect curves and shapely bottom instead of hiding them.

'It's her,' Patty gasped, gripping Betty's arm, her legs threatening to give way beneath her.

'What? Who?' Betty asked, momentarily confused.

'Her,' Patty gestured, turning her head to the carbon copy of screen siren, Greta Garbo — only she was stood in the middle of dirty filthy factory, surrounded by dust, and not on the set of a Hollywood blockbuster. 'That woman — that's who Tommy had wrapped round him like a limpet on Saturday night.'

Stunned, Betty and Nancy couldn't help but immediately turn to look at the girl who was being shown how to direct a piece of steel into a huge machine by an older man.

Jeepers! Betty silently thought. She is certainly a

looker. Her legs go on forever.

I bet she's turned more than a few heads in her time, Nancy mused, a mixture of sympathy for Patty fused with even more anger towards this chuffin' Tommy bloke, who had clearly been stringing Patty along for the sole purpose of hedging his bets.

'Right, come on, luv,' Nancy said, propelling herself back to the situation in hand. 'You don't need to torture yourself any longer. Let's get going before we're late and Frank has our guts for garters.'

'Nancy's right,' Betty encouraged, gently coaxing Patty along the shop floor.'You're only punishing yourself and we have no idea what Tommy claimed or didn't claim about you. I would bet my last shilling, though, that he's been stringing the pair of you along.'

In a state of shock, Patty allowed her workmate to guide her into the next warehouse, sharp salty water filling her eyelids, blurring her vision.

Wasn't it bad enough that Tommy already worked at Vickers without having to see him purr all over this beauty of a woman right in front of m' nose? Patty thought to herself.

'I'm going to have to leave,' she muttered, her voice breaking. 'I should never have left Woollies. I'll have to go back to Mr Watson with m' cap in me hand and beg for me job back.'

'You will do no such thing,' Betty scolded. 'You have as much right to be here as this woman, so you are going to carry on with dignity and your head held high.'

'Oh, Bet, I'm not like you,' Patty said, sighing. 'I'd love to be as strong but I'm just not. Starting here was a big mistake. I'll tell m' dad tonight that I can't spend another day here.'

Betty looked to Nancy for support, running out of words to bolster her heartbroken friend.

'Look, why don't we have a chat after work and see how you feel then,' the older of the three women suggested. 'Things might not seem half as bad when the shock has worn off.'

'No,' Patty replied firmly, shaking her head to reinforce the point, 'there is nothing you can say to convince me. After today I'm done at Vickers — it's caused me nothing but flamin' heartache and pain.'

Her mind well and truly made up, Patty picked up her pace, her decision giving her the speed and adrenalin she needed to get through what she was certain would be her final shift at Vickers.

'I'll see you both later,' she said to Betty and Nancy, as she marched over to Marlene where Archie was waiting at the bottom of the ladder, a look of exhaustion etched across his face.

'You ready?' he stated more than asked.

Something about his morose and slightly brusque tone pinched Patty once again. After the last forty-eight hours she had endured it was the last thing she needed.

'Yes!' she snapped back. 'And you will be pleased to hear this is the final time you will have to work with me.'

'What?' came the quick reply.

'I've had enough. I'm quitting as soon as my shift is done.'

Afraid that Patty might somehow penetrate his mind and work out what he was really thinking, Archie darted towards the first rung of the ladder, unusually taking the lead up to 'their' crane cab as opposed to following Patty in case her nerves took over.

252

Well, at least I won't have to watch her and Tommy Hardcastle fawning all over each other, he thought to himself, trying but failing to convince himself that Patty leaving would be doing him a giant favour. How had he got himself into this ridiculous predicament when his true thoughts were in stark contrast to his actions? Why didn't he have the courage and conviction to say what he really wanted to say: how he thought of Patty day and night; how she consumed his every thought?

The gap between them getting ever wider by the second, Patty was also becoming increasingly disgruntled.

Well, he obviously doesn't give two hoots if I stay or go! she thought. In fact, he's probably counting down the seconds until this shift is over.

Already mapping out the conversation in her head with Frank and then her dad, Patty knew the late afternoon's events were going to be far from a walk in the park but her mind was made up. Her highfalutin ideas about what a stint in Vickers would bring had been exactly that — naive and fanciful — and encouraged by no one but herself. She had as much chance of finding a bloke here who would sweep her off her feet than she did joining the crowds of shoppers walking down The Moor on a Saturday afternoon.

How did I get it so wrong? Patty wondered. She gasped aloud, the tears she had been holding back finally breaking free from behind her tired eyelids, streaming down her flushed cheeks.

The silent sobs of frustration and self-pity caused Patty's vision to cloud over, her focus blurring, the narrow rungs of the ladder becoming less and less distinct.

Less than four hours left, she thought, and I'll be out of this place once and for all.

But as she slowly raised her booted right leg, instead of moving a step closer to what she could only envisage as her final hellish afternoon of incarceration, she somehow missed the rung, lost her balance and with it her nerve.

Suddenly she was grasping at the sides of the ladder, her hot and clammy hands offering no help, their grip rendered useless on the smooth and slippery columns.

The next few seconds seemed to play out like a scene from one of the many pictures Patty had been to see at the Gaumont. Everything happened in slow motion, as though she was a member of the audience watching, clinging to the cushioned armrest of her seat.

Desperately trying to grasp hold of the ladder, Patty screamed out in horror as she realized she was tumbling backwards, her feet clanging against each rung, as opposed to finding their natural grip, her arms flailing in mid-air as she struggled to regain her balance.

But it was no use; the speed with which Patty was perilously falling downwards left no opportunity to steady herself.

'Help!' came her terrifying high-pitched screech as gravity did what it did best and propelled Patty's waif-like body to the ground. Her right foot crashed onto the hard concrete floor first, breaking her fall with a sickening twist.

'Aargh,' Patty cried, red-hot pain searing through her, as the rest of her body landed in a crumpled heap at the foot of the treacherous ladder. For a moment, she thought the razor-sharp needles in her ankle would cause her to be physically sick, but instead dizzying stars flashed before her eyes, then everything went black and her head finally fell with a sickening bang to the warehouse floor.

24

'Patty!' Nancy cried, as she rushed over to her friend, who was now lying in a crumpled heap on the floor, one of her feet twisted at an awkward angle. She had just been about to start the ascent to her crane cab when she watched, aghast, as her young colleague fell to the floor in slow motion.

'Frank, over here!' came Nancy's shout for help, as she gently rubbed Patty's soft and floppy arms, all colour drained from her normally rosy freckled cheeks as she lay lifeless on the floor, her body twisted at an unnatural angle.

'Quick, someone, get help. Patty's unconscious,' she bellowed, suddenly finding herself taking charge of the situation.

'Come on, Patty. Wake up — please,' she whispered, her voice cracking.

This isn't the time to get upset! she mentally chastised herself. Remain focused. Your friend needs you.

Within seconds, a crowd of people were hovering around the scene.

'Give me some space,' came Frank's concerned face. 'Come on, Patty duck,' he coaxed, taking hold of his youngest recruit's hand. 'Wake up now,' he pleaded.

'Do we need to get her to hospital?' Nancy asked, trying in vain to calm the fear that was coursing through her.

'Let's just see if we can rouse her first, duck,' Frank replied, unable to contemplate losing another worker, especially the daughter of one of his oldest mates.

'Oh, Patty, no!' another voice shouted.

Nancy looked over her shoulder. Archie was stood white-faced as he took in the sight before him.

'This is all my fault,' he whispered, his voice breaking. 'I should have let her go first. I'd have caught her.'

'Archie, why don't you go and get a bowl of warm water and see if you can round up some towels?' Nancy said, hoping to distract him by making him useful, knowing he was no use if he got himself in a state.

'I can't leave her,' came his shaken reply. 'I'm to blame.'

'I'll go,' another worker said.

'Come on, Patty,' Frank said, kindly but firmly tapping her ice-cold cheek. She wasn't the first to come flying off those ladders and there was a damn good chance she wouldn't be the last. The steelworks weren't a place for the faint-hearted and Frank knew, better than most, that on any given day you were taking your life in your hands.

'Come on, duck,' he urged, secretly praying he wasn't about to witness yet another catastrophic fatality on his watch. He'd seen grown men lose limbs, suffer horrifying life-changing burns and been the first on the scene to others who had lost their lives after clothes had become tangled in the deathly machines or had been hit by a giant slab of steel.

I can't tell Bill his daughter has become the latest victim at Vickers. I just can't. After all, it was he who had persuaded Patty's dad to let her come and work at the factory in the first place, assuring him she would be in safe hands and come to no danger — yet here she was, flat out on the floor.

'Patty, I'm so sorry,' Archie whispered again, placing himself next to Nancy on the concrete floor, who was firmly rubbing Patty's hands in a bid to get her circulation going again. 'Please wake up. I swear on my life I will never let her out of my sight again,' he pleaded, looking to the older of the three female crane drivers in desperation.

'We will do everything we can,' Nancy said reassuringly, seeing the look of sheer terror in Archie's normally sparkly eyes.

Was this how it felt for the colleagues of her late neighbour, George, when he'd had his accident? Nancy quietly thought. Did his workmates rush to try and save him?

'We won't lose her,' Nancy said out loud, subconsciously hoping that if she said the words, they would miraculously come true.

But as she and Frank attempted to coax Patty back to life, while trying to stay calm, Nancy was beginning to worry. Her young workmate had been out cold for a couple of minutes now, with no sign of life.

'I got the water and towels,' an anxious-looking young lad said, as he gently placed the top and the brown cotton bundle next to Nancy.

'Thank you,' she said kindly, giving him a nod.

'Right, Frank,' she instructed, 'let's see if we can gently ease some of these under Patty's head, without moving her too much, and pop the rest over her. Otherwise her body will go into shock and she will go cold.'

Although Nancy had never done any first aid training, she recalled Bert telling her how he'd come to the aid of a passenger who had lost her footing as she tried to board a tram and knocked herself unconscious as

258

she hit the pavement. He'd used a pile of coats to keep the injured women warm until help came.

'Archie, why don't you carefully lift Patty's head just off the ground while Frank and I pop some cushioning underneath,' Nancy gently commanded, hoping it would help focus the distraught-looking lad.

'I won't hurt her, will I?' he asked. 'I've done enough harm already.'

'Hold her steady and don't lift her head a fraction more than you need to,' Nancy said, hoping beyond hope she was doing the right thing.

Positioning himself at the top of Patty, Archie did as he was asked, carefully holding the nape of her neck, which was now a mass of soft strawberry-blonde curls that had come loose from her bun when she'd fallen.

With her patient's head looking a little less awkward, Nancy dipped one of the spare towels into the cool water and dabbed it on Patty's cheeks and forehead.

'Come on, luv,' she whispered. 'Open your eyes for us. Let us know you are okay.'

At the other side of her limp body, Frank was holding onto his youngest recruit's wrist. 'There's definitely a pulse,' he said, forcing a smile. 'She must have just knocked herself out with a bang.'

But before Nancy could answer, a familiar voice sent a shiver down her spine.

'Oh, Patty, sunshine,' Bill, gasped, hurrying over towards his daughter. Word had got round the factory fast that there had been another accident and as soon as the steelworkers had realized it was Bill Andrew's daughter who had been hurt, he'd been sent for immediately.

'I'm sorry, Bill,' Frank said, guilt soaring through

259

him as he looked up at his friend's horrified and shocked face. 'It looks like she slipped on the ladder.'

'It was all my fault,' Archie reiterated. 'I should have taken better care.'

'Let's not worry about that now,' Nancy said, determined to keep some sense of calm. 'But maybe we need to get Patty somewhere a bit more comfortable. It can't be doing her any good lying on a stone floor.'

She was conscious that quite a crowd had now pooled around her stricken workmate, and if she needed medical attention, they had better take her somewhere more private. She was also terrified Patty might not wake up. She had been out cold for a few minutes and the last thing the workers needed to witness was another fatal accident.

'How about we take her to my office?' Frank suggested, as unaware as everyone else that moving Patty could do more harm than good. He'd never been given any first aid training or a manual on how to keep his workers safe; it really was just a case of doing what you thought was best. 'There's a couch in there — it's gotta be better than leaving her laid out here.'

'I'll lift her,' Bill said assertively. Patty may have been seventeen, but she was still his little girl. It was his job to now look after his daughter.

Nancy looked up. 'Of course,' she said with understanding.

'Right,' Frank said, standing up, 'come on you lot. We need some space here. Get back to work and I'll come back and let you know as soon as Patty comes round.'

They knew their foreman well enough to know when he meant business, and they started to disperse, making their way back to their machines and the blazing furnace.

But as the steelworkers moved away, one was dashing towards them.

'What's happened?' Betty puffed, out of breath from dashing across the factory floor in the blistering heat. One of the lads had got her attention by yelling up to the cab and telling her what had happened. 'I've just heard Patty . . . ' But her words trailed off as she saw her new friend lying in a twisted heap in on the floor. 'Oh, gosh,' she exclaimed. 'Is she going to be all right?'

'I'm sure she will be,' Nancy said reassuringly, conscious that both Bill and Archie were already scared out of their wits.

'Okay, let's get her moved,' said Bill, anxious to help his daughter and get her to somewhere less public. He couldn't allow himself to say out loud what he was really thinking: 'I will never forgive myself if she doesn't wake up.'

25

Five minutes later, Patty was laid out on the old brown leather couch in Frank's office, wrapped in towels.

'Come on, luv,' Bill said, desperately willing his daughter to come round. The thought of telling his wife that their eldest daughter had been taken at the hands of Vickers was too much. He'd fiercely fought against Patty joining Vickers, knowing all too well what a dangerous place it was to work, with little training given and no guidance on safety; it really was more often than not a lottery as to who survived.

'Think of our Tom Tom,' Bill whispered, holding Patty's hand. 'He'll be waiting by the door for you tonight.'

Betty and Nancy looked at one another. With every passing minute, like Bill, Frank and Archie, who were also stood looking over Patty, their fear for her grew. Her limp and fragile body was perfectly still, her cheeks drained of colour and now her lips had a frightening blue tinge.

'We need to get her to hospital and quick,' Nancy said. 'We can't waste any more time.'

Bill nodded, mentally trying to work out the quickest way to get one of his youngest wards to the Northern General. 'There will be a works car we can use,' he started. 'I can get one of the drivers to take us.' But just as he was about to dash out of his office to alert a chauffeur, he yelped. 'Look!'

Everyone in the cramped room suddenly turned to Patty.

Her normally bright and vibrant hazel eyes started to flicker to life, the muffled voices entering her semi-conscious state.

'Where am I? What happened?' she muttered, the pain in her head pounding, forbidding her from talking above a hushed whisper.

'You've had a nasty fall, luv,' came her dad's soothing tone. 'Don't try and move just yet,' he added, no longer able to fight back the tears that had been threatening to erupt for the last twenty minutes since he first saw his daughter sprawled across the filthy factory floor. 'We need to work out what damage you have done to yerself first.'

Patty obediently stayed still but, as she looked around, her eyes fell to Archie, who looked as white as a ghost and as though he was about to burst into tears.

Despite his fear and the state of shock Patty was in, the intensity in their gaze was undeniable.

'Thank God you woke up,' Archie whispered, trying to stop his words from faltering. 'It's all my fault. I'm so sorry, Patty. I should never have gone up that ladder ahead of you. I should have been there to stop you falling. Will you ever forgive me?'

'In a heartbeat!' Patty wanted to say, but her whole body ached from tip to toe and somehow the words wouldn't come out.

'All right, Archie, that's enough for now, lad. Let the poor lass come round first,' Frank said, equally relived one of his newest wards was back in the land of the living. 'Why don't you go and grab a cuppa and see what needs doing on the factory floor?'

'Okay,' Archie said solemnly, still furious with himself. As he left the office, he turned round and glanced back at Patty, relieved she was okay but devastated he hadn't looked after her, all due to his own pig-headedness.

'Do you think you can sit up?' Bill asked Patty tenderly in his usual fatherly tone, as Archie gently closed the door.

She slowly nodded. 'I'll try,' she said, but as Patty pressed her hands into the worn sofa next to her hips to try and lift herself upright, she felt light-headed and instantly drooped sideways, her body as heavy as the steel girders that filled the factory around her.

Bill was on his knees and by her side in a flash, instinctively catching her as she lolled to the side, berating himself for allowing his precious daughter to step one foot in Vickers in the first place.

'Steady now,' he said gently, wrapping his strong arms around her, preventing her from falling off the sofa. 'Just relax for a minute.'

Patty didn't argue, allowing her aching body to fall into her father's arms, her eyelids heavy and sleep once again beckoning.

'Maybe we should give Patty some space now?' Nancy suggested in her motherly and soft-spoken manner, acutely aware Bill would probably appreciate some time with Patty; she knew, despite her being seventeen, she would always be his little girl.

'I think that would be wise,' Betty agreed, relieved their friend had come to.

As the two women left, they spotted a distraught-looking Archie hovering outside the office. The three of them looked back at Patty, whose lips had thankfully returned to their normal colour and a hint of pink could just be seen in her cheeks.

'Come on now,' Nancy soothed, as she led Archie

back onto the factory floor, 'this isn't the time to get yourself in a fret. We all know you would never deliberately let Patty come to any harm.'

'But I did, didn't I? And now look what's happened.'

'Patty's okay and that's all that matters,' Betty said, smiling encouragingly. 'Nancy's right. You mustn't get yourself in a pickle.'

But as Archie made his way back to Marlene alone, he looked as though he had the world on his shoulders.

★ ★ ★

Back in Frank's office, the concerned foreman, who had witnessed more accidents than he could care to remember, had given Patty's foot as thorough an examination as his limited medical knowledge allowed. In all the commotion, one of the lads had taken it upon himself to fetch a bucket of ice from the canteen, which Bill was now pouring into one of the towels.

'It looks like a nasty sprain,' Frank said with a sigh, secretly relieved that apart from a nasty headache and her ankle now resembling a golf ball, Patty had escaped relatively lightly. 'But you might want to get it checked over at the Northern General. One thing's for sure, though, duck, you won't be climbing any ladders for the foreseeable.'

'Oh, I'm so sorry, Frank,' Patty said, guilt instead of relief flooding through her.

All morning Vickers' youngest crane driver had been planning how she could tell her kindly foreman and dad how today would be her final shift manning Marlene, but now, when she had the ideal opportunity to call it quits, the thought couldn't be further from her mind.

In the moments since she'd come round, despite seeing stars and feeling as sick as a dog, Patty had witnessed first-hand how much her colleagues at Vickers cared for her: Nancy, like a second mom, holding her hand; the look of sheer terror in Frank's eyes; and, dare she think it, Archie had looked as though he was going to break down in tears.

I'll never understand men! Patty thought to herself with a sigh.

Tommy flaming Hardcastle had flirted with her and then monumentally humiliated her, and now, after Archie ignoring her, she was sure he wasn't putting on an act when he said how sorry he was.

Why can't they just say it how it is? Patty asked herself, her mind in a complete quandary.

'Don't you worry, duck,' Frank said gently, breaking Patty's daydream and transporting her back to the old but comfy office sofa, 'you take all the time off you need. I'm just glad you're still here to tell the tale. I've seen more fatalities than I can shake a stick at and my heart was in m' mouth when I saw you in a crumpled heap on the floor. My only concern now is that you get yerself right before you attempt to climb that ladder again.'

'Thanks, Frank. I promise I won't take a minute more than I need,' Patty replied, still in a state of shock that she had done such a huge U-turn about her new role.

'Are you sure, sunshine?' Bill asked. 'Maybe you should take a bit of time to really think about it?' He'd secretly hoped that the fall might have been the last straw for Patty, and that she would reconsider going back to Woollies, where, despite how much she disliked her grouchy manager, Mr Watson, she was as safe as could be.

'It's okay, Dad,' Patty said with a nod. 'I know what went wrong today. I was distracted and my mind wasn't where it should have been,' she added, recalling what a fluster she had been in when she set about climbing the crane ladder, annoyed with Archie for paying her no attention. 'I wasn't concentrating but I've learnt m' lesson and I want to come back, as soon as I'm fit enough.'

'Are you sure?' Bill quizzed, perplexed by his daughter's new committed attitude.

'Yes. I've never been more certain of anythin' in me life.'

'If you're sure,' Bill replied, feeling utterly confused, wondering if he would ever be able to fathom how his daughter's mind worked.

'That's m' girl!' Frank grinned, delighted that his youngest recruit hadn't been put off by the nasty accident. He wouldn't have blamed her if she had never wanted to step foot inside Vickers again — many a steelworker would have been put off for life. He felt proud of his girls; they might not have had the physical presence and muscular build of many the blokes who were employed in the works, but they certainly had a steely resolve that was hard to break. They were good workers and worth their weight in gold.

'Right, how are we going to get you home, duck?' Frank mused.

Although Patty only lived a twenty-minute walk away, there was no way on this earth she could manage it with her tender ankle now swollen to the size of an apple and already a frightfully shocking shade of purple and green.

'I think there's one of those old wheelchairs in the stores,' Bill suggested. 'I'm sure my lads can cope without me for an hour. I'd like to make sure my daughter gets home in one piece.'

'That sounds like a plan,' Frank agreed. 'I can nip over and keep an eye on your team too. It's the very least I can do,' he added, still feeling immensely guilty his old mate's daughter had been injured on his watch. 'Right, I'll go and grab that chair,' he said, 'and then you can get this poor lass home so she can rest up.'

As the sweet-natured foreman headed out of the canteen, Bill turned to Patty. 'Are you sure you want to come back, sunshine?' he asked, already dreading telling her mom, Angie, what had happened.

'I am, Dad,' Patty said with a sigh. 'Obviously, not tomorrow. But yer know, when me ankle is right.'

'Okay, luv,' he conceded, 'but just promise me you will take more care in future. You gave us all quite a shock there. For a second, when I saw you lying on the floor, I really thought I'd . . .'

But Bill couldn't actually bring himself to say the words, his eyes once again filling with tears.

'Oh, don't think like that,' Patty gasped, suddenly realizing for the first time the impact her near miss had had on her poor old dad. Patty had never really thought about how much he worried about her, assuming he was being over-protective when he'd aired his reservations about her starting at Vickers.

'It's just, well . . .' Bill started, kneeling down next to Patty, 'you will always be my little girl, no matter how big and grown up you get.'

'Oh, Dad,' Patty said, throwing her arms around him, her own eyes now threatening to leak. 'I never meant to scare you. I'm so sorry.'

'It's okay,sunshine,' Bill muttered,his voice breaking.'I just couldn't bear the thought of — '

'Don't say it, Dad,' Patty interrupted, squeezing her dad a little bit tighter through his mucky brown overalls. 'I'm all right and that's all that matters.'

'Thank goodness,' was all Bill could manage between stifled sobs, pulling his daughter closer to his chest, eternally grateful she was here to tell the tale.

'Oh, I'm sorry,' Frank muttered as he crashed into his office, cross at himself for disturbing what was clearly a private moment between a man and his daughter.

'Don't be,' Bill said, letting his daughter relax back into the sofa as he wiped his eyes.'I'm just being a sentimental old fool.'

'You have every right to be,' Frank said, knowing he'd be exactly the same. He and his wife Mary had always wanted children of their own, but life hadn't turned out how he'd planned. Instead, Frank had become a surrogate dad and uncle to more young steelworkers than he could recall, taking each one of them to his heart. The thought of any of them getting hurt, or even worse, pained him as if they were his own flesh and blood.

'Anyway,' the tired and weary foreman announced, keen to lighten the mood as he endeavoured to manoeuvre the oldest and dustiest looking wheelchair the three of them had ever seen, 'your chariot awaits.'

No matter how hard he tried to push the odd-looking contraption in a straight line, the huge spoked double front wheels seemed to go in the opposite direction to where he was directing the wooden-seated chair.

Bill laughed, unable to hide his amusement.'Thank the Lord that's not a crane yer operating.'

'Yer not — wrong,' Frank puffed. 'This thing makes old Myrtle feel like a dream to control.'

'I'm not complaining Frank,' Patty added, touched her boss had gone to so much trouble to help her, 'but that has to be the oldest contraption I've ever seen!'

'Well, yer probably not wrong there, duck,' Frank quipped. 'I'm not sure how long it's been in that mucky storeroom but, looking at the state of it, I'd say it's as old as Vickers itself.'

That was saying something, considering the company had been manufacturing steel in Sheffield since the late 1920s but the factory itself had first been erected in the 1860s.

'Well, I'm grateful regardless,' Patty smiled. 'I'm really not sure I could walk home on this flamin' foot. It ain't 'alf giving me some jip.'

'Like I said earlier,' Frank reiterated, a look of concern once again appearing across his slightly wrinkled face, 'don't come back to work until you are right. You'll do yerself more harm than good otherwise.'

'Thanks, Frank,' Patty replied, knowing her boss meant every word, despite the fact it would leave him a much-needed pair of hands down.

'Right, on that note,' Bill said, 'let me get you to the hospital to have you checked out, just to be on the safe side.'

'That sounds like a very good idea,' Frank agreed, sure a doctor's opinions would reassure Bill as well as easing his own weary mind.

'Right then,' he said affectionately, turning his attention to Patty, 'shall we try and get you in this monstrosity?'

'That would be grand,' she said.

'You hold on to the back of the chair,' Bill said,

indicating to Frank. 'I've got this.' And for the second time that day, Bill bent down and swept Patty into his arms in one careful fatherly movement, folding her willowy frame to his chest, and gently placing her into the ancient chair.

'Right, you two,' Frank said, 'get yourselves off — and Bill, don't rush back. We will manage.'

Then turning his attention to Patty, he added, 'And as for you, duck, I don't want you hotfooting it back here before yer fully better.'

'But Frank,' Patty started, already impatient to be back in her crane so she could try and fathom if Archie really did have a soft spot for her, 'I know you need all hands on deck.'

'I do that, lass, but you are no good to me injured. I'd rather have you back fully shipshape than risk you coming back too early and not being fit for the job.'

'Okay,' Patty said, trying to ignore the shooting pains in her ankle, 'but I'll do me best to make sure I'm back as quick as possible.'

With that Bill took control of the clumpy wooden chair. 'Let's get you home,' he said attentively, carefully manoeuvring the old-fashioned contraption towards the office door.

★ ★ ★

A couple of hours later, after Patty had been given the once-over at the Northern General, and had her ankle tightly wrapped in a white bandage, Bill was wheeling her home, the warm early-autumn sun on their faces. 'I dread to imagine yer mom's reaction when she sees you,' Bill sighed. 'She's going to have kittens.'

Despite the couple having vowed to bring their five

271

children up as independently as possible, the pair of them had always been as soft as owt when it came to their kids. They'd hadn't wrapped them in cotton wool as such but had always been there with a heaped serving of love and tenderness when any of them needed a bit of TLC.

'Well, hopefully I don't look quite as pitiful now.' Patty tried to avoid wincing as the clunky wheels violently jolted over the pebbled paving.

Before Bill even had chance to call his wife as they reached 56 Thompson Road, the pristine black door flew open, and Angie was stood on the immaculate white step, with Tom Tom perched on her left hip, looking completely aghast at the sight she faced.

'What in God's name has happened?' she gasped, taking in Patty sat in what looked like some form of Victorian hospital wheelchair.

'Oh, Mom, I'm okay,' her daughter said, 'but I only went and slipped down the chuffin' crane ladder.'

'Flamin' 'eck, luv,' Angie gasped, her naturally protective maternal instinct kicking in. 'Are you badly injured? Is anything broken? Are you in a lot of pain?'

'Pat Pat,' Tom Tom cried at the same time, looking bewildered at the unexpected vision of his beloved big sister.

'No. Not really. Dad took me to the hospital and the doctor said I've sprained my ankle and I'm a bit bruised and battered,' Patty said, grimacing, tears filling her eyes now she was home, 'but it does hurt a right lot.'

'Maybe we should get you inside,' Bill quietly suggested. 'The doctor also said you need to rest up for a few days.' He paused. 'I think it might be more problematic than it's worth to try and lift the wheelchair

272

into the house. 'Do you think, if you lean on me, you can manage to get into the house?'

'I'll give it my best shot,' came her reply.

Moving round to the side of the chair, Bill offered Patty his arm to lean on, but as she tried to stand and put weight on her damaged ankle, another shooting pain coursed through her, causing her whole body to slump.

Just in the nick of time, before Patty was in danger of landing in a heap on the floor, Bill instinctively scooped her up, like he'd done countless times when she was a toddler and threatening to go head over heels.

'I think we better get her laid up on the sofa before she does herself any more damage,' Bill said, looking at his wife, who was alarmed to see her daughter in such a state.

Bill carried his daughter into the impeccably kept front room. Just like most living rooms throughout the city, not a thing was out of place, always kept pristine and only used for best.

On the mantelpiece of the rarely lit open coal fire, on either side of a gold-plated carriage clock, proudly stood a pair of matching black-and-white photos of Angie's and Bill's parents in silver frames. The blue, pink and cream floral wallpaper looked as good as new, despite it being over ten years old.

'That the lord for that,' Patty said with a sigh, easing into the mock Chesterfield couch. 'I can't say that wheelchair was the comfiest thing I've ever sat in. Not that I'm complaining — I just felt every pebble!'

'Right, well,' Bill said, 'I'll let you fill your mom in on what happened, while you get comfy and rest up then, madam. If yer sure you're going to be okay, I really should be getting back. We've got orders coming out of our ears and I don't want to leave the lads all afternoon.'

'I promise I'll be fine.' Patty smiled. 'And Dad . . .'

'Yes, sunshine?'

'Thank you for looking after me. I really didn't mean to give you a scare.'

'All's well that ends well,' Bill said with a nod, once again relieved his precious daughter had escaped with relatively minor injuries.

Angie threw her daughter a quizzical glance but didn't say a word, knowing her conscientious husband wouldn't want to let his team down, and she had no doubt Patty would fill her in on how she'd ended up in such a state.

'In the meantime, get some ice on that ankle and keep it elevated — hopefully it won't be 'alf as sore by the time I get home later. We need you back shipshape — these Spitfires aren't going to make themselves.'

Bending down and planting a kiss on top of his daughter's crown of wild curls, Bill finally conceded nothing was going to keep his headstrong daughter away from Vickers.

26

'Thank you, Mrs Wallis,' Betty said, smiling weakly as she picked up her lunch — wrapped in brown greaseproof paper and tied with string — which her landlady had kindly made every day since she'd stared at Vickers.

'Is everything all right, dear?' Mrs Wallis asked. Betty had barely touched her bowl of home-made porridge and honey for breakfast and it was obvious from how red her eyes were that she'd spent most of the night crying as opposed to sleeping.

'Oh, I'm fine. Just ignore me,' Betty said, shaking her head. 'Nothing a brisk walk and a busy day at the factory won't cure.'

But as her young ward rushed out of the door, grabbing her gas mask and scarf from the hooks by the front door as she left, Mrs Wallis couldn't help but feel an overwhelming sense of concern. She'd never been blessed with children of her own, but she'd come to view Betty as a surrogate daughter, so seeing her so visibly distraught made her heart ache too.

In a world of her own, Betty somehow made her way to Brightside Lane. By the time she got off the tram at Attercliffe, she couldn't actually recall her journey — she had been so engrossed in her own thoughts, trying to work out why she hadn't received a letter from William for a fortnight. It wasn't like him; when he'd first left for Doncaster, his lovely handwritten mail arrived nearly every day.

Has he forgotten about me already? Betty silently fretted.

'Morning!' came Nancy's familiar soft-spoken greeting, breaking Betty from her daze, as the two women joined the queue to clock in, but there was no denying it felt odd without the incessant chatter from their youngest colleague.

'Have you had any updates on Patty?' Betty asked, more wearily than normal.

'I have actually,' Nancy replied. 'I walked to work with Bill and he said they looked her over at Northern General and there was nothing broken, but she's suffered a nasty sprain and will need a couple of weeks of complete rest before she can come back to work.'

'Oh, the poor love,' Betty said, 'but thank God she's okay. It could have been much worse if she had been any higher up that ladder.'

'You're right, the consequences don't bear thinking about. But on the bright side, I don't think she's the only one to have had a trip. I reckon from the state Archie was in after the fall, he has well and truly fallen head over heels for our Patty.'

'Yes,' Betty grinned. 'Well, that alone will have her racing back to work as soon as she can. The only reason she started at Vickers was to find the man of her dreams.'

'There is that, but I bet she didn't expect to literally fall for someone!'

'No, I'm sure,' Betty answered, but her cheery tone was now replaced with a disheartened tone, telling Nancy something wasn't quite right.

'Has something happened?' she asked.

'Oh, it's nothing,' Betty said, shaking her head.

'Yer going to have to do better than that!' Nancy replied, raising her eyebrows. 'Penny for them.'

'I'm probably just being daft, but I've not heard from William for a couple of weeks. It's not like him.'

'Oh, luv — ' Nancy sighed, taking her workmate's arm, knowing how much it would upset her too if Bert's letters didn't arrive as regularly as they did '— he's probably just that busy with all his training that he hasn't had a minute to himself. And the mail can be so unreliable — you know what it's like.'

'I hope it's that,' Betty started, 'I'm just worried that his new life is such a big, exciting adventure that I might become a distant memory.'

'Now, listen up,' Nancy said firmly, stopping and pulling a tearful-looking Betty round to face her, 'you are letting yer imagination run away with itself. From what you have told me, your William is a very loyal fella and utterly in love with you. Take it from me, he's not going to just forget about you. If anything, it will be the thought of seeing you again that's keeping him going and getting him through each day.'

'Do you think?' Betty asked, shocked at her own self-doubt. She was normally so strong and independent, refusing to rely on others. But she had played William's months of excitement over and over in her head; in fact it had kept her awake until the early hours the last few nights. He'd been so looking forward to soaring off into the skies in the months leading up to the outbreak of war — maybe he had now fulfilled his biggest dream and found he didn't need her any more.

'Yes I am,' Nancy replied authoritatively. 'You've got yer-self in a tickle and putting two and two together and getting seven. I can guarantee William is just so exhausted and is being pushed to the limit with his training that, by the end of the day, all he can do is collapse into bed. Flaming Hitler is causing havoc and they need as many pilots as possible to put a stop to his godforsaken antics.'

It was true the power-hungry German dictator, who had now formed an allied relationship with the Soviet Union, had all but annihilated Poland, reducing the city of Warsaw to streets of rubble, despite his promise not to engage in indiscriminate attacks.

'Thanks, Nancy. I'm sure you are probably right. I just can't help but worry that the one man I really love will just forget about me.'

'I know I'm right,' Nancy added, giving Betty's trembling hand a little squeeze.

'It's not all bad though,' Betty told her. 'Last night when I couldn't sleep, I came up with an idea to help Patty.'

'That sounds intriguing,' Nancy said, as they started walking towards their respective cranes. 'Why don't you tell me over a cuppa and a sandwich at dinnertime?'

Betty nodded. 'That sounds like a plan.'

'Now you get on this morning and keep yer chin up. I don't want you worrying yerself sick while yer up that crane by yerself. We can't have you hurting yerself too. It's bad enough there's only two of us today, I definitely don't want to be here without one of you girls by my side.'

Secretly, though, Nancy wished she was now operating Mildred alone. She wasn't sure how much more she could take from Harry. His incessant snide and sexist remarks were really beginning to wear her down.

'Don't you worry. I promise I'm not going anywhere in a hurry,' Betty vowed, as they approached Myrtle.

'Well, that's good to hear,' Nancy replied as she gave Betty a quick wave goodbye and headed over to Mildred where Harry was waiting at the foot of the ladder.

'Do yer reckon yer up to shifting a few slabs of steel today?' he asked with an arrogant smirk on his face.

'I think I can manage that,' Nancy snapped.

'I'll be the judge of that,' Harry snarled, turning his back on Nancy as he raced up the ladder two rungs at a time.

'Here we go again,' Nancy muttered to herself, not sure whether she was going to burst into tears or finally give her cocksure workmate a piece of her mind.

'Are you all right, duck?' Frank said, as he paced across the factory floor. 'You look as though you've got the world on your shoulders.'

'Oh, sorry. I just didn't get much sleep. The kids had me up in the night,' Nancy lied, determined to try and get through this battle without having to run to her boss and tell tales.

Frank smiled. 'Well, you just take it steady up there today. I don't want another of my three musketeers injured — one is bad enough.'

'I will,' Nancy said, cautiously heading up the ladder after Harry.

The morning passed as she'd expected, with Harry barking condescending instructions at her, over-exaggerating his more than audible sighs and grunts of horror every time Nancy manned the controls, despite her near-perfect precision.

She was sure she wasn't making any mistakes but

Harry seemed to be taking great pleasure in knocking her confidence with his continual narky quips of 'keep it under control' or 'go lighter on the swing — you'll have some poor lad's head off'.

By the time midday came, Nancy was at her wits' end and couldn't wait to get as far away as possible from Harry. As soon as the hooter sounded, she didn't even glance sideways at him as she climbed out of her cab as fast as possible and descended to the factory floor.

Five minutes later, she and Betty were stood in their normal lunchtime spot, but it felt strange to be unwrapping their sandwiches without their youngest partner in crime beside them.

'Dare I ask how Harry's been this morning?' Betty asked, pouring herself a cup of steaming tea from her flask.

'Oh, the same as ever,' Nancy sighed, utterly exhausted by his constant insults. 'He just can't help himself.'

'Are you sure I can't persuade you to talk to Frank? He's ever so kind and very fair. I'm sure he would sort it out for you,' Betty asked.

'No. Although I don't particularly feel it, I'm a big girl. I need to handle this myself. I'll think of something. I just wish Bert was here — he would know exactly what to do.'

Betty could relate to that — she was missing her William more than ever and would feel so much better if she just received a letter from him.

'Anyway,' Nancy said, breaking the low mood that had descended upon the pair like a heavy black cloud, 'what's this great plan you have?'

'Well,' Betty said, her downturned lips now curling

upwards, 'I do have an idea and would love to hear what you think.'

'Come on then, let's hear it,' Nancy prompted, taking a bite of her very thinly sliced beef sandwich — courtesy of a leftover roast dinner Doris had made at the weekend.

'Do you think a Care Club might work?' Betty asked.

'Ooh tell me more,' Nancy said, intrigued.

'I just thought with Patty being off sick now she won't earn any money, but if we had a whip-round and asked if people would be willing to donate a penny or two each, it might all add up. What do you reckon?'

Nancy grinned. 'That's a brilliant idea, luv; you are so clever for thinking of this, as well as very kind. It really is a lovely plan.'

'Would you help me?' Betty asked. 'I'm not really sure how to go about setting it up. I was going to check with Frank that he doesn't mind and get his thoughts too.'

'I bet he will be delighted,' Nancy replied. 'He seems such a kind soul. And I will happily donate the first penny for our Patty,' she added, digging her hand into her bag and pulling out her little square-shaped black leather purse. 'If I can't spare a penny or two, then life really isn't worth living.' As she handed over a couple of coins, she and her workmate swapped excited smiles. 'This could be the start of something really rather wonderful,' she said. 'Times are tough and I have no doubt they are going to get a whole lot harder before they get better, but your little plan could give us all something to focus on and bring a bit of cheer.'

'That was exactly my thinking,' Betty said. 'I'm so

glad you agree. I was a bit worried you would think I was being a bit daft.'

'Not at all,' Nancy said, shaking her head. 'Quite the opposite — I think it's rather splendid. If there is one thing I've learnt over the past month or so, it's that there are some really good people in the world. Look at my neighbour, Doris. I wouldn't be able to do this job without her, and she's now cooking most of my evening meals. She's an absolute treasure.'

'I know what you mean,' Betty agreed. 'Mrs Wallis has been a real gem too. Not only does she make my pack up every morning, but I've noticed my evening meals are getting bigger. She keeps telling me I'm going to waste away — more like I'm going to put on half a stone at this rate.'

Nancy laughed. 'I don't think there's much fear of that; there's not a pick on you. Right, shall we head back a few minutes early and see if we can catch Frank to tell him about your idea?'

'Well, I suppose there's no time like the present,' Betty said excitedly, secretly in her element, always at her best when she had a project of one description or another on the go.

A few minutes later Betty was repeating her plans for a 'Care Club' to Frank, whose kind eyes lit up as he listened to his most skilled female crane driver.

'What a good 'un you are, duck,' he said, as she set out her plan. 'I think that's a smashing idea. I'll start spreading the word amongst the other foremen straight away and I'm sure the canteen will have an old tin we can use for a whip-round.'

'Aw, thank you, Frank,' Betty said, smiling. 'I'll make a couple of posters at home tonight if you would be happy to stick them up around the factory.'

'It would be my pleasure. And I bet our Patty won't be the only one in need before this blasted war is out. There's always someone in need, whether times have fallen hard or they've had an accident. It would be nice to start a little pot of help for them,' Frank added. 'Some of them don't have a penny to their name. They will have to tip up all their wages to their mom just so they can make ends meet and keep the tallyman from the door.'

'Oh, thank you, Frank,' Betty added. 'I wasn't sure if you would go for it or not.'

'Don't be daft, duck.' The burly foreman's face reflected his kind-hearted nature. 'Anything that helps during these hard times will get my support; you'll get no arguments from me on that score, that's for sure.'

'I told you,' Nancy said, delighted for her pal, hoping it would give her something to stop her worrying about William — although she knew only too well how hard it was to stop your mind wandering when your loved one was away. Barely a minute passed without Bert taking over her thoughts as she constantly prayed he would be okay, wherever he was.

'Well, I'm grateful nonetheless,' Betty said. 'Right. I'd better get back to work before you change your mind,' she added, throwing Frank a big grin. For the rest of the afternoon, in between shifting slabs of steel and waiting for orders from below, she whiled away the hours thinking about how to make a success of the Care Club. Like Frank said, there were bound to be families in real hardship — it would be good to build up a reserve for anyone that was really struggling. As well as an occasional whip-round, they could maybe start knitting for families who could do with some extra clothing, or baking the odd loaf of bread if rations allowed. Betty's mind was a whirl of ideas and, before she knew it, the end-of-shift hooter echoed through the factory, indicating the end of another day.

As Betty carefully made her way down the ladder, she couldn't help but feel grateful. Ever since her sister Margaret had moved to Nottingham, she had missed her immensely, but now she had found a new sisterhood with her fellow workers at Vickers. In the past she had always looked to her big sister for help and support and she'd been worried how she would cope after Margaret left, but it was quickly becoming apparent to Betty she was surrounded by a whole group of people who she could draw strength from.

I really am very lucky, she thought to herself.

Once on the ground, Betty spotted Frank waiting for her out of the corner of her eye, a smile as big as the moon on his face.

'You really do look like the cat who's had the cream,' she said, wiping away the clumps of dust that had settled on her cheeks and were making her eyes water.

'I have a surprise for you,' Frank said, grinning. If Betty hadn't have known better, she would have thought all his Christmases had come at once!

'What is it?' she asked, enjoying seeing Frank looking so excited. He was normally rushing about, checking his shop was in order and always worrying about someone.

'Look,' he said, rattling the tin that had once contained fruits in syrup but now was clanging with the sharp tinny sound of metal against metal.

'Really?' Betty gasped. 'Already?'

'I've not counted it up yet, but I reckon there must a be a couple of quid in here, and I only passed it round a couple of shop floors. We're off to a smashing start.'

'Wow. That's incredible,' Betty exclaimed. 'I didn't think for a minute we would get that much so quickly.'

'Let's give it a couple of days and see if we get any more, then maybe you and Nancy can take it to Patty,' Frank suggested.

'Oh, that would be lovely,' Betty said, stunned by the generosity of Vickers' workers, most of whom wouldn't have had much, if any, spare cash at the end of the week. 'I'm sure it will be a great help to Patty's family. Her mom certainly has enough mouths to feed without losing Patty's wages. I can't imagine they have a secret hoard under the mattress.'

'I suspect you're right, duck, but you might need to tread carefully. I know Bill and Angie are a proud pair. They might see this as charity and be too embarrassed to take it.'

'Oh, of course,' Betty mused. 'I was so hell-bent on doing something useful, I didn't think of that. I remember my dad being the same after my mum died. He didn't want anyone to think he couldn't cope. Let me have a think and see if I can come up with something. The last thing I would want to do is cause any offence.'

'Okay, duck,' Frank said with a nod. 'I know you'll do the right thing. I have every faith in you.'

'Thanks, Frank. I really mean it,' Betty said, putting her hand on the foreman's thickset muscular arm. 'Not only are you constantly looking out for us all, I feel so touched you have helped me with this too. It's good to know people can be so kind.'

'Ay, they're a good bunch,' Frank replied. 'I wouldn't want to work or live anywhere else.'

And for the first time Betty started to think the same. For so long, she had dreamt of becoming a solicitor, to work for a well-respected legal firm and make her mark in life, but despite only being at Vickers for a fortnight, she'd realized she didn't have to wear a suit or be surrounded by legal bundles in a big fancy office to do some good in the world.

'Do you know, Frank,' she mused, 'I'm beginning to think exactly the same.'

All she needed now was to hear from her William and know he still loved her as much as she loved him, and then — despite this awful war and Hitler's best efforts to tear the country apart — life would feel pretty good.

27

Friday, 6 October 1939

Her cloth bag containing her lunch and flask of tea in one hand and her boxed-up gas mask in the other, Betty trundled up Brightside Lane and into Vickers where she knew Nancy would be waiting for her by the clocking-in machine.

Right on cue, as she got in line — which now seemed to be filling up with an increasing number of women and teenage girls — she heard her workmate's cheery greeting.

Seeing a smile emerge on her friend's face, Nancy added: 'You seem a lot brighter this morning.'

'I am,' Betty said.

'Did you get a letter from William?' Nancy asked hopefully.

'Still no word,' Betty sighed. 'As much I would do anything to hear from him, I'm trying not to fret and mope about, so I'm determined to throw myself into the Care Club.

'I've been thinking about what Frank said to me too, about how Patty's family might think we are offering them charity. Do you think they might feel slightly less upset if we bought them some food instead? It might not be such a dent to their pride that way?'

'That's a really lovely, and I'm sure very wise, idea,' Nancy said, pleased to see Betty looking back to her normal self.

'Well, I can't cry into my pillow every night,' Betty

287

said. 'Besides which, I need my energy to get me through a day in the crane.'

'That's the spirit,' Nancy replied. 'I'm sure William will be in touch soon enough, and you're doing a really good thing for Patty and others to take your mind off it.'

'Betty here is just thinking of buying food and a few essentials with the money from Care Club,' Nancy announced proudly.

'Folks round here don't take charity too kindly, but that sounds lovely. Well, anything you need, just give me a yell,' Frank said, delighted to see how the women were rallying around to support one another. There had always been a strong camaraderie in the factory but his new recruits were certainly injecting a warmer touch, especially when it came to helping those in need.

'Oh, Frank,' Betty cheered, 'you are a true diamond.'

'I've also made these,' Betty said excitedly as she pulled half a dozen letter-sized sheets of card out of her bag, with 'Care Club' penned across them in bright-red block capitals.

Just below, in slightly smaller dark-blue letters, Betty had written:

NEW CLUB STARTING.
SPARE A PENNY IF YOU CAN FOR
THOSE IN NEED.
SEE CRANE DRIVER BETTY CLARK FOR
MORE DETAILS.

'What do you think?' she asked.

'It's wonderful,' Nancy said, beaming. 'You have

done a marvellous job.'

'I can't take all the credit,' Betty replied. 'I roped Mrs Wallis in, too. She was delighted to be able to help.'

'Well, I think you are really on to something here, duck,' Frank chipped in. 'Now, I don't mean to rush you, but the gaffer will have it in for me if you aren't on those cranes soon. But I'll take these off your hands,' he said, taking the posters.

'Oh, that's ever so kind, Frank. Are you sure you don't mind?' Betty checked.

'No bother, I'll do it. It makes sense, I know where the busiest spots are. But you may need to make a few more. It's a big place and we are taking on more women by the day.'

Betty smiled. 'You really are the best.'

But as the two women walked towards their cranes, she noticed Nancy's cheery demeanour quickly vanished and she once again looked as though she had the world on her shoulders.

'Oh, gosh, I'm sorry,' Betty said. 'Here's me harping on about the Care Club and I haven't even asked how you are. Has something happened?'

'No, it's nothing like that,' Nancy replied. 'The kids are fine. They've settled into a good routine now, thanks to Doris. It's the thought of spending yet another day with flaming Harry that's filling me with dread. His attitude is really wearing me down. I know you think I should speak to Frank, but I just want to find a way of dealing with it myself but, if the truth be told, I'm really at my wits' end. I've started to dread coming to work every day.'

'Oh, Nancy,' Betty lamented. 'You can't carry on like this. Life is hard enough without Harry making it a million times worse. Have you tried being firm with him and letting him know you won't tolerate any more of his nonsense?'

Nancy wished she had an ounce of Betty's fiery and determined spirit, but she wasn't actually sure it would make a scrap of difference with the likes of Harry. 'I think he would just laugh at me,' she said, taking a deep breath. 'He seems to have absolutely no respect for women at all. I've never met anyone as arrogant. He has such a high opinion of himself and doesn't seem to give a flying monkey about what I think.'

'Oh, he really is a joy, isn't he?' Betty fumed, furious about how appallingly Harry was treating her new lovely and kind friend.

'You could say that,' Nancy muttered, wishing the day away before it had even started.

'Try and stay strong,' Betty said, tenderly rubbing Nancy's arm. 'Get through to dinnertime and we can at least have a cuppa and recharge for the afternoon.'

'Thanks, luv, I'll do my best,' came Nancy's somewhat despondent reply as she headed towards Mildred.

Less than ten minutes later she was safely encased in her crane cab, positioned next to Harry, who as always had a face like thunder. Judging by the stench of stale beer oozing from him, Nancy suspected he'd spent the night before in his local boozer and was now nursing a steaming hangover.

'Looks like we have a heavy day so I hope you're feeling up for it,' Harry barked.

I don't think it's me you need to worry about, Nancy fumed to herself, but she refused to give him the satisfaction of a reply.

The first orders from below were bellowed up.

'Over to the furnace,' came Frank's instruction.

'I better take this,' Harry grunted. 'Looks like a heavy load.'

Turning her head to look at the slab of steel, Nancy rolled her eyes, confident she was more than capable of doing what was needed.

Don't bite, she thought.

But as she watched Harry take to the controls, it was obvious it was him who wasn't up to the job. His hands were visibly shaking, and he didn't seem to be moving as swiftly as needed.

'Get a move on,' Frank hollered up. 'There's a backlog that needs shifting today.'

'You know what these women are like — they're just not on the ball,' Harry yelled back, throwing Nancy his usual arrogant smirk, which doubled up as a warning not to say a word unless she wanted her day to get even worse.

Deep breaths, she told herself, and count to ten. He will get his comeuppance soon enough.

Eventually, after what felt like an eternity, Harry managed to manoeuvre the heavy slab of metal to the waiting workers below.

Half an hour passed in what felt like deadly silence, despite the deafening noise reverberating around the factory. Nancy nervously picked at the cuticles around her fingernails, which were now red raw, with specks of crimson-red blood rising to the surface as she subconsciously scratched away at her broken skin.

'Next lift,' came Frank's command, instantly snapping Nancy out of her anxious bubble.

As she looked down at the white-hot furnace, she could see the now heated piece of steel was ready to be moved so it could be worked on by the turners in the adjoining warehouse.

She knew there was no point asking her antagonistic but clearly flagging workmate if he wanted her to do it, knowing she would be met by another of his condescending comments.

Sure enough, he took charge of the crane handles without giving Nancy a second glance.

Instead she kept her eyes on the scene below as Harry dropped the enormous crane hook into position for it to be attached to the dangerously hot piece of waiting steel. By the impatient look on the faces of the workers below, she knew it was taking Harry longer than normal to do what was needed.

No doubt I'll get the blame for that too, she thought.

As soon as the steel was loaded on, Frank lifted both his arms, palms facing upwards, in his typical gesture, indicating that it was ready to be moved.

But instead of lifting the hook directly upwards, suddenly the whole contraption, including the now roasting slab of metal, started swinging from left to right.

'Watch out,' came a piercing holler from a worker, who miraculously managed to dive out of the way just in the nick of time, saving himself from being taken out by the perilously hot cargo.

The next few seconds seemed to happen in slow motion as the group of men who had been manning the furnace ducked and scarpered across the factory floor to avoid being struck by the boiling steel or even worse.

'What in God's name is going on?' Frank yelled, an unmistakable mixture of anger and terror echoing through his voice.

Stunned, Nancy looked to Harry, all the colour

drained from his face, his cheeks now grey and ashen.

Speechless, he fumbled with the solid metal controls as he stared down in shock at the almighty havoc he had caused.

As quick as the chaos had erupted it was over, as Harry somehow managed to bring the now steady hook and load under control and deliver it to its intended destination.

But the shockwaves that were now crystal clear below were far from over.

'Harry,' Frank shouted up to the cab, 'what the chuffin' hell happened there? Someone could 'av been killed.'

White as a ghost but obviously thinking fast, his conniving brain ticking over, Harry glared at Nancy, his sly eyes bestowing a sinister warning.

'Sorry, gaffer,' he called down, an unbelievable calmness in his apology, 'I warned her to take it steady, but she got a bit carried away.'

'What?' Nancy gasped, utterly stunned by his inconceivable lies. 'You can't blame me for that!'

'Who's going to stop me?' He shrugged, not in the least bit bothered by the impact of his deceitful actions. 'Just be glad that hook didn't kill anyone, otherwise you would be in real trouble.'

'No!' Nancy stormed, something finally snapping inside her, her tolerance breaking. Maybe the fact she had taken control when Patty had fallen had given her the confidence to stand up to Harry and his chauvinistic and arrogant ways. 'I am not taking the blame for your irresponsible actions.'

'What are yer going to do about it?' he crowed, with a playground bully-like demeanour, convinced his softly spoken female co-worker wouldn't have the courage to stand up to him.

'Watch me,' came Nancy's fierce reply, and with that she lifted herself out of the cramped cab and hauled herself down the crane ladder quicker than she could say her name.

Stunned by her response, Harry was hot on her heels, determined Nancy didn't land him in it. He'd been given his fair share of warnings over the years from Frank, and today of all days he wasn't in the mood for a bloody great rollicking.

But just as his inept actions behind the crane controls had revealed, the skinful of beer Harry had indulged in the night before had left him the worse for wear. He stumbled as opposed to climbed down to the factory floor in time to hear Frank demand: 'What on earth happened up there?'

Despite his flustered appearance and ruddy cheeks, Harry was still convinced he would be able to salvage his own reputation.

'I've been trying to tell Nancy she needs to be more careful,' he said, the despicable lies naturally rolling off his tongue. 'What with Patty and now this, I really don't think women are up to the job.'

'How dare you!' Nancy lambasted, the anger and frustration she had been feeling for weeks finally erupting. 'You know only too well that you were manning the controls, and maybe if you hadn't drank enough to sink a ship last night, you wouldn't have nearly killed someone.'

For a split second nobody said a word, the shock of the normally timid and reserved Nancy exploding with fury leaving them frozen to the spot.

Momentarily stupefied, Harry's mouth dropped open as he gawped at his workmate, horrified she'd had the guts to drop him in it.

'Is this true?' Frank quizzed, breaking the silence, his eyes revealing his annoyance.

'I might have had a couple but, as I say, it was her who couldn't manage the job in hand,' he spat venomously.

'That is an out-and-out lie,' Nancy responded. 'You and I both know the chance would be a fine thing.'

She turned to a very flustered-looking Frank. Her voice now threatening to break, exhausted by how she had been treated, she added: 'Harry has barely let me near the controls since I started, taking great pleasure in telling me repeatedly, as a woman, I wasn't capable. I've endured one insult after another and only been allowed to do the simplest of tasks.'

'It's true,' came Betty's voice. She had witnessed the near miss and the commotion that had followed and come to her friend's aid. 'I've been pleading with Nancy to tell you how appallingly Harry has been treating her, but she refused, not wanting to cause any trouble. Harry has made her life a living hell.'

Blood rising to his cheeks, Frank clenched his fists, trying to contain the surge of disgust that now flooded through him.

'Harry,' he bellowed, despite the fact the now worried-looking steelworker was stood less than a metre away. 'I have just about had enough of your cocky attitude. I have given you more warnings than I've had hot dinners. Now I want no more lies. I have no doubt, by the bedraggled state of you today and the fact you reek of beer, who is telling the truth here. Go to my office; I will deal with you in a minute.'

Furiously glaring at a shell-shocked Nancy, who was now visibly shaking, he stormed past the two women, shooting Betty a filthy look as he went, and marched towards the end of the factory floor.

As soon as he was out of earshot, Frank gently put his arm around Nancy's shoulders.

'You should have told me sooner, duck,' he said, his voice now calm and tender. 'I promised you all I would look after you, and I meant it.'

'I'm sorry, Frank,' Nancy said. 'I thought I could sort it myself. I never for one second thought he would be selfish enough to put someone's life at risk. If I had, I promise I would have said something sooner. I really am sorry.'

'Now, you listen up, duck,' Frank started, 'you have absolutely nothing to apologize for. Harry is lucky he hasn't had his marching orders. He was told in no uncertain terms to look after you, not to alienate you. This flaming war means we can't afford to lose a pair of hands, but I assure you, Nancy, you won't have to work with him ever again.'

At that very moment, a cheery-looking Archie walked past, his normal happy-go-lucky smile once again etched across his kind face, knowing Patty was on the mend, even if she wasn't his girl.

'Aha, just the fella I'm looking for,' Frank said, beckoning him over. 'It would appear you are the only decent male crane driver I have right now.'

'Really?' Archie asked, slightly bemused by the unexpected compliment.

'Yes,' Frank said, reaffirming his point. 'So, I need you to take Nancy under your wing until Patty is back and show her the ropes.'

'Of course, boss,' Archie replied. 'But where's Harry gone?'

'Let's just say he won't be stepping foot in this

warehouse ever again. So, I need you to get Nancy up to speed so she too can go solo in the next couple of weeks. Our workload is getting bigger by the day, thanks to chuffin' Hitler, and we are being spread far and wide.'

'Not a problem,' Archie answered. 'When would you like me to start?'

'Well, I'm giving Nancy and Betty a well-earned half an hour tea break so they can grab a cuppa and Nancy can settle herself, but after that there's no time like the present.'

'Got it, boss,' Archie said, grinning. Turning to face a now settled-looking Nancy, he added: 'Come and find me over at Marlene when yer ready, and we can get going.'

'Thank you,' Nancy said, a massive weight finally lifted from her shoulders.

After Nancy had supped a sweetened mug of Brooke Bond tea with Betty in their normal courtyard watering hole, the early-autumn sun warming their faces, the two women headed back into the factory, a huge weight lifted from Nancy's shoulders.

★   ★   ★

That afternoon, Archie proved himself to be an able teacher, patiently directing Nancy while constantly complimenting her attention to detail, as she carefully manoeuvred great hunks of steel across the yard, never once over-swinging the hook or dropping the potentially fatal loads.

'Yer a natural,' the young amenable steelworker said at the end of their shift as they made their way down to the factory floor. 'Yer won't need me by yer side for much longer.'

'That's very kind,' Nancy said. 'You have been so kind and patient. It certainly makes the world of difference and I have learnt so much quicker and feel far more confident now I haven't got Harry barking at me all the time. Now tell me, have you thought about popping in on Patty?'

With that Archie's normally vibrant smile was replaced by a frown.

'I'd love nothing more, but I thought she'd be too busy with Tommy Hardcastle looking after her.'

Nancy didn't know whether to hug the poor lad or shake him.

'Oh, Archie. You've got it all mixed up, luv. Patty isn't stepping out with Tommy. That ship has well and truly sailed, but I'd bet my last shilling she would love nothing more than a visit from you.'

'Really?' he asked, the twinkle in his bright-blue eyes appearing. 'I was sure she and Tommy had become an item after him asking her to go to the dance.'

'Let's just say Patty saw that deceiving little toerag for what he really is.'

Overhearing the back end of their conversation, Betty, who had come to see how Nancy's afternoon had been, interjected, 'Ooh, do you think she is up for another visitor? Now we've had a bit of a whip-round, I wanted to pop in and deliver Patty and her family a little surprise.'

'I'm sure she would love to see you,' Nancy replied. 'Bill was only telling me this morning, as we walked to work, that she's missing us all.'

'Typical Patty. One minute, threatening to leave, and the next can't get enough of us.' Betty laughed. 'Well, I'll nip to the butcher's and greengrocer's on

298

Saturday afternoon after I've finished here and get a food parcel put together, and take it over to Patty's house.'

'Maybe you should pop in too?' Nancy added, turning to Archie, who looked as though a weight had been lifted from his shoulders.

'Do you really think Patty would want me to?' he asked, his self-confidence battling against him once more.

'Yes!' Nancy and Betty replied in unison.

'Okay, if you're sure.' Archie smiled, a burst of colour flushing his cheeks.

Betty and Nancy threw each other a knowing smile but didn't say a word, not wanting to cause Archie any more blushes.

Instead they bade the lovesick crane driver goodnight and the two women, gas masks in one hand and their handbags in the other, made their way out of the factory.

'Can you imagine if Archie turns up to see Patty on Saturday too?' Betty said as they exited the big heavy doors onto Brightside Lane.

'I can see her eyes lighting up now,' Nancy said, laughing as she envisaged their youngest workmate coming face to face with Archie again. 'They are clearly both smitten with one another.'

'They certainly are,' Betty agreed. A few seconds later, the two women hugged goodbye as they prepared to head home in opposite directions. 'It's good to see you looking happy,' she said, as they parted.

'Thanks, luv,' Nancy replied. 'I must admit, Vickers feels a lot less daunting without Harry to deal with.'

And as she made her way back to back to Prince

Street, for the first time since she'd been moved onto the main factory floor, things seemed to settling into a good routine.

28

After what felt like a rollercoaster of a couple of weeks, the hooter finally signalled the last shift of the week. Despite how calm the last couple of days had been, Betty and Nancy didn't need to be told twice to climb down from their crane cabs. Both were in need of a relaxing weekend and an early night.

'Are you two ladies off to see Patty now?' Frank asked, as he walked across the busy factory floor towards the women, who were simultaneously pulling on their jackets to protect themselves against the early October weather, which had brought with it a sharp chill.

'We are indeed,' Betty said.

'Well, please do give her my love,' Frank added. 'And tell her not to rush back until she is right as rain. I'd love to come with you, but I need to put in an extra few hours here, sorting out the orders for next week.'

'Oh, don't worry, Patty will understand,' Betty said, fighting back her pang of jealousy that she didn't have much else to keep her busy. She couldn't even face writing William yet another letter considering he hadn't sent her a single note in weeks. It didn't seem like two minutes ago since they were counting down the minutes until they saw one another for a late-afternoon stroll around the park or a trip to the Empire on a Saturday night. But all of a sudden she was

301

questioning whether the man she was sure she would spend the rest of her life with even remembered who she was. She'd spent too many nights awake fretting, and every day when she returned home after her shift, she always had to fight back the tears when Mrs Wallis announced there had been no post again before she dished out a hot dinner and told Betty she needed to keep her strength up.

'Besides which,' Betty added, 'according to Bill, it sounds like she will be back soon, and you can catch up with her then.'

'Well, please tell her not to come back before she's shipshape. I don't want her having another accident,' Frank replied. 'And while yer at it, try and find out how she really feels about our Archie. I'm not sure what else I can do to persuade him, on the basis of how she looked at him after her fall, that she definitely has a soft spot for him.'

'Oh, I'm sure I won't get any choice,' Betty replied. 'I can't imagine for a minute Patty will want to keep her feelings for Archie a secret!'

'No, knowing Patty, she'll be bending our ears all afternoon wanting to know if he's uttered her name while she's been away.' Nancy grinned, knowing her young workmate's biggest wish in the world was to be swept off her feet by a dashing knight in shining armour, and she had a feeling it wouldn't be long before her dream came true. From Archie's devastated reaction after Patty had gone crashing to the floor, you would have to be as blind as a bat not to notice how smitten he was with the youngest of the three crane drivers.

Betty and Nancy made their way down Thompson Road, each of them carefully balancing a huge and heavier than expected cardboard box in their arms. Breathing a sigh of relief, they finally reached number 56, with its immaculate white doorstep that had been scrubbed to within an inch of its life.

Carefully placing one of the precious bundles of goodies on the floor, Betty went to knock on the equally spotless black front door, but before her hand reached the brass knocker, it swung open.

'Betty. Nancy!' Patty squealed excitedly, holding on to a walking stick with one hand and the door handle with the other. 'It's so lovely to see you both,' she said, her voice rising another octave. 'I've missed you so much. How are you both? I'm so happy to see you. Please come in. Oh, and what's this?' she asked, finally stopping to draw breath.

'Give them chance to get a word in edgeways,' came Angie's voice as she bustled down the hallway after her giddy daughter. She smiled at a bemused Betty and Nancy. 'It's lovely to meet you both. As you can imagine, our Patty here has told me all about you. Now, why don't you come in and I'll make you each a cuppa? You look parched.'

'Well, as long as it isn't putting you out, Mrs Andrews, I wouldn't say no,' Betty accepted gratefully.

'Call me Ang or Angie at the very least, please. Mrs Andrews makes me sound far too old.'

'Okay,' Betty said, bending down to pick up the heavy box of groceries.

'What's that, luv?' Angie asked, suspiciously eyeing up the huge collection of food.

'It's just a little something,' Betty replied, starting to worry she may have made a mistake. 'I can explain.'

'Okay, well leave them there,' said Angie tentatively,

who was wearing her usual floral apron with a white trim, which wore the marks of many a Sunday dinner. 'Bill will lift it in just a minute, duck. And you too, Nancy. Come on in and I'll get the kettle on.'

'I really can't stay long,' Nancy said politely. 'I've left my kids with my neighbour, so I'll just have a quick cuppa if that's all right and get myself off.'

'Of course, luv, that's okay. But I really would like to thank you for what you did for our Patty, rushing to her side like that after the accident.' Angie smiled. 'The very least I can do is make you a hot cuppa.'

'That would be lovely,' Nancy said, nodding. 'I'll never turn down a good cuppa.'

Right on cue, Patty's dad, who had now changed out of his mucky khaki-brown Vickers overalls into a pair of navy slacks and a light-grey knitted pullover, appeared behind his wife.

'Hello, you two,' he said, beaming. 'To what do we owe this pleasure?'

'They've come to see me, of course,' Patty chirped up to a chorus of laughter from everyone.

'Right, let them in,' Angie insisted. 'The poor things haven't even got through the front door yet.'

Ten minutes later, Betty and Nancy were finally seated at the family kitchen table, a cup of tea in Angie's best china in front of them, accompanied by a home-made shortbread biscuit, with Tom Tom clambering at Nancy's legs, eager to see what treats may be on offer.

'Oh, don't mind him,' Angie said. 'He's like a bottomless pit. I've never known a child to eat as much.'

Nancy laughed. 'I bet my Billie could give him a run for his money. I'm sure he's got hollow legs.'

'They must have,' Angie agreed. 'I have no idea

304

where they put it all. Now, are you going to tell me what these two parcels of food are all about?'

Secretly praying she had made the right decision, Betty explained how there had been a bit of a whip-round at the factory after Patty's fall, knowing she wouldn't be able to bring a wage home.

'Oh, luv, that's very kind of you and all, but we don't need charity,' Angie interrupted, trying her hardest not to sound harsh, but her fierce Yorkshire pride taking over.

Her normally milky porcelain cheeks instantly reddening, Betty looked from Angie to Bill. 'We didn't mean to insult you,' she said, all too aware that Angie's response replicated exactly how her own dad would have reacted.

'It was done with the best intentions,' Nancy added, knowing she would have reacted in the same manner.

'I came up with this idea to start a Care Club to help anyone who needed a little extra support and it all stemmed from there,' Betty explained, trying to justify her good intentions. 'I didn't want to offend you by offering you money but would really like to offer you some bits to help out. Patty has only been at Vickers a short time, but it would appear she has already made a big impression, and after her accident people just wanted to do something to help.'

Angie turned to her husband, her pink lips straightening and her brow furrowing, deep worry lines appearing. 'Did you know about this?'

'I'd heard a rumour,' he confessed, knowing how proud his wife was, 'but didn't know the details.'

Turning to Betty and seeing how anxious she now looked, he added: 'We shouldn't knock Betty's kindness, luv. She's done it with a good heart, and aren't you always the first to give away our last bowl of sugar?'

'It really was done for the right reasons,' Nancy reiterated, her soft voice reflecting the goodness of all those who had wanted to help.

A wistful look came across Angie's gentle face. 'I'm sorry,' she started, 'I didn't mean to sound so rude and ungrateful. I just didn't expect it but what you've done is incredibly thoughtful. Now, why don't you tell me what mountain of goodies you have so kindly delivered?'

Relief soared through Betty, and, her cheeks gradually returning to their normal shade, she took a deep breath. 'Well,' she started, 'the collection came to over a week's wages so Nancy and I nipped to the butcher's on Station Road and then to the greengrocer's next door and asked them what would be most useful to feed a family of seven.'

Angie brought her prematurely aged hand — weathered by hours of scrubbing her doorsteps and mountains of weekly washing — to her eye, and quickly wiped away the couple of watery tears that had appeared, before looking into the box.

'Well, it looks like we're in for a feast fit for a king this week,' Angie said gratefully, her voice revealing how touched she was. Inside lay a dozen of the best pork sausages, a generous portion of beef, a pound of back bacon, a tray of eggs and enough fruit and vegetables, including three huge blood oranges, to keep even the hungriest of families satisfied.

'Apple,' Tom Tom called, never one to miss out on the opportunity to get his hands on something to keep his tummy from rumbling.

'Trust you,' Patty said, laughing, 'but I think we

306

can spare a Granny Smith for you.' She smiled, pulling out one of the shiny green gems.

'We really can't thank you enough,' Bill added, turning to Betty and Nancy. 'I will send a thank you message round the factory on Monday, and I'll be contributing to your collection in future.'

'That's really very good of you,' Betty replied. 'I'm hoping if we get a little fund together it can help anyone in need with a few essentials when they need it, especially after an accident. Winter can be hard enough without worrying about money, too.'

'I can't believe people were so kind,' Patty added, another surge of guilt coursing through her as she thought back to how the morning of her accident she had been adamant she would never step foot in Vickers again, but in just a short space of time her feelings couldn't be more different.

She had done exactly what she'd been told, resting her sprained ankle, keeping it elevated while she scrubbed and peeled veg for her mom or kept Tom Tom entertained, but now she was determined to get back to the factory, where she could discover if Archie really did like her after all.

'Oh, before I forget,' Betty said, transporting Patty back to the present. 'I have a little something for you too.'

'Oooh, have you?' Patty exclaimed. 'What is it?'

Reaching into her over-the-shoulder handbag, Betty pulled out a small package that she had carefully wrapped in a piece of delicately fragranced pink tissue paper that Mrs Wallis had in one of her many drawers of knick-knacks.

'Here you go,' she said, handing the parcel to an eagerly awaiting Patty, whose hazel eyes had lit up in anticipation. 'I got you a little get well soon gift.'

'Thank you!' The young steelworker beamed as she carefully unwrapped her unexpected gift, revealing the satin powder-blue neck scarf. 'It's beautiful. I love it,' she said, placing it around her slender neck. 'You really didn't have to do this,' she added, getting up from the kitchen table, hobbling over to Betty to give her a hug and a huge kiss on her cheek.

'It's only a little something. I know how you love fashion and I thought it might cheer you up,' Betty told her.

'Well, it really is perfect,' Patty said, beaming. 'Now I just need an excuse to wear it.'

'Oh, I'm sure one will come round soon enough,' Nancy said, knowing that if Archie had listened to a word she'd said earlier, her little plan to get him and Patty together might start to take shape.

'Well, I'm ready for a good night out. It feels like an age since I got dressed up and let my hair down,' Patty said, grinning, her mischievous personality making an appearance once again.

Reaching for another lightly sugared shortbread biscuit that Angie had left on the pink and white rose-patterned plate that she kept for special occasions, Patty placed her other hand to her lips.

'I've had an idea,' she almost squealed. 'Why don't us girls all go to the City Hall next Saturday?'

'What about your ankle?' Betty asked, the idea of Patty tottering around in a pair of heels conjuring up all sorts of worrying scenarios in her mind.

'Oh, it will be fine by then,' she said, dismissing her more sensible friend's worry.

'Are you sure?' Angie asked, backing up Betty's thoughts.

Patty laughed. 'You are a pair of fusspots. I'm sure I could actually go tonight — '

'No!' Angie, Betty and Nancy gasped in unison.

'All right, all right.' Patty laughed, holding her hands up in a gesture of surrender. 'I was only joking.'

'Mmm, I'm not so sure,' Angie replied, rolling her eyes. 'I wouldn't put anything past you.'

'I'll definitely be okay next week, though,' Patty insisted. 'So, do yer fancy it, girls?'

'You are a case, Patty Andrews.' Nancy shook her head in mock horror. 'Let me speak to Doris and see if she will have Billy and Linda for a couple of hours, but I don't like to take advantage of her; she does enough for me and the kids. Speaking of which, I better get going,' she added, standing up and pulling her navy mackintosh on. 'I don't want to be rude, but Doris has had my two since the crack of dawn.'

'You can always send them here, luv, if you need a break,' Angie offered. 'It's really no bother.'

'Oh, that's so kind of you,' Nancy replied, taken aback by Angie's kindness. 'Thank you so much and thank you for the lovely cup of tea too. It was just what I needed.'

After Patty, Angie and Bill had all bid Nancy goodbye, and many thanks had been repeated by everyone, the two remaining female steelworkers sat back down at the table.

'It would be good to have a night out, so you can count me in,' Betty said, returning to Patty's suggestion. Anything had to be better than spending another Saturday night wondering what William was up to, torturing herself that he had found someone else and was just ignoring Betty until she took the hint that he was no longer in love with her. 'I'll try and persuade

Nancy on Monday, but I know she feels guilty about leaving Billy and Linda and putting on her neighbour so much.'

'I meant it. Her kiddies can always come here,' Angie repeated as she portioned off the bacon and sausages and popped the fruit into bowls. 'I don't mind at all. What's another two?'

'You really are very generous,' Betty said, in awe of how one woman could juggle so much.

Patty and Betty excitedly chattered away, pleased to be back in each other's company again. Once Patty had heard about everything she'd missed, she couldn't help but ask after Archie.

'Has he mentioned me at all? Do you really think he cares for me? He did look sad when he saw me on the floor. Do you think I really stand a chance?' Patty barely stopped for air. 'I was just so flamin' infatuated with that good-for-nothing cad Tommy Hardcastle, I couldn't see the wood for the trees. I could kick myself for being so stupid.'

'Well, let's see how things pan out,' Betty said, as she stood up and hugged Patty goodbye. Despite her own niggling worries about William, she was excited for what seemed to be on the horizon for her new friend.

'Now just take it steady,' she added, pulling on her tweed overcoat and slipping her boxed gas mask over her arm. 'We miss seeing you at work, so don't go and do anything daft — we want you back in one piece.'

'And I need to be fit for next Saturday.' Patty grinned, her eyes glinting.

'Of course,' Betty said. 'See you then.'

'Thanks again, luv, for everything,' Angie added, following Betty to the door. 'It really was very kind.'

310

'It was no bother at all,' Betty said, waving the compliment away. 'I'm just glad it's of some use to you all.'

With that Patty hugged her friend once more and opened the front door but to their utter surprise, there in front of them was a very coy and nervous-looking Archie, who'd been pacing up and down on the pavement in front of the house, holding a bunch of pink carnations in one hand and a box of what looked distinctively like chocolate caramels in the other.

'Oh, hullo,' he said, taken aback by the door swinging open before he'd worked up the courage to finally knock.

'Right, I'll get off,' Betty said, not wanting to embarrass Archie any further and keen to escape so she didn't spoil the moment for him and Patty.

'Thanks, Betty. See you soon,' Patty said, waving her off but barely taking her eyes off Archie, who was equally transfixed by the girl he'd fallen for the moment he'd set eyes on her.

'Please come in,' Patty said, finally finding her voice.

'Only if you're sure?' Archie said, hoping beyond hope he wasn't about to set himself up for another fall.

'Yes,' Patty squeaked, trying to stay calm but struggling to hold back her excitement.

'Have you got another visitor?' Bill's voice came down the hallway, a split second before he appeared in person. 'Oh, Archie lad, it's you. Do come in, son. Patty's very popular today; it's like Piccadilly Circus here this afternoon.'

'I don't want to intrude, Mr Andrews,' Archie said hesitantly.

311

Bill smiled. 'Don't be daft, lad. I think Angie has just popped the kettle back on the stove. Come and grab a cuppa.'

In a state of shock, Patty led a bewildered Archie into the family kitchen.

'Mom, this is Archie,' she announced, looking intently at Angie as if to say: 'Please do not say a word to embarrass me now'.

'Hello, lovely to meet you at long last,' Angie gushed. 'Patty has told us so much about you.'

Mom! Patty silently screamed, wanting the floor to open up and swallow her whole.

'I hope you don't think I'm being rude, Archie — do make yourself at home, luv, but I just need to go and change this one,' Angie said, lifting a very grubby-looking Tom Tom into her arms, who had black blotches all over his face and down his hand-knitted green jumper. 'I turned me back for one minute and he was in the coal bucket.'

'Of course,' Archie said, secretly grateful to be left alone with Patty.

'I'm so sorry,' he said as soon as the kitchen emptied out. 'I bought you these,' he added, holding his hands out, offering Patty the flowers and chocolates. 'Please tell me you're okay. I feel so terrible about what happened. It's all my fault.'

'It's not at all,' Patty protested. 'I was in a foul mood and wasn't concentrating. I've got no one to blame but m'self.'

'Hear me out,' Archie said. 'I really would like to explain.'

'Well, in that case, you better sit down.' Patty smiled, indicating with her arm for Archie to pull out a chair.

'It's just,' he started, sitting upright, looking as

though he was about to deliver a formal speech, 'I saw you with Tommy Hardcastle when he was asking you to the dance, and I assumed you were now stepping out together.'

'Oh, no,' Patty said, grimacing, once again internally chastising herself for being so easily led by that blasted man and offending one of the nicest blokes she had ever met at the same time. 'I've been such a fool.'

'You haven't,' Archie kindly interrupted. 'I was just sure that you wouldn't give me a second glance if you were with Tommy, and I suppose I was sulking with you. So, the day you fell, I was deliberately ignoring you because I guess I'd hoped one day you would be my girl.'

'Aw, Archie,' Patty whispered, her tummy turning somersaults at his heartfelt confession.

'So, I was hoping, after Nancy told me I'd got completely the wrong end of the stick, you would consider letting me take you out on a date?' Archie nervously shifted in his seat as he clenched his fingers together and bit down on his bottom lip, knowing he'd either made a complete and utter fool of himself or was about to become the happiest man alive.

'Yes! Of course,' Patty squealed with delight, jumping up a bit too quickly, jarring her already delicate ankle, her grin quickly replaced by a grimace.

'Oh, Patty, are you okay?' Archie asked, also on his feet in a flash and rushing to her side.

'I think so,' she said, half-laughing, tears of happiness and red-hot pain filling her eyes.

Gently taking Patty's arm, Archie eased her back onto the wooden kitchen chair. 'I really will take better care of you from now on, I won't let any more harm come to you,' he vowed, concern etched across his face.

'You haven't,' Patty reassured him, once again cross with herself for being so preoccupied with Tommy chuffin' Hardcastle, she hadn't seen what had been staring her in the face all along. 'But you must let me explain too. I feel so stupid.'

'There's really no need,' Archie said, taking Patty's hand in his as he perched himself on the chair next to her. 'I'm just glad you don't hate me.'

'Hate you!' Patty gasped, partially out of shock Archie could ever think she disliked him, the other part of her tingling all over as a result of this lovely bloke gripping her hand, which was causing waves of excitement to soar through her. 'You couldn't be further from the truth,' she finally said. 'I thought you had a girlfriend and that's why you started ignoring me but now I realize I've been an utter dimwit. It really is me that should be apologizing. In fact, I *am* apologizing: I am so sorry.'

'Well, why don't we agree to simply forgive and forget?' Archie grinned, his smile lighting up his face and his dreamy blue eyes twinkling once again.

'Okay,' Patty replied, with an identical look of sheer delight.

'So,' Archie started, 'when you are better, can I take you out?'

'Well,' Patty teased, 'the girls and I were planning a trip to the City Hall next Saturday. Would you like to be my escort?'

'I couldn't think of anything I'd rather do,' Archie replied, throwing his arms around Patty. 'You have just made me the happiest lad in Sheffield.'

Letting herself fall into Archie's warm muscular

chest, Patty had never felt so content. She might have made an utter fool of herself but thankfully Archie wasn't angry with her, and, with a bit of luck, he might just be the knight in shining armour she had been searching for.

29

In the blink of an eye it was Monday morning and Betty was clocking in again, with Nancy just a couple of minutes behind her.

'How was the rest of your afternoon with Patty?' she asked, as the two women made their way through the colossal factory, barely noticing the ear-piercing noise and vibrations, which, only last month, had felt so horrifically overwhelming.

'Well,' Betty replied, 'just as I was leaving, you will never guess who turned up.'

'Who?' Nancy asked, secretly hoping it would be the one person who would be guaranteed to make Patty the happiest girl alive.

'Archie,' Betty said, grinning. 'I didn't stay to find out what happened but, by the expressions on both their faces, I should imagine they will both be on cloud nine today.'

'Oh, I am pleased,' Nancy replied, delighted Archie had taken on board what she'd said. She'd worried his less-than-confident side might have stopped him taking her advice. 'Let's hope Patty's grand plan to find Mr Right has turned out well after all.'

'Talking of which,' Betty added, 'have you given any more thought to coming to the City Hall this Saturday? I realize it might be difficult for you to make it with Billy and Linda, but even if you can only come for a couple of hours, it would be lovely if you can

316

make it.'

'I would love to — ' Nancy sighed '—but I'm still not sure I can leave the kids. I feel so guilty that I'm not there for them after school or on a Saturday morning. Can I let you know in a day or so? I'll have a think and mull it over.'

'Of course.' Betty smiled. 'And please don't feel under any pressure — that's the last thing any of us want.'

'Thank you,' Nancy replied as they reached Myrtle and Betty stopped, taking off her overcoat and popping it down next to her gas mask and the cloth bag that held her lunch. 'You really are a good friend.'

The day passed quickly as Nancy gained her confidence under Archie's encouragement, in between him revealing how he too would be going along on Saturday night to the weekly dance in the heart of Sheffield's city centre.

Not wanting to embarrass the lad, Nancy didn't pry too much about his afternoon with Patty, but it was strikingly obvious it had gone well. Archie was back to his normal cheery self, unable to wipe the permanent lovesick grin off his face.

As they broke for dinner on Friday at midday, Frank was waiting at the foot of the ladder as they descended to the factory floor.

'Is everything all right?' Nancy asked, suddenly filled with self-doubt, worried she'd made a mistake.

'It's more than all right, duck,' the cheery foreman beamed, his signature deep-set frown disappearing. 'I was just coming to see how you felt about going solo on Monday when Patty comes back.'

'Do you think I'm ready?' Nancy asked, her eyes

darting between Frank and an equally pleased-looking Archie.

'Yes!' they both replied in unison.

'Does that answer your question, duck?' Frank smiled. 'I've been watching you this week, and, like our Betty, you treat this crane with the attention and precision required. Archie will back me up, won't yer, lad?'

'Absolutely, gaffer,' the young, fresh-faced steelworker nodded. 'I've barely had to lift a finger this week — you're more than ready,' he added, turning to face a delighted but modest Nancy.

'Right, well, that's that then,' Frank concluded. 'On Monday you will be in charge of old Mildred while Archie concentrates on getting Patty back up to speed.'

'Oh, I'm sure that won't be a problem,' chirped in one of the nearby young lads, who had overheard the back end of the conversation. 'He might not get much work done, mind!' News had clearly travelled fast around the factory about Archie and Patty's blossoming courtship.

'Oi!' Archie called, his cheeks now the colour of the red-hot flames in the nearby furnace.

'Now then, boys,' Frank said, chuckling, bemused by the light-hearted banter and secretly delighted to see one of his top-notch workers looking happy again, 'I'm sure Archie knows the score, don't yer, son?'

'Yes, yes,' Archie stuttered, quietly swearing blind he would give his mate what for later on.

'Right then, go and grab yer snap and I'll see you all back in here in twenty minutes or so,' Frank added, throwing Nancy a conspiratorial wink. 'Let's make sure your partner in crime here is more than ready to take control of Mildred on Monday morning.'

As she always did, Nancy went and found Betty so they could have a quick catch-up over a sandwich and a cuppa in their normal courtyard spot. 'We might have to find a new spot soon,' Betty shivered as she pulled up the collar of her overcoat, the early October chill replacing the Indian summer they had become accustomed to.

'I was just thinking the same,' Nancy replied, offering her workmate the first cup of steaming hot tea from her flask, a welcome gift as the cold air quickly turned their increasing work-weary tingling fingers pink.

'I nearly forgot,' she added, 'Doris has persuaded me to meet you all on Saturday night.'

'That's wonderful news,' Betty said, beaming. 'It will be lovely to just relax and let our hair down, let alone socialize outside these factory walls.'

'It will,' Nancy agreed. 'I will probably only stay a couple of hours, mind — I just don't want to abuse Doris's good nature — she already does so much for me and the kids.'

'Of course.' Betty took a mouthful of the tea before unwrapping the meticulously prepared beef sandwich Mrs Wallis had carefully enveloped in brown grease-proof baking parchment. 'And on a purely selfish note, I now don't have to worry about playing gooseberry to the new lovebirds!'

'Well, yes, there is that,' Nancy said with a laugh, but she suspected Betty, like her, would give her right arm to be escorted to the City Hall by the man she loved and missed constantly. Doris had been right: the job at Vickers had been the distraction she needed. If she had been at home all day every day, she knew she would have had far too much time on her hands, sending herself mad worrying about her Bert, who was now somewhere in France, defending the country against Hitler's troops.

'So, shall we meet on the steps outside the City Hall at seven o'clock?' Betty suggested, breaking Nancy's trance.

'Yes, that should be fine, I'll let Archie know too. I'm sure he will be collecting Patty. Talking of which, any news from William on how his training is going?'

'Sadly not.' Betty sighed, looking down, trying to fight back the tears she had shed every night for the last week or so into her lavender-scented pillow from flowing once again.

But Nancy wasn't daft. 'Oh, luv, I'm sure he's just working long hours and will be in touch very soon.'

'That's exactly what Mrs Wallis said, and I'm hoping it's true. I just can't help worrying . . .'

But Betty couldn't bring herself to say the actual words that tormented her every minute of the day and interrupted her sleep, convinced if she dared say them out loud, her worst fears would come true.

'Come on,' Nancy said, taking one of Betty's trembling hands, 'that lad is smitten with you. There will be a perfectly reasonable explanation. I don't want you overthinking this.'

Betty nodded slowly but her controlled response to Nancy's well-meant and kind words was at odds with her true feelings.

'Right,' Nancy encouraged, 'let's get back to work. If there is one positive about manning those cranes, it's that it'll keep your mind busy.'

Betty didn't argue; whether it was down to her hard-working conscientious attitude to always do her best, or the fact she knew Nancy was right, it didn't really matter — she couldn't allow herself to fall to bits, no matter how much her heart was aching.

Instead, as the two women walked back through the factory to their great waiting cranes, Betty told herself — just like after she lost her precious mum as a ten-year-old little girl — she would find a way to carry on. After all, as the old saying goes: what doesn't kill you makes you stronger.

30

The following afternoon Patty was skipping around the family kitchen as though she was walking on air, counting down the minutes until Archie arrived to collect her. At long last she was sure she had fallen for a fella who was going to treat her right and not break her heart.

'Why don't you make yerself useful and soak me some oats in water ready for the morning, and that dough in the pancheon could do with one final knead,' Angie said, keen to occupy her daughter, who had been as giddy as a kipper all day as she willed the kitchen clock to strike six.

'What was that, Mom?' Patty asked, mid-daydream, as she ran through her outfit in her mind for the hundredth time that day.

'I give up!' Angie mock sighed, pretending to whip her blue-and-white-checked tea towel at Patty's arm. 'Just go and grab the bag of oats from the parlour.'

Thankfully the next hour went quickly with the odd jobs she had to help with around the house and it was soon time for Patty to go upstairs and get ready for her first real date with Archie, even if Nancy, Betty and her friend Hattie from Woollies would be joining them.

The last time the two good pals had gone to the City Hall it had ended in disaster after Tommy Hardcastle had not only stood her up but had blatantly flaunted his latest conquest, the strikingly beautiful Greta Garbo lookalike, in front of her very eyes.

Tonight was going to be different though. Ever since she had fallen down the crane ladder, Archie — who she had taken a shine to the second she had clapped eyes on him but had been too blinkered to do anything about — had shown her nothing but love and affection. There was no need to put on an act when she was in his company or try and compete with the latest movie-star sex siren, with her crimson-red lipsticks, enviable cheekbones and legs that went on forever. Archie had seen her in a heap on the dusty floor at Vickers, without make-up, dirt smudged across her blotchy tear-stained cheeks, and instead of recoiling, he'd run to her aid and revealed he had fallen for her the moment he'd seen her walk across the noisy factory floor.

But now as she stepped into her pretty powder-blue and white flowery skirt, partnered with the beautiful satin scarf Betty had given her, Patty was determined Archie was going to see her at her best. Carefully sweeping a couple of her long strawberry-blonde curls away from her face and pinning them into place with the diamanté clip he had given her a few days after her accident, Patty smiled back at her refection in the mirror, despite the millions of butterflies that were fluttering around her tummy.

Patty had been blessed with a perfect creamy porcelain complexion, but, wanting to feel that extra bit special, she took her Max Factor panstick — another one of her Woolworth buys — and dabbed some of the creamy foundation into her skin, before applying a few dots of pale-pink rouge on to her cheeks and a lick of candy-pink lipstick. 'Well, that should do the trick,' she told herself, feeling like a million dollars.

As Patty made her way down the two flights of narrow wooden stairs from the attic bedroom she shared with her youngest brother, Tom Tom, to the bottom floor, there was a gentle tap at the front door.

She knew instantly it was Archie. She'd been waiting for this exact moment all day.

'I'll get it,' Patty called giddily, almost skipping to welcome her date for the evening.

Pulling the door open, Archie burst into a huge smile, temporarily taken aback by how stunningly beautiful his equally smitten sweetheart looked.

'You look amazing,' he whispered, holding up a posy of pale-pink and cream chrysanthemums.

'Thank you,' Patty whispered back, her cheeks instantly flushing. 'You look pretty dapper yourself,' she added, taking in his smart navy slacks and perfectly crisp white polo shirt, which she could just make out from underneath his dark-blue jacket.

The pair certainly made a dashing couple out of their mucky Vickers overalls and not a speck of dirt in sight.

'Aw, I assumed it was you at the door,' Angie said, making her way down the hallway from the kitchen, with little Tom Tom on her hip. 'Now you two go and have a lovely evening.'

'But make sure you are home for ten thirty,' came Bill's light-hearted but firm warning, as he followed his wife to see off his daughter and Archie.

'Don't you worry, Mr Andrews, I will have Patty here home safe and sound in plenty of time.' Archie was clearly determined to show Patty's parents he was good enough for their eldest daughter.

'Just ignore him,' Angie replied, rolling her eyes,

324

and pretending to tap her husband's arm with her free hand. 'We know you're a good lad. Now go before you waste another minute.'

'Thanks, Mom. Would you mind popping these in a vase?' Patty asked, handing her mom the lovely bunch of flowers Archie had brought her.

'Just before you do,' Archie politely interjected, gently snipping one of the cream flowers with his finger and thumb, carefully tucking it in between a couple of Patty's curls to the front of the slide he'd given her.

'Aw, you big softy,' Angie said, 'but you do a look a picture, Patty,' she added, beaming with pride at how lovely her daughter looked. 'Now, go on and get off before it's time to come home.'

Doing as they were told, Archie linked Patty's slender arm and led her out of the house and up Thompson Road.

'I really couldn't wish for a better date,' he whispered, pulling her a little closer as soon as they were out of earshot from Patty's parents, the side of their bodies now skimming each other, creating ribbons of electricity.

'Well, I feel pretty lucky myself,' Patty said, turning to face Archie, a smile on her face. He swiftly took the opportunity to plant a tender kiss on her right cheek. 'And I could definitely get used to that,' she said, grinning.

'Oh, hello you two,' came a familiar voice. 'I'm not interrupting anything, am I?' Nancy teased.

'No, not all,' Patty mock-gasped, endeavouring to save Archie's blushes. 'What sort of girl do you think I am?'

'Well, it's good to see you back on your feet and looking so well,' Nancy said. 'We've missed you at the factory. It's not been the same without you.'

'You'll be fed up with the sight of me soon,' Patty replied. 'I'm getting back up that crane on Monday if it kills me.'

'I'm sure Archie here will look after you,' Nancy said.

'I absolutely will,' the protective steelworker reassured the pair. 'But let's not think about that now,' he added. 'We've got a night out to enjoy.'

* * *

A few miles away on the other side of the city, Betty had just made her way downstairs from the room she rented.

'Oh, now, you must try and keep your chin up dear and enjoy your evening,' Mrs Wallis sighed, taking one look at Betty. Despite carefully applying her panstick and a slick of rouge, it was obvious she'd spent the last hour in tears. 'I'm sure a letter will arrive soon, and I promise if anything comes in the evening post, I'll pop it on your pillow for you.'

'Thank you,' Betty said sadly. 'If I'm honest, I'd rather stay here tonight, but I promised the girls so I don't want to go back on my word.'

'No, you mustn't,' Mrs Wallis replied. 'Besides which, it will do you good. Now paint that smile on and go and have a good time. I assure you, it will do no good moping about here. Time will only pass slower.'

'I know you're right,' Betty said, forcing a weak smile. 'I promise I'll do my best.'

'That's my girl,' Mrs Wallis said, opening the front door for her youngest lodger, who, with each day felt more like the daughter she'd never had. 'You'll enjoy yourself once you are there.'

'Thank you,' Betty replied, even if she wasn't feeling as optimistic as her landlady would have liked.

★ ★ ★

Half an hour later Betty was making her way across the precinct at Barker's Pool, in front of the City Hall, with Hattie, who she'd bumped into near the bus stop, when she caught sight of Archie, Patty and Nancy.

'You're here,' Patty squealed with excitement, delighted to spot Betty and her best friend, Hattie, as they reached the bottom of the steps that led to the dance hall, their coats pulled tightly around them, protecting them against the autumn evening chill.

'We haven't kept you long, have we?' Nancy asked.

'Not at all,' Betty answered. 'We've only just got here.' What she didn't add was the pang of envy she'd felt when Hattie had explained how, just that morning, she'd received a letter from her boyfriend, John, who had been sent to France to fight Hitler's troops. Betty had felt so deflated when yet again she had waited for the postman to arrive but had been left with tears stinging her eyes when nothing dropped through the letter box.

'Well, let's get you ladies inside,' Archie encouraged, 'before you all freeze to death.'

'I won't argue with that,' Patty replied, suddenly realizing she had rushed out of the house without her jacket, the cold causing her to come out in goose pimples.

'Where's my manners?' Archie said, chastising himself. 'I should have given you my jacket.'

Patty laughed. 'Don't be daft; I hadn't felt the cold until now, but I might take you up on the offer on the way home.'

'I think I can manage that.' He smiled, wrapping his arm around Patty's back to protect her against the cold, as he ushered the four women inside the majestic venue.

Heading down the grand wooden staircase, Archie led the women towards the long mahogany bar, which was already lined with a sea of Saturday-night revellers, all dressed to the nines, the girls in their best dresses, and the men suited and booted, with Brylcreem-quiffed hair.

'First drinks are on me. My treat,' he insisted, speaking up to be heard over Glenn Miller's 'Blue Orchid'.

'That's very kind,' Betty replied, courteous as ever, but inside really wishing she hadn't agreed to come. Everywhere she looked there were happy lovesick couples holding hands, or blokes throwing flirtatious glances at girls they were keen on — it acted as a cruel reminder of the love she was now convinced had gone forever.

Taking their orders of a port and lemon for Betty and Hattie, half a shandy for Nancy and a dandelion and burdock for Patty, Archie left the women chatting as he found a place at the busy bar.

But as soon as Patty saw the look on Betty's face, she knew her new, normally much more stoic, friend, was on the edge of tears.

'Oh, Bet, what is it?' she asked, rushing to her side.

'I just can't pretend to be happy,' she gasped, her voice breaking. 'I'm so sorry. I don't think I can be here. I really am sorry.' And with that, Betty turned on her immaculate cream Mary Janes and dashed through the sea of bodies towards the doors and into the downstairs lobby.

'Did I say something wrong?' Patty asked, horrified at the thought of upsetting her friend. 'Should I go after her and make sure she's okay?'

'No,' Nancy replied. 'You stay here with Hattie and Archie. I'll go. I think I have an idea what's bothering her and hopefully a good old hug and chat will be just what she needs.'

'Okay. If you think that's the right thing to do?' Patty sighed, still anxious she might have offended Betty in some way.

As Archie headed back to the now diminished group of women, carefully balancing five glasses on the plastic tray, Nancy followed Betty, keeping an eye on her pale-blue overcoat as she zig-zagged through the scores of revellers.

Only as Betty, her shoulders now shuddering, entered the ladies' loos, did Nancy manage to catch her up.

'Hey, luv,' she said, gently taking hold of her arm, 'it's okay. You don't have to do this alone.' Nancy had accurately guessed her friend was struggling after not hearing from William.

'I just miss him so much,' Betty cried, finally succumbing to the tears that had been stinging the back of her big brown eyes all day.

'Come on, luv,' Nancy said, wrapping her in her arms. 'I'm sure there will be a reasonable explanation.'

'Like what?' Betty said between heartbroken sobs, her cheeks now a blotchy mess and the rouge she had so carefully applied smeared. 'Surely he could have sent me a letter?'

'His letters are probably all sat in a pile in the post

office,' Nancy said, praying to God she was right, and William hadn't left Betty high and dry.

'If you don't mind, I think I might just catch the bus home,' Betty muttered. 'I don't really think I'm going to be much company and I don't want to ruin Patty's special night.'

'You do whatever you need to,' Nancy said kindly as she pulled a clean white handkerchief from her handbag and passed it to Betty. 'I'll let them all know, but at least let me walk you out. I don't want you going home feeling this upset.'

'Thank you, Nancy, you're such a good friend.'

'I'm quite sure you would do the same for me if the shoe was on the other foot,' Nancy said, as she gently ushered Betty from the loos — where they were getting sideway glances and raised eyebrows from the other women who were waiting in line — towards the cloakroom.

But as they pulled on their coats and walked through the double doors into the square, Betty stopped midpace, frozen to the spot.

'What is it? Is everything okay?' Nancy asked, at a loss as to what could be bothering her friend. When she didn't get a response, Nancy turned to face Betty, who was staring straight ahead, her eyes wide, silent tears freely flowing down her red-raw cheeks.

Nancy followed her friend's gaze and there, just a few metres away, was a handsome dark-haired man, dressed in a mid-blue RAF uniform, who was also stood stock-still.

'William,' was all Betty could manage in the quietest of whispers.

The trance broken, the dashing but exhausted-looking military man rushed towards her, his arms out wide.

'Betty, my lovely sweet Bet,' he said as she willingly fell into his arms. 'I've missed you so much.'

'William,' was all Betty could manage as she sank into her sweetheart's chest, tears once again cascading down her cheeks, her make-up replaced by streaks of mascara, which were now being absorbed by his brass-buttoned jacket. 'I thought you had forgotten about me.'

'Never,' William whispered. 'You are the only thing that keeps me going. I have been counting down the days and hours until I could see you. I went to your lodgings, but Mrs Wallis told me you had come to the dance. I got here as fast as I could.'

'But why haven't you sent me any letters?' Betty asked, trying to make sense of why she hadn't heard from her beloved William.

'Oh Betty, I did. Did you not receive my note, explaining I was busy but would write as soon as I could?'

'No,' she sighed. 'But, let's not worry about that now.'

Smiling, Nancy silently slipped away, not wanting to disturb the intimate moment, and made her way back inside to Patty, Hattie and Archie.

'Is Betty okay?' the youngest of the three steelworkers asked.

'Well, she is now. You will never believe this, but William has just turned up!'

'Really?' Patty gasped. 'But where's he been and why didn't he write to her?

'I think he did,' Nancy replied. 'Betty just never received the letter. William certainly looked horrified at the thought she hadn't received it.'

'Oh, how romantic,' Patty said, grinning. 'Maybe he will propose too.'

'Patty!' Hattie laughed, nearly choking on her port and lemon. 'You really are a case. It's not a scene from the pictures, you know.'

'You never know . . . ' Patty said, her mind working overtime. 'He has just turned up completely out of the blue.'

'Well, we won't be kept in suspense for too long,' Archie said, averting his gaze to the dance floor, where, arm in arm, with smiles as broad as a Cheshire cat's, Betty and William were walking towards them.

'Oh, don't they look lovely together,' Patty sighed. No one could argue with that. William's chiselled handsome looks and Betty's classic beauty — with her high cheekbones, the tears now dried up and a natural flush in their place, complementing her carefully coiffed hair — ensured they looked an absolute picture.

'I'm so sorry I dashed off like that,' Betty said as the happy couple approached the waiting group, 'but I would like you all to meet William.'

'We've heard so much about you,' Patty squealed, nearly bursting with excitement, wrapping her arms around the somewhat taken aback but amused William.

'Sorry, pal,' Archie said, laughing, when she finally let him go. 'Patty hasn't been out for a while. I'm Archie,' he added, shaking William's hand. 'Pleased to meet you. And this is Nancy and Hattie.' He gestured to the pair, whose smiles revealed how utterly delighted they were for Betty, who'd looked as though her heart was about to break in two not half an hour earlier.

As though right on cue, Glenn Miller's 'Moonlight Serenade' filled the hall. 'I think Betty Clark, this is where I sweep you off your feet and onto the dance floor.' William grinned, glancing towards the throng of couples who were already entwined in one another's arms.

Just when Nancy didn't think her friend's grin could get any bigger, Betty's now sparkling eyes smiled too. 'I definitely won't say no to that,' Betty said, blushing.

'Here, let me take your coat,' Nancy said, realizing they still hadn't managed to get to the cloakroom.

'Thank you,' Betty said gratefully, taking off her jacket to reveal a beautiful figure-hugging A-line lilac-and-cream-flowered dress.

'Will you give me the honour of allowing me this dance?' Archie said to Patty, sensing her desire to also be swept off her feet.

'Yes!' Patty giggled, living out her own fairy tale.

As the two couples made their way onto the polished wooden dance floor, finding their own private spaces to enjoy a few precious minutes together in each other's arms, Nancy turned to Hattie. 'Shall we sit down?'

'Yes, that sounds like a good plan,' Hattie said. 'I've been on my feet all week at Woollies and could do with sitting down.'

As the two women took a pair of seats at the table on the edge of the dance floor, where Archie had placed all their drinks, Nancy felt a sense of calm. The last month had been the hardest of her life. Kissing her Bert goodbye, leaving Billy and Linda to take a dangerous job at Vickers and then having to cope with Harry and his arrogant, condescending sexist comments, had tested her to the limit. She'd spent many a sleepless night questioning how she would face the next day. But now, despite not knowing when she would next see her beloved, caring husband, she felt whatever tomorrow brought, she would find the strength to cope.

★ ★ ★

An hour later, as her newfound friends and their sweethearts chatted away, Nancy quietly slipped away, making her way back out into Barker's Pool, not wanting to leave her children a moment longer than she had to.

As she pulled the collar of her navy mackintosh up around her neck, she quickly made her way to the bus stop. It had been a funny old night but one she was sure none of them would forget in a hurry. The last few months had certainly thrown them all some unexpected challenges.

Becoming a crane driver wasn't something Nancy had ever dreamt she would do, but for so many reasons it had been the best thing she'd ever agreed to. She had made two new friends in Betty and Patty, who were already beginning to feel like sisters, as they all pulled together to help one another whenever they needed it. And, like her steel factory workmates, she was doing her bit to ensure Bert — like Hattie's boyfriend, John, and eventually, no doubt, William — would have the munitions and aircraft they needed to fight Hitler and his troops.

Watching Patty and Betty, madly in love and full of hope, dance the night away affirmed that, together, at each other's side, they could tackle whatever this dastardly war sent their way.

Nobody knew what Hitler might throw at them, but Nancy had no doubt in her mind the women of Sheffield were steelier than anyone would ever guess and were certainly not to be underestimated. Hitler might think he could break the morale of those he was aiming to attack, but he really didn't have the first clue how hardy and determined Nancy and her band of female factory sisters were.

She had every faith that, whatever they were faced with, they would tackle it together as one.

Author's Note

I started *The Steel Girls* after spending two years researching the true-life stories of the women who worked in the factories that lined the River Don during the Second World War. Their tales of hardship, strength and resilience left me humbled and in complete admiration of what this tremendous generation endured.

Many were mothers or young girls with no experience of what it was like to be employed in one of the big windowless factories, which were described on more than one occasion as entering 'hell on earth'. The deafening, ear-splitting cacophony combined with the perilously dangerous but accepted working conditions, alongside the relentless and exhaustingly long shifts, was a huge culture shock for so many of the women who walked through those factory doors for the first time.

Those who had young children had no choice but to hand their precious sons and daughters over to grandparents or leave them in the care of older siblings, some of whom were just out of school themselves, but were expected to grow up fast and also do their bit to help.

What struck me in the course of my research, though, was how little resistance was offered to this new arduous, strangely unfamiliar and frequently terrifying way of life. 'We were just doing what was needed,' was an all-too-common answer when I asked the women to whom I had the pleasure of talking why they so eagerly took on the somewhat risky roles they'd volunteered for. 'We had no choice. It was what was needed to keep the factories going.' This is true; the foundries desperately needed workers, with so many men enlisting in the armed forces to begin a 'new adventure'.

It soon became clear to me that this band of formidable, proud and hard-working Yorkshire women were not going to just stand by and let Hitler and his troops wreak havoc across Europe and beyond, without them doing what they could to aid their husbands, brothers, sons and uncles who were off fighting someone else's war.

Over and over again, I was left in complete awe of how much the women of Sheffield sacrificed, day in and day out, for six long years. It's hard for most of us to comprehend now what a difficult and seemingly never-ending length of time this was. As well as working night and day as crane drivers, turners, making camouflage netting or labouring next to a red-hot, and at times fatal, Bessemer Converter, they lived with the constant and all too real fear they might never see their loved ones ever again.

One lady, Kathleen Roberts, told me whenever a shooting star was seen going over a factory, it was a sign another soldier had fallen and a telegram bearing the bad news would be delivered soon afterwards. To live with that level of sheer terror, let alone cope with the ominous air-raid sirens that indicated the Luftwaffe could be on their way, is truly unimaginable. But this was the harsh and constant reality that thousands of women lived with across Sheffield.

It wasn't all doom and gloom, though. The one thing that struck a chord with me while talking to the women and their families was the way in which they counteracted the harshness life had thrown at them. They created unbreakable bonds with their new female fellow workmates — a camaraderie which even Hitler himself couldn't break. In a determined bid to 'keep up morale' our feisty factory sisters focused on nurturing a warm community spirit to keep them all going when times got hard. Friendships were created in the most unlikely of circumstances, often amongst women who would never normally mix; lipsticks were snapped in half and divided between colleagues, and a single wedding dress could be worn a dozen times to ensure no Sheffield bride had to walk down the aisle not looking her absolute best. It really was the era of sharing what you had with your neighbour and never letting someone in need go without.

Of course, it would be easy to romanticize this period, or hail it as 'the good old days', but the reality is it wasn't that either. It was simply a case of facing head-on the hardships life was dealing out and getting on with it as best you could. Some had it easier than others but, no matter what, all these women woke up in September 1939 to a new life, and somehow managed to take it in their stride, though they really didn't have much choice. With no savings to fall back on to tide them over, or a welfare state to lighten the load, it was a case of 'cracking on' and doing what was needed.

In 2009, after watching a TV show on the land girls, Kathleen Roberts rang the *Sheffield Star* and asked why she and others like her, who had sacrificed so much of their lives, had never been thanked. What started as a frustrated phone call developed into a campaign by the local paper to ensure the women of the city who had worked day and night in the steel-works were finally recognized. Kathleen, alongside Kit Sollitt, Dorothy Slingsby and Ruby Gascoigne, representing this whole generation of women, were whisked down to London to be personally thanked by the then Prime Minister, Gordon Brown. Afterwards a grassroots campaign was launched by the *Sheffield Star* to fundraise for a statue commemorating the female steelworkers to be commissioned and erected in Barker's Pool, in the city centre — directly outside the dance hall they would often visit on a Saturday to escape the drudgery of their lives.

In June 2016, the larger-than-life bronze statue — paid for entirely by the people of Sheffield — was unveiled to the rapturous delight of the surviving women of steel, their contribution to the war effort now eternally immortalized.

Although the characters in this book are entirely fictitious — their experiences a result of my creative imagination — the truth is that every page is based on the interviews I conducted and the ongoing research I'm still undertaking. I hope within my books I can also help keep this generation's memory alive. I inter-viewed women who flew up crane ladders, others who were scared witless and many who remember only too clearly what it was like to live in absolute poverty, the tallyman a regular visitor to their door. So, despite the poetic creation of Betty, Nancy and Patty, I can pic-ture their real-life counterparts, hear their voices and recall their experiences — the reality of it is, the raw bones of some of these stories are so remarkable you couldn't make them up. Only after hearing first-hand how terrifying it was to be hauled up to the terrify-ing heights of the factory heavens in a crane cab or listen to the raw heartbreak of not knowing if your husband was dead or alive in a faraway country, hundreds of miles from home, could I put pen to paper and deliver our real women of steel the justice they rightfully deserve.

I truly hope, as a Sheffielder (well, just about — I've been here twenty-five years), I have served the women of this hardworking industrious city well and you have enjoyed reading this book as much as I have writing it.

Michelle x

Acknowledgements

Firstly, I would like to thank every female steelworker of the First and Second World War and their family members, who over the course of the last three years have so generously given up their time to talk to me, recalled memories and answered my endless questions. Without these women, *The Steel Girls* would not be possible. Although, the characters are fictional, they are created from the real-life experiences and true stories that have been shared with me. In addition, I am so grateful to the women and their relatives for their ongoing and tremendous support, which means so much. At every step of the way, they have been there to cheer me on, and for that I will be forever grateful.

I am indebted to every author, historian, journalist and social commentator who enabled me to look at this period of time in extra detail, allowing me to understand the wider issues and feelings of the women who lived and worked through the Second World War, creating a new way of life in the most troubled and hardest of times.

Special thanks must go to Kate Thompson and Amanda Revell-Walton, who in different ways have inspired me and supported me, something I am incredibly for.

I must also say how grateful I am to book blogger, Nicola Smith, from Short Book and Scribes, who has been so kind and has continually shown enthusiasm and encouragement from the moment she discovered

The Steel Girls was happening.

Enormous thanks must be given to the extremely dedicated Hannah Weatherill, at Northbank Talent Management, who not only believed in me, but offered reassurance, encouragement and invaluable advice throughout the process of writing this book. Her dedication is second to none.

I must also offer the greatest of thanks to my wonderful editor, Katie Seaman at HQ Stories, without whom this book would never have seen the light of day. Katie believed in me from the very start, when *The Steel Girls* was just an idea, and then became the wisest and most patient of sounding boards whenever I needed a little natter or a brainstorm. Katie's enthusiastic passion for *The Steel Girls* can only be described as the shiniest and brightest star in the sky, guiding me through the writing and editing process with such dedicated care and compassion. Our chats over character development and plots has always been a joint, joyful, and fun process. Not once did it feel like a gruelling pressured chore, but more of lovely chat over a cup of Yorkshire tea, as we bashed out ideas until they came to life and jumped off the page.

Alongside Katie at HQ Stories, I must offer my sincere thanks to copyeditor Donna Hillyer, whose knowledge on the nuances of the Yorkshire accent is exemplary, to proof-reader Anne O'Brien, to Kate Oakley and the HQ design team for designing the most evocative and beautiful of covers. I'd also like to extend my gratitude to Lily Capewell and Becca Joyce for helping create the publicity and marketing for *The Steel Girls* and to Harriet Williams and Fliss Porter in sales, for getting this book on actual shelves.

I am so grateful to each and every one of my family members and truly amazing friends, who have offered unfaltering support in writing the book. My very proud dad, Kevin Smith, who along with my equally proud and inspirational aunt, Anita Knight, brothers Gavin and Neil Smith, and their wives Bilika and Chloe, have been my biggest cheerleaders. I can't fail to mention my good friend and running mate, Leanne Hawkes, who has lived this book with me at times, listening to me as we ran up mountains (well, small hills), and kept me sane throughout. I must also thank Ann Cusack, Grace Macaskill, Sheron Boyle, Deirdre O'Brien, Polly Rippon, Lisa Bradley, Claire Rifkin and Susan Cotter for listening to me as I continually told them how I was getting on and always offering relentless support.

I cannot end this passage of gratitude without saying thank you to my husband, Iain, who never once moaned about doing far more than his fair share of dog walks for our crazy Cavapoo, Mabel, and making endless cups of tea and coffee when my eyes were drooping. As for our two amazing children, Archie and Tilly, who know come 7 p.m., I had to start work again, their enthusiasm and excitement that 'Mum is an actual author and really writes books' is the best reward. I sincerely hope I have instilled in them the belief that, if you work hard enough for something, you can achieve your dreams, no matter how big or insurmountable they might feel.

There is one person whom I constantly thought about while writing this book and that is my late mother-in-law, Coleen, a Woman of Steel in her own right. I would give anything for her to still be here to see this book. I can imagine her shouting from the rooftops about it, telling all her friends they must read it. Coleen was an avid local history fan and I wish she was still here for so many reasons but would have loved her to check the minutiae of this book, the accents, the landmarks, the Yorkshire traditions. I know she would have been there, going through the details with a fine-toothed comb.

But I derive so much happiness and comfort from the thought of how proud and excited she would have been to see little old me writing a book, steeped in historical fact, about the remarkable women of the city she loved so much. Coleen, like our hard-working and caring Steel Girls, you will never be forgotten.

We do hope that you have enjoyed
reading this large print book.

Did you know that all of our titles
are available for purchase?

We publish a wide range of high
quality large print books including:
Romances, Mysteries, Classics
General Fiction
Non Fiction and Westerns

Special interest titles available in
large print are:
The Little Oxford Dictionary
Music Book, Song Book
Hymn Book, Service Book

Also available from us courtesy of
Oxford University Press:
Young Readers' Dictionary
(large print edition)
Young Readers' Thesaurus
(large print edition)

For further information or a free
brochure, please contact us at:
Ulverscroft Large Print Books Ltd.,
The Green, Bradgate Road, Anstey,
Leicester, LE7 7FU, England.
Tel: (00 44) **0116 236 4325**
Fax: (00 44) **0116 234 0205**

Other titles published by Ulverscroft:

A SHOP GIRL IN BATH

Rachel Brimble

Hardworking and whip-smart, Elizabeth Pennington is the rightful heir of Bath's premier department store — but her father, Edward Pennington, believes his daughter lacks the business acumen to run his empire. He is resolute that a man will succeed him.

Determined to break from her father's hold and prove she is worthy of inheriting Pennington's, Elizabeth forms an unlikely alliance with ambitious and charismatic master glove-maker Joseph Carter. They have the same goal: bring Pennington's into a new decade while embracing woman's equality and progression. But, despite their best intentions, it is almost impossible not to mix business and pleasure...

Can the two thwart Edward Pennington's plans for the store? Or will Edward prove himself an unshakeable force who will ultimately ruin both Elizabeth and Joseph?